KILL ZONE

KILL ZONE

GUNNERY SGT.
JACK COUGHLIN,
USMC (RET.)

with

DONALD A. DAVIS

St. Martin's Paperbacks

This is a work of fiction. All of the characters, organizations, and events portrayed in this novel are either products of the author's imagination or are used fictitiously.

KILL ZONE

Copyright © 2007 by Jack Coughlin with Donald A. Davis.
Excerpt from *Dead Shot* copyright © 2008 by Jack Coughlin with Donald A. Davis.

Cover photograph of soldier © Lynsey Addario / Corbis
Cover photograph of gun © Jim Sugar / Corbis

For information address St. Martin's Press, 175 Fifth Avenue, New York, NY 10010.

ISBN: 0-312-94567-1
EAN: 978-0-312-94567-1

Printed in the United States of America

St. Martin's Press hardcover edition / November 2007
St. Martin's Paperbacks edition / December 2008

St. Martin's Paperbacks are published by St. Martin's Press, 175 Fifth Avenue, New York, NY 10010.

10 9 8 7 6 5 4 3 2 1

PROLOGUE

A DUSTY HAZE HUNG OVER the little cluster of mud and brick huts just before dawn, and the smell of cooking fires filtered back to the snipers. A boy with a stick herded a few goats across stony ground to the east, trying to find something on which the animals could graze. The land was barren and bleak, like the lives of the few people who lived here. A single guard with an AK-47 walked about, trying to stay awake.

It had taken Gunnery Sergeant Kyle Swanson and his spotter, Corporal Eric Martinez, seventy-two hours since being dropped by helicopter to reach the hidden overlook position. They had humped through valleys and steep ridges, following faint trails that led them to a rough road running through the no-name village.

They had moved only during darkness, for although they wore the same sort of clothing as the locals, they obviously were quite different. Swanson was a Massachusetts Irishman with reddish-blond hair, and Martinez was an olive-skinned Mexican. With such distinctive faces, plus being weaponed up, they could not take the chance of being examined too closely.

They made scheduled radio checks every two hours. Swanson led the way in silence as they closed in on the road until they spotted the lights of the village in the distance. He looked at the map for a final time, smiled, folded it up, and put it into a pocket.

It was still the darkest hours of the night when they discovered the deep cave on the ridge above the village. It had an exit at the far end, which allowed them to crawl in undetected. They gathered weeds and bushes from the rear side of the ridge and stuffed them into the folds of their loose clothing to create crude ghillie suits, and became invisible in the night. They took their positions, set up the rifle and the spotting scope, and lay motionless fifteen yards back in the gloom of the small cavern.

The target was in one of those huts below them on the road that led from Afghanistan into Pakistan.

At 5:00 A.M., Martinez reported on the radio that the hunter-killer team was on station and expected the target to move soon. Swanson gave him some map coordinates, and a routine confirmation was returned. Without contradictory instructions at that final radio check, the mission was to proceed, so the snipers went black. The radio was turned off to save the battery, and the backup satellite phone was also shut down.

They would have preferred to conduct the entire operation at night to help with their escape, but the world isn't perfect in combat. A window of opportunity such as this would be open for a very short time. It had to be done now.

They ran laser ranges on every hut and worked out firing solutions on all of them, including the front door of the target hut, its single window, and the old pickup truck parked out front. There was a scramble of junk in the bed of the pickup to make it appear to be just another vehicle carrying scavenged items for resale at some bazaar.

Kyle Swanson smoothly glassed the area, the huts, and truck. The images jumped in magnification, seeming close enough to reach out and touch. He looked at the guard wandering aimlessly about. Still good.

A light came on in the window, the yellow flicker of a lantern. "We have movement," whispered Martinez.

A big man came through the door. The snipers, working from a picture, examined him closely through their scopes to get positive identification. The bearded face of Ali bin Assam was unmistakable in the brightening morning light. "It's him," said Martinez.

Ali was a top military operative of al Qaeda, one of the operational guys who planned the dirty work, then had others carry out the attacks. He was responsible for a lot of innocent people being dead, and American intel had picked up his scent after a suicide bomb attack in Baghdad had misfired a week earlier. Swanson and Martinez were assigned to hunt him down and kill him.

Now Swanson laid the crosshairs of his rifle on the dark figure.

"I see the target," said Martinez. He quickly glanced at the logbook. "Four hundred eleven meters to the doorway."

"Wind?" Swanson asked softly.

Martinez looked at the smoke drifting over the hut. "Two minutes left."

Swanson fine-tuned until Ali bin Assam filled the scope. "I'm holding center mass."

"Roger. On scope."

The terrorist looked up at the brightening sky and seemed pleased with the coming of morning. The new day held the promise that he would soon be safe in the tunneled sanctuary of Pakistan's forbidding Tora Bora mountains. He raised his big arms and stretched, his back bending.

"On target," said Swanson as he took up the slack on the trigger.

"Fire when ready."

Swanson exhaled and gently pulled straight back on the trigger, and the long rifle fired. The 7.62 mm bullet tore through Ali just left of center, ripped through vital organs and arteries, and took out a chunk of the heart. He staggered back and collapsed against a dirty wall as blood poured out of him.

The guard stared down in surprise at his fallen leader, and Swanson turned the rifle on him, jacked in a new round, and hammered the gunman with a chest shot. The body crumpled to the ground, where it quivered briefly like a piece of Jell-O.

"Two hits," Martinez confirmed. "Two targets down."

To make sure, Kyle Swanson put another round into Ali's head.

The shots echoed across the little valley, but no other fighters emerged from the huts, and no return fire came searching for the snipers. In this harsh land of easy death, no one wanted to get involved in whatever had just happened, and they all stayed inside except for the little boy, who had abandoned his goats and taken off running. They let him go.

Martinez backed out of the rear entrance of the cave and ran down to the fallen targets while Swanson covered him. He opened a kit containing test tubes, snipped a hair sample from Ali, and shoved a long cotton swab to the back of the dead man's tongue for a saliva sample. He bottled them both and locked them in the small box. The DNA would be used later for positive identification.

When he was clear, they started to hump back to a flat area about 800 meters away, where the daylight extraction could be done by a Black Hawk helicopter accompanied by a pair of Apache gunships. There was no need for secrecy now, just speed. The jig was up and the snipers had to get out of there.

Martinez turned the radio back on and gave the map coordinates to call in the birds, but a raspy and angry voice broke into his transmission. "Where have you been?" the voice demanded. "We've been trying to get you for the last thirty minutes! Abort the mission. Say again, abort the mission!"

Martinez stared in shock, but Swanson winked at him and grabbed the receiver. "Too damned late! Mission accomplished."

"Fuck!" There was panic in the disembodied voice. "You gave us the wrong coordinates on that village. You were on the wrong side of the border. *Fuck!* Choppers are inbound. We'll deal with this when you get back." The transmission was terminated.

Swanson handed the receiver back to Martinez. "Let's go

home." They set out in a trot down the ravine toward the landing zone.

"Gunny, we in trouble?"

"Eric, you just remember we took out a real bad motherfucker today. We may get some shit for it, but when they quit shouting, old Ali's still going to be real dead, and that's a good deal. He was a worthless piece of shit who had a lot of American and Iraqi blood on his hands. Anyway, we can't unshoot him, can we? Can't change a thing. I'll take any blame, but my guess is they will just bury it. The CIA never admits mistakes."

"Did you know we were on the wrong side of the border?" They heard the buzz of the approaching choppers, and Swanson popped a smoke grenade to signal their location.

"I was always lousy at map-reading," Swanson grinned. "That bastard needed killing and now he's dead. That was the job. Fuck the border."

CHAPTER 1

THE BOATMAN STOOD WAITING *in the cold fog, a ragged apparition resting against a long oar that disappeared into the black water. He smelled of death, and his robe pulsed in the stiff wind. "Do you have another one?"*

"No. Not this time." Kyle Swanson recognized the five silent passengers seated in the low craft, for he had brought them all here, one by one. They stared at nothing, with empty and lifeless eyes, and did not know him.

"Then I still have an empty seat," said the Boatman. "Will you furnish someone else soon?"

"I don't know. Probably. Maybe not." Over the Boatman's shoulder, he saw tongues of fire raging along the far shore. "No."

The spectral figure shook its head and exhaled a foul odor. "I cannot leave with an empty seat."

"Yeah. Okay." Swanson looked about, but there was no one else around. He carefully put down his fully loaded M40A1 sniper rifle, unsnapped the web gear, and let the pack fall away. He took off blocks of C-4 explosive and tossed them aside. Two razor-sharp knives, gleaming blades streaked with blood. A silenced 9 mm pistol. A sawed-off shotgun. An M-16 and an AK-47 and a Claymore mine and its clacker. Smoke, fragmentation, and thermite grenades. A small satel-

lite radio. All the tools of the sniper's trade. He wanted to hold on to something. "Can I keep my boots?"

"You will have no need for boots, but it does not matter."

"They're comfortable. I just got them broken in good."

"Keep them." A favor. Bare, cracked teeth showed in the skull. The Boatman usually had little to say, but he and Kyle Swanson had known each other for a very long time.

Swanson took off his boonie cover and put it on top of the stack, tucking it so that the eagle, globe, and anchor emblem of the United States Marine Corps remained visible. Then he removed the plastic-laminated photograph of a beautiful young woman with dark hair and eyes, kissed it, and placed it on the pile.

"Is there anything else?"

"No."

"Very well." The Boatman extended a long, bony hand. Swanson grabbed it for support as he stepped aboard and took a seat among his latest five kills. Ali bin Assam, looking gray and with a big hole through him, was beside him.

Swanson felt the small vessel rock gently as the Boatman shoved off, pushing hard on the oar to begin the passage across that black river to whatever was over there where the flames danced along a brimstone beach.

At least I still have my boots, *he thought.* At least I still have my soul.

Then the hand grabbed his shoulder.

CHAPTER 2

KYLE! LET'S GO, LAD." Time to do some shooting." Sir Geoffrey Cornwell pushed gently on Swanson's shoulder, awak-
ening him with a start. As a former colonel in the British
Special Air Services, Jeff understood that warriors sometimes have dreams, and his keen gray eyes beneath bushy
brows studied the sniper, who had been twitching in his
sleep.

Swanson blinked in the bright sunshine that made the
Aegean Sea glow like burnished copper. The boat was rocking
gently, but this was not a death cruise. The fucking Boatman
didn't get him this time. Instead, he was safe aboard the
Vagabond, one of Jeff's favorite toys. One hundred and eighty
feet long and twenty-nine feet wide, the yacht was as sleek
as a needle and carried five luxurious cabins and a crew of
eleven, plus a full-time captain. A pair of 3,240-horsepower
engines thrummed quietly somewhere below the polished teak
decks.

Swanson yawned. "Okay," he said. "Let me wash up and
grab something wet to drink and I'll be ready." His mouth
was dry. "Go tend your flock. Five minutes." Jeff smiled and
slapped him on the back and returned into the air-conditioned
main cabin where three venture capital money men, two
Americans and one Brit, were having drinks, and resumed

promising them an opportunity to buy into a river of gold. When Jeff retired from the SAS, he had made a quick fortune as a consultant to defense industries, then raked together an even bigger pile of money by designing, producing, and selling high-tech weapons on his own. At the age of sixty, he had a knighthood for his outstanding, although undisclosed, services to the Empire, a Bill Gates-size checkbook, and better hair than Donald Trump.

Kyle Swanson got up, stretched, adjusted his bathing suit, and walked to the hot tub area.

Jeff's wife, Lady Patricia, was in a lounge chair. She wore a big white straw hat that provided a circle of shade that protected her face. She was drinking neat whiskey and smoking a thin cigar as she read a Danielle Steel novel. Her shimmering blue one-piece bathing suit was covered by a gauzy wrap. Lady Pat had put up with being a military wife for years and now openly enjoyed the good life. In Kyle's opinion, she had earned it.

The venture capitalists had brought along the eye candy for the week of cruising among the Greek islands, their stunningly beautiful young trophy wives, who had been topless almost since the yacht left Naples two days ago. Now they lay bronzing on large towels beside the pool, toasting magnificent plastic breasts that gleamed with oil. Kyle wondered if there was a factory somewhere with an assembly line that stamped out these kids for rich old farts.

He sat on the edge of the hot tub, stuck his feet in the warm water, and nodded in their direction. "You ought to do that," he told his girlfriend, Lieutenant Commander Shari Towne. "You know, take off your top for a while. Looks comfortable."

"No," she said, protectively adjusting the top of her red bikini.

"You're already way out of uniform, ma'am." Her long black hair lay wet against her dark shoulders, and just looking into her black eyes made his stomach do flips, because he considered Shari to be the most delectable intelligence officer in the U.S. Navy. She had been born in Jordan to an American father and a Jordanian mother, both of whom worked for their respective governments. Shari was only six years old when her father, a young diplomat based in Amman with the State Department, was killed in a plane crash. Her mother was a public relations and tourism specialist and worked at embassy postings in Cairo, Paris, and Tokyo before her current assignment as head of the public relations department for the Jordanian Embassy in Washington.

Shari was fluent in several languages by the time she entered George Washington University and accepted a U.S. Navy commission upon graduation. It did not take long for her to land in Naval Intelligence, where, after compiling a sterling record, she was snapped up to be an analyst for the National Security Council. Her office was only a desk in a basement cubicle, but the address was still the best in town, 1600 Pennsylvania Avenue: the White House.

"Go away," Shari told Kyle, closing her eyes and leaning against the high-pressure jets that churned the water into frothy bubbles around her. She lifted her face to the sun.

"Hey," Swanson argued. "Your boobs are real! We ought to show them off."

"*We?* You don't get a vote on that. You want tits, go over there and ogle the Desperate Housewives." Her breathing rate had not increased and her eyes remained closed as she insulted him. She added, in Arabic, "Screw you."

"Screw me? Now there's a thought," Kyle replied in the same language. His smooth line wasn't working, but the evening held promise. Swanson splashed water on his face, wiped it with a soft towel, and stole a few sips from the glass of iced tea at Shari's side.

On the deck above, Jeff herded the potential investors to the railing and explained what was going to happen.

Kyle glanced at them. Soft men in shorts and bright shirts. "I gotta go to work now," he said. "Blow up some shit for Jeff's pals."

"So go," Shari ordered. She opened her eyes and gave him a smile.

Lady Pat lowered her steamy novel, peered at him above her sunglasses for a moment, and also got in a barb. "And

Kyle, dear, please remember that these ladies and gentlemen are Sir Geoffrey's dear friends, important guests and investors. So do be a good boy and try not to kill anyone, at least until after dinner, would you please?"

"Does that include smartass broads, m'lady?"

CHAPTER 3

THEY WERE FAR OUT IN OPEN WATER, the horizon an unbroken straight line all around. Through an optical illusion, it appeared to be above them, as if they were at the bottom of a saucer.

Swanson made his way to the broad lower aft deck, where he found a tall, thin man working beside three fifty-five-gallon drums. "Hey, Tim," he said, and opened the protective, cushioned box in which a pristine big rifle lay like a jewel. "You ready?"

Timothy Gladden had been a captain with the elite British Parachute Regiment for more than a decade, leaving the Paras only because a broken right leg did not heal properly and doctors would not allow him to continue jumping out of airplanes. He resigned his commission and launched a vigorous new hobby as a triathlete, principally to prove the British Army diagnosis wrong. There was nothing wrong with his leg, nor with his Oxford-trained brain, and Sir Jeff had hired him into the corporate side of his growing weapons development business. Once a poor farm boy in Wales, Tim was now deputy chairman.

"Of course, old boy," he said. "I'll toss in the blue barrel first, then the red and the yellow at fifteen-second intervals, steadily increasing the visibility problem. The blue one is going to present you with a very difficult shot." He thumped one barrel, which gave back a hollow clanging echo. It contained only ten gallons of gasoline, so the remaining space was packed with explosive fumes. "The captain is making a steady twenty knots and will hold her course straight whenever you are ready. Make all three shots from prone, if you will."

A section of the aft railing had been removed, and Swanson slid into the familiar position flat on his stomach and dug the toes of his deck shoes into the rubberized mat. One problem with designing a new generation of sniper rifle was that he had not been allowed to actually shoot an enemy soldier with it in a combat situation, which made all the difference. Range targets cannot think and react or shoot back, while a human being might turn, duck away, trip, or break into a run in a microsecond and spoil an otherwise perfectly good solution. This field test was designed to duplicate those sorts of unexpected movements, as the floating colored barrels would rise, fall, spin, and bounce unpredictably in the waves.

Jeff came down the ladder, his eyes bright with excitement. "The lads upstairs are primed and hungry for adventure, so don't get nervous on me now, Kyle," he said in a tight voice.

Kyle pushed the cool fiberglass stock of Excalibur, the best sniper rifle in the world, hard into his shoulder. It had been molded to fit him like a custom-made Armani suit. "Be quiet, Jeff," he said.

The aristocratic British voice repeated, "Really, there is no pressure, Kyle. Just take your time, lad, and do it right."

He brought his eye to the scope and clicked a button with his thumb. That activated a BA229 lithium battery and engaged the heads-up display, and the scope came alive with numbers that paraded in a steady, changing readout. The range to the target, measured in meters by an infrared laser, showed in the upper right-hand corner, while digits at the top left gave the wind compensation. Barometric pressure was in the lower right, and the bottom left figures summed up all of that and gave the exact setting to dial in the scope. The weapon was doing the algorithms that he normally would have had to do in his head.

"We will be videotaping this test," Jeff said, rubbing his hands in anticipation.

It had taken a while for Kyle to become familiar with the moving avalanche of numbers, but with practice, they had become part of the background and did not distract from his concentration. He took a deep breath and steadied Excalibur in his left palm, exhaling slightly and tightening his finger on the trigger. He did not want to move in any way that might change his position. "I got it, Jeff. No pressure! Videotape! Now will you please be quiet?"

No pressure. Only that he was being watched by a line of venture capitalist vultures along the stern rail of the yacht with drinks in their hands and fat checkbooks in their pockets. If Swanson could make Excalibur sing today, they would invest millions of dollars and pounds with Jeff to build secret weapons with dream-world technology. Even so, Kyle thought, this was just dollars and cents. Pressure came in battle, when if you missed, your buddies died.

"I can't believe I'm putting the future of my entire corporation in the hands of a bloody Marine," Jeff complained.

"The SAS eats shit for breakfast," Swanson growled. "Now shut the fuck up, get this tub steady, and drop the barrels." He wiped the world from his mind and concentrated on the scope, settling into his personal cone of silence. Things slowed down, his senses increased, and background noises became whispers. He was becoming one with his rifle.

Tim Gladden said, "Trust the numbers, Kyle. Trust the numbers." He felt the big yacht, which handled like a sports car, settle into a smooth glide.

Kyle had gotten to know Jeff Cornwell while running joint special operations, and their friendship had grown tight over the years. When Cornwell had set his engineers and scientists to work designing a state-of-the-art weapon for long-range precision firing, he asked the Pentagon to loan him Kyle Swanson as a consultant periodically when he was not on other assignments, and the generals had agreed.

Swanson had loved the weapon from the moment he saw

the raw diagrams, and Jeff knew how to speak sniper talk. Together with the engineers in a span of three years, they built a sniper's wet dream.

It was a very smart weapon, and fired a hand-crafted .50-caliber round that increased the power of a punch over longer distances. Developing experimental material, with Kyle and Jeff insisting on a lightweight weapon that would be easy to carry in the field, the engineers had developed a super epoxy for the stock and a special alloy for the trigger assembly. The rifle was surprisingly light, only 19.9 pounds with a full magazine, a critical factor for the man who would have to lug it around all day in combat. The normal .50-caliber sniper rifle weighs in at 37 pounds unloaded. The free-floating barrel provided space and could whip up and down when fired but not throw off the sight, which was further strengthened with an internal gyrostabilizer. The gyrostabilized infrared laser worked with a small geopositioning satellite transmitter and receiver in the stock to triangulate the precise distance between the rifle and the target. The GPS provided a further element of safety by letting a sniper know his exact position anywhere in the world. When the sniper is out there all alone, that little bit of information can mean a lot. The rifle, therefore, was more than the sum of its mechanical parts. It was an incredibly accurate weapon system that reduced the chance of a miss by at least 75 percent. In many tests, Kyle put a shot group within a half-minute of angle, an eight-inch circle, at up to 1,600 meters in daylight and 1,000 meters at night. The average human head measures ten to twelve inches. If he could see an enemy a mile away, he could kill him with a shot right to the head.

They named it Excalibur, after King Arthur's magical sword, and it was more than strong enough to end any bad guy's day.

Jeff counted down from five and whispered, "Go!" Tim pushed the blue barrel overboard and it hit the water with a loud splash. Twenty knots may not seem fast, but the twisting target rushed away from the boat, tumbling in the wake, already growing smaller. Kyle could not fire until all three were in the water. He heard the red one go over, watched it through the scope as it wiggled into the distance, and the final fifteen seconds seemed like an eternity before the yellow one splashed overboard. "You may fire in five seconds," Jeff said, and did another countdown.

He looked for the yellow barrel, but already the water had snapped it out of the frame of the scope. It was just too close, and he lowered the magnification by fine-tuning the focus ring. As he brought it back into the picture, he punched the laser button once to lock onto the target and a second time to get the range. Exactly 547 meters. That alone was amazing, since he did not have to consult any written tables of mathematics nor wait for a second man, the spotter, to come up with the information. It was all right there in the scope, and the rifle was making its own adjustments. The laser locked on and talked to the GPS system, which had a brief chat with the gyrostabilizer, and it didn't matter what the barrel did now as long as Kyle kept it in view. Excalibur automatically computed any changes and adjusted the firing solution. The barrel squirmed in the water and the rifle tracked it, numbers whirling in the scope.

"You may commence firing," said Jeff. The scope gave a microsecond flash of a bright blue stripe down one edge that meant everything was ready. Kyle gently squeezed the trigger straight back, for to press it even slightly sideways could screw up a shot.

Excalibur barked a sharp, keening sound and the bullet smashed hot and hard into the yellow barrel, detonating the collected gasoline fumes inside like a small bomb. The container disintegrated in a loud explosion and pieces of shrapnel showered down, some almost reaching the *Vagabond*. Lady Pat was not going to be pleased about that.

Swanson was already looking for the red barrel that was somewhere on the other side of the ball of orange fire and gray smoke. Some movement contrasted with the ordinary motion of the water, and he found it out at 893 meters, about nine football fields behind the boat. This time he didn't wait for the blue stripe, but just locked on the laser and squeezed the trigger. Another explosion shook the water to prove the hit, followed by a ball of fire and more smoke as he jacked in a fresh round.

Jeff was dancing a little jig off to the side. He had stolen a look at the money men and their wives at the rail, and they were pointing and talking excitedly. "They're wetting their knickers up there," he said. Tim Gladden held a pair of big binoculars to his eyes.

But when the smoke cleared, Kyle couldn't see anything but water. The damned barrel seemed to have vanished, but he did not dare remove his eye from the scope. "I don't see it, Kyle," Gladden said.

Swanson slowly glassed the wake directly behind the boat and let the laser scan the surface, looking for something solid. The laser blinked momentarily when it found the steel surface of the bobbing barrel, and Kyle saw a little blue dot that was not much different from the color of the water, ducking and weaving behind low waves.

"There!" said Gladden. "About a thousand meters or so and off to the port side ten degrees."

The laser measured and the computer did its thing. Exactly 966 meters. Tricky-ass shot. *Follow the bouncing ball and trust the numbers.* Swanson exhaled and took up slack on the trigger and the blue stripe flashed in the scope. *Squeeeeze.* Excalibur barked in triumph and he could see the disturbed air trailing the bullet, which ate up the distance in an instant. This time everyone saw the fireball detonate before the sound of the explosion reached the boat.

"Yes!" cheered Tim. "My, what a fine shot!" It was as high a compliment as could be expected from another warrior.

"Beautiful," said a relieved Jeff. "You got them all."

Swanson lowered the rifle to a little stand beside the mat and realized that he was drenched in sweat. "Boys," he pronounced, "this puppy works."

His part of the demonstration was done. Now he and Shari could totally relax for the next ten days. Tim would run things for the next few days while Jeff wrung cash from the impressed investors. The rest of the cruise would be a treat, with opportunities to sample the local wines, food and grapes and cheese, and fire-breathing ouzo in places like Piraeus, Monemvasia, and Mykonos. The two of them planned to spend a few days alone in Venice, walk over the Bridge of Sighs, visit the Doge's Palace, slip through the canals in one of those big canoes called gondolas, and dance in the moonlight on the wet stones of St. Mark's Square. Time for fun.

CHAPTER 4

TWO MERCENARIES RESTED their elbows in pockets of loose sand and held large binoculars steady as they watched the oncoming Thursday morning traffic. Only their hands and heads, covered by desert-brown camouflage, were visible above a small hill crowned by scrub brush about ten meters from the highway between Riyadh and Dhahran in Saudi Arabia. AK-47 assault rifles were strapped across their backs and rocket-propelled grenade launchers were at their sides. Between them, a radio transmitter lay sealed in a plastic bag that protected it from sand. Everything was in place for the snatch-and-pull ambush.

They had worked through the night, digging into the gravel beside the highway. By dawn, passing vehicles had whipped up enough dirt and debris to erase almost all traces of their work. The only evidence that a bomb had been planted was a needle-thin wire antenna that stuck up six inches above the dirt.

The night had ended suddenly, and the brilliant summer sun rising behind them punished the eyes of oncoming drivers. It was hot, already in the low nineties, and sweat trickled down their faces, but they would not lower their binoculars.

"Gettin' hot, Vic," observed former U.S. Army Ranger Jim Collins. He stood six feet tall but was the smaller of the two.

"No shit, Jimbo? Hot in Saudi Arabia? You're fuckin' brilliant." Victor Logan's rumbling voice was more like a low growl. The former chief petty officer in the U.S. Navy SEALs never let Collins forget who was in charge of this Shark Team.

"Just sayin'," Collins replied, then shut his mouth and thought about the money instead. They were getting fifty thousand dollars each for this job. He wanted to talk about what he planned to do with the cash. Definitely a new truck. When they got back to the house, he would log onto eBay Motors and shop for a while.

Vic Logan and Jimbo Collins were part of an elite group of hand-picked former special ops warriors who were used only for high-risk, off-the-books jobs by a multinational private security company. Logan grinned. *If we're Sharks, then I'm a Great White and this dumbass is a fucking Hammerhead.*

The big American was pissed at everyone, including himself. He had been less than six months from retirement, with twenty years in the navy, when his career went down the toilet. The body of a badly beaten young prostitute was discovered in an alley in Naples, and the shore patrol found him passed out a block away, drunk as a skunk. Since the only witness was dead and no evidence tied him to the girl, the cops had to cut him free, but Vic Logan was through as a SEAL. They had kicked him off the teams so fast it had made his head spin. *And I hadn't done anything all that wrong!* There was not enough evidence for a court-martial, but some sea lawyers picked through his records and found enough dirty laundry for fighting, drunkenness, assault on an officer, and suspicions concerning another dead whore in Olongapo, that dirtbag town right outside of Subic Bay, to lay an Administrative Separation hearing on his ass. The AdSep ruled Logan to be morally unfit for service, which was the navy's chickenshit way to get rid of him. It took everything—rank, loss of pay, benefits, and retirement—and he was told to consider himself lucky that there was no jail time and no federal conviction.

Fuck the navy, the SEALs, and the whores, including the ones they never found. In his view, the AdSep was trumped-up bullshit. If he killed enemies of his country, he got medals. Stop a couple of whores trying to rip him off and he was framed. Within six months he hired on as a merc. This was payback.

The most difficult part of the job was waiting, and their patience was rewarded when three boxy, shiny black Hummers came into view, heading toward them like a line of big beetles.

They knew exactly who was in each vehicle. A radio update had come in moments after the convoy had departed the U.S. Embassy compound in Riyadh. Brigadier General Bradley Middleton of the U.S. Marine Corps was alone in the back of the big vehicle in the middle of the small convoy. A Marine guard was in the front seat, along with the Saudi driver.

Another armed Marine rode shotgun beside the driver of the lead Hummer, with two Saudi security troopers in the rear. The trailing vehicle had a driver and another Saudi guard, and its passengers were a young woman Marine captain who was the general's aide, and a civilian escort from the foreign ministry.

On they came, arrow-straight along the broad road. A mile. Half a mile and coming fast. On the ridge, Vic Logan readied the little radio transmitter.

In the lead car, Staff Sergeant Norman Burroughs was glad the trip was almost done. He felt naked in the unarmored, civilian-style Hummer. Cool air-conditioning blew on his face, but he would have preferred to be sweating and uncomfortable inside a Marine armored vehicle with a .50-caliber machine gun up top. Burroughs did not like this place. Trouble just seemed to ooze from the desert sands. The Saudi guards and the driver were joking and smoking cigarettes instead of paying attention. Security was for shit. The staff sergeant tugged the brim of his hat lower, adjusted his sunglasses, and continued to stare into the morning sun as he counted off the

miles back to the real world, which for him was the Marine
Expeditionary Unit aboard the task force cruising in the Per-
sian Gulf. His fingers unconsciously traced the trigger guard
of the M-16 rifle propped between his knees, locked and
loaded.

The driver smirked at the nervous American. Dhahran
and Riyadh were the two safest places in the kingdom, and
the long road between them was smooth as glass and totally
safe. He had driven it a hundred times or more just in the
past year, and knew that he would soon be away from this
unpleasant heat, spending the day at a villa in the cooler
Dhahran Hills, waiting to pick up a government official for
the return trip to Riyadh in the evening.

Burroughs kept his eyes moving, looking for possible
threats, but by the time he saw a glitter of sunlight bouncing
off the thin wire antenna, the speed of the Hummer had
taken them into the kill zone. The staff sergeant started to
yell a warning, but didn't make it.

The bomb detonated with a horrendous roar, and the
first Hummer catapulted into the air, flipped twice, and
crashed down on its roof. The fiery wreckage skidded and
ground forward on the pavement, bathed in churning smoke
and flame.

When the blast wave rolled over them, Logan and Collins
moved smoothly into kneeling positions with the rocket-
propelled grenade launchers on their shoulders. They triggered a pair of missiles that rushed with low hissing sounds
toward the last Hummer, and the car exploded in a ball of fire.

They tossed the launchers aside and ran down the slope
with AK-47s in hand. Collins broke away to check the rear
vehicle, while Logan opened fire on the middle Hummer, a
careful fusillade that destroyed the tires, crashed into the engine, shot out the front windshield, and killed the driver and
the guard in the front seat. Bullets sang in ricochets, glass
shattered, and a smell of burning rubber and oily smoke
oozed from the destroyed vehicle.

Jimbo Collins returned from the rear vehicle dragging the

general's aide, Captain Linda Hurst, by her arm. She was dazed. Her face and short blond hair were caked with sticky blood, her ribs ached, and a leg was broken. She had barely been able to focus when she was pulled from the wreckage, and thought for a moment that she was being rescued. Instead she was jerked from the car and pulled down the road, the pavement peeling away bloody strips of skin from her legs. She was dropped at the feet of a large man wearing old blue jeans, a brown T-shirt, tan desert combat boots, and a brown scarf that masked his face. Captain Hurst could not hear her own screams, because the RPG blast had destroyed her eardrums.

"General Middleton! Get out of the vehicle right now, or I kill this bitch!" Logan pointed his rifle at the wounded and bleeding woman.

Middleton, gasping for breath in the smoke, had his pistol out, but recognized the situation as hopeless. He had seen the lead Humvee evaporate in the explosion, and when the RPGs took out the car in back, he dove to the floor for safety as his own vehicle was shot to pieces. His entire security detail was dead and all he had left was his Colt .45 pistol, while the attackers had automatic weapons, RPGs, and a hostage. Although he knew all of this, he still hesitated, because Marines don't surrender. Why hadn't they killed him, too?

A few seconds later, another burst of AK-47 fire tore into Captain Hurst's right arm and her screaming rose. Several cars that had slowed on the far side of the highway scurried away when the drivers saw what was happening.

"I SAID GET OUT OF THAT DAMNED CAR!" Vic Logan roared again.

Middleton hardly knew the young officer who lay out there. She had been assigned as a temporary aide at the start of the trip, and had done little more than carry his briefcase in Riyadh while he talked with the Saudis. Had he been alone, he might have chosen to fight, but he could not let the kid be murdered. "All right! I'm getting out!" he called, and dropped the pistol. He opened the car door, raised both hands above his head, and stepped into the bright sun.

Jimbo Collins jerked the general's arms behind his back and expertly slapped on steel Smith & Wesson handcuffs. Once he was secured, Vic Logan casually double-tapped Captain Hurst. Two 7.62 mm bullets blew off the back of her head.

The Shark Team pushed and hauled the general away from the burning pyre of the highway, over the sandy ridge, and down to where a dark green Land Rover was parked in the dry gulch. They threw him into the back seat and Logan got in beside him. Collins slid behind the steering wheel and started the engine, and the strong Land Rover surged forward in four-wheel drive.

Middleton flinched when a hypodermic needle plunged into his arm. He felt the morphine circulate through his system, and hissed through gritted teeth: "I'll kill you both."

"Shut up," said Logan. "You ain't gonna be killing nobody." He tossed the needle out of the window.

As he collapsed, Middleton's mind finally registered what he had been too busy to comprehend. The general's last thought before the morphine swept him into blackness was, *My God, these are Americans!*

CHAPTER 5

YOU ARE A VERY TROUBLED PERSON," said the sniper to the knight, pointing at a beautifully presented Hearts of Palm salad that was the first course of a fantastic lunch aboard the *Vagabond*. It was an old Special Forces thing. In desert survival training, with no food, you could chop down a palm tree to get at the tasty, edible centers. Anyone who endured the experience would have done it so many times that they would swear never to eat another Hearts of Palm salad as long as they lived.

"You ungrateful American! My chef will be crushed," said Jeff with an easy laugh as he pushed away his own salad. "Perhaps you would prefer a peanut butter and jelly sandwich?" Tim Gladden also passed on the salad.

The others at the table had no idea what the three military men were talking about, so Jeff steered the conversation into areas in which his business guests could glitter and glow. As if wound up mechanically, they soon were rattling on about new companies preparing IPOs, who got how much of a bonus for leading a company into bankruptcy, and who had been indicted. It was too easy to get those guys to talk about themselves. They did not include or need anyone else in their conversation about finances and the venture capital world. The ladies switched to serious relationship chatter about the breakups and marriages of supermarket tabloid celebrities, and when Lady Pat and Shari tuned in to the gossip, Jeff hauled Tim Gladden and Kyle Swanson out on deck.

They toasted with cold green bottles of Heineken beer and lit fresh cigars that Jeff vowed had been rolled on the thighs of Cuban virgins who afterward were personally deflowered by Castro himself.

Kyle said, "You know, I swear that little blonde was giving her husband a hand job beneath the tablecloth. His eyes were crossing."

"Gawd. How does one control newlyweds? She's thirty years younger than he. I hope she doesn't give him a heart attack before we can cash his Excalibur check," said Tim.

"Our bank already confirmed it," said Jeff. "If he dies, he dies with a smile, we bury him at sea and console the grieving widow." He turned to Swanson and put on his serious face. "So, what's your answer?"

"Same as always. Thanks but no thanks." The wind pulled the smoke away, toward the distant lights that marked towns along the heel of the Italian boot.

"Kyle, you are not getting any younger. You cannot do your sort of work forever."

"I like what I do, Jeff. I'm a pretty fair sniper, and somebody has to do it."

Tim spoke up. "I have news for you, old man. You are not indispensable. When you leave, another Marine will step into your place. I didn't see how Ten Para could possibly get along without me, either, but somehow they did just fine."

Jeff agreed. "The biggest hurdle is the first one, hanging up the uniform. You know it's going to happen sooner or later."

"The time isn't right. I'll know when. Not yet."

"Don't wait too long," said Gladden. "Thanks to this grumpy old man, I found a new and worthwhile career. I used to think a hundred thousand dollars was a lot of money, but with the patents and proprietary interests the company has developed, there is much, much more available. And we desperately need your help on new projects."

Jeff emptied his beer, tossed the bottle overboard, and uncapped a new one. "You and Tim and I are the only people who know everything about the Excalibur project. We had the engineers work only on specific sections. Once we finish the field trials, those guns are gold, Kyle. After that show you put on yesterday, those investors couldn't write checks fast enough. You have more than earned a share."

"I worked on it as part of my job, guys," Swanson replied. "The Marine Crotch would throw my ass in the brig if I got paid extra for it." The sideways offer had caught him off guard. They were willing to put up part of the action on the future licensing and sales of Excalibur. A fortune.

"We only bribe politicians," Gladden said. "We are just pointing out that you would be an extremely valuable asset to our company, and also that we could make it worth your while financially."

Jeff looked at Swanson like a priest at a sinner and abruptly changed the subject. "Damn it all, man, why don't you and Shari *both* just get out of the military business? I know you want to get married, but you're wedded to your jobs instead of each other. That is not good at all, lad. You must grab time before it passes you by. Anyway, I want a grandson."

"Been talking to her, have you? And you can't have a grandson by us because we're not related."

"I was speaking in general terms. A granddaughter would be just as welcome. No, we haven't spoken with her about it, although Pat has been planning the wedding for some time, something terribly romantic and worthy of a pop diva. You may not have reached the point yet where you want to make the change to private enterprise, but you will, my friend. When you do, I promise you a soft landing. We just want you to hurry up."

"You'll be the first to know."

Tim gave him his unsmiling commando look. "Maybe we have a competitor for your highly marketable skill? Has one of those dreadful PSCs come a-knocking on your door, offering some big money to the super sniper?" He was talking about private security companies, the modern mercenaries.

"Oh, hell, no. I would never be a merc. There are a ton of

those jobs out there, but you can never trust them because you don't know where their loyalties really lie. They're like Doctor Frankenstein's monster, and could just as easily spin out of control. Anyway, if I kill somebody while I wear the uniform, it's okay. I don't know how that would play out if the mercs take part in combat ops."

Gladden laughed. "Oh, Kyle, you are so naïve. They're already running combat missions. Have been for years. Some PSCs have armored vehicles, choppers, and even some old jet fighters now. Bleedin' private armies, they are, for sale to the highest bidder. And with the U.S. military heading toward privatization, it's only a matter of time before they are authorized and paid to fight an entire war by themselves. It just plays better to the public if some South African merc is lost in action for a noble cause rather than the boy next door."

"If it's so great, why aren't you two in on it?" It wasn't like Jeff to pass up a good business opportunity. There were hundreds of millions of dollars in the PSC game.

Jeff shrugged. "Like you, chum. We were professional soldiers for much too long. I'm more than satisfied with my company and its products, and I'm old-fashioned enough to enjoy being in the service of my queen and country."

"So, as you Marines would say, 'Fuck the Frankensteins,'" said Tim Gladden, holding his beer aloft.

Jeff raised his bottle, too. "Fuck the Frankensteins."

Kyle Swanson touched theirs with his own. "Fuck the Frankensteins."

CHAPTER 6

THE IMMACULATE PILATES, a Swiss single-engine private aircraft painted midnight blue with gold trim, lifted smoothly away from a dry riverbed, its powerful turboprop engine leaving a triangle of sand hovering momentarily in the air behind it. By the time the dust settled back onto the desert, the beautiful plane was gone, building to a cruising speed of two hundred knots while skimming no more than two hundred feet above the sand to avoid radar. In the two and a half hours since taking off from a crude airstrip, it had flown northeast from Dhahran, and then dashed out of Saudi Arabia and into Jordanian airspace without being spotted by the air defense commands of either country. It was just another private executive plane in a region that had fleets of them belonging to rich and powerful princes and sheikhs. Even if it had been seen, no one would have questioned it, nor paid it any mind. The color scheme was recognized as that of a powerful Iraqi, Ali Shalal Rassad, the Rebel Sheikh of Basra, and it was best not to be too curious about him.

A dirty truck was waiting when the Pilates landed on a macadam road outside a village, and the unconscious General Bradley Middleton was carried off the plane by his two American captors and stuffed into the rear seat of a waiting car for a ten-minute drive to a specific address. Vic Logan pulled another hypodermic needle from his kit and injected Middleton to start bringing him up from the blackness.

Dull colors, garbled words, and a sense of awkward, jerking motions blended in Middleton's drug-muddled mind. His brain could not separate the individual things happening around him, nor grasp any meaning. The only thing he felt was a pounding headache. Pain got through. Strong hands held his arms and propelled him forward. His feet would not respond; his legs were rubbery. The dragging stopped, and he was forced to sit in a chair. More words he did not understand, and a sensation of something wet cooling his face. Scrubbing hard. Words. He shook his head to clear the cobwebs of scrambled thought, with no result. Laughter. Hands worked with his clothing, tucking in his khaki shirt, smoothing his collar, straightening his tie, and adjusting the shining single star on each collar point, half-inch and centered.

Pinpoint flashes of shifting light danced at the edge of his consciousness, blinking like a field of fireflies. Then they were gone. The fireflies had flown. A smell of something rotten rose in his nostrils. Camels or goats close by.

A soothing female voice spoke English words with a lilting accent, and a gentle hand tilted his chin back. *"Here, General. Drink this. All is well. Just drink this."* A cool stream of water went across his tongue and down his throat. He gulped it in relief. Thirst. *"That's enough for right now, because we don't want to make you sick. You can drink more in a few minutes."*

His arms were tied around the back of a small chair to keep him from falling. He sensed other people.

A moment of total silence was followed by the blazing lights of a dozen suns, strong enough to make him wince. He began to breathe fast, and unreasoning panic set in, bringing a childhood nightmare of a monster, frothing at the mouth, that chased him. He struggled momentarily, and then settled.

When he was calm, a soft command was given and a video camera began to record the image of the Marine general bound to the chair, the shining single star of his rank leaving no doubt as to his identity. A man's voice read a statement in Arabic. The camera caught it all the first time, but the statement was repeated just in case. The lights went out.

Middleton felt a tiny prick in his arm as another needle went in to return him to the dark world, then strong hands lifted him. A fist slammed into his stomach, doubling him over. He gasped for air, then vomited. Another blow, and he was on his knees, being kicked to the floor. Laughter, fading. Blackness. Pain still got through.

The cameraman reviewed the scene to be sure his Panasonic PV-GS250 had done its job, and nodded in approval. The low-light problem had been solved by stealing a rack of huge bulbs that a road crew had been using for night work. He plugged a USB cord between the camera and a Dell computer and downloaded the images and soundtrack onto a small disc, which he slid into a protective hard plastic case and handed to the woman. She folded a written copy of the statement and dropped it and the videodisc into a common brown envelope that she taped closed. Licking it would have left traces of her DNA. In an hour, she was in Amman, Jordan, where she handed the package to the front desk clerk of the hotel that was the residence of the local correspondent for the al Jazeera television network. She walked two blocks, paused beneath a tree, and called the correspondent on a cell phone. "This is the Foreign Ministry's press office, sir. We have delivered a news release to your hotel," she said in French, cut the connection, and tossed the phone into a trash bin.

The correspondent recognized her voice, and knew this had nothing to do with the Jordanian Foreign Ministry. A confidential contact had resurfaced, one who had never given him a bad story. He hurried downstairs, retrieved the envelope, returned to his room, and dumped the contents onto his desk. After reading the statement, he watched the video. *Unbelievable!* He pulled a bottle of Jack Daniel's bourbon from a suitcase, and only after two stiff shots of whiskey did he call the busy al Jazeera newsroom in Doha, Qatar. It was two o'clock, plenty of time for the evening newscast, but he knew they would not hold the story until then. It was too important.

When it was broadcast, the sedated General Middleton was finishing a smooth hop aboard a twin-engine Cessna 421 into Syria. A Land Rover hauled him on the last leg of his journey, and he slept for fourteen hours.

CHAPTER 7

GOOD DAY, LADIES AND GENTLEMEN. I have to brief the President in a few minutes, so let us get right to it. What's happening with this kidnapped general?" National Security Advisor Gerald Buchanan swept his gray eyes around the White House Situation Room at nine o'clock in the morning. Every chair was occupied and staff members hovered nearby. "CIA. You start."

John Mueller, the deputy director of operations for the Central Intelligence Agency, flipped open a folder branded with a diagonal Top Secret red stripe, hunched forward in his chair, and read the cover sheet that distilled the basics. "General Bradley Middleton of the Marine Corps was abducted just outside of Dhahran, Saudi Arabia, about 0300 hours this morning, Washington time. His two Marine bodyguards, his aide, and the Saudi security team were all either killed in the explosion of the roadside bomb or executed during a follow-up attack. Witnesses saw two men take the general away over a ridge beside the highway. Tire tracks led to a nearby paved road, where they could have gone either way. Al Jazeera was broadcasting the story only a few hours later. An anonymous caller to al Jazeera, after the broadcast, claimed credit in behalf of the Holy Scimitar of Allah. The Holy Scimitar, of course, is the name of the militia of the

Rebel Sheikh in Iraq. The caller said the kidnappers would cut off the general's head unless all U.S., British, and NATO troops and citizens leave the Arabian Peninsula." The CIA man closed the folder and pushed it away. "The demand is obviously ridiculous, so we conclude there must be some other reason or reasons." Mueller quit speaking and crossed his arms on the big table. He had learned to keep his mouth shut when he didn't know anything.

Buchanan glared at him and swore. "Holy Jesus Christ! I heard the same thing on CNN and Fox before I came in here. Does anyone have something that hasn't been on live television? FBI? Talk to me."

"We have a team working with the Saudis on forensics. Nothing conclusive yet. It's just too early." The FBI director also knew not to go too far with Buchanan. Answer the question and shut the hell up.

The National Security Advisor ran a palm across his neatly trimmed hair and sighed. Then he removed his rimless glasses and wiped them with a handkerchief. He wanted these people to stew for a while.

"Anybody?" Buchanan snapped. "How about you, Homeland Security? NSA? DIA? Pentagon? State Department? Anything other than what al Jazeera has been showing to more than fifty million people in their part of the world? The domestic networks and cable over here are going to run it forever."

No one wanted to challenge him. Gerald Buchanan would end a career without a second thought if he detected weakness or a lack of political loyalty, and the fuse was burning on his infamous Irish temper. He unscrewed a fountain pen with a gold nib and scribbled a note to himself, closed the pen, and folded the piece of paper. Everyone wondered if their name was on it. "Ladies and gentlemen, I am not pleased. The President will not be pleased, and our countrymen will not be pleased that after spending billions of dollars to build a global intelligence apparatus, you have once again failed. I would strongly suggest that when we gather again later today, you have some facts for me. Is that clear?"

"Excuse me, Mr. Buchanan. May I?" General Henry Turner, the four-star Marine general who was chairman of the Joint Chiefs of Staff, was not afraid of Buchanan's bluster. He had seen civilians come and go through many administrations and had served them all to the best of his ability. Hank Turner was as close to untouchable as anyone in the room.

Gerald Buchanan detested him. Turner had almost as many advanced degrees as he, plus the general had a heroic reputation, could do more push-ups than a boot camp private, and had even penned a volume of poetry. Still, Buchanan enjoyed recalling that Turner had stood third when he graduated from Annapolis while Buchanan was first in his class at Yale the same year. And his poetry was not all that good.

It was personally satisfying to Buchanan that the highest-ranking officer in all of the military services could speak only with permission in this room. He said, "Go ahead, General. Please. I grow weary of this silence."

"Sir, it is frankly too early for anyone to know much about what has happened to General Middleton. It will all be discovered, but it's going to take some effort and some time. My point is that I really don't care much about what happened *before* Middleton was snatched. I am confident that the intelligence agencies represented around this table will discover that. I want to focus on getting him back as soon as possible."

To Buchanan, the military mindset had always seemed very limiting. Good to have the uniforms around to carry out policy, but original thought was not their strong point. All those badges and ribbons meant little in the halls of real power. "And how is that going to happen? Do you have a plan?"

"With all respect, sir, at the Pentagon, we plan for almost everything, all the time. As soon as we find out where Middleton is being held, we will pull out something suitable and adjust it according to present conditions, and when we receive the authority of our civilian leadership, we will execute it."

"So you don't have a plan."

"Not a detailed one, no. Of course not. But preparations are in motion. The air force has offered its assets, the navy SEAL teams are on alert, the army is spooling up Delta, and the Joint Special Operations Command is on board. We all want the same thing."

"Well, at least that's something that I can take into the Oval Office," said Buchanan. "Thank you, General." He inwardly recorded Turner's condescending *Of course not* as a debt of rudeness to be repaid later.

But Turner was not quite through. "Only this, sir. General Middleton is a Marine. He's one of us. We welcome the support of all branches of service, but we will be the ones to bring him home. I have issued an alert to MARCOM, the Marine Forces Special Operations Command at Camp Lejeune in North Carolina. They are passing the word to the Marine Expeditionary Units in both the Arabian Sea and the Mediterranean. The MEUs are always on a short leash, ready to go."

"You really believe you will be able to do it?" Buchanan raised an eyebrow. "Pull him out of hostile territory?"

"We don't just believe it. We *know* we can." The chairman did not wilt before Buchanan's stare.

"Very well, then. We meet again at noon." Buchanan rose and left the room, annoyed with the arrogance of the Marine. Once back in his office, he dialed the number of Samuel Shafer, his deputy, whose office was across the street in the Old Executive Office Building, and asked if everyone in their shop was present for this emergency. There must be no holes in his own operation that some rival might exploit. He was told that five staff members were absent, for reasons ranging from maternity leave to scheduled days off, but the only one who was really needed was their top Middle East analyst, Lieutenant Commander Shari Towne.

"Then get her in here," Buchanan ordered.

"Sir, she's vacationing on a boat somewhere! Greece, I think. Maybe Italy," exclaimed Shafer.

"I did not ask where she was! Just get her!" He slammed down the telephone, then exhaled slowly and rested both palms on his polished desk. He rubbed it, the smoothness of the shimmering old oak grain almost sensual to his touch. It had been built from the timbers of one of the navy's first warships, and had been used in the Oval Office by President Lyndon Johnson. Buchanan allowed himself a private smile. Old LBJ. Now there was someone who was never afraid to exercise power. He would thump men on the chest when he was talking to them to make sure they got the message, personally telephone reporters in the middle of the night to harass them, and when a Marine guard once advised Johnson that his helicopter was waiting, the President replied, "Son, they're *all* my helicopters." Maybe, Buchanan thought, some of Lyndon's magic was still in the wood of the ancient sailing ship.

He savored the moment. There was nothing better than this, not even sex. Buchanan had controlled the emergency conference on an international crisis and, with a simple instruction, had set in motion a scramble that would ricochet throughout the U.S. government until a low-ranking naval officer was found on a boat and fetched back from half a world away. He gathered his briefing book and headed toward the Oval Office. Power. Delicious.

CHAPTER 8

SENATOR THOMAS GRAHAM Miller, chairman of the Senate Armed Services Committee, pushed away the remains of a seafood dinner, stood, and gave a crisp salute to the three hundred cheering veterans who had paid $1,000 each to be with him tonight, paratroopers all. He was proud to be one of them, for when he was young, he, too, had worn the distinctive shoulder patch of the 82nd Airborne Division. He could always count on his fellow vets to help fill the election coffers, but they were more than cash cows to him, just as Miller was more than just another politician to them. This was his Band of Brothers. It irritated him that the Screaming Eagles of the 101st always got the good publicity.

Miller had used his military benefits to get his college education, then a law degree, and became an aggressive prosecutor. He rode a record of achievement, impeccable behavior, and honesty to a seat in the House of Representatives for six years before he was fifty years old, then vaulted to the Senate, where he was in the middle of his third term. He still had the build of an airborne trooper, ran every morning, and was a bachelor. His wife and infant daughter had died when the birth went horribly twenty years ago, and he never remarried. The image of such a strong and handsome man also being a brokenhearted husband and father made the ladies wilt.

Instead of family, Miller devoted himself to the men and women of the armed forces of the United States, even the damned 101st.

He had begun this long day in Washington, and after lunch he went down to Fort Campbell to view an afternoon jump, some five hundred troopers pouring out of the fat bellies of transport planes from five thousand feet. Miller could almost feel the familiar jerk of the parachute harness as the chutes blossomed like sky flowers and the soldiers drifted to earth. When they landed, formed up, and conducted a maneuver, he felt a tear in his eye, as if he saw himself as one of those strong youngsters who could leap out of a plane, fight, and have energy left over.

After the drop, Miller had scheduled three "political events" across the state, which meant he was grazing for campaign money, and was ending the day at this fine dinner in Louisville. He rolled out his tried-and-true stump speech for a friendly audience, bounding to the podium with gusto, smiling and saluting and waving and pointing to individuals. The senator squinted into the bright lights and made a slightly off-color soldiers' joke to put everyone at ease. The lapel bar of a Silver Star flashed in the light, and the slight limp in his right leg silently proved that he also had been awarded a Purple Heart. He did not need notes, for he knew this speech cold.

"The armed forces of the United States are the finest the world have ever seen, just as they were when you and I wore the uniform," he declared, and leaned close to the microphone and give the guttural fighting call of the clan: *"HOOO-AH!"* Although the audience had just resumed their seats after his introduction, they leaped up again in a standing ovation. It worked every time. He could have filled a bucket with checks after just that opening. But Miller had more to say, and launched into firming up their important support for his current battle.

"The biggest threat we face is not an external enemy. None at all. There is no one, and I mean no one, out there today who can match our planes, our ships, our technology, and the spirit of our fighting men and women. We own the sky, and the space above it. We own the top of the seas, and the waters beneath the waves. When our soldiers put their boots on the ground somewhere, well, we own that, too. Yes, we have a huge budget, one worthy of a superpower, but we spend it wisely, from communications satellites to bullets and beans, and we can take pride in what we have bought. Have no doubt, my friends, that we are still number one. Anyone who messes with us is going to lose.

"But we don't have time to relax and go to Disneyland. Our biggest threat is not from terrorism. We will do our part, and the intelligence and law enforcement agencies of this great land will do their part, and we can keep control of those maniacs. They will occasionally make a splash and create terrible headlines, but they cannot even hope to shake our government or our will. The United States of America and our allies will root out these cockroaches and squelch their evil. That job will take years to complete. It will be done.

"No, my brothers, we face a much more serious threat today, and it comes from inside the Beltway. That's right, in Washington, D.C. There is a crisis facing our military that could be the equivalent of another tsunami or 9/11 or Hurricane Katrina in the danger it poses. I tell you this both because it is true, and because you, as veterans, can see it better than anyone.

"Private security companies threaten our base of funding. In fiscal 2003 alone, the United States spent twenty billion—BILLION!—on contracts with PSCs, which back then were called PMCs, or private military companies. They changed the name from 'military' to 'security' companies to polish their image, but no matter what name they are called for public relations purposes, they are still mercenaries, soldiers of fortune, and professional adventurers. That is our money, dollars that should be going to support and protect our troops. The glossy literature and the K Street lobbyists have found friendly ears, and have changed the debate. Mercenaries have been around for centuries, fighting for whoever paid them the highest dollar, and their reputation was that of guns for hire. Now private enterprise has put the old merc into a clean shirt and tie, scrubbed his face and reputation, and, behold, we have the private security company.

"They started small, just supplying minor logistical support, and we let them take over the preparation and serving of meals in mess halls. They said they could do it cheaper and free up soldiers for more duties. Step by step, as our money flowed their way, they expanded into everything from transportation to ferrying aircraft to providing personal security to VIPs in hot zones. You see that merc in the news pictures all the time—the beefy and bald guy with the Fu Manchu mustache, wearing dark sunglasses, jeans, and an armored vest, and carrying an assault rifle as he escorts some civilian to a meeting. Again, the arguments were cost-effectiveness and not having to assign troops to those duties.

"Now, my friends, the PSCs are taking the next step. The same companies are now running private combat teams, some in the pay of small countries with lots of money but little military expertise. Other units are being inserted into our own areas of operations. The PSCs are back to their basic tricks of being the gunslingers who fight for hire and give short-term loyalty to whoever pays them."

Miller paused for dramatic effect and let his eyes sweep his audience as he took a sip of water. The room was silent, and the audience knew what was coming. He made the same speech almost every day, and it was often shown on television.

"As you have read in the newspapers and seen on the talk shows, I have been making a big deal with the Senate Armed Services Committee, for we are being pummeled to further loosen the rules on the use of mercenary fighters. I have been shown proposals that would make any professional soldier tremble in anger. The Pentagon would turn over entire sectors of our fighting force to the private sector, and give them the most modern equipment to meet today's battlefield challenges. Some argue that these men are also professional soldiers, trained former members of the SEALs and Marines and Rangers and other elite units such as our own 82nd

Airborne, and that they are volunteering for hazardous duty. The wage and benefit packages are attractive to a soldier on active duty.

"By hiring these people, the United States would not have to put as many of our soldiers in harm's way. In other words, they are making a play to take over the armed services. If we surrender in this fight, they will grow stronger while our uniformed services would grow weaker, because all of that money comes out of the same budget. And when the crunch comes, my friends, we won't have soldiers like you out there defending America. Instead, there will be a line of mercs who look tough on film but answer to the call of their paymaster, not to any flag, not even the Stars and Stripes. Some PSCs already hire foreign soldiers whose own armies no longer exist. To whom are they loyal? Would a merc from South Africa or Ukraine or Libya really lay down his life for the USA? Are you willing to bet the lives of your family on them?"

Now he gripped the podium so tightly that his knuckles whitened. The friendly, famous smile was replaced by a grim face that had seen battle. Everyone in the audience detected the change and responded with hushed attention.

"In two weeks, my committee will vote on the first important set of these privatization proposals, and rich lobbyists are swarming around us like sharks. Billions and billions of taxpayer dollars are at stake, but so is the safety of our country. I want you to pull every string you can, call your congressmen, wave the flag, write letters to the editors, call up talk shows, chat with your neighbors. I am traveling the country to alert Americans to this new and unique danger, and I need your help. I am counting on it. We must not allow that bill to pass."

He leaned forward again. "Stand up and hook up, troopers. Stand in the door. Your country needs you to make one more jump."

Tom Miller was exhausted. His press secretary had been dismissed after handing him the typed itinerary for tomorrow's activities during the elevator ride up to the top floor. He closed the door, clicked the television set to CNN, and neatly hung his coat and tie in the closet. He undid his collar and washed his face in the bathroom, letting the cold water rinse away the fatigue. Long days like this made him feel his age.

He groaned when there was a knock on the door. This was supposed to be *alone* time. "Who is it?"

"Trish Campbell, Senator. I'm the night concierge, and the hotel manager asked me to be sure you had everything you need for tonight and tomorrow morning." The voice was pleasant.

The senator peered through the viewing glass in the door. A pretty young woman was smiling, knowing she was being inspected. Her dark hair was in a ponytail, and she wore wire-rimmed glasses and a blue blazer buttoned at the waist. She held a clipboard against her chest. "I'm fine, Ms. Campbell. Just a moment." He opened the door.

Trish Campbell shoved him backward, hard, and a huge man hiding beside the wall spun into the room and immobilized Miller, slapping a big hand across his mouth. Miller tasted rubber and realized the man was wearing latex gloves.

Trish closed the door. "Sorry for the intrusion, Senator. This is Big Lenny," she said. "We will be brief." She also pulled on a pair of gloves and removed from her pocket a plastic bag containing a syringe with a long tube on it instead of a needle. Trish clicked the stopwatch function knob on her big wristwatch, then fed the tube into Miller's mouth between Lenny's fingers and pushed the plunger.

Miller tried to struggle as liquid flowed over his tongue and down his throat. Big Lenny held him like a steel clamp.

Trish Campbell returned the syringe to its sealed bag, which went back into her pocket. She watched him closely with intelligent eyes. "If you're wondering what is killing you, it's a particularly bitchy little strain of shellfish toxia along the lines of a solvent-based tropodotoxin and ricin. I don't know the details because I'm not a scientist. Big Lenny and I are just the messengers. In addition to poisoning you, I am to bid you a fond farewell from Mr. Gordon Gates."

Senator Miller struggled as fire spread through his veins, the heart pumping hard. *Gates!*

"The short version, as I understand it, is that chemical agents are busy shutting down your central nervous system right about now and that is going to cause your heart to fail." She looked at her watch. "You will be dead in a couple of seconds. By the time your body is found tomorrow morning, the toxins will have evaporated and you will be ruled to have croaked from a simple old heart attack." She leaned close and peered hard at his eyes, which were rolling back. "Let him go, Lenny."

Senator Miller fell to the floor and went into convulsions. A vicious spasm arched his back at an impossible angle, he gargled, and his hands flailed at his chest. A final breath was exhaled. Trish Campbell felt for a pulse. There was none. She clicked the stopwatch. Thirty-two seconds, start to finish.

She took a hotel vacuum cleaner from the closet and ran it over the area of carpet that she and Lenny had occupied, returned it to the closet, then opened the door and checked the hallway. It was empty. Lenny went out first and Trish pulled the door closed. When it locked, she hung a plastic white-and-blue DO NOT DISTURB sign on the handle and the Shark Team left the hotel.

CHAPTER 9

SIR JEFF WAS IN A GOOD MOOD. To mark the success of the Excalibur demonstration, which had won over the investors, he decided a celebration ashore was in order on the bright afternoon. His captain found a quiet, rocky cove on the northeastern coast of the Greek island of Corfu and dropped anchor into perfectly green water. The ladies and the venture capital guys went ashore in the runabout first, and Jeff promised that he, Kyle, and Tim would be right along when the inflatable motorboat made a return trip. The sneaky Brit had a surprise for the money men, who planned to leave soon and make their way up through Italy to Florence before returning home.

When the little boat sped away, Jeff ducked into his cabin and returned with three bell-shaped bottles of thick glass containing a dark amber liquid. "Gifts for our departing friends," he said. "Two-hundred-year-old Hennessy Richard Cognac. I picked it up from a wine merchant in Paris just for this occasion." He handed one of the heavy bottles each to both Tim and Kyle, with a stern warning to handle them gently. Each cost $2,000. He liked to keep his business associates happy.

The sheer green beauty of the island was stunning as they approached in the little runabout that bounced fast over the water. Olive trees were everywhere, millions of them, from the heights of Mount Pantocrator down to the white sandy beaches. Kyle was looking forward to a fresh salad with cheese from the local goats as Gladden swung to a smooth stop at a narrow pier. They tied up, grabbed the cognac, and headed ashore to where their group was seated on an odd collection of stools and wooden chairs around little tables at a *psaro taverna,* a fish restaurant. Like most eating establishments in Greece, this one was called the Café Olympia. Irregular weathered stones spread along the front, and tan walls were shaded by the spreading olive branches.

There was a problem with the idyllic scene. Four rough-looking men also were at the tavern, obviously drunk and taunting the guys and making lewd passes at the women. The money men were sitting there, embarrassed, while the girls were trying, without success, to ignore the drunks.

"Oh, my," said Jeff, who wore cream-colored linen trousers, a soft blue shirt, and leather sandals. Tim Gladden had on a lightweight white short-sleeved shirt, creased white pants, and Converse sneakers. Swanson was barefoot, in wrinkled khaki cargo shorts and a brilliant blue Hawaiian shirt with orange palm trees. They looked as threatening as three lost missionaries.

"I say, chaps," Jeff pleasantly addressed the men as he carefully placed his precious cognac bottle on a table. "Would you please be off now? We are just here for a quick and a pleasant lunch and then will be on our way."

The four Greeks stopped pestering the visitors and stared at the newcomers, knowing that playtime was over. Kyle shifted his weight a bit as the drunks rose from their table, pushed aside the chairs, and formed a line, one-two-three-four. In any street fight, the tough guys lead, and the biggest of the bunch was slightly forward in the two position, shoulder-to-shoulder with number three, a husky man with a face scarred like an Ultimate Fighter. The remaining two flanked them. Kyle glanced at Shari and winked. Lady Pat sat back, took another sip of ouzo, and lit a thin cigar.

The largest guy, around six-two, spoke. "You will fuck off now, you rich bastards, and take these three other queers with you. The women can go back to your big boat when we are done."

"Ah, I see," said Jeff. "Well then, lads, I guess we are for it. I'll take this big fellow, if you don't mind."

"No," Tim disagreed. To free his hands, he also put his bottle on a table and moved to a fighting stance. "I want Mr. Big. You can have that ugly one. Scarface."

Kyle smashed his heavy bottle over Big's head, catching him on the left side of the forehead, and raked the jagged edge down across the eye, cheek, and mouth for a maximum cutting effect. Deep inside Swanson, the switch had clicked into combat mode and he was running on automatic. Speed and surprise. Don't let them regroup. Eliminate the threats in descending order of importance.

The first guy collapsed to his knees with a scream, the strong alcohol biting into the deep and bleeding cuts. Kyle already had spun away to his left and slammed his left elbow into the nose of Scarface, knocking him backward across a table. Blood spurted from the fractured nose, and the man's head cracked against the paving stones.

"He is going to be even uglier when he wakes up," Shari said to Pat.

Kyle's momentum was still at work and he finished the spin facing number four. He locked Four in a bear hug, slid his clasped hands up behind the man's head, and pulled the body weight toward him. When the man leaned back, thinking Swanson was going after his face, Kyle drove his right knee deep and hard into the crotch, sending the ruptured balls somewhere up between the eyes. The man gasped for breath and crashed over a chair.

"An emergency surgical suite for that one," Pat commented. "Kyle is very messy today."

Number one, who had been at the far end, came on fast as Kyle came to rest in a squared position, perfectly balanced. The man's right leg locked as he ran forward, and Swanson leaned back, lifted his own left foot, and came straight down with a kick on the knee. The leg snapped sharply, with a sound like breaking wood.

"Kyle! My God, man!" Sir Jeff screamed in anguish. *"You broke a bloody two-thousand-dollar bottle of cognac!"* He gathered the two remaining bottles, looking at Swanson with horror in his eyes.

"Sorry," Kyle said. The whole thing had taken about ten seconds.

Tim walked to the stunned guests. Lady Pat and Shari were already standing and stepping over the bleeding debris on the stone slabs. "I think we had all best be leaving now," said Gladden. "We will finish lunch aboard the *Vagabond,* all right?" He escorted them to the waiting small boat.

The owner of the taverna was standing in his doorway like a statue, with fresh bowls of salad in each hand. Kyle took one, gave him more than enough money to cover the damage, and walked away. The big guy, number one, stirred and looked up with his bloodied face as if he was determined to rise. Since the man was no longer a threat, Kyle felt there was no need for a lethal blow and settled for kicking him in the sternum to take away his air. The large man passed out, gasping for breath. Kyle thought the goat cheese was delicious. He wished he had not had to eat it with his fingers.

One of the Desperate Housewives looked back over her shoulder as she walked down the pier, her blue eyes wide in shock. She could not believe what she had just seen. "How did he do that? He was like a crazy man," she asked Shari.

"It's the way he is trained," Shari replied. "He doesn't think, just reacts on instinct. Believe me, those guys got off easy."

"Do you mean he might have killed someone? There were four of them. Wasn't he afraid?"

"This is what he does," she said, stepping into the runabout. As she took a seat, she gave a tight smile to the woman, who lived in pretty places far from the dirt of the real world. "Kyle is not afraid of anyone . . . but me."

Late that night, the *Vagabond* cruised through the narrow Strait of Messina. Since the dawn of written history, those waters had gobbled up ships, with the deadly whirlpool Charybdis at the edge of Sicily forcing captains to sail close to the very toe of the Italian boot, where the mythological monster Scylla prowled the rocks. Now the electronic eyes of radar and satellite navigation systems defeated the dangers of superstition.

Shari leaned against Kyle's chest as they stood at the port rail, and he buried his nose in her silky hair. It carried the gentle scent of an English flower garden. He wrapped his arms around her and she covered his hands with hers as they watched the boiling bowl of the distant volcano, Stromboli, erupt in flashes of bright orange, with red flame illuminating the underside of passing clouds.

"I love this," she said. "My favorite guy, a luxury yacht, a beautiful night, and an exploding volcano. What could be better?"

He squeezed gently and she turned her head enough to give him a kiss. They were alone on the deck at two o'clock in the morning and the churning fire on the distant island made it seem that they might be the only people left at the end of the world. "Being able to stay out here with you a while longer would be better."

"Did Jeff offer you a job again?"

"Yup. Says we ought to get married and make a lot of money and beget him and Pat some godchildren they can spoil rotten."

"Sounds like a plan. You turn him down again?"

"I told him it was all your fault, because you make that white uniform with all the gold stripes look so good and you like people to salute you."

She sighed. "I make anything look good. Really, does he understand that we're just not quite there yet?"

"He understands. Both he and Tim put the full-court press on me tonight and threw in the promise of a share of Excalibur sales."

Shari turned in his arms, and the glow of the volcano reflecting off the water seemed like a halo around her. "Maybe we should reconsider, Kyle. I've had the strangest feeling that something bad is going to happen. And that I won't see you again."

Sixth sense, witchery, hunches, woman's intuition, or whatever, she had it in spades. Her ability to not only connect the dots, but the spaces between the dots, was what made her such a great intelligence analyst. Shari's brain dwelled in a place where one and one did not necessary always equal two, and Kyle always paid attention when she got one of her feelings. This time, he downplayed it. "Fat chance. I'm like a boomerang. I always come back to you."

"Yes. But after that last mission, the cross-border incident, you caught a lot of flack and they tried to make you the scapegoat. A lot of people would just like for you to go away, Kyle. Who know what they may hand you next time? Maybe something where you're not supposed to come back."

"Never gonna happen, Shari. I know how to play their game too well."

She kissed him, pulled away, and looked around. The deck was empty. "Then maybe I should give you even more reason to come home." She slipped the straps of her black dress from her shoulders. "So look at me, I'm Sandra Dee!"

"Who the hell is Sandra Dee?"

"You know. *Gidget*?"

"What's a *Gidget*?"

"Shut up before you ruin the moment," she said, and slid the loose folds of her dress down to her waist. Her breasts gleamed gold in the volcano firelight. Kyle brought her close and lowered his lips to her nipples. Shari moaned softly, and he ran his hands over her soft skin. Then her hand moved along his leg.

"Unless you want to be screwed right here on this expensive teakwood deck, young lady, I suggest we retire in great haste to our suite," he whispered. Kyle saw a familiar impish look come into those dark eyes.

"In a minute, Marine. In a minute." Shari pushed him against the chill steel of the bulkhead and dropped to her knees, reaching for his zipper while Stromboli painted the night. In a few moments, Kyle thought that the volcano was not the only thing erupting that night. When he finished panting, they rushed off to wrestle between white silk sheets.

There was a loud pounding on the door, and Kyle heard Tim Gladden calling loudly from the passageway. "Kyle! Shari! Geoffrey wants you in the main cabin right away to see this incredible news report on television! A Marine general has been kidnapped!"

CHAPTER 10

UNITED STATES SENATOR RUTH Hazel Reed of California—called Ruth Hazel by her friends and Rambo by her enemies—would replace her very dear colleague, the late Senator Graham Thomas Miller of Kentucky, as chair of the Senate Armed Services Committee. She was an attractive woman with blond-going-gray hair that was as stylish as her tailored wardrobe. The slender body was kept under strict control through rigorous exercise three times a week and a delicious diet provided by her private chef.

"Congratulations, Madame Chairwoman," said National Security Advisor Gerald Buchanan, lifting a glass of seventy-five-year-old scotch in a toast. They were standing before a warm fireplace at the mansion of Gordon Gates, deep in the fox country outside Culpeper, Virginia. The huge room had thick wooden ceiling beams. Old furniture, old staircases, old books, old money. Lots of it.

"A bit premature, Gerald, but thank you." She clicked her glass against his. "The Senate president will make his decision in a few days."

"Oh, that's just a technicality. I've already told him that the White House will be pleased to work with you." Buchanan had reviewed her file again before coming out here tonight for the meeting. So much depended on this woman! Was she really up to it?

She had graduated from Stanford and married a helicopter pilot who was killed in Vietnam. Ruth Hazel buried her grief along with her pilot, obtained her real estate license, and opened an agency in Del Mar just as the sunny coast of San Diego County became the hottest housing market in the nation. She made a fortune before turning her boundless ambition and energy to politics. A single term on the Del Mar City Council led to a big leap into the House of Representatives for two terms. Reed had been in the Senate for the past eleven years.

Land speculation and the military, the twin engines of the dynamic San Diego economy, formed her primary political base. The senator was adamant in getting tax breaks for land developers and big business and voted for any military spending proposal. Nobody gobbled up more taxpayer dollars for the Pentagon than Rambo Reed of California. The defense contractors and housing industry tycoons at the receiving end of the money pipeline showed their gratitude with campaign contributions.

Despite all of her money, power, good looks, and adroit phrasing, Buchanan considered Reed to be just another politician to be used like a sweet-smelling bar of soap until there was nothing worthwhile left to be used. There was always another Ruth Hazel Reed out there waiting to be groomed like a colt in training for the Kentucky Derby. This filly might break out and actually win the race for the roses, but a wise owner would have a lot of colts. She had been carefully selected for the role she was to play.

Senator Reed moved to a soft chair and sat down, putting her drink on a small Chinese-style table with a polished marble top inlaid with intricate stonework of precious gems. She considered Buchanan to be a competent number-cruncher and an above-average strategist. It was quite helpful to have him around, and he could be discarded the minute he did not deliver the goods. Headlines hailed him as a genius, but these guys were plentiful in Washington. Arrogant, too. She hoped that Buchanan did not let his pride get in the way of the job he had to perform. Was he up to it? The senator wondered how much the table was worth.

Reed had also spoken with the Senate president, and knew her appointment to succeed Miller was a done deal. Buchanan had to make a big show of everything. To chair that committee was definitely another rung up the ladder, but it should be only temporary. Reed had no plans to run for re-election. By this time next year, she planned to be President of the United States.

"As they say, Ruth Hazel, we live in interesting times," mused Buchanan.

"True enough. And during such difficult times, our country needs very careful guidance. Not knee-jerk action based on snapshot poll numbers."

Buchanan caught the insult. He was the most famous consumer of polls in Washington. "Indeed. That is precisely why you will be so valuable in your new position. From the untimely death of one senator can come progress for all." Unspoken was the barb that Reed was also just one senator of fifty. Only one-fiftieth of one-half of one-third of the United States government. They were even.

Buchanan poured himself a refill and offered her one with a smile. A peace offering. He found politics rather loathsome and did not want public office of any sort. He was a scholar and much too good, too intelligent, to have to explain himself to common voters and fools. Nothing lasted forever, including what he viewed as the American Empire. Buchanan believed that it was his destiny to shepherd the troubled nation to a new level of political evolution, which included writing a new Constitution. *His* Constitution would replace that antique Jeffersonian piece of parchment displayed under glass in the National Archives. What had been unique and powerful ideas for a democratic republic in the eighteenth century simply did not apply in today's complex world. It would be even less relevant in tomorrow's. Thomas Jefferson had been dead for a long, long time.

Rambo Reed could sit in that big chair in the Oval Office, but Gerald Buchanan would run the government.

"You two should hear yourselves talk! What total bullshit!" A slight, whippy man with the build of a marathon runner came into the big hall, walked over, and gripped their hands with the enthusiasm of someone who relished life. "We're the first of a new generation of leaders, my friends, and we are going to kick a lot of ass and make a ton of money while we save our country."

Gordon Gates IV had an easy, confident smile that indicated he did not have a care in the world. He wore a loose white shirt of Chinese silk, dark Armani trousers, and soft black Prada boots. A slim, clean Louis Vuitton Tambour chronograph was on his left wrist, and thick sandy-blond hair swept down over his forehead. He was fifty-five years old and looked ten years younger. The intelligent green eyes missed nothing.

He was very rich. His great-grandfather, the original Gordon Gates, was a grease-stained machinist who had invented a tiny part for aircraft engines before World War II, built on that modest success as aviation grew, and within five years owned a giant corporation. America's fighter planes and bombers could not stay in the sky without Gates equipment. Gordon Gates Jr. expanded military production when jet propulsion came along, established offices abroad, bought a shipbuilding company to make nuclear-powered submarines, and renamed the international company Gates Global. When "GG III" came along, a brilliant engineer in his own right, he seized the early days of the rocket age. Gates Global helped man walk on the moon, provided the electronic brains for missiles that could reach anywhere on the globe, then got into Area 51 secret weapons development with lasers and sound. Markets were locked up and money poured in. When politicians spoke of the military-industrial complex, they were talking about Gates Global.

The company always rewarded its friends on Capitol Hill, and its executive ranks were loaded with former generals and admirals, and ex-members of Congress.

The family groomed Gordon Gates IV to carry on the torch. He was a very bright kid when he was attending an elite prep school, but he had a vision of his own. All he had to do was say the word and he could step out of prep school and into Harvard, Yale, or Stanford, and then be prepared to take over Gates Global when his flashy playboy father was ready to pass the baton. But with the added bonus of aggravating his old man, young Gordon joined the U.S. Army as a private, determined to start at the bottom and get the kind of on-the-ground experience that would help him know what the hell he was talking about when he finally joined the family business. He still planned to run it someday, but Dear Old Dad wasn't anywhere near ready to voluntarily give up the throne. GG IV detested GG III, who felt the same about his only son and heir.

The smart kid from the mansion in Mission Hills, Kansas, enlisted in the U.S. Army as a grunt soldier, became a Ranger, and was a sergeant in the 101st Airborne when he was qualified for Delta Force. After two years as a Delta operator, he allowed the Army to pay for his higher education and was scooped from the ranks to attend West Point. Once commissioned, he took a Rhodes Scholarship at Oxford and then got back into the mud with a year's secondment to the British SAS.

He returned to Delta deep-selected as a major, and served three more years on special missions to the dark holes of the world. The Pentagon loved having Gordon Gates on the payroll, brought him to Washington, made him a light colonel, and buried him deep undercover to plan and implement black operations. It was said around the E-Ring that Gates was a slam-dunk for his first star. Then Daddy GG III wrapped his Ferrari 512 Berlinetta Boxer and his mistress around an oak tree alongside a curving, wet road.

And he was always bitching at me about taking risks in the army! Gordon thought as the casket of Dear Old Dad was lowered into the grave in the family plot in Kansas. It was his turn to take over Gates Global, and he came to the job totally ready as a dues-paid-in-full member of the Pentagon Gun Club.

He established his supreme authority by bringing a squad of lawyers to his first meeting with the board of directors, and fired most of the men and women who had been his father's staunchest friends and allies. He told the survivors what was coming. The Berlin Wall is a pile of old rocks: there was never going to be a battle between Soviet and American tanks for the Fulda Gap. Continuing to manufacture thousands of new tanks was stupid. Nuclear-powered aircraft carriers were sailing toward a horizon of obsolescence and the giant submarines crammed with world-crunching missiles were outdated. Whole generations of fighter planes had nobody to fight. That really didn't matter, he said. Gates Global would continue to build the steel and titanium dinosaurs as long as the profit margin remained solid.

Gates would leave a hand-picked CEO in place to run the public face of Gates Global. That person would be a technocrat and use terms like "littoral battle space" and "netcentric communications" and "transformational combat force projection" to lasso contracts for new ships and planes and weapons systems. "Build whatever the fuckers want," Gates said. He would have nothing to do with that side of the company, as long as it made a lot of money.

In return, he demanded an unlimited budget that would not be answerable to them. Let the lawyers and accountants figure out how to hide it from the IRS, but it had to be a totally black account and available when he wanted. "Gates Global is expanding and you don't need to know the details," he told them. "Stop thinking in millions and start thinking in billions. You all will make a lot of money and nobody will ever be indicted for anything if you keep your mouths shut and stay out of my way." He stared around the room and then abruptly walked out, leaving no doubt about who was the company's new leader.

Gates's vision was that the United States military was

going right back to where wars are always won, with boots on the ground. It was the topic he knew best, because he had walked many miles in those boots, humping a pack and carrying an automatic rifle. Teams of highly trained Special Operations soldiers would fight the country's future conflicts because the national defense could not be entrusted to acne-pimpled National Guard soldiers or fat-ass regular army colonels. In his plan, the private units could be combined in any size, from the lethal two-man Shark Teams that did special jobs all the way up to battalion size or even bigger. Gates was building the preeminent private security company in the world, and that was only the first step.

Gates, Buchanan, Reed. The three people standing before the fireplace, holding crystal glasses of scotch, would redirect the enormous and ever-growing Pentagon budget to fund private armies, with Gates Global positioned to provide everything from bullets to beans, transportation to firepower, for a nice price. Other major corporations could handle infrastructure needs or be front companies to keep the Gates name out of tricky situations. PSCs were the future. American soldiers did not need to spill their blood abroad when mercenaries could do the same job better, faster, cheaper, under no political restraints, and without press coverage. He would draw upon the Pentagon's resources as needed for the big stuff like close air support and satellites and aircraft carriers, but all of that eventually would come under his umbrella, too.

Just a little tinkering was needed to get the plan past the Democrat and Republican politicians and the media howlers. That should be simple enough when America endured the worst siege of terrorist attacks in its history and thousands of U.S. citizens were slaughtered in shopping malls and hospitals and homes. Enraged and frightened citizens would demand that they be kept safe!

Civilian police were not up to the task. American troops would be needed to protect American shores and borders and cities and towns when martial law was imposed. To fill the vacuum abroad, Gates Global would be given the grateful appreciation of the nation to fight Washington's foreign battles. After a few years, the door would open wider for stateside operations as well. Martial law would morph into a new, firmer way of running the country under a banner of national security.

It was time to implement Operation Premier while Senator Reed had the legislative clout and Buchanan could deliver the executive branch.

"So, Ruth Hazel, now that Senator Miller is out of the way, where does it leave our privatization bill?" Gates brought those harsh eyes to her.

"I will bring the American Defense Act before the subcommittee next week and fast-track it through the full committee, both in closed sessions. When Operation Premier creates a significant domestic terrorist strike just before the vote, the House of Representatives will respond with a similar bill and a conference committee will rubber-stamp it. It will be political suicide for any of them to oppose defending America while the blood of innocents is in the streets. Gerald should see the bill come down to the White House in no more than thirty days."

Buchanan nodded. "I will brief the President and endorse the act. That crap in the Middle East has tortured him enough, the media is always bitching about it, and he's anxious to get out of there. There are a lot of fronts in the war on terror, and something decisive hitting in the American heartland will give him the political cover to readjust his sights and bring our troops home."

"You're sure that he will sign the privatization bill?"

"Absolutely." Buchanan lifted his own eyes and looked at his comrade's. "If we wrap up the one remaining loose end."

Gates laughed out loud. "You mean with General Middleton?"

"Middleton cannot be allowed to testify before my committee!" Senator Reed said firmly, putting down her glass and crossing her arms. "He's only a one-star, but he is influential as hell with his books and lectures about the value of a professional military that answers to elected civilian officials.

Together, he and Miller would have stopped us cold. They were planning a public relations offensive on this, including getting television networks to cover the hearings. Open hearings!"

"Which is exactly why they are not in Washington today," said Gates. "We have gotten rid of Miller with the heart attack, and the general has been kidnapped and will not survive the adventure. Neither can be traced to us."

Buchanan shuffled a toe of his tasseled loafer into the thick carpet. "I have been riding the Pentagon and the intel services hard. When your people reveal the location, the Marines will launch a rescue operation, just as you predicted, Gordon. I will let them do it, of course, reporting the plans directly to me."

Gates nodded. "The Sharks and some of the Rebel Sheikh's militia boys will be ready when Force Recon guys arrive in Syria. Cameras will record the destruction of most of the assault force, but a few Marines will be allowed to fight their way into the house where Middleton is being held."

"And they will all be killed together in the shootout, on video," Reed said. "Another military debacle."

Gordon Gates smiled. "I want to add one last piece to the scenario, Gerald. Just imagine that in the middle of the shootout, a U.S. Marine is actually shown to be the one who kills General Middleton."

"How could we possibly arrange that?"

"Simple. You, my friend, take one of the best snipers on the CIA roster and order it done. Remove him from the chain of command. When the rescue fails, the sniper is to make certain that the general's vast knowledge of homeland security information does not fall into enemy hands."

"How does he survive that initial ambush?" Buchanan scratched his ear.

Gates knew the capabilities of a good operator and waved away the question. "The firing will not be very heavy, and if he is any good at his job, he won't have much trouble being among those getting to the right house."

"Would he actually do it? Shoot the general?" asked Senator Reed.

"Only if it was a direct order from his commander-in-chief in the White House," said Buchanan. "When the last members of the rescue team are being wiped out, the sniper becomes both our insurance policy and a fall guy for any blame. Then he is also taken out. End of a tragic fiasco."

"You boys can take care of that, Gordon. All I care about is that Middleton not show up before my committee." The senator brought the conversation back to center point. "He could wreck everything."

"Excellent. Excellent," said Gates. "So that brings us to decision time on Operation Premier. Senator?"

"It has to be done," said Reed.

"Don't go vague on us, Ruth Hazel. Say exactly what you mean, not some political bullshit. You agree that we will prepare the Shark Teams for the theater attacks. We must be absolutely plain with each other. After all, the three of us essentially are staging a coup."

"Yes," she replied.

"Gerald?"

"Yes. Do it."

"Me, too. Yes. It's unanimous." He flashed that enigmatic smile again. "Now let's have a nice dinner and a good bottle of wine to salute this historic creation of New America."

CHAPTER 11

KYLE SWANSON WATCHED the television report silently, his arms crossed. Bradley Fucking Middleton! The general's picture came on the screen, a stock photo of him in full dress uniform and an American flag in the background. It was not a face that Kyle ever enjoyed seeing. Every time they met, something bad seemed to happen, until finally Middleton had tried to cashier Swanson out of the Marines. As the news reader droned on, Kyle's mind rolled back to his first clash with Middleton years ago during Desert Shield, in the abandoned town of Khafji, on the border between Saudi Arabia and Iraq.

It had been two days into the new year of 1991, and there was something happening in the black desert night. The growl of engines and the clank of tank treads, out where there was supposed to be nothing but sand. "Multiple heat signatures, Sergeant. More than ten vehicles. Hard to say with this piece-of-shit night vision gear," the spotter said quietly after looking hard and long through his thermal imaging glasses. "Lots of movement, though."

Kyle Swanson pulled the ten-power Unertl scope of his M40A1 sniper rifle to his eye. Nothing but darkness across the border between Saudi Arabia and Kuwait. "Call it in. Tell 'em it sounds like more than just a recon."

Iraq had overrun Kuwait, and the Iraqis were not sitting still while an American and international coalition of forces was building up to take it back. Kyle had been a scout-sniper sergeant at the time, heading a two-man observation team hidden between the floorboards of a building at the edge of town. Several other OPs were scattered throughout other buildings, but until now, Saddam Hussein had kept his people out of the area. Boredom had been the biggest enemy.

A chill crawled up the back of his neck that had nothing to do with the cold temperature. All that noise meant armor. Saddam was about to expand the playing field, and the OPs were right in the path, with the closest friendlies about thirty minutes away, a very long time in a firefight.

They remained motionless as the mumble of impending battle moved closer, and the first light of dawn brought the startling truth. The sun outlined Iraqi T-62 tanks and a herd of other alphabet armor—MBLTs, tracked personnel carriers on the main chassis of a battle tank; BDRM recon scout vehicles; and the BMPs with anti-armor cannon. A bit of everything. This was no probe, but the advance guard for an entire armored division, and they were already on the outskirts of town, moving closer by the minute. Dismounted Iraqi troops hustled around the vehicles, darting like a swarm of ants going after a picnic basket as they cleared the abandoned houses. The spotter called in radio reports while Swanson ran a final check of his rifle, ammo clips, the clackers for the Claymore mines, and grenades.

To try to leave would be suicide; a tank and the supporting infantry would make quick work of anyone they saw. Swanson glassed potential targets with his scope, and his mouth watered with anticipation. Behind the troops coming into the town there were guys riding atop the vehicles, talking in groups and moving in the open, lacking discipline as they pressed forward, for they expected no opposition. Careless ants. He put the crosshairs on an officer wearing a red beret and standing in the turret of a tank, gripping a handle so he could get a better view of Khafji. He had a big thick mustache, a pressed uniform, and a pistol on a polished belt of brown leather. Kyle thought: *He's mine*.

"Mike Tango three niner, this is Hunter One. Fire mission. Over." The spotter had headquarters on the net and was quietly lining up an artillery strike. He pinned his finger on an exact spot on the plastic-covered map folded before him. "Grid. Six two niner four. Niner eight seven six. Direction: five niner one one. Twenty to thirty Iraqi tanks and APCs in the open. Fire for effect."

Swanson tracked the officer, waiting for a sound louder than that of his rifle. The first 155 mm artillery rounds came in like loud zippers in the sky, and when they exploded, throwing dirt and debris into big mushrooms of destruction, he finished squeezing the trigger. His bullet took the Iraqi officer in the throat and knocked him from the tank. Soldiers were scrambling for cover and paid no attention to the fallen officer, thinking he had been hit by the artillery. Kyle fed a fresh round into his rifle and looked for a new target, found one, and waited for another big round to explode and mask his shot.

The Iraqis opened up with everything they had, shooting wild. There was no enemy visible, but the artillery salvo had been so precise, it was obvious that someone was watching them. Their entire line surged forward, firing as they came, and violent explosions blew walls apart. The soldiers rushed to find shelter from the artillery, and Swanson and his spotter shrank back into the shadowy hide. A squad of Iraqi infantrymen ran into the main floor of the small building for cover. One came up to the second floor but could not see them between the floorboards, and stomped back downstairs to the rest of the squad, which moved on to clear another building. "Sloppy," Kyle whispered.

The Iraqi tanks and armored personnel carriers prowled the streets, unleashing cannon and machine-gun fire on anything suspicious, and small-arms fire rattled on both sides and to the rear of the observation team. The bad guys had the town, and Kyle, his spotter, and the other Marines were trapped inside it.

The situation was beyond serious, and Swanson made the decision without conscious thought. If they were going to survive, they needed help in a hurry, because those enemy soldiers soon would be prowling about in a more thorough search for the observation teams. He grabbed his spotter by the shoulder. "Call Broken Arrow!"

The emergency signal meant that U.S. forces were being overrun. Every warplane in the sky that morning diverted immediately from its mission and accelerated toward Khafji, afterburners thundering to pour on more speed. The spotter started guiding them in, while other OP lookouts adjusted the artillery strikes. Nearby buildings vaporized with concussion blasts that shook them like a couple of gerbils in a cage.

Swanson cleared away debris that fell in the front of their hide and got back to work, taking targets of opportunity whenever an artillery round came in or a plane made a bombing run.

It was all now in slow motion. The chaotic sounds and sights passed through his mind only as parts of the mathematical equations he needed to figure out the next shot. He was an emotionally empty vessel, without fear, mentally shutting out any personal feelings for the targets—not men, but targets—and became an extension of the rifle. He wasn't counting, he was killing, and hoping to avoid getting killed in turn.

The morning grew brighter and the allied planes circled like fast vultures to pounce on the exposed Iraqis. Kyle's world shook and burned as bombs rocked the city, and the artillery punished the Iraqi infantry troops who had taken cover in some of the same buildings in which the Marine observers were hidden.

Finally, U.S. and coalition ground troops and armor showed up. A Saudi National Guard unit was allowed to roll into the town first, for symbolic reasons, but the big chase was conducted by a Marine light recon battalion that roared through the broken town like it was Saturday afternoon at the Daytona Speedway. TOW missiles and 25 mm Bushmaster cannons obliterated any Iraqi vehicles that were too slow.

Kyle and his spotter climbed from their hide like filthy moles, covered with dirt and debris. Only then did he realize that a big splinter had punched into his left bicep. Blood stained his uniform. He had been too busy, and the adrenaline was pumping too hard, to notice when it happened.

A medic yanked out the splinter, cleaned the puncture, and tied on a quick bandage. "You'll get another Purple Heart for that one, Sar'nt," the medic said.

"Forget it," Kyle responded, rubbing the sharp piece of wood, about three inches long, between his fingers, then tossing it away. "Ain't worth nothing."

As the other teams emerged, similarly battered and bruised, Kyle walked off to get some water and find a quiet place to be alone.

It was part of his routine that let his mind disengage from the combat mode and come back into the real world. He found a cool, dark room in one of the empty houses and sat down as his body began to quiver. He thought of that big gaping hole he had blown in the throat of the first officer. Of the infantryman who believed he was safe behind a wall until Kyle shot out his liver in splash of blood. Of the driver of the armored personnel carrier who popped out of his hatch and caught Kyle's bullet through the left eye. Sights of inflicted death paraded before him, and he knew that in future months, those Iraqis would visit in his dreams. Kyle Swanson, exhausted, curled into a fetal position and grabbed his knees tightly while his mind dealt with the carnage of his trigger finger. Tears streaked the dirt on his cheeks.

A hand touched him on the back. "S'arnt Swanson? You hit?" A Marine major had found him, saw the bloody shirt, and thought he was wounded.

Kyle relaxed. His eyes were still unfocused. "No, sir. I'm okay." He swiped a hand across his dirty face, the sweat and tears leaving muddy tracks. "Just catching my breath. It got kinda intense out there."

It took a few moments for Kyle to recognize the face of Major Bradley Middleton, the executive officer of the Force Recon battalion. The major was a veteran but had little experience with snipers, and had never seen one personally deal with the aftermath of a day of battle. Ordinary soldiers shoot almost anonymously and seldom see what they hit. Pilots never view the bodies blown away by their bombs, and tankers have limited visibility. But with a powerful scope, a sniper sees every strand of hair in an enemy mustache, the color of an eye and the movement of a finger. They also see the gory holes they make in a man, and after the battle is over, that has to be dealt with. Every sniper has his own way of adjusting.

Kyle told his shooters when they were in training, "We have to be peculiar, or we wouldn't be snipers in the first place. None of us do what we have to do simply because we enjoy killing people. That would be crazy." Some, the lucky ones, would just get drunk and wash away the images with beer and whiskey. Nightmares and divorces were common. Others would be gripped by unreasoning anger and fight whoever came along and end up in the brig. Kyle's own habit was to shake and bake a little bit and be done with it.

Middleton just squatted there beside him, mystified at the quaking Marine sniper. He had invaded Kyle Swanson's private world uninvited, and after a minute he rose and walked back into the sunshine and left Swanson alone.

Neither of them forgot the incident. Then Middleton saw him do it again after a brawl in Somalia, by which time Swanson was a staff sergeant and Middleton had risen to light colonel. Middleton considered the continued strange behavior to be important and gave Kyle a negative evaluation report. "Shaky," he wrote of Swanson in an evaluation report, by which he meant undependable, unworthy, and unreliable. He recommended that Swanson undergo psychiatric evaluation and be retired from the Marine Corps because he was a walking time bomb. Who in their right mind would want a shaky sniper around?

Kyle had come within an inch of being ruined until other

officers and senior enlisted types jumped to his defense and forced the potentially career-ending piece of paper to be withdrawn. But the term "shaky" leaked out and his fellow snipers loved it, for they gave no quarter in busting balls. "Shake" stuck, an unwanted nickname.

As he watched the news report aboard the *Vagabond* that Brigadier General Middleton had been taken hostage, Kyle felt conflicting emotions. It made him angry because he hated that kidnapping shit. Terrorist assholes could not just go around snatching American generals or anyone else without consequences. That anger was on principle alone.

Personally, the moment also made him proud to be an American, because he knew the United States had a firm policy of never bargaining with terrorists. Well, almost never. So there would be no deals made to get the general back. Kyle believed that the unwritten rule book on international terrorism was very clear on that point.

Therefore, now that terrorists actually had taken Middleton, Kyle reasoned that they had to keep him. That was just fine with the sniper.

CHAPTER 12

TWO OLD MEN LEANED UPON the railing of the bridge on which the Boulevard de la Gare crossed the Seine. Clouds had rolled in to chase the sun and a chilly afternoon breeze swept up the river, warning of coming rain. Sweaters protected their shoulders. Automobiles swarmed behind them on the roadway, and trains clattered into and out of the Gare de Lyon and the Gare d'Austerlitz stations on either side of the river. It would have been impossible for either to have been followed by someone without being seen, and the noise drowned out their soft voices.

They had been competitors, enemies, partners, allies, and opposing spies in their younger years. After retirement, both stayed in Paris and a friendship followed. It was enjoyable to pass the time talking about the good old days of the Cold War over cups of hot café, particularly since they could now laugh at the absurdity of six decades of spying for the United States and France.

Buzz Higbee had grown up in the Minnesota woods and could have returned to the U.S. of A., but found the thought of retiring to a cabin beside a lonely lake that was frozen half the year to be unattractive. He had lived most of his adult life in Paris, and his wife, children, and grandchildren were all French. Minnesota had become the foreign land. He was a healthy eighty-two years old, with white hair, weak blue eyes, high blood pressure, and a hearing aid.

Higbee had ventured out today to meet Jean-Paul Delmas, who was only eighty. Delmas walked with the help of a cane, but his intellect remained sharp and since his spy days he had devoted himself to an extensive collection of rare stamps. Buzz called him "the Kid."

"This is rather delicate," Delmas told Higbee.

"*Merde,* Jean-Paul. Where our two countries are involved, what is not rather delicate?"

"It is true. But I was quite pleased when your people in Washington changed the name of French Fries to Freedom Fries. What awful things you Americans have done to food."

"I'm glad that we were able to please the republic in our own little way, Kid, but that was bullshit and anyway, they changed the name back. You eat them, too, but with a Frenchified name. *Pommes frites.*"

"Entirely different."

"Same thing. Now why are two over-the-hill spooks like us meeting clandestinely? Everybody knows who we are, what we were, and that we hang out together. My landlady calls me the 'old American spy who lives upstairs in 2B.'"

Delmas laughed and looked down at the fast-moving dark water. "Which is why we have such excellent cover, no? No one would suspect that we had any worthwhile missions left in us."

"They may be right. How are you doing?" Higbee knew that Delmas had undergone chemotherapy for lung cancer.

"It may be coming back."

"Jesus. Sorry to hear that, my friend."

Delmas shrugged. "Life. Death." His wife had died twelve years ago, and the way he spoke those words showed that he no longer cared about living or dying, and probably would choose death if it meant a chance to reunite with his love. He turned in a circle, as if watching a passing pigeon, but checking to be sure no one was loitering nearby. "I have been asked to give you something to relay to your former masters at Langley. My people wanted to keep this affair as back-channel as possible, and nothing can possibly be any more back-channel than you and me."

Even when governments are locked in extreme disagreements over international policy, sometimes even while at war, their intelligence services maintain unofficial contacts. Such was the case with the current strain between Paris and Washington. The French could not afford to be seen as helping the Americans in the Middle East, so passing an urgent and sensitive message was better done through very unofficial means.

Buzz put on his CIA game face for the first time in many years. It felt good. Jean-Paul had been an agent with Le Service de Documentation Extérieure et de Contre-Espionnage (SDECE) back in the dirty days of Algeria, and since 1982 with its successor, the Directorate of External Security. He was retired over his protests.

A crash of thunder rolled over the city, and raindrops began to fall from the churning, slate gray sky, speckling the bridge. In unison, they raised black umbrellas.

"It is your missing general. You heard about him? This Middleton?"

"Been all over the television. Yeah. What about him?"

"As you know, we depend heavily upon human intelligence sources, where you Americans rely more on technology. We don't have your capability in that field, but we have been growing agents in Africa and the Middle East for better than a century."

"Tell me about it. If somebody was about to fuck a sheep in Algiers, you knew about it before the sheep did." They both laughed. The rain fell steadily, lightly.

"Buzz, the Directorate has been contacted by one of our people, a former soldier in the Foreign Legion. He now lives in southern Syria, travels all around the area for us, and he saw your general being taken into a house in a village called Sa'ahn. The general appeared unconscious, but our man recognized that distinctive Marine uniform."

"Whoa, partner. You have a man on the fucking scene?"

Jean-Paul reached into the pocket of his sweater and

pulled out an envelope. "*Oui*. Here is his name, photograph, and the location of the village and the house he maintains there. I am authorized to tell you that the Directorate persuaded him to stay where he is to help guide any rescue effort, and to point out the house where the general is being held. You'll have to pay him some money, of course. Probably a lot of money. He wants a million dollars, U.S."

"Damn. Just a mil? He'll have to buy a couple of new camels to carry all the gold they will give him to get Middleton back safe." Buzz Higbee put the envelope in a deep sweater pocket. "How does Washington contact this asset if they want to do something?"

"Get a quiet message to our military attaché in Washington. Paris will pass it on through a coded microburst transmission to the asset."

"Sounds almost too good to be true, Jean-Paul, which means it probably isn't. What's the catch?"

"I considered that and asked about it. There is nothing that we know of," the Frenchman said. "Nobody wants to see still another flareup in that region. This isn't Iraq, and Paris is more than willing to work with Washington on the problem. So I believe the only downside, as you say, is that you are now in my personal debt. I demand a lunch."

"Anywhere you want, and make it somewhere expensive. CIA is buying."

Jean-Paul smiled. "I was hoping you would say that. I will call you in the morning to name a place. Tell Marie that I send my love."

They shook hands and parted, heading toward opposite ends of the bridge, hurrying to reach shelter before the storm broke.

CHAPTER 13

THE CIA REPRESENTATIVE AT the meeting of the National
Security Council wore a private, satisfied smile. He had
something that would get Buchanan off his ass. CIA tapped
the keys on a laptop computer and the photograph of a
middle-aged man with dark hair and a thick brushy mustache flashed onto one of the wall screens. "His name was
Pierre Falais when he served in the Foreign Legion. He became a Muslim after his enlistment was up and took the
name of Abu Mohammed. Father was French, mother Alger-
ian. Studied to be an engineer in France, but gave it up, did
the military stint, and then moved to Syria in about 1985 and
worked as a skilled carpenter. Injured in a fall from a ladder
and couldn't do the high work anymore, so he moved to this
village and set up shop. Does a little carpentry, a little farming, and a lot of spying for the French."

"Why should we trust the French on this?" asked National Security Advisor Gerald Buchanan.

"They controlled the area for years in the colonial times,
and French roots run deep there. The information was given
to us through a totally reliable channel, Mr. Buchanan. Our
own contact agent is retired, but has known his French coun-
terpart for many years. He believes the information is valid."
CIA stopped briefly to consider his next words. "Paris has

done an extremely rare, timely, and thorough breakout on this guy for us."

"So this Abu Mohammed actually saw General Middleton and knows precisely where he is being held?"

"We consider the information to be accurate as of this moment. It could change at any time." CIA replaced the large photograph with a map, satellite imagery of a small town just to the east of the rugged Mount Druz. It was only a couple of streets and blocky buildings. "This is where the informant claims Middleton is being held . . . right . . . here." He tapped a key and a red circle blinked around one of the small buildings near the edge of town.

Buchanan tapped his fingers against his pursed lips. "Anyone care to comment?"

The table remained silent for a few moments as he watched them all carefully. Finally, the woman from State gathered her nerve. "I'm uncomfortable with it."

"Why?" Buchanan had never liked her. One of those faceless drones who had lived overseas too long, enjoying the good life and throwing embassy parties. She had been in Rio until she came back home to that roost of diplomatic vipers over on C Street, for God's sake. What would she know about the Middle East? "What troubles you?"

"It all seems too easy. Too convenient," State said, keeping her voice quiet and level. Buchanan was trying to move too fast, she thought, and nobody was willing to buck him. "Any time there is a major incident, we start getting walk-ins to embassies, our intel communities see their switchboards light up, and the FBI has to beat informants away with a stick. These potential informants all smell money and want to swap information for cash. On the Middleton kidnap, however, the secret world has gone quiet. Nobody got anything until this retired old CIA guy is contacted by his buddy, a retired senior French intelligence officer, and the whole thing falls into our laps. We get a local guide, his picture and history, and the address where the victim is being kept."

"So you think they are lying?" Let her dig her own grave.

"No. But it's possible that both Washington and Paris are

being used. I have been in government service more than twenty years, Mr. Buchanan, and it has never been this easy. Problems of this magnitude do not just resolve themselves."

"Your concern is duly noted," Buchanan said, knowing her comments were true. The contact in Syria was working with the Shark Team there and the information was intentionally being fed in from the field. He had to sidetrack her. The others at the table remained silent as Buchanan smirked. "This one indeed has come out of the blue. I think Paris realizes just how deep in the crapper they are with us on other things, particularly Iraq, and are offering this up as a goodwill gesture without having to do so publicly. That's why they used the old boys. Okay, so everybody knows where we are. What's the next step?"

General Henry Turner, chairman of the Joint Chiefs, leaned into his microphone. "We want to go in and get him as soon as possible. The navy is moving a task force into position in the eastern Med, and we can fly a Force Recon rescue team in over Israel and plop right down on these people. Thirty minutes on the ground and we bring out both Middleton and the informant. All we need to green-light the mission is the President's authorization."

Buchanan nodded once. Good, the general had shifted the attention of the group from questioning the "how" to the "what next." He stood abruptly. "Sounds good. Make your final plans and prepare a briefing for the President."

"Yes, sir. We will get him everything he needs to know."

"Then let's go and get your general," said Buchanan. He turned and left the room.

State caught up with CIA on the way out. "This is too damned easy," she repeated.

CIA shook his head almost imperceptibly in agreement. "I just work here," he said. They left the White House together.

Gerald Buchanan stood at the window of his office with the door closed, ready to sign the death warrant. A high position carried burdens. He, and he alone in this building, including the fool who sat in the Oval Office, had the guts to sign an order of the sort he contemplated. Few men in the entire city would be willing to sign it. That bitch from State certainly could never do it. They were weaklings who did not understand putting higher needs over the survival of one man. For the good of the United States of America, General Bradley Middleton had to die.

General Turner had made a tactical verbal mistake in his eagerness to rescue Middleton by unveiling his determination to use only Marines. Buchanan had captured one of Turner's pawns in that move, because he would now be able to confine his search for just the right man, someone qualified to carry out the order, to a handful of Marines to put U.S. military fingerprints on this assassination.

He moved to his wall safe, placed his right palm against the biometric reader, and dialed a combination. When the heavy door swung open, he pulled out a file that had been secretly ordered from the CIA on a dozen Special Forces operatives who were occasionally used for unique missions. "The wet stuff," CIA had explained.

Taking it to his desk, sitting in the black high-backed chair and studying the papers under the bright light, he flipped to a section that identified three Marines who were employed for such work, and saw that two of them were already on other assignments.

The remaining candidate was an expert scout sniper and gunnery sergeant. The statistics and the photograph showed that he was five-nine, 160 pounds, with gray eyes and short brown hair; a combat veteran; age thirty-four; single; and numerous decorations including awards from foreign governments and letters of commendation that were marked TOP SECRET. Buchanan read the biography with some interest, for it seemed that the man had been in almost every hot spot around the world for the past ten years, including special missions with the Israelis, the British, and the Russians. He was officially credited with eighty-one confirmed kills, but the real figure was much higher, for the number included only his victims who had been confirmed, and not any killed in special secret operations. Interestingly, the file also had a couple of letters of reprimand that indicated problems with authority. His last mission had involved a questionable kill on the wrong side of the Pakistani border, which had caused a serious diplomatic incident. The shooter was reprimanded and temporarily banished from the active list of covert agents. This would be a good time to bring him back. Not only was he finishing a contract job with some weapons company and was free for new orders, but he also might be wanting to prove that he was still up to doing clandestine work. Buchanan underlined the name: last name Swanson; first name Kyle.

The National Security Advisor possessed one of the most secure computers in the entire U.S. government, but Buchanan refused to believe it could not be hacked. All of those whirring and clicking sounds only meant that the hard drive was storing and shuffling information. There was no such thing as a really secure computer. He did not want anyone to someday unveil his secret correspondence to a Senate investigating committee or have it become a headline in *The Washington Post*. He would not even trust his secretary on this one.

From his middle desk drawer, Buchanan slid out a single sheet of expensive stationery that bore THE WHITE HOUSE across the top in simple blue letters, and began to write in a neat, precise longhand. There would be only this one original, and it would rest in a briefcase locked to the wrist of a special courier. Once the instruction was read by the Marine sniper, the courier would destroy the document. No copies, no paper trail.

Buchanan finished the note, sealed it in an official envelope, and put it into a light blue file folder with a red stripe diagonally across the front and WHITE HOUSE TOP SECRET stenciled in big black letters. He sealed that, too.

Then he told his aide Sam Shafer to locate this Gunnery Sergeant Swanson and get him to that fleet Marine unit in the Mediterranean as soon as possible. Shafer would also fly out to the task force, carrying the letter in a burnished aluminum briefcase handcuffed to his wrist, to personally deliver it. By using his private staff and a CIA cover, Buchanan would bypass General Turner and the others in their fancy uniforms.

As he worked, Buchanan once again had to grudgingly approve of Gordon Gates's enterprising and farsighted ideas. Sending in a bloodthirsty robot like Swanson was indeed a good insurance policy.

CHAPTER 14

ALI SHALAL RASSAD KNEW THAT sometimes just a little shove was all that was needed to force friends and enemies alike to do something they would later regret. He was a master of that quiet tactic, and was about to employ it against the United States of America. Rassad was known as the Rebel Sheikh not so much for being a great fighter, although he was, but because he refused to be consumed by any higher political power. His streak of stubborn independence made him an ally of convenience from Baghdad to Tehran to Washington. He worked with all, trusted none, and worked only for himself.

He had agreed to perform a very precise role in the drama involving the American general, the sort of multilayered deception that he most enjoyed. He was being paid well to lend some of his militiamen to the mission, then to hold a single brief meeting with the Pentagon correspondent from a major American television network. The reporter had been in Iraq many times and had great credibility within the United States. His story would be accepted as fact.

Rassad sipped a cup of strong tea as he scanned the *International Herald Tribune* and other newspapers and magazines that were brought daily to his office in Basra. A staff that monitored the Internet furnished its hourly report: the blogs were busy, but had nothing significant. Just braying opinions of people who didn't really know anything. Three television sets ran CNN, al Jazeera, and Sky News, and stories about the disappearance of General Middleton and the peculiar demands made by the Holy Scimitar of Allah dominated the news.

There was nothing in the papers or on television to match the fresh information on a decoded message that was also on his desk. Task Force 32-A of the U.S. Navy's Seventh Fleet was moving into position in the western Mediterranean. Israel had granted flyover permission for the Americans. The Marines were coming. Rassad intended to spur everyone along with a renewed sense of urgency to prevent them from having second thoughts that might breed caution.

Rassad loved the game. He pushed aside the papers, finished the tea, and snapped his fingers for an assistant to clear the desk and incinerate all of the papers. Some posturing politician someday might send a raiding party to his palace in attempt to find and seize incrimination information. That would fail, of course, and the politician would soon be assassinated, but Rassad kept his most important information in his head. Everything else was consigned to ashes.

He returned to his living suite, where a barber waited to trim his beard, eyebrows, nose, and ears. The valet had laid out clothing chosen for the interview, a dark gray suit from London, an off-white dress shirt with a muted silk tie, and highly polished Italian shoes. The trousers were tailored to help offset the fact that his left leg was an inch shorter than his right, a reminder of the year and a half he had spent in Abu Ghraib prison for the crime of defending his beautiful girlfriend when Uday Hussein's thugs had come for her. Uday himself, laughing, had wielded the long steel crowbar that smashed Rassad's bones while telling in great detail how the girl, a virgin, had been fucked and how she screamed and how when Uday tired of her, he tossed her to the guards in a rape room, where she died. Rassad would be allowed to heal for a while after one of the torture sessions, only to undergo a repeat performance with the crowbar when he had recovered enough. He was not beaten to get a confession, for he had nothing to confess. Uday just enjoyed beating him. In the end, when the Americans had released him, Rassad could not walk on the mutilated leg.

The limp became a badge of honor for his new life as it healed, an unspoken reminder that he had paid dearly for opposing the dictator Saddam Hussein. When he was taken to prison, he had been just another bureaucrat in the Ministry of the Interior, but he emerged as a new political force, for he had channeled his powerful mind away from the pain and into how he could capitalize on his experiences. There were days now when he could almost thank Uday for the cruelty, because no one ever questioned Rassad's loyalty to his country. It was a wonderful political bargaining chip. In the end, Rassad had the final laugh on Uday by directing the Americans to the location of the Hussein brothers, where they were killed. He kept a picture of Uday's misshapen dead body in a folder in a desk drawer, and he looked at it often.

Today, Rassad would wear the fine suit instead of the comfortable robes in order to appear as a reasonable, moderate, westernized Iraqi leader. He did not want the American television audience to equate him with some ordinary Koran-thumping radical mullah. He had graduated from MIT, for Christ's sake.

A sleek Bell helicopter, ornate in its coat of glistening midnight blue with gold trim, skimmed in to land at the palace after a smooth trip from the big American base in Doha, Kuwait. Jack Shepherd unfolded his lanky frame from the comfortable seat and stepped out, shielding his eyes against the rotor blast. He was disoriented. Something was missing. Something was wrong, a sense of incompleteness. It wasn't until an escort shook his hand and helped his television crew load their gear into an air-conditioned limo that Shepherd could put his finger on what was different. It was quiet! He had heard others speak about the eerie feeling in the broad neighborhoods around the Rebel Sheikh's palace, but he had not been here for at least a year. In Iraq, he usually came in tense and expecting danger, with bomb blasts echoing throughout the countryside, something somewhere always blowing up with the erratic constancy of a popcorn machine, but this area of Basra was an oasis of calm.

The escort gave them a quick tour before going to the palace. Shops were open, private cars jammed the clean streets, children played soccer on neat green fields, and women walked freely in the street markets, some with heads uncovered, with bags of goods on their arms. Police without sidearms directed traffic, and men in robes or open-necked shirts and trousers sat around the tables of sidewalk cafés. There was laughter.

Shepherd saw a sign giving directions to the new Toyota plant, and passed other signs of German, French, British, Japanese, and Russian companies. Foreign investment was flowing in. The new buildings being erected were not slapdash brick-and-mortar jobs, but well-engineered concrete and steel. Shepherd flipped through his mental index cards until he found the comparison—Beirut, and how the older correspondents described it back when it was a pearl of a city and not a terrorist hellhole. Military units stayed outside Basra, and some of the Rebel Sheikh's feared private militia had been transformed into civilian police. This area of the city had been good last year when he visited, and was better today. Whatever the sheikh was doing was working.

"Jack Shepherd! It is good to see you again." Ali Shalal Rassad stepped from the shade of an arbor of trees beside a fountain in the courtyard of the palace and extended his hand. "Thank you for coming on such short notice."

"Thank you for the invitation," Shepherd replied. "This is a big story and I appreciate getting your comment."

Rassad nodded and led the correspondent into the coolness of the palace. "Indeed. Please have your crew set up right away. I fear that time is not on our side. After the interview, you can use my press office to feed your story back to your editors. My technicians will help in any way they can."

As they took their places and were miked up, and lights were arranged and tested and the camera was prepared, Rassad steered the off-camera conversation toward what Shepherd had observed on the way in.

"I must say I was quite impressed," the reporter answered. "Everywhere else this country is torn by violence, but your zone shows none of those signs. Why is that?"

"Many reasons, my friend, and I will be happy to discuss them when we have lunch after the interview. The easy answer is that we just want to live in peace, and the Prophet, may his name be praised, is leading us in that direction. Foreign armies have invaded our country over the centuries, and we know how to rebuild," he said as a technician adjusted his suit and tie and a makeup artist applied a little powder to a bright spot on his forehead. "The problem this time was that the Americans wanted to do everything their way, and not our way. Luckily, we drew the British as occupiers, and they were more understanding. Once we endured the violent time and proved we could provide our own security and were no danger to others, London was glad to allow us room to grow and so withdraw some of their troops."

Rassad suddenly looked grim. "No American contractors are allowed to come in and pay fantastic sums to their U.S. employees while giving our people slave wages, and making decisions in Dallas that should have been made in Iraq. We wanted equal pay for equal work. If they didn't want to oblige, they would learn that they were not the only outside nation on this earth that had contractors wanting to help us. The hubris of the American administrators was their downfall. We were building an entire nation, not some shopping mall. The result was that we were able to establish security, clean water, adequate food, electricity, and a civil government that is quite secular and that emphasizes fairness and tolerance. There is no reason that the rest of our nation cannot be the same way, if the foreigners—all of them, including our fellow Muslims from other countries—will simply go home."

He did not mention his personal militia, the feared Holy Scimitar of Allah. They were kept out of sight at distant bases and trained daily with the deadly specialists from

Gates Global, one of the world's best private security companies. One reason things were so quiet in Basra was that everyone in town knew that stepping out of line would result in a quick trip into the desert, never to be seen again.

Shepherd made notes. "That sounds rather like a threat," he observed.

"Not at all. They will leave sometime anyway, for they have done so throughout our history. The sooner the better. Let us get on with our lives."

Shepherd got a nod from his cameraman. "Okay, we're ready to roll if you are."

Rassad's manner changed dramatically, the facial expression eased, and he became a quiet diplomat. "I will make a brief statement, then you can ask questions."

The cameraman pointed and Rassad began. "The people of Iraq have been greatly shocked by the news that Brigadier General Bradley Middleton of the United States Marine Corps has been kidnapped. We also have been shamed by the outrageous claim that this crime was committed by the Holy Scimitar of Allah. As a humble representative of the Holy Scimitar, I want to denounce that falsehood in the strongest way possible. As everyone knows, the Holy Scimitar is a benevolent society, much like the American Red Cross, and is dedicated to the health and welfare of the Iraqi people. It has no connection whatsoever with any terrorists. We were not involved with the kidnapping of General Middleton and we reject those who have tarnished our good name. They are thugs and beyond the protection of the Koran's teachings." The sheikh paused and stared into the camera. "We had no hand in this."

Shepherd had a hard time keeping his face straight and professional. Great stuff, and the sheikh had adroitly danced around the Holy Scimitar's violent history. "Do you know who did it?"

"Unfortunately, no, we do not. But our security people have uncovered something which we feel we must convey publicly to your government. We did not contact them directly because while we wish the general no harm, we do not work for the

Americans. I contacted you, Mr. Shepherd, because I consider you to be an honest broker of this information."

"What is the message?" Shepherd was glowing inside. That unsolicited compliment, plus this invitation to interview the sheikh, would play well in the upcoming negotiations to renew his contract. He damned sure was not going to screw this up now by challenging the sheikh about the real reputation of the vicious militia.

"Evil men are planning to execute General Middleton before a television camera at noon on Tuesday. He is to be stoned to death in symbolic retribution for the destruction American forces have wrought. The true villain in this horrible episode is al Qaeda."

Shepherd was shocked. "Can you prove that, Sheikh Rassad?"

"Yes." He removed a white envelope from the inside pocket of his jacket. "After we finish speaking, the Holy Scimitar will turn over to a Swiss diplomat this written message that was delivered from an al Qaeda messenger only a few hours ago. It claims to contain details known only to someone who participated in the kidnapping. Beyond that, it gives only the time of the execution and says there will be no negotiations."

Rassad eased back into his chair as Shepherd said something inane to close the interview. As the lights went off, both men unclipped their mikes and Rassad took him by the elbow, steering him away. "Now you must go to our press center and file your report, John. Please hurry, for I consider this to be extremely important, and perhaps you can save the life of General Middleton. When Washington calls, as I am sure they will, you can tell them from me personally that we are digging hard for any information that could be helpful and will pass along anything we find immediately. Now go, go! When you are done, we will have lunch. I want to talk about the coming football season."

Sheikh Ali Shalal Rassad was satisfied. This was Arab politics at its best, built on shifting sands, bargaining in which something could be nothing, or anything. Gordon

Gates had paid him a hundred thousand dollars for assisting in the capture of General Middleton and meeting with the reporter. Buying Rassad's help was not the same as getting his allegiance. Gates was a comrade of convenience. Rassad was now moving to convince Washington that the danger to the general was great, but that he wasn't involved at all. They were always ready to believe that al Qaeda was at fault, which meant that those radical fools who were trying to weaken his hold on Basra would be hit hard again by the Americans. As a further goodwill gesture, he would have the Holy Scimitar sweep up a couple of al Qaeda operatives tonight and turn them over to the CIA and further rid him of that nuisance.

Ali Shalal Rassad walked down a cool, tiled hallway toward his living quarters, pulling at the confining necktie. He had time for a nap before the reporter finished filing and joined him for a late lunch.

CHAPTER 15

PREPARE FOR LANDING." THE anonymous voice on the public address system woke him up, and Swanson tightened the belts holding him in the uncomfortable seat. He was aboard a twin-engine Grumman C-1A, technically called a Carrier On-board Delivery System, but familiarly known to all as a COD. Many of the twenty-eight passenger seats were occupied by young sailors and Marines returning to the huge CVN-71 after spending a shore leave as drunk as skunks. The seats faced the rear of the plane, which created a disoriented feeling of flying backward and severe cases of motion sickness and a need for extra barf bags. A hangover combined with a COD ride is just too much for most human stomachs to handle at dawn on Sunday morning.

The pilot lowered his flaps and gunned the twin Allison engines, and the COD fell out of the sky, the tailhook catching the three-wire across the deck of the USS *Theodore Roosevelt*. Swanson was jerked hard against the seatbelts as the plane went from 120 knots to flat zero in only 60 feet. Since the insides of the passengers underwent the same rate of instant deceleration, it felt like the stomach was coming out of the mouth, and a young sailor down the aisle puked noisily, starting a chain reaction.

It took a few minutes for the COD to be released from the

wire and taxi to a parking place on the broad deck; then the side door opened and sea air poured inside to remove the stench of fresh vomit. The awkward-looking CODs ran regular missions out to the carriers to deliver personnel and supplies, and Swanson was just part of the day's cargo being hauled from the U.S. Air Force Base at Injerlek, Turkey, out to the carrier battle group steaming in the western Mediterranean Sea.

Shari had received her summons to return to Washington two hours before a duty officer called on Kyle on his cell phone, ordering him to return to the fleet as soon as possible. All leaves were cancelled. Shari pointed out that she was called first because she was much more important to world peace and protecting the nation. Sir Jeff had directed the *Vagabond* to Naples at a speed that would allow Shari and Kyle to catch flights out first thing Saturday morning, yet slow enough to make time for a final fantastic dinner aboard and a night together. The yacht trip had been a balm for both of them, a rare occasion that stitched their relationship even tighter, and leaving her in Naples had been difficult, but they parted knowing they would have plenty of tomorrows. For now, it was time to get into a warrior frame of mind and concentrate on business.

He waited until everyone else was off the COD before waddling down the aisle, carrying Excalibur in a gun case in one hand and a Val Pak suitcase in the other. Swanson stepped out through the hatch and down the small metal stairway. Wind howled across the flight deck, which was busier than a Wal-Mart at Christmas and smelled like jet fuel and oil.

"Are you one Gunnery Sergeant Kyle Swanson?" The question was yelled in a deep voice that pierced the chaos of the flight deck by a Marine top sergeant whose head was scraped clean of hair.

"Who the fuck is asking?"

"I am God Almighty as far as you are concerned, you piece of pond scum. Fear me!"

"Fear. Right. Here, Double-Oh, catch." He tossed him the

Val Pak. The other Marine grabbed it with one big paw, laughed, and clapped Kyle on the shoulder.

"Come on. We ain't waiting around on this barge. They sent me over from the *Wasp* to fetch you, and our chariot awaits over yonder." Master Sergeant Orville Oliver Dawkins of Pratt, Kansas, pointed across the deck to where a boxy UN-1H helicopter was warming up, the big rotor whomping the air around it. They went over to the port edge and down a couple of ladders and entered the subterranean, pipe-laced caverns that were filled with planes and busy crew members in different-colored jerseys. Mechanics and technicians burrowed into the parked aircraft.

The two Marines did not speak openly with so many people about, but Kyle's curiosity was running away with him. He had learned in Turkey that for some reason he was a high-priority item, and now he had been met personally by a top sergeant with a private helo. Kyle thought for a moment that maybe he was as important as Shari after all.

"So what's this all about, Double-Oh?" Their boots thudded on the steel deck.

"I didn't catch the whole conversation, but the colonel said something about either giving you another Navy Cross or finally kicking your skinny little ass out of my beloved Corps. I forgot which."

"Some god you are. A top who doesn't know what's going on? What is our world coming to?" Swanson said.

"I know all. The beasts of the field and fishies in the ocean do not move without my knowing."

"It's just 'fish,' not 'fishies.' 'Fish' is both singular and plural."

" 'Fishies' sounds better, and since I am God, I can say it however the fuck I want to." They stepped out of the way of a little yellow tractor that crawled toward them, pulling a wings-folded F-14 Tomcat.

"So you really have no idea what's going on, do you?"

"Not a clue, Kyle. Just bet your ass something big league is coming down involving your old pal General Middleton. Why else would you get a private whirlybird ride?"

Dawkins looked back over his shoulder long enough to give him a smile that contained no warmth whatsoever. "And a 'special guest' is waiting for you."

They started up the stairs and ladders to the main deck. "Shit. A spook?"

"Spooky as Freddy Krueger on Halloween. As Jason with a chainsaw. As *Scary Movie 3*. CIA dude straight from Langley. Got here last night."

By the time they reached the deck, the Huey was ready to go. The bird was primarily used as a command-and-control platform, which meant it had cushioned seats. Neither Double-Oh nor Swanson buckled in, because they made a living jumping out of helicopters and hated being confined inside one. The Huey smoothly lifted away, the open doors letting the fresh morning air swoosh through the cabin. The giant *Roosevelt* grew small in size, and then disappeared behind them as the green Med rolled gently underneath, five hundred feet below.

On the way over to the *Wasp,* Kyle considered the unexpected appearance of the "special guest." Last he had heard from the CIA, he was standing at attention in front of some civilian and a bird colonel and being told that he had fucked up the border mission, that he was more trouble than he was worth, and that he would never get to play with them again.

"What?" he had asked the spooks. "Did that asshole Ali bin Assam come back to life or something? You wanted him dead. He's dead."

He was then chewed on for a while for constantly violating accepted doctrine in the field, and told that the agency had no room for renegades. Kyle shrugged it off. He had heard it all before, just the usual complaints made by the office weenies when they had given him their unspoken blessing before the black mission began to do whatever was required. They were just covering their asses for the files, and he knew those loud threats to absolutely, positively, never, ever use him again would last only until the next time he was needed.

Now it seemed that time had arrived. Something had

changed their little bureaucratic minds, which probably meant he was going to get shot at and that a snatch raid was planned to get Middleton back. Kyle reached between his boots and gave the gun case an affectionate pat, quite happy that Sir Jeff and Tim insisted that he take Excalibur along and give it a real field test. Somebody shot at him, he was going to shoot back.

CHAPTER 16

SWANSON KNOCKED ON THE hatch and heard a sharp command from within the VIP cabin: "Enter." His boots made impressions on the soft carpet covering the steel deck of the well-decorated room. Prints of sailing ships, old admirals, and sea battles hung on the walls, flags stood in the corners, and the curtains were pulled away from a large porthole that lit the room with sunshine. A civilian with an astonishing helmet of black hair slicked straight back stood to meet him. He wore a moderately expensive dark suit with a white shirt so starched that he probably stood it up in a corner at night. The guy reeked of ego.

"Gunny Swanson, I'm John Smith," he said with an easy smile that showed a lot of even teeth. "Please feel free to call me John."

How original, Swanson thought. "I'm not working for the CIA anymore, Mr. Smith. I've been back with the MEU for about a year, after a, uh, dispute about my last mission."

Smith sat down on the large sofa and crossed his legs carefully. "I flew all the way out here from Washington to personally hand you some new orders. You stay with the Marines on paper, but there will be a temporary and a simultaneous mission for the CIA."

Swanson went silent, considering the situation. The

squeaks and thumps of an aircraft carrier under way filtered into the quiet. "Who knows about this?"

Sam Shafer lied. "Myself and my boss, the National Security Advisor, Gerald Buchanan. The commandant of the Marine Corps and the President of the United States." Actually, Shafer did not know, but admitting that would lower his sense of importance. Neither did the President or the commandant know, because Buchanan was running this on his own. Shafer was itching to get a look at the letter. Buchanan had only given him crumbs of information and terse instructions about how to handle this interview.

"What about my MEU commander?"

"This is a *need* to know situation, Gunny. Not a *want* to know."

"That sort of complicates the hell out of things right out of the box, Mr. Jones."

"Smith."

"Smith. Jones. Who the fuck cares? It's not your real name anyway. So this is a black job that even my commanding officer will not know about? That sucks big-time. How can it work if he doesn't know what I'm doing?" Clearly the mission had been dreamed up by people who had never served in a combat role. That made Kyle suspicious about whether the Marine commandant was really in the loop.

"As far as your commanding officer is concerned, you are going along on the mission to rescue General Middleton as a sniper for extra firepower. If everything goes smoothly, this other order is to be disregarded."

"So what's the job?"

Sam Shafer walked to a small desk on which lay his aluminum briefcase, and dialed the combination to open it. He handed Kyle a sealed white envelope. Swanson took it over to the porthole and read it in the bright light. The first thing he noticed was small blue printing across the top: THE WHITE HOUSE. The order took his breath away. He read it a second time. Same result. "Shit," he said. "You're out of your fuckin' mind."

"I assure you, Gunny Swanson, this is as serious as a dozen

heart attacks." Shafer was bluffing, but he knew Buchanan was not playing a game. The instructions, whatever they were, meant what they said.

"And if I refuse to carry out this order?"

"Then you will be held in isolation in the brig aboard this ship and we get somebody else to do the job. You are forbidden to discuss it with anyone. After the mission is over, you would be thrown out of the Marine Corps."

"And if I do it, not only do I probably still get run out of the Marines, but maybe I also face a firing squad for having done such good work for the CIA. Fuck this."

"Are you refusing the mission?"

"Let's just say I have some big questions. For starters, I don't know you. You haven't shown me any identification, which leads me to believe you're not CIA at all. So let's start at the beginning, Mr. Smith. Who the hell are you?"

The civilian's brown eyes went cold as he reached for his wallet and pulled out a laminated government identification card. His real name was Samuel Shafer and he worked at the White House as assistant to the National Security Advisor. That clicked, for the mission order was signed by Gerald Buchanan. Shafer was a messenger boy.

Kyle handed the order back to him. "Now I want you to tell me face-to-face, so there is no misunderstanding. What are my orders, Mr. Shafer?"

Shafer had a difficult time keeping a stone face and maintaining his glee. At last he got to see the order. When he read it, he was shocked, too, but buried the reaction to pretend he knew what was going on.

"Just what it says, Gunny. If things go wrong on this mission to rescue the general, you are instructed by the White House to shoot him dead."

"And why would we want to do that?"

"We don't *want* to do it at all." Shafer was thinking on his feet. "Middleton is too valuable to stay in enemy hands. He knows too much about certain highly classified projects that are time-sensitive. We cannot risk him being made to talk.

Too much is at stake to take the chance that the torturers may pull the information out of him. He knows that, too."

"They wouldn't get anything from Middleton," Kyle said. "I hate his guts, but he's a tough bird. He would die before giving up a secret."

"Drugs and torture could leave him no choice. He would be interrogated in a hospital somewhere, with an IV drip in his arm and his mouth running like a motor. If we can't bring him back, they cannot have him, either. Simple as that." Swanson handed the letter back to Swanson. "Gunny, this is obviously a difficult assignment, but we have to put our country's security first. It is a national security emergency."

Swanson studied the authorization letter again. "If that's so, why is the order signed by this guy Buchanan and not the President himself? You said he knows about it."

"Are you being intentionally naïve? Deniability. The President's name can't be on anything like this, even though this is the only copy and I'm going to destroy it right after you tell me whether you are taking the job or not. So, Gunny, time's up. Consider that to be an order to you directly from your commander-in-chief. You in or out?"

Kyle paused, then walked away from Shafer, folding the letter and buying moments to think. *Since there was no way the Marine commandant would be in on this, was the President's involvement also a lie?* Murdering a general was huge! But the order came straight from the White House. Swanson made a decision.

"Okay. I'll do it, Mr. Shafer. But you're not going to destroy this letter. We'll have the captain put it in the ship's safe until the mission is complete. If I have have to pull the trigger, the order is transferred into a secure safe under the control of the CIA director of operations. I won't be left hanging out to dry with no way to prove I was following orders."

Shafer reared. "Out of the question! Give me the letter, Gunny. I will burn it and then you go off and do your goddam job as you have been ordered to do." He put on his angry face, raised his voice, and pissed Swanson off.

"No. The letter goes in the safe."

They stared at each other for fifteen silent seconds and Shafer spun on the heel of a highly polished shoe. "I'm going to get a secure radio link back to the White House, and you will be ordered directly by senior civilian authority to surrender the letter to me. Take it from me, Gunny Swanson, you do *NOT* want to have that kind of conversation with Gerald Buchanan."

Kyle moved to the desk and plopped into the seat. He shoved the telephone toward the visitor. "I'll wait here for you, Mr. Smith. Patch the call to this extension."

Shafer went through the hatchway and stormed down the corridor.

Swanson jumped up and found Double-Oh waiting outside. "Problem, Double-Oh. Catch up with that dude and lead him around for about ten minutes. He's looking for the comm center, so steer him through the berthing areas or engineering spaces or whatever, then bring him back here. I'll explain later." The big guy took off after the angry civilian.

Kyle went the other way, down a ladder, and made his way aft to the little shop where the ship's daily newsletter was printed. A yeoman was clicking the keyboard of a computer.

"You got a copying machine?" Swanson waved the folded letter.

The sailor didn't reply, just pointed to a big beige box in a corner, a Xerox that would have been at home in any civilian business office. Kyle peeled back the flexible lid, pressed the letter flat, lowered the lid, and hit the green COPY button. After a brief hum and a flash of rolling light, the machine spit into a side tray a copy that was indistinguishable from the original. "Thanks," he told the swabbie, who had not looked up from his computer. Back in the VIP suite, Swanson found an envelope in the center drawer of the desk, put in the original letter, and sealed it. The envelope went back into the drawer. He folded the copy just as the original had been folded, and laid it on the desk.

Within two minutes, Double-Oh delivered the exasperated Sam Shafer back into the room, where Gunnery Sergeant Kyle Swanson was standing at a sharp parade rest position. Shafer closed the door, his face red with anger, but before he could speak, Kyle did, very formally.

"Sir. I have reconsidered my position. I was confused about the chain of command, but if you were willing to get Mr. Buchanan on the horn, then this order is obviously valid. Therefore, I apologize and accept the mission, although with reluctance."

Shafer, having won the point, calmed down. He was back in control and oozed White House power. "And the order?"

Swanson pointed to the paper. He did not want to allow Shafer too much time to examine it. "Right here, sir. Burn it and get it over with. It would be best for me that it is never seen again."

Shafer placed the paper in a large ashtray and took out a cigarette lighter, and a quick flame nibbled the corner, then fire ate the entire page. Shafer took the ashes into the bathroom and flushed them down the toilet.

"When will you be returning to Washington, sir?" Kyle asked.

"As soon as they can launch me. I've been assigned a two-seat F-16 for this trip," he said.

Swanson gave him a sharp salute. "Yes, sir. Have a good trip back, sir."

"And good luck to you, Gunny. I know this is a tough one." He extended his hand and Swanson shook it, then stepped outside as Shafer left. Double-Oh had been waiting, and after Kyle retrieved the letter, they went to get some coffee and find a quiet corner.

"You ain't going to believe this shit," Swanson told his friend, and Double-Oh didn't, until Kyle gave him the envelope for safekeeping. "Now I have you as a witness *and* the original letter, and Mr. Shafer from the CIA or White House or wherever he works can go fuck himself and the F-16 he rode in on."

CHAPTER 17

IN THE MIDDLE OF THE NIGHT, Kyle Swanson stood in the well of a portside gun turret next to the flight deck and let his thoughts roam away from the mission at hand. The irony of the job struck him. He was aboard the USS *Wasp,* a small aircraft carrier designed for special operations, sailing in the eastern Med beneath a massive umbrella of protection. It was part of an entire battle group that spread around the nuclear-powered carrier USS *Theodore Roosevelt,* about a hundred thousand tons of steel and one of the biggest ships ever to sail the seas. Needle-nosed destroyers, daunting cruisers, and big submarines also were slicing the waters, and there were enough missiles, planes, bullets, torpedoes, and sailors on hand to take care of anything that any enemy could throw at them at sea, and also to strike deep into hostile nations. So if this mighty task force, the best the squids had, was so tough, why was he standing here, dressed all in black, his face smeared with grease, and decked out with his personal firepower, getting ready to head out once again on a raid against some low-tech ragheads not all that far from the shores of Tripoli? The Marines seemed to keep coming back to this part of the world that was part of their hymn, as if there was some magnet for them in the desert sands.

Swanson felt rested. He had caught a couple of hours of

sleep following a late operational briefing, and then test-firing and cleaning his weapons for a final time. He rolled out of his rack at oh-dark-thirty and joined up with the Force Recon team that would be the assault force on the TRAP, the initialized way of saying "Tactical Recovery of Air Personnel." A longer acronym labeled them as part of the Marine Expeditionary Unit, Special Operations Capable, or MEU-SOC. The mission was a frequently practiced operation designed to rescue a pilot downed in enemy territory and had therefore been easily adapted to pull out a hostage. Two helicopters would go in, and the first to land would have the mortar platoon aboard, which would spread out and secure for the landing zone. A TRAP moved so fast that heavy mortar tubes were not part of the attack, so the Marines normally assigned to them were free for other jobs like protecting the LZ. The second helo carried the attack force. This package was built for speed, not total firepower.

The mess table was crowded with young Marines packing in big, greasy breakfasts of eggs and sausage, biscuits and bacon, and bragging and shouting insults and curses to cover their pre-battle jitters. Kyle found a place on a bench and satisfied himself with cereal and hash browns to load up on carbohydrates, and some fruit. Juice instead of coffee, to avoid the caffeine. Then he went to the war room on the second-level hangar deck of the *Wasp,* found a soft chair, and fell asleep while the younger dudes, eager to rock and roll, continued their grabass. When the noise abruptly stopped, Swanson awoke and saw a cluster of officers filing in to conduct the confirmation briefing.

In moments the room was totally silent, and the briefing officers began flashing photo recon pictures on the screen and putting up transparent overlays of maps. Swanson perched on the edge of his seat, watching closely. Only a few hours ago, the mission had still been vague on many points, but now it had slammed together like the hatch of a tank. Kyle had been through many briefings, but never had heard such a rapid-fire discussion of precise targets, operations, and methodology for exactly who was to do precisely what. No significant opposition was expected, since surprise would be total and only two guards were with General Middleton. *How the hell do they know that?*

The intel geeks claimed to have pinpointed the exact location where Middleton was being held, right down to the specific house, had downloaded satellite pictures and maps, and even had a photograph of a local guide, some French Arab who was a veteran of the Foreign Legion. Small pictures of the man were distributed with both of his names, Pierre Falais and Abu Mohammed, printed on the back. Having an inside operator should certainly make the mission a lot easier. The briefer predicted a smooth snatch-and-grab with little action, if any.

Kyle never liked planning for the easy scenario. There were always sudden twists and turns in combat, the enemy never reacted exactly as predicted, and really good intelligence was usually bad. To top it off, Murphy's Law always clicked in: If something can go wrong, it will, and at the worst possible time. A damned goat wanders into the wrong place, or a woman decides to string a laundry line across the landing zone, or somebody breaks a leg. He settled back into the chair. Sometimes it is best not to look a gift horse in the mouth and just accept what the man says. Occasionally, the bullshit works.

There was a stir among the senior combat-seasoned guys in the room, and Kyle exchanged a quick glance with the major who would lead the assault force and received a nod of silent agreement. *Here we go again. No enemy on the ground. Don't worry about it. Yeah, right. In the Middle East, land of fairy tales and mirages.*

Judging by the briefers who were taking turns at the podium, every government and spy in the Middle East had been working to find General Bradley Middleton, because his death would bring down the wrath of this big task force on somebody's head. For him to be executed in a television spectacular would make all Muslims appear to be savage maniacs before an unsympathetic world audience. Maybe some king or prince had dropped the dime on the bad guys,

Kyle thought. Middleton was being held in Syria, and the leaders in Damascus well remembered the shock-and-awe campaign that opened the war with Iraq. Whoever these kidnappers were, their security sucked.

Still, this was a hell of a lot of information to have been gathered in such a short time in a part of the world where hostages and kidnap victims regularly were missing for weeks before any word surfaced about them.

The briefing done, Kyle slung Excalibur over his shoulder in a zippered drag bag and wandered up to the gun turret to find some privacy. Noise and movement assaulted him as soon as he stepped through the hatch, for it is never quiet on a ship. The pungent smell of oil, grease, and jet fuel hung over the carrier despite the stiff wind, and grease-stained sailors looking as dirty as coal miners were working everywhere. He punched the button on his cell phone for frequently dialed numbers, hit the SEND button, and listened as the *beep-beep-beep* sounded on the East Coast of the United States.

"Hey, you." Shari Towne usually was annoyed if she received a personal call during working hours, but the incoming number showed it was Kyle.

"Hey," Swanson said. His voice was soft, distant, concerned.

"You okay?"

"Yeah. I'm good. How was your trip home?"

"Quick and comfortable, but boring. Some kind soul laid on a little jet plane just for me. The movie was a chick flick that you would have hated."

Kyle paused, visualizing her sitting in her tiny office, surrounded by papers while intel reports pumped out of the computers. She would speed-read them, unconsciously translating as she went, remembering almost everything. "What are you wearing?" Swanson asked.

"The shoulder boards of a lieutenant commander in the United States Navy, you horny jarhead." She laughed.

"I just needed to hear you," Kyle said, turning serious. "I'm going to be gone for a little while." The conversation was a struggle. They wanted to be intimate, but professionalism and the need for security would not let them. Just hearing her voice was the best he could hope for.

"I know." Her mood shifted, too.

"You do?"

"Umm. Been working on it at this end. It's a strange one."

"You don't know the half of it."

"I don't? I'm supposed to know it all."

"Well, you don't. Trust me."

"Kyle? What's wrong?" Her voice was tinged with genuine concern. "Should I get involved here?"

Swanson caught himself. He had said too much, and telling her more might put her in jeopardy, since the letter containing what he considered an illegal order had come from her boss. "No, no. Absolutely not. Forget it, and please don't say anything to anyone about my bitching. It's just some Pentagon backseat driving, and nothing I can't handle. That's why I get the big bucks."

"But you're okay?" she asked.

"Oh, yeah. All dressed up for the prom, and the limo is waiting."

He ducked below the level of the flight deck as the launch crews moved an AV-8B Harrier II Plus attack jet into launch position, their purposeful ballet underscored by the plane's two screaming engines. Tongues of blue-white fire spit back from the exhausts and illuminated the darkness. Kyle told Shari to wait a moment while the plane built to a thunderous roar and lifted straight up from the deck, its exhaust rolling out in an engulfing cloud of heat. The plane hovered and changed the position of its wings and engines, then thundered away. Two Harriers, loaded with everything from iron bombs to cannons and missiles, would orbit near the target zone as part of the TRAP package, ready to zoom in if things started going to hell.

"I love you, girl," he shouted into the phone as a second Harrier was rolled into place. "I gotta go now."

"I love you, too. Call me when you get back. The very instant, you hear me? You understand?"

"Yes, ma'am."

"And be care . . ." She stopped talking. "We better stop."

"Yep. I'll call you in a while. Love ya." He thumbed the OFF button and the connection was broken, leaving Kyle feeling empty and alone as the plane wound up its roar to launch. Shari knew more about this rescue mission than she was able to say on an open line, which meant that one hell of a lot of people were involved, from the guys putting the Harriers in the air all the way up the ladder to the White House. The more people who know, the bigger the chance for a fuckup, the bigger chance of losing the cloak of secrecy.

He came up the ramp and walked onto the deck after the second Harrier had cleared out. The hostage rescue raiders were gathering near a pair of giant CH-53E Super Stallion heavy transport helicopters that were waiting with the rear ramps down and the big rotors starting to turn.

Twenty-four Marines were split into two groups, with a lieutenant already leading his stick of men up the ramp of one chopper. Kyle checked in with the major leading the assault force as it also moved to load. Double-Oh appeared at his elbow.

"Fuck if I shouldn't be going on this job," he told Kyle. "You get all the fun."

"Piece of cake, man. Didn't you pay attention to the briefing?" Kyle had a small bag of personal items in his hand, including his watch, cell phone, and wallet. He handed it to the big master sergeant. "Instead of all of us, maybe they should send a taxi to pick him up, huh?"

"Or maybe the briefers should go." He accepted the personal items, to hold until Kyle returned.

"An officer would never lie. You still got the letter I gave you, right?"

Dawkins tapped the chest pocket of his battle dress uniform and said, "I'll keep it right here until you get back." Kyle noticed that his friend had also put on a shoulder holster rig with the butt of a pistol in easy reach. Nobody was taking that letter.

The last Marines were stepping onto the ramp, and it was

his time to board. "Look, Double-Oh, I just talked to Shari. If you need to show that note to someone later, bring her into the loop. Just remember, she works for the asshole who signed it."

"You're going to disobey a direct order from Washington, aren't you?"

"I'm not going to murder a Marine, even an asshole like Middleton," Kyle said. "I'm going to bring him back alive, just to piss everyone off." He tapped fists with Double-Oh and vanished into the dark cavern of the big helo.

"Hey, Swanson!" Master Sergeant O. O. Dawkins bellowed, his best parade ground voice cutting through the racket as the ramp began to close. "If you die, can I have your girl?"

CHAPTER 18

FIVE MINUTES OUT." THE PILOT'S scratchy voice came into Kyle Swanson's ears through the internal radio net as the two CH-53E helicopters lurched through the night sky. The interior of the birds was deafening because each had three powerful GE engines and little insulation. Everyone wore special flight helmets fitted with thick earmuffs that contained radio receivers. The team was all on a single frequency, but the assault leader and Swanson could also communicate with the aircrew.

It was uncomfortable and cold in the narrow compartment where he sat scrunched among a dozen Marines, for although the huge helicopters were almost a hundred feet long, the cabin was thirty feet long, less than eight feet wide, and not even seven feet high. Looking around, the scene of the young warriors with painted faces and weighted with gear reminded Swanson of the old pictures of American paratroopers jammed aboard ancient C-47s going into the D-Day invasion.

The helicopters had flown an impeccable mission, and had gone "feet dry" over Israel right on schedule. From that point, they were wrapped in a protective embrace by Israeli jet fighters that just happened to be conducting a night exercise along the same path. Any hostile radar would have a hard time picking the two helicopters out of the clutter on their computer screens.

The assault force members had gone silent, each man alone with his thoughts, when they flew out of Israel, moved into unguarded airspace over Jordan, and finally reached the edge of Syria. They spent the long passing minutes checking their equipment or leaning back against the vibrating bulkhead, eyes closed and lost in thought. The first CH-53E would land about two kilometers from the village and the mortar platoon Marines would pour from it to form a protective cordon for the landing zone. The second one, which Swanson was aboard, would come in simultaneously and the raiders would hustle off, conduct the rescue, and bring the general back to the safe LZ and they would all be away.

The choppers hurtled along at their cruising speed of 175 miles per hour, the pilots handling the huge machines as surely as if they were driving their own cars, with hardly a wiggle in the flight path. The change in the pitch of the rotors, the sinking feeling in Swanson's stomach, and the pressure in his ears confirmed the beginning of the approach run, and he unbuckled his seatbelt. "Four minutes," came the warning call from the cockpit.

There were two open hatches near the front of the cabin, and a crew member was at one, perched behind a .50-caliber machine gun. At the three-minute alert, Swanson unplugged his commo line from the net and made his way forward to the second hatch, trying not to step on anyone as he sidled past the small motorcycle lashed in the aisle. The dirt bike was to be used by a scout if the mission commander wanted extended reconnaissance.

A typhoon of wind rushed through the open hatches, blowing hard when he reached the opening and looked out. The darkness had a deep vastness, and a little slice of moon provided the only glimmer of light. He adjusted his night vision goggles and watched the green world pass below him. Swanson was to be the last man to leave the helicopter, remaining out of the way while the other Marines charged out. Positioned in the open hatch, he could provide extra firepower until it was time for him to join them. He plugged the commo line in at the new position in time to hear the pilot say, "One minute."

Swanson put his hands against the sides of the hatch and shifted his fifty-pound pack and other equipment to be able to sit down. His stubby M-4 assault rifle hung across his chest, and Excalibur crossed his back, safe in its padded bag. With thirty seconds to go, the major ordered, "Stand up! Lock and load!" and the other Marines unbuckled, exchanged their flight helmets for real ones, and formed rows in the narrow aisles.

Kyle removed the night vision goggles, pulled the M-4 into firing position, and put his eye to the scope, which could penetrate the darkness. He could engage with precision shots at up to eight hundred meters and switch to rapid fire if necessary, but he saw nothing of interest. He kept the sight moving, searching for threats as the two aircraft jockeyed for the final descent, sharply reducing their altitude and bleeding off speed.

The rear ramp began to lower and the wind through the chopper increased to gale-force proportions. The tail dipped as the helicopter flared to almost a complete stop in the air, braking its forward momentum less than twenty feet off the ground and barely moving forward. With the more stable platform, Swanson stood and continued parsing the LZ with his rifle and night scope. Nothing out there.

A loud scream erupted over the crew net. The two helicopters were hanging almost motionless in the air when a freak wall of wind that had swept unimpeded across a hundred miles of desert tore through the LZ and threw the birds together with train-wreck violence. The churning seventy-nine-foot-long rotors chopped like long swords, and both aircraft were instantly out of control, tangling with each other.

The standing Marines went flying and crashing about the spinning cabin like dolls, breaking necks and spines and limbs as the helicopter blades dug through the thin metal sides of the helicopters and went after the men like sharp knives. When his helicopter lurched onto its left side, Swanson was propelled straight out of the open hatch by the centrifugal force, like a piece of trash thrown from a car on a highway. The force of the ejection tore the helmet commo line free to prevent him from being lynched. The M-4 assault rifle snapped from its strap and flew away. His last sensation as his body was pulled into the void was of the cold wind caressing his face. He tumbled toward the desert floor.

CHAPTER 19

SWANSON SLAMMED BELLY first onto the downward slop-
ing side of a small sand dune and skidded, rolled, and
bounced over and over before his tumbling body came to a
stop at the bottom of the wadi. An explosion that would be
heard for miles detonated behind him, and pieces of the dis-
integrating helicopters whizzed overhead and whiplashed
the sands. He lay dazed, almost unconscious, trying to get
some air into his lungs.

He lay motionless for about thirty seconds before coming
out of his stupor, choking and gasping while his brain reeled
and his face felt as if he had been punched by a young Mike
Tyson on his best day. He pushed into a sitting position and
used two fingers to dig gobs of sand out of his cheeks, then
found his canteen and poured water over his face, sluicing it
in his mouth and spitting it out. He doused his bandanna
with water and rubbed his aching eyes. Blood came away on
the cloth, and he explored his face until he found the gash
across the bridge of his nose where the helmet had cracked
him. In times of dire emergency, he knew, it was best to take
a moment to gather his wits before doing anything at all, so
he pressed the bandanna against the cut, flopped back
against the sand, and took deep breaths, repeating his personal mantra softly: *Slow is smooth; smooth is fast.*

When he felt able to move, he crawled to the top of the dune and looked in horrible fascination at the wreckage that only moments before had been two powerful transport helicopters loaded with combat-ready Marines. It was hard to tell one of the birds from the other now because they had come down in a heap, cutting each other into chunks and merging into a single pile of smoldering wreckage. Twisting columns of red and yellow and orange flames spun into the dark sky.

Swanson dropped his gear and ran to the wreckage, stepping through the hot, sharp metal and pockets of burning debris to check for signs of life and finding only bodies and parts of bodies. There were no moans, no cries for help. Had the Marines been seated and strapped in, some might have survived, but he found nothing but carnage. The machines had slaughtered each other as well as every human being aboard except him.

Almost thirty men had been killed, and the scene sickened him. "Fuck me," Swanson said. He turned away, took a few steps, and threw up.

It was a fiery end for the ambitious plan that the briefers had predicted would be a cakewalk. Motherfucking Mr. Murphy and his bad-luck law had shown up early on this one, and Kyle, breathing deeply, forced himself back into the cold reality of the moment. *Get your shit together!*

He could see if there was a workable radio and call the Fleet, where everyone would be listening to the net. But Washington probably was also plugged into the radio chatter, and the White House would simply hand the assassination job to someone else. If Swanson called for help, General Middleton would surely die.

Think, damn it, think! If he didn't call, everyone would think that he was dead, too. But that would allow him to work alone, and although Buchanan would probably still assign another assassin, Kyle stood a good chance of reaching the general first because he was already on the ground.

Hell, he should be dead anyway, so why not continue the mission by himself, in total secrecy? The odds were astronomical, but Kyle would not allow himself to think of it as a suicide trip. *That's it, then. Just get on with it! Go!* New confidence surged through him like electricity.

He looked toward the village, which was about fifteen hundred meters away. That distance had not been changed by the crash. The helicopters had come down right where they were supposed to, just in a terribly wrong way. With the crash, the jig was up as far as surprise went, and everybody in the village might be temporarily stunned by what happened, but they would be coming his way in a hurry. Time was not his friend.

He went back into the wreckage and gathered canteens of water, more ammo, plenty of blocks of C-4 explosive, a couple of Claymore mines, a portable satellite telephone that still had power, and a survival radio from one of the pilots. He snapped them both off. Even when not in active use they would still send electronic signals, and when the little green power lights vanished, Swanson could no longer be tracked. On the screens, he was dead. He found an M-16 rifle, locked and loaded.

A glance at his watch showed him that three minutes had flown by, and he still had two more important chores.

Kyle stepped over bodies and debris until he was beside the little Kawasaki motorcycle. He gave it a quick check and it seemed undamaged, having been held tight on the deck throughout the disaster. Unlike the Marines, it had been professionally secured, and Kyle unsheathed his big knife, cut away the loading bands, and pushed it out. He loaded everything he had on it and rested it on the kickstand.

Now came the hard part, leaving a clue for Shari, something only she would recognize. She was in the informational loop about the mission, and would assume that he had died in the crash. He wanted to let her know he had survived, but also to provide some misdirection for anyone else.

He scanned the dead Marines and found one in the jumble of corpses, someone whose face could not be recognized but was about Kyle's size. The rubber-rimmed dog tag identified the man as Lance Corporal Harold McDowell, and his neck had been snapped when he was thrown against the bulkhead. A Marine Corps tattoo was inked on his right forearm. The kid had been proud to be a warrior and would not object to doing one more job.

Kyle exchanged the neck dog tag with his own. "It's this way, McDowell," Swanson whispered while he untied the kid's left boot, then his own, speaking to the pale face. "I need your help here. The bad guys are going to be looking for survivors. If they figure out some crazy sniper is missing, they'll really start hunting. If a radioman is missing, no offense, they won't give a rat's ass and think you will holler for help and get picked up sooner or later. You would pose no threat to them."

Kyle unbuckled the big radio from the dead man's shoulders. He would dispose of it later, but he needed to take it along to complete the disguise and misdirection play. The pursuers would logically believe that a missing radioman would have kept his radio. "And for the good guys, well, Harold, some of them ain't so good. For this plan to have any chance of working, we need those assholes to also think I'm dead. That's where you come in, Harold. What did they call you: Hal? Mac? So convince them that you are me, okay, Lance Corporal McDowell?" Swanson stood and threw the youngster a quick salute. "Semper fi."

He hustled over to the bike, hooked the radio pack over the handlebars, straddled the motorcycle, and, with a prayer, pushed the starter button. The little engine coughed once, then kicked to life, ready to run. His wristwatch showed that he had used up his time cushion, about six minutes since the helos went down.

He adjusted his night-vision goggles and drove away from the wreckage, the muffled exhaust helping avoid making any more noise than necessary. In the unlikely case that someone from the village figured out there was a survivor, Swanson steered the motorcycle to the east, leaving clear tracks that would indicate he was running to the Israeli border.

A minute later, he was on the paved road that ran through

the village behind him, and far enough away from the wreckage to pile on a little more speed with the 1,200-cc engine. Dawn was coming, and he had to be invisible by then.

When radio contact was broken between the operations center aboard the USS *Wasp* and the TRAP team helos, several minutes elapsed while the sailors at the consoles tried to reestablish a voice link. A download from a stationary satellite watching the area showed a flash in the darkness and the lingering bloom of immense heat at the landing zone.

Colonel Ralph Sims, commander of the 33rd Marine Expeditionary Unit, chewed a fingernail. "Get the Harriers in there to take a look," he ordered, and the pair of fighter jets broke out of their orbit over Israel, heeled over from 40,000 feet, dropped to the ground, and sped into Syrian airspace riding their afterburners. Nearing the scene, they saw the fire, cut their speed, coasted over the wreckage, banked into a sharp turn, and ran past it again.

Aboard the *Wasp,* the speakers crackled in the quiet commo room. "Henhouse, this is Rooster One. They're down and burning," a pilot reported.

"Survivors?" Sims asked. The radioman relayed the question.

"Negative. No sign of life or movement at the scene, but there are bad guys coming out from the target zone. Request permission to engage."

Sims wanted to say, "Hell, yes," but could not. An attack run by the Harriers would probably result in casualties among Syrian civilians, which would make a bad situation a lot worse. It was time to call it a day. "Negative," he barked, and turned to the commander of the ship's Marine Air Wing. "Get those planes back home."

The Tactical Air Center sent the order. "Egress! Egress! Egress!"

The pilot hesitated. "Henhouse, Rooster One. What about a bombing run on the wreckage? I can torch the scene."

"Negative," came the immediate reply from Colonel Sims.

He needed higher authority for that, and didn't have time to get it. He would message Washington for permission to send in a Cruise missile for that demolition job. "Repeat. Negative. Return to base."

"Rooster One. Roger that. I copy egress, return to base." The Rooster Flight headed home.

He heard his wingman come on the air. "Rooster Two to Rooster One, push to Rooster freak." Both pilots switched to another frequency so they could talk without being overheard.

"Go ahead, Two, this is Rooster One."

"Boss, did I copy that last right? We really leaving these guys behind?"

"You heard the same thing I did."

"I know, but what about 'Marines don't leave their own'?"

The flight leader's temper was simmering. He felt the same way, but because he was in command, he could not agree with his friend over an open radio channel. "One to Two. You saw it as good as I did. They're all dead!"

"Well, if they weren't then, they are now. Or worse."

"That's enough, Rooster Two. Follow your orders. Rooster One out."

The Harriers hugged the ground as they dashed back to Israeli airspace, where they would climb high for the rest of the return flight to the *Wasp*. The pilots remained silent, lost in thought about a rescue raid that had flipped into total disaster. Rooster One knew that by flying away, they were erasing any chance American survivors might escape captivity, torture, or death. "Please, God, don't let me see one of those kids show up on Al Jazeera," he said in a soft prayer, words that would never leave his cockpit.

Aboard the *Wasp*, Colonel Ralph Sims sent the message about the cruise missile to Washington, then walked rigidly out of the command center, seeking fresh air and a moment of privacy. He lit a cigarette and thought about his Marines lying entombed in the helicopters in Syria. There would be a lot of investigations, and people, including him, would probably lose their jobs. At the moment, he didn't really care, for he had a bigger worry, one that was much more personal. *What the hell am I supposed to tell their families?*

The sky was losing its blackness, and the first rays of the new day crawled across the Middle East.

CHAPTER 20

ROOSTER ONE. ROGER THAT. *I copy egress, return to base."*

The Harrier flight leader sounded calm and professional as he was heard in real time over a satellite linkup straight into the Situation Room of the White House. Members of the National Security Council had been there for an hour, monitoring the Middleton rescue raid. Now they were immobilized in shock.

Lieutenant Commander Shari Towne brought both hands to her mouth, fighting not to cry out in anguish at what she heard. Both helicopters down. No signs of life. Unknown people moving in fast. *KYLE! NO!*

National Security Advisor Gerald Buchanan was at the head of the long table in his big chair, tapping a yellow pencil against a legal pad as he listened to the disembodied voice. This was something he had not counted on, and he was busy weighing the up sides and the down sides. He looked around at the military people and detected an advantage. Make it their fault.

The chairman of the Joint Chiefs of Staff, General Turner, was chewing a knuckle, and lines of thought creased his forehead. He was, after all, a Marine, although he represented all of the military services. He had previously been the Marine Corps commandant, so those were *his* men who had lost their lives. He was emotionally involved.

A definite advantage! Grab it! Buchanan, however, spoke quietly. "Your Marines failed, General, so we now have a situation."

Turner had to agree. He had watched the crash via the satellite feed and had heard what the pilots had to say. "Yes, sir. It does appear the mission was unsuccessful."

Buchanan did not follow up his first jab. He stared at the satellite picture of a glowing hot spot in the Syrian desert. He could remain the consummate professional. "A tragedy, but we must move ahead. I need to hear options. Right now."

An admiral joined the conversation. "It's too late for an emergency rescue extraction. A team of Special Forces would not be enough at this point, with the Syrian military obviously going on alert. I would expect the Syrians to be controlling the scene within hours. We would have to insert nothing less than an airborne battalion, and that probably would not be enough. They would soon be surrounded and chopped up without massive air cover, and that would really up the stakes." He paused. Looked directly at General Turner, then Buchanan. "No further troop deployment is advisable."

"You can't just leave them there!" Shari Towne exclaimed, and all eyes in the room were drawn to her. She was the lowest-ranking officer present, in charge of nothing.

"Stay out of this, Lieutenant Commander," the admiral, her immediate boss, growled impatiently.

Shari caught the warning and flipped the pages of a red three-ring binder. "Yes, sir." She stopped at a page. "I was referring to the protocol in the operations manual."

Nice recovery, girl, the admiral thought. He knew of her personal relationship with Kyle Swanson and that Swanson was on the mission, but he wanted her to shut up before she went too far. The admiral liked them both and believed that their personal life was no business of anyone else at the table.

"What would that be, Lieutenant Commander" asked Buchanan. Had he caught some distress in her voice? More than normal? *Why?*

"Standard operating procedures instruct the incineration of wreckage, just as the pilot suggested."

"And how would that be accomplished?"

The air force general at the long table answered. "We can get some fast movers in there, either from the carrier in the Med or up out of Iraq, sterilize the area with napalm before the Syrians can plant ground-to-air missile batteries around it. We would have to move pronto."

The admiral interrupted. "No use putting more of our people in jeopardy. We can spin up a Tomahawk on a ship in the Med and get it in there even faster, and the missile would have a bigger clout. That's what the Marine mission commander recommends. He's waiting for a decision."

Buchanan kept tapping his pencil like a little metronome of menace, seconds ticking away in a crisis. "Why do we need to do that? What is the benefit?" he asked.

"There is a lot of sophisticated equipment and material aboard those helicopters, sir. Everything from secret commo gear to night-vision goggles. Crypto. Maps. Weapons. Even avionics. Maybe some classified papers. We have no way of knowing if it all was destroyed," Hank Turner replied. "The Syrians will strip them bare, and we cannot take the chance of all that material falling into their hands."

"So you people are telling me that now that rescuing General Middleton is beyond your reach, that disaster may be compounded by still yet a bigger disaster? Jesus Christ."

Everyone noted that Buchanan had stopped tapping the pencil and had used the phrase "*your* reach," not "*our* reach."

"That sort of criticism is beside the point, Mr. Buchanan," Turner responded, his voice terse, growing angry with the man he considered nothing more than a political predator. "Right now, we have to decide between a missile and a bombing run, and there's not a minute to lose."

Buchanan abruptly stood and buttoned his coat. "Very

well. Then my decision is the *third* option, something that none of you suggested, I might add. We do nothing. We will not, repeat not, strike the wreckage with either the bombers or a missile." He looked directly at Shari. "What was the protocol term that you used, Lieutenant Commander Towne? Incinerate? No, absolutely not. Sending a rescue attempt into Syria was one thing, but conducting an air strike on a sovereign nation that has not attacked us could be considered an act of war. God knows whether it could be contained."

He gave a little bow to the woman from the State Department. "We have to go the diplomatic route now, ladies and gentlemen, and hope that State can pull the Pentagon's nuts out of the fire."

Shari's last wall of reserve was cracking. She had to get back to her office before she broke into tears, and it would take every ounce of strength to make that short walk. But the professional side of her mind kept turning over her intuition. Something was not right. Buchanan had driven the point home hard that the military efforts had failed, but he had hardly mentioned the deaths of American Marines. There was no anger or sorrow. *Why?* She put the thought aside as the admiral stepped beside her and whispered, "Get out of here, Shari. Take the rest of the day off. We'll let you know if we hear anything about Kyle."

Buchanan walked back to his office mentally chalking up a most beneficial outcome. He had put those military morons in their places again, particularly the crew-cut, spit-and-polish General Turner. The raid had not gone as planned, but the unexpected crash of the helicopters had resulted in a total, dreadful, and irreversible failure that would be shown in the starkest light all over every news program in the world within a few hours. The world's most professional and powerful military establishment had failed. Shades of the mess in the desert of Iran back in 1979.

This could definitely help the privatization act. With his office door closed, Gerald Buchanan rocked back in his chair and propped his feet on his desk. There was a broad smile on his face as he picked up his secure telephone to brief Gordon and Ruth Hazel that he had sidetracked the bombing run or any further rescue attempt. Those bodies would be coming home in flag-draped coffins. It would make great television.

CHAPTER 21

VICTOR LOGAN PRESSED HIS face hard against the cheek pad of a Russian-made Dragunov SVD sniper rifle to steady the four-power telescopic sight on the place where the helicopters had crashed. His partner, Jimbo Collins, scanned the rest of the area with night-vision goggles, looking for infrared heat emitters. Since kidnapping General Middleton, they had been waiting for the rescue attempt that was sure to come, ready to ambush the Marines, only to have it all go to hell right in front of them.

"Nothing but the wreckage," said Collins as he put the goggles away. "The fire and the hot metal just kills this heat-sensitive imagery. All I can pick up are those damned ragheads running around." He glanced at the brightening sky. "Think the Harriers will be back to burn it?" Collins had a shoulder-fired Stinger ground-to-air missile beside him. Other Stingers lay scattered in the other trenches.

"That's the SOP. Makes no sense to leave all that gear for the sand monkeys to pick over, but the Harriers seemed to be getting out of here in a hurry." Vic Logan had been in too many emergencies, in too many places, too many times, to let shit like this bother him. "Let's go see who's what. Big fuckup, this."

The American mercenaries moved from the sandbagged

trench and walked around a large ZSU-23-4 antiaircraft weapon. The gunner had abandoned his position behind the ammunition feed trays immediately after the helos went down, leaving the powerful radar-guided gun useless in his run to get to whatever booty he might steal from the helicopters. The quad rack of 23 mm cannons was still locked into position, useless if the Harriers returned.

Logan and Collins walked easily, not bothering to keep distance between them, because they were in no danger. "Too damned bad, Vic," said Collins. "This was a good ambush configuration."

Logan's big strides ate up the ground. His head was on a swivel and his hard eyes captured the tactical situation. The ragheads from the trench to the right, which would have supplied a cross-fire, were also out of their holes and heading toward the wreckage, along with women and children from the village. From soldiers and civilians to scavengers in the blink of an eye. A verse of Kipling came to him: *"When you're wounded and left on Afghanistan's plains, And the women come out to cut up what remains, Jest roll to your rifle and blow out your brains An' go to your Gawd like a soldier."* Afghanistan then, Iraq yesterday, Syria today, who knows where tomorrow? These people were going out to the crash site to do what they had been doing to foreign soldiers for centuries. *Fuckin' vultures.*

Logan sort of hoped none of those jarheads were still alive, although the idea of killing Americans had not cost him a moment of sleep. It was a business deal, sweet payback for being screwed over by the navy, and Logan was determined to come out of all this rich. He had shopped his services around until he discovered that being part of a Shark Team paid better than any of the other private billets. He was pulling in ten thousand dollars U.S. a month, and complicated things like this brought more. For these big bucks, he didn't give a fuck if he had to kill the pope.

The fact that the birds went down by themselves made no difference to Logan, because the result was the same. He got fifty thousand for snatching the general and now the rescue mission had failed, which meant still another fifty would flow into his bank account. He figured to retire when he topped two million.

He clicked his AK-47 to full automatic and fired an entire clip into the air while shouting in Arabic for the ragheads to clear out until he and Collins were done searching the area. Reluctantly, the crowd pulled back away from their looting and stood in sullen groups while the two American mercenaries got to work.

"Get the camera going," Logan said as they approached the twisted wreckage. "I'll look around the perimeter. You take pictures of every one of those Marines, get the dog tags, and read off the names loud enough to be recorded, clear enough to be understood. Any funny names, spell them out. I want a stone-cold positive ID on every one of those dudes."

"Got it." Collins stepped into the wreckage. It was a mess in there. He started photographing.

"And make sure all the arms and legs add up!" Logan called, then began a slow walk around the site, circling from the nose of one of the choppers out to about a hundred meters. That put the helicopter in the center of an imaginary clock, with the nose pointed to twelve o'clock, and Logan switched on a powerful flashlight as he worked back and forth in pie-shaped segments. One o'clock. Two o'clock. Raghead footprints and chunks of debris from the aircraft reached out in all directions. He would have missed the puddle of vomit near the seven o'clock position had he not smelled it before locating it with the bright beam of his flashlight. Nothing much more than some discolored yellow bile. A raghead sickened by the sights and smell of new death? Not likely, but possible. He walked on, and two slices of the clock later, almost obscured by the scuffed footprints of the scavengers, he found the unmistakable tire tracks of a motorcycle. He did not recall hearing any. How old was the track? Some civilian ride through yesterday? It led toward the road, east.

"Hey, Vic!" Collins hollered from the ruptured end of one of the helicopters. "Take a look."

Logan was there in a couple of big strides. "What?"

Collins was squatting down and had the loose end of a big strap in one hand. He tugged on it to show that the other end was secured to the deck of the fuselage. "Three more of these straps. There, there . . . and there."

All four ends had been sliced clean. Something had been secured here. Had the ragheads already stolen it? Something large? No, he would have noticed. Logan backed out of the wrecked bird and Collins followed, putting away his camera after photographing and identifying the final two bodies. They went to the fuselage of the other helicopter. A little Kawasaki dirt bike, badly damaged, was still lashed to the deck with straps like the ones that had been cut on the first helo.

Logan scratched his neck, came to a conclusion. He waved to the onlookers and they poured back into the wreckage like honeybees after a lump of sugar.

"Somebody survived that mess," he told Jimbo as they returned to the village and their satellite radio. "We got a runner."

CHAPTER 22

HE HATED NOISE. KYLE SWANSON valued silence, for stealth was his cloak of protective comfort. On a wide battle-field, there was so much racket in a raging shootout of tank cannons, masses of small arms, machine guns, grenades, and artillery that soldiers talked in shouts for a week afterward, long after the fighting stopped. As a sniper, he preferred to be far from that chaos, out on his own, where making sounds could spell doom. Swanson was the ghost at the party, able to move unseen and unheard. Noise weakened snipers and made them vulnerable, almost like normal human beings. The only noise he liked to hear in combat was the single *POP* of his silenced rifle being fired.

So although the dirt bike had a silenced muffler, the steady throbs of the engine still reverberated in the desert night. Kyle believed any fool with ears could hear him. Combined with the coming dawn, that would leave him exposed and vulnerable. He weaved slowly, deliberately along the pavement, steering through patches of loose gravel normally avoided by motorcyclists because bikes have a tendency to skid. A mistake could dump him in a heartbeat, but he wanted those tracks to be found.

His mind was also busy on another level, thinking about possible places where he might hunker down for the day, when people would be everywhere. Being caught near a population center, even a small village like this one, was never good, plus people were probably going to be out searching for him when they figured out someone had lived through the crash. The flare of a match straight ahead snapped him back to reality.

Someone had lit a cigarette. Swanson took his hand from the throttle and coasted the motorcycle to a halt. He turned off the engine and sat balanced on the dirt bike with a boot down on each side. Focusing his night-vision goggles, he saw two men about two hundred meters ahead, a pair of careless Syrian soldiers at a road checkpoint. Both were watching the area where the helicopters went down instead of paying attention to their jobs.

Kyle laid the bike down along the hardball highway and carefully dropped his gear, except for the M-16 and a couple of hand grenades. On his arms and knees, he low-crawled until he was within twenty feet of the guards. They were cooking something in the guard shack. Smelled like rice and lamb. The guards were jabbering like tourists about the crash and had stacked their rifles against a wall when they climbed onto the flat roof of the shack for a better view. Controlling his breathing, Kyle circled behind them, moved in close, rose to a sitting position against the wall, and pulled the pin on a hand grenade. He let the spoon flip away, held it for a count of two, and then tossed it onto the roof and sprawled to the ground next to the structure.

The explosion blew both of them from their perch, and Kyle quickly checked the bodies, which were riddled with shrapnel. Not good enough. The people back at the crash site were more than a mile away and probably would not have heard this small explosion, so he had to leave enough information to convince whoever eventually investigated the deaths that the work was sloppy enough to have been done by a rookie Marine. A young radioman would have done the easiest thing available and smashed right through the checkpoint, using the basic weapons at hand, in his haste to escape. Kyle wanted to leave this scene as American as possible. He clicked his M-16 to full automatic and raked an entire magazine of bullets across the chests and stomachs of the dead men, and the bullets dug through the bodies and into the hardpan pavement beneath them. Shiny brass cartridges flipped and bounced wildly everywhere. He walked in the sand to leave bootprints. Window dressing. He could easily have taken them both out with Excalibur, or up close with his knife, but this was a stage show. As a final touch, he ducked inside the small bunker and gobbled down some of the meal the men had been preparing. He was right. Spicy lamb and rice.

He reassembled his gear, remounted the bike, and rode past the checkpoint, spiking a piece of cloth torn from his camouflage uniform on the barbed wire. The track of the dirt bike then continued west, again toward the border.

A hundred meters later, he made sure he was on clean pavement, stopped the bike, got off, picked up the bike, and turned it around 180 degrees. Now he would disappear and leave no tracks at all. He pushed the motorcycle through the roadblock, past the dead men. Swanson propped the bike on the kickstand long enough to pull up some bushes and sweep away any prints that might give away his direction change, and then headed back toward the village.

When he entered the vicinity of the crash, people were milling around the wrecked choppers. Kyle knew that meant they might see him, too, but he knew human nature had them in a near frenzy. They were only looking for booty. A lone man in the distance was of no interest. Still, every moment he was out there was a risk because the first hot curve of the rising sun had crested the eastern horizon and painted the underside of the morning clouds in a sheet of shining gold. When Swanson was working, he hated the arrival of daylight as much as a vampire like Count Dracula, for he, too, was a creature of the night.

Swanson went off-road and skirted about a kilometer to the right of the scene, keeping low in the wadis to avoid being spotted. Within a mile, the country flattened again.

The village of Sa'ahn had the familiar, compact look of any other desert town he had ever seen, houses and shops

that had grown up over the centuries around a water source.
Rainfall in this section of Syria was adequate to feed fields
of sugar beets that were bordered by tight patterns of apricot
trees in the east. North of town, he could smell as well as see
and hear the feed lots where sheep and goats were being fat-
tened for market. Irrigated rows of ragged cotton were
planted on the western side. Mount Druz dominated the
land, and a carpet of desert stretched to all horizons.

The homes all looked alike, squat and square, with low
walls that corralled the family's chickens and goats. Droop-
ing lines between poles carried telephone lines and delivered
electricity from a dam about twenty miles away. One large
building near the center appeared to be the town's administrative center. Lights were on in a few windows of the private
homes, brightening colorful small curtains of green and red,
so people in those homes were already moving about. He
had to hide.

Kyle stopped the bike about three hundred meters from
the nearest building. He had run out of darkness and did not
have time to bury the motorcycle, which he preferred to do.
So he hid it in a deep wadi and covered it with bushes, hoping that the obscure location, the crude disguise of weeds,
and the camo paint job would keep it hidden.

With the M-16 locked and loaded and his finger resting
on the trigger housing, Swanson moved closer to the village
until he found a forlorn and bare hillside that overlooked the
approach road. A berm lined with thick brush rose like a
dirty pimple near the top, and he ducked down to keep it between himself and the town. This was it.

He circled to the back side and dug a shallow trench
straight up to the rim of the berm. The rising sun was already
heating the dirt, and Kyle sweated the last few meters, but
when he came up in the middle of the bushes, he had a clear
view from the high ground.

Dumping his gear, he wiggled back down, gathered more
brush from random spots in a radius of about twenty meters,
and swept his tracks, then planted the foliage around his new
hide until he was sure that it would look to a passersby like a

single big bush. Time would slow down for him now, so he arranged things in his shady nook to get some rest. Real sleep was not an option, not alone in hostile territory, but he could allow himself a light doze, just under the edge of total awareness, with his hand always on a weapon.

As the sun cleared the horizon and full daylight arrived, he drank some water and took out the binocs again for a last look at the village before settling down. The homes, the goats, the women and children moving about. Normal tempo. Most of the men were probably still busy stripping the helos. He stopped his sweep with his glasses abruptly when he got to the area where the major road entered the town. Sandbags were stacked along a trench line, and just to his side of the road was another deep trench. AK-47 rifles were laid carelessly over its sandbags, and missile tubes leaned against the sides. Sticking out of a protected hole where the trenches came together were the snouts of the four barrels of a ZSU-23-4.

"Well, now, ain't this a bitch?" he asked himself. "A Zeus, fighting holes with AKs, and lots of guys. We were flying into a fucking ambush."

Kyle put away the glasses, took another drink of water, and let the adrenaline and excitement leave his body. He shifted his shoulders to get comfortable, laid the M-16 across his chest, and felt the heavy exhaustion from the past few hours pull hard on him. His last conscious thought before he passed out was, "They knew we were coming."

CHAPTER 23

VICTOR LOGAN SAT AT A SMALL table, pecking at a laptop computer to input the names of the Marines killed in the crash. His big, thick fingers were blunt instruments, meant for things much more coarse than dainty taps on a keyboard, and he found this work both laborious and somewhat insulting. Clerks did this kind of shit, not warriors. He detested having to wear reading glasses when he worked on this machine. They were a sign of weakness, of getting old, past the prime, but Logan had decided to adopt the modern age to get the technological edge. Just because a gorilla eats leaves does not mean he is any less of a mean son of a bitch.

He could tell the sun was up by the steady increase of the temperature in the room. Finally, he finished copying the names that Jimbo Collins had culled from the dog tags and clicked the key to save the file to a directory. He called up another list that had been downloaded from Washington several hours earlier, did a cut-and-paste job with the one he had just written, and compared the two. He highlighted one name in bright red, increased the font size to make it bold, then pushed away from the screen and studied it. "I was right, Collins. Somebody's missing. The Washington list has one name more than the dog tags on the kill list. You damned sure you got them all?"

"All of 'em, Vic. I pulled the tags off every one of those crispy critters." He held up a plastic bag filled with dog tags and shook it with a definitive rattle of metal against metal. Collins was at his own computer, working with his camera to freeze-frame individual images of each of the dead Marines, inject them into a folder, and adjust the color and clarity.

There was a knock and a shout at the door, and both men grabbed weapons. Security was always on their minds, and they kept an extra AK-47, locked and loaded, on two pegs directly above the front door for emergencies. "What?" called Collins. He went to the front wall and put his back to it.

"Open up! Something else has happened!" The English came in a familiar French accent.

Collins held a mirror to the window and angled it to confirm who was there. "It's the frog. He's alone." Logan nodded, and Collins opened the door.

A small man, thin but muscular, came in. He had a sharp face with prominent cheekbones, dark eyes, and a slit of a mouth that never smiled and was almost invisible in a long, thick black beard. Pierre Dominique Falais was a familiar figure in Sa'ahn, where he had settled after getting out of the Foreign Legion. As a converted Muslim, he was welcome everywhere, despite his European background, and he would drive to other towns and villages to buy crafts, wool, and rugs and load them into his white Toyota truck, then usually find a reason to stay overnight in order to smoke and eat and talk with the locals. The Syrian villagers considered Abu Mohammed to be a most generous man and an honest trader. Success in the little trading enterprise and some carpentry meant nothing to him, for his real money came not from peddling items to stores and bazaars, but by selling his intelligence services to the governments of Syria, France, and Russia. He was able to work openly with all three countries because their policies were seldom in conflict.

For the time being, however, these two large American mercenary soldiers, who had deposited five thousand dollars into his bank account in Damascus, had his total cooperation. A similar amount would come in when the task was completed.

"The fuck you want, Pierre?" snapped Logan, turning back to the name on the laptop screen. *A radioman lived through that and escaped?*

The Frenchman stepped inside and closed the door. The place stank. These little homes were usually kept very clean by the women, with the pungent aromas of hard tobacco and cooking food welcoming visitors like a pleasant cloud. In here, the smell of human waste, sweat, and filth offended him. He shrugged it off. They were, after all, Americans, a disgusting people. "Two guards at that checkpoint a few klicks to the west have been killed. Bullet holes all over the bodies, and a villager described some open wounds that sound to me like they may have been made by grenades. I'm going out there."

"Sounds like our runner, Vic. Somebody had to have some firepower to do that," said Collins. "Want me to check it out?"

Logan grunted and waved them both away, absorbed by his work. *A radioman fought his way through two armed sentries? Yeah, he was a Marine, but that was a good piece of work.*

"Okay, Pierre. Lead on." Collins followed the Frenchman into the light and over to the pickup truck, a well-maintained vehicle with extra suspension and wide desert-quality tires with deep treads. The custom heavy-duty engine turned over on the first try and the straight exhaust pipes rumbled low. Falais wheeled the Toyota onto the road and sped away. Jimbo Collins immediately started talking to him about different kinds of shock absorbers.

Vic Logan kept staring at the name in red and studying the kill list: McDowell, Harold. Lance corporal. Radio operator. Twenty years old. He had heard lots of stories about people walking away from a plane crash or an automobile pileup that killed everyone else. It was possible. So the kid grabs the bike and takes off for Israel and just surprised the lazy guys at the checkpoint. It was the logical play. "Fucking Syrians can't even stop a damned radio operator," he grunted.

The Marine would be picked up soon. He probably had a little spec ops training in escape and evasion, but it was a long way to the border, and most of it was either over open territory or on busy roads. He was good as caught and just didn't know it yet.

Logan opened an encrypted file to transmit to Washington. Collins could send the pictures later. It took him only fifteen more minutes at the keyboard to finish his report, and he saved the work, leaving space at the bottom to add whatever details Collins picked up at the roadblock.

There was nothing more he could do now. Logan felt he had earned some relaxation. He rose, stretched his six-foot-five frame, and peeled off his clothes as he went into the small bedroom. It was a little cooler there.

On the bed lay a terrified, wide-eyed girl, tied to the four corners, spread-eagled and naked. A piece of gray duct tape was across her mouth, and although she could not scream, she wiggled in terror when she saw the huge American approach. He had first spotted her at the local store, where the fourteen-year-old beauty worked with her mother and father, and had checked her out as best he could while he bought a few items. Not really much to see, since the small girl wore one of those damned black bedsheets. But the flashing eyes were unafraid of the foreigner, and Vic imagined there was a flawless body with long, coltlike legs and budding breasts under all that cloth. He snatched her the first night he was here. Knowing the ragheads really thought their women were something special, he went to great lengths to keep her out of sight and quiet. She was tight that first time, struggling, fighting hard, just like he enjoyed his women. A little tiger. Lots of blood. When he was through, the young body was no longer virginal and wore a number of ugly bruises, varying shades of green and purple and yellow. The eyes were no longer unafraid. She had been taught respect.

The only question for Logan at present was whether to feed her or give her a chance to pee before he raped her again. The hell with it. Those helos going down had changed everything and he would be out of here as soon as Gates decided what he wanted done with the general, who lay trussed up in the next room.

Just thinking about the general pissed Logan off. The mercenary was angry that he couldn't hit that one-star ass-hole in the face or anywhere that would show a bruise, be-cause they were going to need him looking good for another television show. So he turned his frustrations on the girl in-stead, and went to her again, his hand moving to his penis. He wasn't hard yet. This dirty whore was going to have to work to get him aroused.

He struck her hard across the face with his right hand, just to make sure she was paying attention. Her head snapped to the side like that of a doll, and the tears began to roll. Too bad he had to leave the gag on, he thought as he rolled his belt around his fist, leaving the sharp brass buckle dangling free. He slapped it on her thigh and a bloody gash opened in the smooth olive skin. Again, and a crimson streak flowed down the ribs as her body arced in pain. Again, click-ing the metal buckle across both nipples. The screams would have been nice.

He looked down at himself with growing frustration. He still wasn't hard, because she wasn't working to satisfy him. "Bitch!" he yelled, and the belt came down again, on the side of her head, and dark blood oozed through the tangle of black hair. "Move it, damn you!" Logan's fury grew like the heat that cooked the room, and he beat the girl without pity. No matter how hard he struck her, no matter how much he made her bleed, his goddam dick would NOT get hard.

A pounding sound drew his attention. The damned gen-eral was kicking the wall. Tied up like a turkey and still a pain in the ass. Logan shouted, "Shut the fuck up! I'll be in there and beat your ass soon as I'm through with this little bitch!" The pounding continued, even harder.

And still the girl just lay there, moaning, refusing to help even though he had total control over her worthless body! *Little whore! It was her fault!* He had taught others, and he would teach her, too. With his free hand, he balled up his big fist and slammed her in the mouth. *Her fault!* Finally, he got hard, grabbed his penis, and ejaculated on the small breasts before falling across her, exhausted, into the pool of blood and semen.

Then Logan, still naked, went into the other room, where the general was handcuffed to the steel frame of a cot. Middleton's eyes were filled with fury at having to sit there helplessly while a young woman was torn apart.

"You got a problem? Kickin' on the wall like that?" Logan asked with a sneer.

"You sick shit." Middleton spat on the floor in disgust. "You're going to die under my knife!" He wore a loose and dirty Arab robe, was totally under Logan's control, and yet still was making threats.

"Assholes like you got me kicked out of the Teams," Logan said, squatting down beside Middleton. "I expect that we are going to get permission soon to blow your ass away. I'll enjoy it." He rolled Middleton over, grabbed the little finger of his left hand, and bent it back until it broke.

The general exhaled a sharp groan, then sucked up the rest of the pain, refusing to give Logan the satisfaction of hearing him cry out. When the sharp wave of having a bone snapped ebbed, he glared at the big man. "That changes nothing, you psycho."

"Don't judge me, dickhead. You've got nine more fingers I can break before I start on the toes." He left the room, slamming the door behind him.

Logan was washing up in the small, stinking bathroom when Jimbo Collins returned. The water had cooled his body and the demons within.

Collins called out, "Vic? You in there?"

Logan walked back into the main room. "Well?" He was wiping himself with a towel.

"The frog had it right. A grenade apparently was used first, and there was a bunch of brass all over the place. M-16 cartridges. I found tracks of the motorcycle for about a hundred meters on the other side of the checkpoint. The runner took those Syrian dudes out without hardly slowing down."

"Okay." Logan sat down and added the checkpoint incident to his report, then hit the transmit button. The names and the details of what happened before dawn near the little town of Sa'ahn zipped into the morning sky and were relayed by satellite to a computer that was waiting far, far away.

Collins tossed his weapon aside and kicked off his boots. "Say, Vic. It's gonna take some time for me to finish the video. How 'bout you let me have another piece of that kid first? We'll probably be leaving soon anyway."

"Be my guest, Collins," Logan replied with a sweep of his arm toward the bedroom door and a dark laugh. "And when you finish screwing that dead pussy, you can feed and water the general."

"She's dead?"

Logan grinned, his eyes almost sparkling. "Little whore just laid there like a pillow. No enthusiasm at all. The scrawny bitch didn't earn her life."

Jimbo Collins looked into the bedroom. The girl and the bed were covered in blood. This was not the first time that he had thought there was something really wrong with Logan, but it was wise to keep that thought to himself. A few more hours and he probably would never see the asshole again. Concentrate on the money, not the corpse. "Good thing we got dirt floors," Collins remarked as he turned to his camera equipment. "We can bury her right here, then burn this shit-hole to the ground."

CHAPTER 24

THE ASSHOLE OF THE WORLD sounded like a pig going after slops, snorting in his pleasure, so she just let her mind drift that way. Sprawled in the pigpen, down in the muck, a worthless piece of pork wallowing in a place where feelings were meaningless and the next "oink" meant only that she was still alive to hear it. A surge, heat, a final groan, and her father released her wrists and rolled off, spent. "I'm going downtown," the Asshole muttered, wiping himself on her bunny sheets. *Like I even care.* Ruth Hazel Pierce blinked her blue eyes and came out of the pigpen stench enough to hear that. On this night the fourteen-year-old girl decided to care very much, a moment of decision that changed her life and ended his.

Usually she curled into a fetal position for a while, safe in her happy place, a pretend enchanted castle, surrounded by good friends and fire-breathing dragons that protected her. Only after an hour or so would she return to the real world of fear and shame and hate and get cleaned up before her mother came home from her late shift as a waitress. On that final night, however, Ruth Hazel exhaled a big sigh and headed for the hot shower and sweet bath soaps and freedom. From her dresser, she removed the tight one-piece black swim team suit she wore for school meets, stretched into it, and then put on old jeans with torn knees, a bulky San Diego State University sweatshirt, and jogging shoes. Out the door and down the hall to her parents' room, where the Asshole of the World, the gun nut, kept all those weapons loose in the closet. When she was small, before the molestation got really serious, he had taught her how to shoot, thinking that a girl enjoyed the explosions. Respect a weapon, he said. Guns can hurt you if you're not careful. No shit, Pops. She grabbed the Ruger .22, made sure it had a full ten-round magazine, tucked it into her waistband, and walked out of the house to change her future. One of them, either herself or the Asshole of the World, would not be coming back.

She walked along the beach from the trailer park to Oceanside in the early darkness, thinking she could see his footprints, since he always came this way. He walked because he had been picked up too many times for driving drunk. On the edge of the seedy downtown area, Ruth Hazel found a dumpster in an alley directly across the street from the Asshole's favorite bar, a run-down strip joint, and she sat on the concrete in the shadows, crossing her legs and listening to the traffic on the street and the rumble of the surf. He staggered out two hours later, alone. Either he had run out of money or had been thrown out again. She didn't care. It didn't matter. Oink.

He ambled down the sidewalk and cut through a vacant lot to the high, dry ground of the beach. She followed his wavering silhouette against the starry night as the waves nibbled and sloshed at the sand about forty yards away. The tide was coming in. Not a soul in sight. Ruth Hazel pulled out the Ruger and began a little jog that closed the space between them in only a few steps. She stopped and took a firing stance, both palms around the grip like he had taught her. "Daddy?" she called in her little-girl voice as she snapped off the safety.

The Asshole of the World turned. The first bullet caught him in the stomach, but he was a big man, and a single .22 shot was not much more than a hard punch to the gut, not enough to put him down. The other six shots went into the chest, careful shots, one after another, and sprawled him on the sand like a beached porpoise. Ruth Hazel stepped closer. She saw recognition in his eyes, then horror as she deliberately aimed the Ruger at his crotch and fired. He screamed. She put the last two bullets into his eyes.

She rolled him onto his side and snatched the wallet from his back pocket, put the pistol back into her waistband, and jogged smoothly away down the beach. About a mile later, she shucked off her bloody clothes and swam through the surf, fighting stroke after stroke to get past the steep slant where the water went deep and the currents were crazy. Treading water, she pulled the pistol and the wallet from within her stretchy bathing suit and dropped them. As the items settled to the bottom of shifting sand, Ruth Hazel went into an easy butterfly kick and let the waves carry her to the beach. She walked home, her feet light on the sand. Another hot shower, stain remover on the blood spots on the jeans and sweatshirt, and those went into the washing machine. Ruth Hazel was drying her hair with a big blue towel, watching TV and eating popcorn, when her mother came home. "Hi, Mom!" she called.

The small woman who had lived with the beatings for years cast her worried eyes around the mobile home, puzzled as to why Ruth Hazel was in such a good mood. "Is your father here?"

"No. He was in for a little while after work but then went out again a few hours ago. Come on and sit with me, Mom. This is a hilarious movie. Have some popcorn."

"Have you done your homework?" Doris Reed put down her purse and went to the sofa and smiled at her daughter. So much happiness! She seemed to glow.

"Yes, Mom. I did everything I had to do."

Senator Ruth Hazel Reed kept two framed photographs on the long polished credenza behind the desk in her office in the Russell Senate Office Building off of C Street. One was of her handsome young army Warrant Officer Chuck Reed, lounging against a helicopter in Vietnam, the black-and-white picture taken four weeks before he was killed in action. The other was a family photo of ten-year-old Ruth Hazel snuggled between her smiling mother and father during a vacation to SeaWorld in San Diego. All of them were gone now. The Viet Cong had killed Chuck, cancer had taken her mom, and Ruth Hazel had murdered her father. Ancient history.

She never told anyone about the shooting; not her mother, not her husband, not even her hairdresser. The cops did a brief investigation and decided it was a robbery by some Mexicans coming up from the border, although the savagery of the attack, the clear rage, made them suspect a family member had done it. But they had alibis, sitting at home watching TV and eating popcorn together. Had to be Mexicans.

Ruth Hazel had absorbed the lesson that her rapes had not been about sex as much as about her father exerting power over her until she became more powerful than he. Since then, the search for power was her fuel in everything from sex to academics to business to politics. She might allow a man equality, as she had with Chuck, but she would yield to no one, ever again.

That included Gordon Gates and Gerald Buchanan. When she became President of the United States, she would be the most powerful person not only in New America, but in the world. Privatizing the military would give her off-the-books strength that no other President had ever possessed because she would not have to bring politics into play to assassinate a foreign dictator or sink a ship bringing in drugs or make some terrorists disappear. Just a phone call to Gordon would do the job. Under her reign, New America would be secure.

Now discomforting news had come from Syria, and the three powerful people were alone in a long black limousine parked near the Lincoln Memorial. Gates had told his chauffeur to come back when he called on the cell phone.

"Is our plan in trouble, Gerald?" asked Ruth Hazel. "You said it was foolproof." Idiot.

"No, Ruth Hazel, the plan is not in trouble. The Marine rescue fiasco actually plays into our hands," Buchanan responded in a smooth tone, holding his tongue so as not to respond with an insult. "I've been riding the Pentagon and intel services hard. There won't be another rescue attempt, and the Syrian government is in an uproar."

"Middleton is still alive, Gerald. He was supposed to be killed in the rescue attempt. You even sent in that sniper as a backup. But they are all dead, and yet the general lives. Hardly a success so far."

"Easy, Senator," said Gates. "I also think it may turn out to be fortunate for us that the Marines screwed up on their own and did not have to be ambushed." He took a folded piece of paper from his briefcase and handed it to Buchanan. "Look at this. My Shark Team over there just sent this list of all of the Marines who were killed in the crash, verified by their dog tags. I expect to have pictures soon to help with the identifications."

"So what am I missing here, Gordon?" Senator Reed asked.

"Look, Ruth Hazel. We wanted to show your committee and anyone else we could get to listen that while the U.S. Marines created a disaster, two special operators from Gates Global had infiltrated the village so deeply that they were able to go in and get these identifications and even make contact with the French guide. We can now say that if the Pentagon had not intervened and screwed up, my people would already have brought General Middleton out of there, safe and sound."

"Not really."

"Of course not. The only difference is that instead of the ideal of having the Marine sniper shoot him while we take pictures, or having our Shark Team finish the job, we let the jihadists kill him."

"I don't care who shoots him or if he steps on a scorpion. I just do not want him coming back to testify before my committee next week." She pushed back in the soft seat and folded her arms.

Buchanan finished reading the list and handed it to the senator. It didn't add up. "Somebody got out?"

"Apparently," Gates responded with a slight wave. "Some kid who is only a radio operator took off on a dirt bike that was on one of the helicopters. I know that country, and he won't get far. The Syrians will pick him up before he can reach the border, and I predict that we will be seeing him on television soon. We can exploit that when it happens. Not really a bad thing, when you think of it, because his comments will show even further how fucked up the mission was."

Buchanan nodded in approval, pleased that Rambo Reed had been slow to understand how any situation such as this was fluid and one had to adapt to change. "So the senator and I can use the identifications as additional proof of how efficient private contractors can be, and how we can accomplish missions better than rote-memory military teams that court an international incident every time they get involved."

Ruth Hazel read the list without changing her expression and handed it back to Gates. "I don't like it when plans fall apart, but I agree that this problem can be turned to our favor."

Gates switched on his cold voice, totally unemotional. "Good. We're back on the same page. If you two approve, I'll fire off a signal to the sheikh in Basra to have his men execute the general in some interesting and public manner as soon as possible."

"And your team on the ground?" Buchanan raised an eyebrow.

"They will not be seen, nor will they interfere. They will simply hand Middleton over to the sheikh's people and get out. So I expect Middleton will be dead within a few hours, and we can get on with Operation Premier."

CHAPTER 25

HE AWOKE WITH A START. THE tinny recorded voice of a muezzin was being broadcast from a loudspeaker attached to the minaret of the little town's mosque, the summons to morning prayer. Gritty crumbs of sand had fallen into his mouth, and every one of the over two hundred bones in his body felt broken. The fear of falling completely asleep had kept Kyle hovering near the surface until he heard the familiar call: "Hasten to prayer!" Over and over and over, broadcast five times every day. It reminded him of Somalia, where he occasionally would shoot the broadcasting loudspeakers in revenge for the annoyance.

He looked at his watch and cursed. He had been out for almost an hour, much too long, and wondered what he had missed. There was no way to recover anything that might have happened during that time.

Swanson fumbled for a packet of MRE crackers, popped all eight out of the vacuum-packed seal, lumped peanut butter on them, and started chewing. Tasteless, but it would keep the digestive tract well plugged during the coming hours. Dessert was two Motrin tablets for his aches and pains, and some water, and then he exercised with some isometric stretches and told his body to stop bitching about being so thrashed. Swanson never liked that macho line about pain being a friend. He hurt like hell, but nothing was broken, and he would make time to moan later, with a pretty nurse in attendance. Right now, he had to get back to work.

He pulled out the powerful spotting scope that had been on his gear list, only to find it had broken in the crash and was useless. But the Steiner binos had survived, and their 10×32 viewing field would serve him almost as well. At five hundred meters, objects would appear about twenty times their normal size. He removed the lens caps, gave the glasses a quick wipe, rolled onto his stomach, and slowly raised his eyes above the edge of the hide.

He had no specific plan other than to observe for a while and, after that, play things by ear, with the big advantage of the enemy not knowing he was in their backyard. First he would conduct the basic recon to determine the security posted by the bad guys, what kind of patterns the guards had, and determine the weakest point and how to exploit it. After that, he would be able to make realistic, systematic decisions to set conditions of battle in his favor. What he saw through the binos made him smile.

People were going about their business. Shops were opening, goats were in the streets, women were cleaning around their homes, farmers moved to the fields, some dude was selling bread from a cart, and other men were settling down for some early-morning smoking and coffee. It was the normal tempo of a village. The big four-barreled Zeus still sat brooding beside the road, but there was no gunner in the seat. The fighting holes and trench lines were empty, and the guys with the guns were gone, except for two lazy guards sitting on the ground in a patch of shade beside the Zeus.

There was nothing Swanson could do until dark other than gather information, so he took out his logbook and started a detailed sketch of the village. He started with the building to his far left, where a woman swept her front stoop with an old broom, and slowly examined the small house with a left-to-right, up-and-down grid. Then he checked the surrounding streets and pathways.

He laid the M-16 aside and unsheathed Excalibur. After

giving the sniper rifle a quick once-over, he brought the scope to his eye and touched the button to turn on the laser rangefinder. The numbers stopped scrolling when he clicked on the doorway of the woman's house: exactly 680 yards. He jotted the figure on one of the logbooks' green range sheets as the woman finished her sweeping and propped her broom against a side wall. He shifted his attention to the next building.

Someone cursed in Arabic and the two Zeus guards scrambled to their feet. A chubby little man in civilian clothes with an AK-47 slung across his back had emerged from a doorway and moved toward them, shouting that they were worthless pigs and gesturing at them to stand up. Kyle examined him closely. *Who are you, Pudgy? No uniform, but obviously in some kind of command.* Another man, tall and bearded, also with a rifle on his shoulder, came from the same house and stood idly while the sentries were chewed out. *Okay. You're Beanpole.* Assigning nicknames helped Kyle sort out the various players.

They laughed at the young guards, then crossed the street to a café and disappeared inside through a front door shaded by a small cloth awning. Fifteen minutes later they came back out, carrying stacked boxes of food. Pudgy and Beanpole had not had time to have eaten at the little store, so they obviously were taking meals back to the house. Judging by the number of boxes, it was a hell of a lot more food than for just the two of them. Kyle's interest had perked up by the appearance of the Arab fighters, and he sketched their house, did the ranges to the door and windows, and marked it as a probable target.

Beanpole came back out with a couple of the meal boxes and walked casually to another house nearby, where the door was closed and the curtains were drawn. He leaned toward the door, and his lips moved as he spoke to somebody inside. More than a minute passed before the door opened quickly and from the shadows, two arms reached out, grabbed the food, and vanished back inside. The door was shut again. Beanpole walked away, and Kyle saw the man's lips moving, probably in a soft curse at the rudeness of whoever snatched the food. It had only been a momentary glance and at an awkward angle, but Swanson could have sworn that the skin of whoever took the food was light-colored, possibly even white.

He resumed studying each house in the village, taking time out periodically to check around his hide and make sure he was not under observation himself. Not having someone covering his back left him feeling naked and completely alone. Staying busy by building the range card kept his mind off his vulnerability.

Over the passing hours, the normal life of the village became his private reality television show, and he noted the times of all significant movement in the area, looking for patterns, sketching and lasering ranges to important aiming points. Seventy-forty-three to the major intersection. Six-twelve to the right edge of the restaurant. Left, right, and middle distances to suspicious houses. He mapped it all out systematically as time ticked by, and he tried to commit as much as possible to memory. There was no such thing as too much information.

"Hasten to prayer!" The noon call of the muezzin surprised him because he had been so busy that hours had slipped away. Then he got an unexpected break. A group of armed men came from the house used by Pudgy and Beanpole. While most residents simply worshipped within their homes or workplaces, or went to the small mosque in the center of the village, these men wanted to make a public show of their fervent devotion. Each unrolled a small rug or a straw mat in the street, knelt, and performed the rituals of prayer. Kyle got an accurate head count: eight men, all with their weapons. Nobody had come from the other suspicious house, where the door remained closed.

Prayers done, two of the men repeated the breakfast run and went to the store for the group. A small, wiry man tagged along behind a large character with a square head and big shoulders. *SpongeBob and Pee-Wee.* Back to their house with arms overflowing with boxes and bottles, and then Sponge Bob made the delivery run of three boxes and six water bottles over to the second house. This time Swanson was ready when the door opened, and was looking only for the hands that reached for the boxes and bottles. *White!* No damned doubt. Not a damned doubt in the world.

I'm starving out here on crackers and peanut butter while you assholes are having meals delivered.

Swanson turned over to rest. Seeing all those clowns down there made him start to think that he might have bitten off more than he could chew with this. He considered that the eight in the house were probably hard-core fighters, but how many else were down there? Enough to keep shifts of guards around the Zeus. Add whoever was in the mystery house. Round it off to at least a dozen, probably more. Clowns with guns could still shoot. He was strongly tempted to break radio silence and call for help.

It was not fear, for he was not afraid to die. He was just afraid to fail. But if he could get the general, it would take only a moment to light up his phone and get an air strike to take out the main group with a single smart bomb. He could pull Middleton out during the confusion and evade to a landing zone where a chopper could come in under air cover and pick them up. He almost convinced himself that was the way to go.

Then he weighed the down side. His people would be monitoring the cell phones of the members of the TRAP team to see if they had been put into use by the enemy. Using his own would announce his existence. The element of surprise would be gone, and the tactical situation would tilt back to favor the bad guys. Better that they continue to think he was a lone radio operator running for his life. Same thing with the pack radio he had taken from the dead Marine.

He rubbed water over his face to cool it. This whole deal smelled as rotten as a month-old banana. Those people down there had known exactly when, where, and how the Force Recon choppers would arrive, and that meant there was a leak somewhere. Not a leak. A flood! The person responsible had to be high enough up the food chain to have been trusted with details of the plan. *Who?* Kyle dug out another bottle of water. Sweat was pouring from him, even lying motionless in the little bit of shade provided by the bushes roofing his hide. It was probably 120 degrees at midday.

A call to alert the Marines that he was alive would risk that the traitor would also find out and block any new rescue attempt.

How high up the food chain was the leak? The mission had been put together in a hurry, but a lot of people knew about it, both civilian and military. But only one person had done something truly unusual: Gerald Buchanan, the man who wrote out in his own hand the order for Kyle to assassinate the general if things went haywire. Why even issue such an order unless he anticipated that something was going to go wrong? As far as the Marines were concerned, it was supposed to be a rather ordinary in-and-out mission with sufficient speed, troops, and firepower to get the job done. The commandant of Marines would never have approved such a plan. The President of the United States knew? Impossible. The man was a decorated veteran himself. The guy who came to the carrier, Shafer, was just the messenger boy. The circle led back to Buchanan.

He thought about why a man like Buchanan would betray his country, and then he considered what would be a suitable punishment. What would be worse for a deskbound political animal than having to spend the rest of his life cramped in a supermax cell in Colorado alongside big-league terrorists? A bullet in the ear would work, but Kyle felt Buchanan should be brought into public shame and disgrace. Like that Enron guy, he could always have a heart attack after being convicted. Swanson shook his head to clear the cobwebs. The whole thing was irrelevant and had nothing to do with his job at the moment.

He would trust Double-Oh to get that letter into the hands of the right people and that they would take care of the problem. Isn't that what the FBI does? He was a sniper, not a cop, and all he could deal with at the moment was whether to make this fight all alone, or risk using the damned telephone. He was fucked either way. He would not make the call yet. Anonymity was his friend, and the best route, the only route, was straight ahead. He kept the sat phone and buried the pack radio. No use lugging it along, since it had only been taken as a diversion in the first place.

He rubbed his eyes, picked up the binos, and got back to sketching the village.

Boredom set in as the sun baked the town and the lone man watching it, but Swanson would not let himself fall asleep. There would be no more sleep until this job was done, for to sleep would be to yield awareness of the situation, and that could be the end of everything. He began arranging what he knew, planning his attack. He studied the little grocery, putting it on his mental list of places to visit after dark.

About four o'clock, a dirty white Toyota pickup truck came down the shady side of the main street with a throaty rumble and stopped in front of the suspicious place Kyle now called the House of White Hands. Although he had a beard, the driver was not an Arab, but he moved with the loose gait of someone comfortable in the surroundings. He wore lightweight slacks and a long-sleeved blue cotton shirt rolled up at the wrists, with sunglasses pushed up on top of his head. He greeted a few men seated on stools in some nearby shade. *Damn!* Kyle kept his right hand on the binos while his left dug into a thigh pocket and grabbed a plastic envelope. It contained the small photograph of the Frenchman who was to be the contact for the Marine raiders, and he looked at the picture, then back at the man. Pierre Falais. The Frenchman knocked on the door, said something, and was allowed inside. Fifteen minutes later he was out again, and his truck roared to life. Toyotas don't roar, Kyle noted, and they don't wear big desert tires. This was a custom job. He watched it drive to the gate in a low wall that surrounded another flat-roofed house three blocks down the main street, and then he lasered the hell out of the place.

It was finally time to move. Swanson spent two hours backing out of his hide and working his way down the wadi to a new spot a hundred meters to the right to get a better view of the mysterious door before the dinnertime delivery at the House of White Hands. This time, when the door opened, he had a plain view of a big man wearing desert cammie pants and an olive drab tank top. Not only was he white, but he had a line of tattoos on his right arm from shoulder to wrist. He took the food and shut the door.

Swanson was stunned. Who the hell was that and what did he have to do with the situation? The white skin meant westernized: Eurotrash or Aussie or Kiwi or Canadian or Scottish or whatever. Maybe even American. The tattoos helped narrow the field because they indicated a military background. That meant a spook of some sort, or a mercenary, and so much food being delivered indicated more than one in the house. A couple of Frankensteins just happen to be in the neighborhood during a Marine raid? No chance that could be just a coincidence, and it sure as hell didn't help the odds against him.

Kyle crawled back to his hide, ate some more crackers, and checked his water supply before taking a sip. He had taken two one-quart and four two-quart canteens from the other Marines so that he could be liberal in staying hydrated, because he planned to resupply after dark. But he never drank more than half of the water on hand. Water was life in the Middle East, and he judged that he still had plenty. As he ate, he considered his list—the Zeus and its guards; the house with Pudgy, Beanpole, SpongeBob and Pee-Wee, and a minimum of four other Arab fighters; the frog and his souped-up Toyota; and finally the House of White Hands, which contained at least one non-Arab guy who was most likely a merc.

Places to go and things to do, and Middleton was down there somewhere. *The frog will tell me.* Lots to do. He cut chunks of C-4, rolled them into tiny balls and put them in an arm pocket. A handful of pencil-sized detonators went into another pocket. From a full roll of black duct tape in his pack, he ripped off a half-dozen long strips and stuck them along the legs of his pants. He cleaned his weapons. He waited for darkness.

CHAPTER 26

NEWS FROM THE FRONT, GENERAL! Guess what? You're gonna be a fuckin' TV star again!" Victor Logan squatted before his captive, grabbed Brad Middleton hard by the jaw, and turned him so the prisoner had to look into his eyes. Logan laughed, a mirthless sound that echoed in the small room, and he wore a smile of triumph.

As the heat of the day was easing, Middleton, prone on the bunk, was able to breathe a bit easier, pulling air into his lungs despite the aching rib that had been broken in one of the beatings. The broken finger was useless. He had ripped a strip of cloth from his robe and tied it to the next finger to immobilize it. The room stank so badly it had become part of him. His guts were sore, and he had neither bathed nor shaved since they had used him in that earlier rigged media show.

Middleton's right wrist was chained to the metal cot, giving him only enough movement to reach two buckets, one about a third full of fresh water and the other a stinking one that he used as a toilet. The loose full-length cotton robe was filthy.

"We just got some new instructions," Logan said, letting go of the jaw but giving Middleton a medium-strength slap on the side of his head, enough to make the general's ears ring. "I guess you might consider the good news is that this is going to be our last day in this shithole. The bad news, for you that is, comes tomorrow morning. Jimbo and I are going to clean you up, get you all dressed in that spiffy uniform hanging on the door over there, and hand you to the raggedy-heads. The jihadists plan a big show. Might call it the local version of *American Idol.*"

Middleton ignored the flash of pain, slowly swung his feet to the floor, and spat on the floor to disrespect Logan. He wasn't afraid of the giant, because almost by definition a Marine Corps general has a streak of arrogance. His mind had cleared as the drugs wore off and he had thought long and hard about why he had been taken hostage, adding in the snippets of information he overheard through the door as his captors talked. He knew that he would never be released, so damned if he would go down sniveling. Middleton decided to interrogate the big man.

"If you have something to tell me, Logan, just say it. You and your partner: Dumber and Dumbest," the general said with a condescending sneer. "I can't understand why a company as big as Gates Global, with hundreds of pretty good people on the payroll, would stoop so low as to bring a couple of losers like you aboard."

Logan reacted sharply and stood to his full height, glaring down at Middleton. "They came recruiting me, not the other way around! The company uses Shark Teams to handle the uncomfortable side of things."

Middleton gave a wry smile. "And you were stupid enough to sign on. Look. I know Gordon Gates personally. He eats guys like you and Dumbo for breakfast. Sharks. Jesus."

"Jimbo, not Dumbo."

"Right. So Gordon waved his checkbook and you fools jumped on board." With a couple of oblique probes, Middleton had gotten Logan to admit that Gates was behind the kidnapping. He decided to push harder.

"He's paying me a hell of a lot better than the military ever did. Way better. I got more money in the bank than you ever dreamed of."

"Good for you. I hope your 401(k) brings you peace and

comfort for the next few hours, because you're already a corpse, too, and just don't know it yet."

"Bullshit."

The general stretched to loosen his muscles. "You are not going to live long enough to spend it, Logan. I guarantee that a big reward has been put on the street, and your best friends are already looking at you as a piece of meat that is worth about a half-million American dollars, dead or alive." Middleton tugged at the handcuff chain, let it drop, and faced Logan again.

"Also, you and Dumbo are the only links to my actual kidnapping, and Gates Global is going to cover its own ass. You are loose ends. Another one of your gear-queer Shark Teams probably will be sent out to gobble you up. You may be King Kong today, but between the tickle of a big reward among the ragheads and the double-cross coming from your boss, you're going to be just another dead monkey."

DAMN. Logan wanted to hit the general, beat the crap out of him, cut him, make him bleed. That was not allowed. "Shut your damned mouth, Middleton, or I'll shut it for you. You don't know nothing."

"I know it all, Logan," Middleton said, staring at the merc. "It's so quiet around here that I can hear the rats fart, and I've been listening every time you guys talk. You're going to have me killed on TV. Big deal. The Marine Corps is a big organization, and six colonels are probably already fighting for my desk. I'll be missed at the Pentagon about as much as you have been by those wussy SEALs. Let's make a bet: I say your freedom fighter buddies will bury all three of us in the desert tomorrow: you and me and Dumbo together through eternity." The general lay back down as if he did not have a care in the world, but continued the questioning. "No wonder they kicked you out of the shitbird SEALs. You weren't even good enough to meet their low standards."

Logan snapped at the bait. "Yeah? You think your Marines are such hot shit?" He was pissed that Middleton was ridiculing the Teams. SEALs were the best! "Your Spec Op boys couldn't even fly two helicopters without running into each other out here. Wouldn't have mattered if they landed, neither, because we had them in a kill zone even before they fucked up."

Middleton made a point of grimacing as if disappointed and said nothing while he made another mental note. Confirmation that this whole thing was a setup for an ambush. Blabbermouth.

"You think I ain't already got my own escape covered? You may be a general, but I'm as smart as you."

"Sure. That's why we're in here together in this smelly house. Couple of Einsteins, we are. E equals MC squared."

Logan had never liked really intelligent people. He didn't get that part about EMC. "You know why you're really here? Think you figured it all out?"

"Yeah. It's not all that hard. Real terrorists would have gone after an easier target, not a moving convoy with armed Marine and Saudi guards. That's why they snatch schoolteachers, not soldiers. So who would consider me important enough to risk an ambush that would certainly result in casualties and guarantee media coverage and a manhunt? Who profits?"

"What's your answer?"

"Simple. Gates Global. Your job was to put me on the sidelines. The only thing worthwhile on my schedule is testifying next week in Washington before the Senate Armed Services Committee. That is where I intend to stop this nutty privatization of the United States military and keep disgraceful incompetents like you from sneaking back into the tent. Shit, Logan, I wrote the book on privatization while I was at the Naval War College. The PSC concept is long on cost and short on loyalty. The Naval Institute Press published it and we even got some good ink in *The New York Times Book Review.*" Middleton laughed derisively and glanced at Logan. "It helped me get my star. I'm sure you read it."

"Big fuckin' deal."

"You're working for a private security company, but any way you cut it, you're nothing but a mercenary. A gun for hire. You work for Gates Global, which ordered you to kidnap me. Now, for some reason, which I assume is related to the helo crash, the original plan has changed. You never planned to let me live anyway, but Gates was just trying to figure out how he could benefit the most by my death. So it turns out the jihadists will do the honors. Once that is done, you are no longer needed either. Probably just one hole will be big enough for the three of us."

"Not gonna happen, Middleton." Logan moved to the door. "I've listened to enough of your shit. Anyway, let me tell you how it's going to come down tomorrow. Once we get you all pretty again and give you to those Iraqis . . ."

Middleton snorted, a bark of a laugh. "See? You just did it again!"

"Did what?"

"Gave me information I did not need to know. I had no idea those guys were Iraqis. You furnished another piece of the puzzle, you shitbird."

"Fuck you. I'll tell you something else, because you're going to be dead real soon. Not only are they Iraqis, but they work for that badass Rebel Sheikh down in Basra. At eight o'clock tomorrow morning, they are going to prop you up in a chair and cut off your fucking head!" He let the big cocky grin creep back across his face. "And I'm going to be standing there to watch. Gonna really enjoy the show."

Middleton closed his eyes as if bored. "Okay, Logan. See you in the hole." The general turned his back to the mercenary and did not move again until the door closed. Even then he did not move, thinking about beheadings and the alliance between Gordon Gates and the Rebel Sheikh.

CHAPTER 27

MASTER SERGEANT O. O. DAWKINS had not slept since the choppers had lifted off earlier that morning from the *Wasp,* and had smoked a whole pack of cigarettes. What a cluster fuck. He leaned on a railing of the USS *Blue Ridge,* flagship of the Joint Amphibious Task Force commander, and watched the water churning past far below. The entire TRAP team and two helo crews down in the desert, probably dead in the smoking ruins, and then abandoned. Just like that hostage mess back in 1979 with the Rangers and Delta operators in Iran. All of the high-tech toys in the world were bound to screw up sooner or later, and when Marines ride on the razor's edge, Mother Nature gives no second chances. He flipped his cigarette butt overboard and made his way through the chutes and ladders up to Flag Country.

His boss, Colonel Ralph Sims, looked like he had been punched in the gut, and waved Dawkins to a chair in his small but private stateroom. Sims was commander of the 33rd Marine Expeditionary Unit, the first one to work under the banner of the Joint Special Operations Command. Dawkins, an ex-Force Recon platoon sergeant, normally would have been the MEU operations chief, but under the realignment into special forces, he was called the MARSOC team sergeant.

He was an operator, not an administrative type. New generation of titles, same jobs.

Sims and Dawkins had been friends for more years than they cared to think about, and just sat there staring at each other in silence for a time across the desktop that held a small computer, a cup filled with pens, scissors, and a small ruler, and a little nameplate sign carved in the Philippines. They felt helpless, and could do nothing more to either save their men or bring the bodies home for honorable burials. Marines had left Marines behind. Sims opened a locked drawer and pulled out a bottle of Jack Daniel's Black Label bourbon. He poured shots for each of them into black coffee mugs emblazoned with the scarlet and gold crest of the 33rd MEU, and they drank the whiskey in quick gulps.

Outside sounds seeped dully into the quiet room. Ship noises. The creaking and groaning metal, the whines and whops of Harriers and helicopters, water moving through exposed pipes along the ceiling and around the red emergency lighting fixtures. The wall intercom, volume turned low, muttered just at the level of hearing. The stateroom, painted navy gray, was a combination work space and living quarters, so Sims could dash to his station in the Tactical Center only one deck up in an emergency. There was no porthole for outside light, but a small refrigerator worth its weight in gold was wedged into a corner.

"Anything new?" Dawkins asked.

Sims shook his head. "The Harrier pilots were thoroughly debriefed, Double-Oh, and their stories match. All they really saw was a big fireball when the choppers went down and no signs of life afterward when they flew over at low altitude, other than people coming out from the village. We lost 'em all."

"No chance, I suppose, of sending in another mission for the boys and the general?"

The colonel turned around and looked at a map taped to the bulkhead that showed the route. "Washington says it's out of the question. They won't even authorize a missile strike to eradicate the wreckage, and a diplomatic shitstorm is on the way. Syria is yelling 'Invasion!' and our State Department is trying to explain, 'Well, not really. It's this way . . .' "

"Then the fuckin' media and the United Nations will get involved."

"Yup. Too big a development to keep secret. The Muslim world is going to go nuts with demonstrations." The colonel poured more bourbon into the mugs. "We're going to get hammered."

Dawkins nodded his big, crew-cut head. "Not our best day, sir. Looked easy on paper."

"Always does, Master Sergeant. Always does."

"So you think it is a safe bet that Gunny Swanson is dead?"

Sims nodded. "Pilots said no signs of life. With daylight, we got better satellite imagery, but it still shows nothing useful. I don't see how anyone got out of that mess in one piece, even a ghost like Swanson."

A small speaker on the bulkhead crackled, and a quiet voice announced: "Attention all hands. A sunset memorial service will be held on the flight deck at eighteen hundred hours for the men who died on today's mission."

They raised the cups in salute. "To those who won't return. May they rest in peace," said the colonel.

"And to Kyle," responded Double-Oh.

"To Kyle."

"Semper fi."

They downed the smooth whiskey.

"Hard to imagine him gone." Dawkins settled back into the chair.

"What are you trying to tell me, Double-Oh? You didn't ask for a private meeting just to talk about old times."

Dawkins took a deep breath. The colonel had the uncanny knack of reading right through people. "No, sir. Well, since there is always room for more bad news, I guess I need to give you some."

"This has something to do, I assume, with why you have been wandering around the ship wearing a locked and loaded .45?"

"Yes, sir."

"So you weren't really expecting pirates to come charging over the starboard bow shooting RPGs?"

"No, sir. This is for real." Dawkins undid a Velcro snap on the sleeve of his flight suit and retrieved the envelope. "You remember when that spook from Washington came aboard to meet privately with Gunny Swanson?"

"Ummm. Figured he was getting tagged for a special mission when this was over."

"Sir, this *was* the special mission. Kyle was put under some top-secret orders, and his death leaves us with a situation."

"A situation." Sims put his forearms on the desk and leaned forward. He was tall and lean, with dark brows and a beaked nose that gave him the look of a pissed-off eagle like the ones he wore on his collar.

"Yessir. Maybe more a major league fuckup that will make people look back fondly on Richard Nixon after Watergate and Bill Clinton's blow job." He slid the letter across the smooth desktop with his fingertips. "It's all in there, sir."

"Swanson told you about this?"

"He refused to carry out the order until the spook threatened to get the White House to verify it. Then Kyle somehow snuck a copy without that Washington fuck realizing it, and the fool burned the copy, thinking it was the real thing. Gunny gave me the original in case he got whacked. He got whacked. So here it is."

"I don't think I really want to open that."

"No. Probably not, and I don't blame you one bit. But that's why you're a full bird colonel with a bunch of college degrees and I'm just a master sergeant. You decide where it goes from here."

"What's it say?" The colonel held the envelope as if it were scalding hot, turning it over and over in his hands.

"If it looked like the rescue attempt was going to fail, Gunnery Sergeant Kyle Swanson was under orders to execute Brigadier General Middleton."

"The hell you say," said Sims, running a thumbnail under

the envelope flap. His eyes gave away nothing as he read the handwritten note.

"The hell I do say, sir. The reason I went around the chain of command to get straight to you is that we don't know who may be involved in this thing. I guess it is going to be a very special need-to-know category."

Sims dug out some thin plastic map overlay sheets from his desk, folded them around the letter and envelope, and carried them to his private safe to lock them away. "You're right, Double-Oh. In fact, you're so damned right that I'm going to have to think about our next step. A wrong move and we both end up at Gitmo with German shepherds chomping at our balls. You got a suggestion?"

As the colonel resumed his seat, Dawkins stood. His leathery face actually wore a smile. "Yeah, Skipper, I do. The Thirty-Third MEU is an independent Special Ops unit, and as its commanding officer, you report straight to Central Command. I suggest you pack your bags for a routine trip back to Tampa to give the boys at MacDill a 'special briefing' about why the helicopters crashed. Have your staff type up a bunch of papers and make a PowerPoint show for cover."

Sims rubbed his thumb across his lips, which had gone dry. "And while I'm there, I get some private face time with CENTCOM?"

"No, sir. Halfway across the Atlantic, your flight will be diverted because the Pentagon will decide it wants to hear your lame-ass excuses in person. I can cash in some favors and get the Sergeants' Network to cut orders that far and keep you below the official radar. Once in Washington, it will be up to you to snag a meeting with General Hank Turner, our old boss from the First MARDIV. Although he happens to wear four stars and be chairman of the Joint Chiefs of Staff now, he's still an old Force Recon operator at heart. Him we can trust."

Sims agreed. "You're right. Turner will kick in the doors to find out what is going on." The colonel folded his hands behind his head. "Make it happen, Master Sergeant."

"Semper fuckin' fi, Colonel."

CHAPTER 28

ALI SHALAL RASSAD MADE HIS afternoon prayers in one of Basra's crowded mosques, in the midst of a crowd of kneeling, praying men. Afterward, he smiled his way to the door, hugging fellow worshippers along the way and dispensing words of encouragement, a whispered promise of help, a handful of coins. He was a leader because the people considered him to be one of their own, a warrior and a dutiful, humble servant of Allah, whose name be praised. The prayers provided quiet moments during which he often thought about how much he owed to the dictator Saddam Hussein. Without pure evil, how would people recognize good?

Like so many Iraqis, Rassad had grown up in poverty, a product of the Baghdad slums. He caught the attention of his teachers at the religious *madrassa* schools because he possessed an intellectual curiosity and showed a natural leadership ability. They decided he was worthy of more education, with the idea that he might become an Islamic scholar and religious leader. They misjudged the boy. During the day, he piously studied the Koran, but at night he read other books, and led a small gang of thieves through the alleyways of Baghdad. Death was never far away in the slums, and Rassad had gutted several men before his fifteenth birthday. He was a realist instead of a zealot, interested in obtaining his own goals and not simply obeying the rules of any book, not even the Koran.

No one was surprised when Rassad passed the exams to qualify for university study abroad as an engineer, nor that the government let him go to school in the United States. His family would remain in Baghdad as hostage until he returned to take a job with one of Hussein's ministries.

Rassad studied electrical engineering at the Massachusetts Institute of Technology, and also studied the complex organism that was America. He traveled to the oil fields in Louisiana and the West, to Silicon Valley in California, and to the vast farmlands of Kansas in search of understanding how and why democracy worked in Washington, D.C.

The individual experiences started coming together during his junior year, when he drove from Boston to Florida to participate in the annual ritual among students known as spring break. The all-night parties had been quite educational, and several pretty girls had found his dark eyes irresistible. The important lesson came late on a Monday night as he grew tired while driving back from Daytona Beach. A green neon sign of a little diner beckoned near Brunswick, Georgia, and Rassad followed a side road north for two miles. There was only a weathered pickup truck and a little Honda parked in the lot, which was illuminated dully by the ragged circles cast by three lights attached to the eaves of the building. He parked his new BMW 735i SE, went inside, and took a stool at the counter. A disinterested waitress took his order for a glass of water with ice and a piece of the fresh pecan pie that sat in a plastic case.

"Looky here," Myron Hix muttered. He was seated at a table crowded with empty beer bottles. A younger man, small, thin, and unshaven, was pushed back in another chair, a grimy Atlanta Braves baseball cap on his head. Rassad ignored them.

"Give that boy a beer!" Hix bellowed. A thick man of middle age with close-cut hair over a red, round face, he lifted a bottle of Budweiser in a toast. "You look like a man who needs a drink."

Rassad raised his hand to the waitress to signify he did not want a beer. "Thank you, but I do not drink alcohol," he said to the man.

"He 'do not drink alcohol.' " The man laughed, and so did his friend. Both wore dark blue shirts with open collars and name patches sewn above the pockets, the uniforms of a local garage. Scarlet script spelled that the big man's name was "Myron." The other man was "Robert."

The waitress slid the saucer with the pie and the glass of water before Rassad with the clatter of cheap china on thin Formica. Georgia was famed for its pecan pie. He took a bite. Delicious. The waitress, a bored woman with dyed blond hair, vanished into the kitchen through a swinging door.

The man approached him and perched uninvited on the torn leatherette stool. "Name's Myron Hix, boy. You a stranger in this neck of the woods and I wanna buy you a drink. So what'll it be?"

"Just water." Rassad faced the man. Bright eyes and beer breath. Glancing at the table, Rassad saw a stack of empty bottles.

"Ain't polite to refuse a man's offer," said Hix. "Not down 'round here."

"I do not wish to be impolite. My religion forbids alcohol."

"Where is it you from, then? Me and Robert are Baptists. Our preacher don't like us to drink neither, but the Bible says wine is okay. If wine is okay, then ain't beer and whiskey?"

"I am Muslim." He finished the pie, drank the water. "Thank you for your kindness." He fished a ten-dollar bill from his wallet and put it on the counter.

Hix slapped his hand down on the green face of President Andrew Jackson. "Moos-lim? I thought so." He spun on the stool to face Robert. "I tole you he was some kinda sand nigger, din't I?"

Rassad tensed. "Please. I wish no trouble. I will just get in my car and go."

"You damn sure will. And you don't come back. Hear? Go on back to Egypt and fuck your camel." Both of the men laughed.

He had just unlocked his sleek gray sedan when he heard the screen door of the diner slam shut, and tensed just as beefy hands shoved him against the vehicle. Rassad smelled the dirty breath of Myron Hix. Two miles away, a stream of headlights moved north, kids going back to school after the holiday. The lighter steps of Robert approached. "We ain't through with you yet, boy," said Hix. "You need a good lesson in 'firmative action so you don't forget who you are." Hix spun Rassad around and loomed over him like a bad dream.

The Iraqi looked steadily at the bigger man. "I believe that you are what people call a roughneck?" he asked mildly. "No. My English is poor. The term is stupid fucking redneck. Is that correct?"

As he was being turned, Rassad's right hand was hidden long enough for him to pull a sharply honed knife with a three-inch blade from the leather sheath clipped to the back of his belt. He had worn such a knife since he was a boy, and it almost jumped into his hand, like an old friend. He knew exactly what he was going to do with Myron Hix.

Rassad kept the knife shielded just behind his right ass cheek while he rotated the blade into position, then he struck upward in a quick, smooth motion with all the force he could muster.

The tip of the blade slid into the soft flesh under Hix's chin and Rassad shoved it in all the way, up behind the nose until the butt of the knife came to a stop. He ripped to the right and down, hard, cutting the jugular vein before jerking the knife out with the sharp edge toward him in order to cause a maximum of damage. One of the most valuable lessons of his brutal childhood was that once you start an attack, never pause until it is done, and be utterly ruthless.

He held Hix steady and watched the eyes go wide in anger, then surprise, then fade to dimness. Rassad let the body fall, stepped over it, and took three long strides to close on Robert, whose last word was, "Myron?" Rassad plunged the knife in at the belly button, careful to avoid the big metal belt buckle, got his left hand into Robert's hair, and pulled him forward while he stabbed three more times in the midsection. As Robert fell, the blade stabbed into the neck on the right side and was raked across the throat, opening a deep and bloody track.

Rassad wiped the knife on Robert's jeans, returned it to the sheath, got into his car, and started the engine. He wasn't even breathing hard. His clothes were soaked in blood, and he wiped his face clean with a handkerchief.

All the way back to Massachusetts, he drove safely among the hundreds of honking cars of other students, avoiding police attention and notorious speed-trap towns by just being one of the crowd. Friends at his local mosque arranged for the car to be stolen, and for the knife and clothing to disappear. Rassad replaced the Beemer with the insurance settlement. *The Boston Globe* reported a violent double killing at a roadside café in Georgia, identified the victims, and quoted a Georgia state patrolman as saying, "It was the most terrible thing I ever saw, even better than when that truck full of Vidalia onions squashed the Volkswagen crammed with drunk Florida Gator football fans."

Rassad now considered that Myron Hix had been sent by the Prophet to point out the darker side of American political history. More than twenty years later, Ali Shalal Rassad, the Rebel Sheikh, still savored that delicious moment when Myron—he liked to refer to him by his first name—called him a sand nigger to his face.

In his senior year at MIT, he expanded his exploration of United States history to include racial hatred. Signs in Texas restaurants once decreed, NO DOGS OR MEXICANS ALLOWED INSIDE. Native Americans had been slaughtered for their land. Railroad builders hung Chinese workers over the sides of mountains in baskets to blow away chunks of rock with dynamite and created the saying that an unfortunate person might not have "a Chinaman's chance." Japanese citizens were thrown in huge camps during World War II, but German citizens were not. The South was still dealing with the aftermath of slavery. Mexican immigration was a burning issue. The color of a person's skin seemed very important in America.

Rassad was fascinated by the political demagogues. Each brimmed with vices, but rose to political prominence by painting themselves as ordinary men of the people. It was called populism, but extended only to those of their own kind: white voters who were extremely religious. When Rassad attended their churches, the congregation stared. Americans taught him racial intolerance.

His professional degree was as an engineer, but his life was about politics, a thirst for power that increased when Saddam's son threw him in prison, where he somehow endured until the Americans came. Prison always seemed to be a good place for visionaries, and torture was excellent fuel for serious thinking.

When he was released during the first weeks of the American occupation, Rassad set out to perform political magic in Basra because he knew that populism would work as well in Iraq as it ever had in the Southern boondocks. Tribal strength, blind hatred, and fervent religious beliefs inherited over generations proved to be a potent combination. All that was needed was a leader to focus it all, someone to unite the factions.

Within a few years of the occupation, the people of Basra thought they had chosen him for that task, when in reality he had created a political vacuum by getting rid of his enemies. He was trusted by other Iraqis and bridged the gap between the religious factions by showing them there was more to be gained by working together. Peace got the oil flowing, and the oil brought in money enough for everybody. His private militia kept the peace by frequently reminding citizens about the horrors of war.

He had recognized the precise moment to shed his old skin as the leader of violent opposition and be reborn as a strong political savior, the man of peace. Rassad had the grace and intelligence to win the confidence of other foreign leaders, and the Americans were desperately begging for someone, anyone, to step forward and become the Iraqi George Washington. Rigorously managed, democracy could be just the springboard he wanted to expand beyond Basra and take over the government in Baghdad, with all of the levers of power and a treasury that King Midas would have envied.

In the coolness of his air-conditioned office, Rassad again read the urgent coded message he had received from America. It was an instruction to kill the American general Middleton immediately, but gave no details.

He let out a soft, tuneless whistle and smoothed the note on his desk as he let his mind roam free. This was tantamount to an order! Something had changed in his arrangement with Gordon Gates, and he had not been informed in advance for approval. It was irritating.

Therefore he had to examine the entire plan again. The game obviously had entered a new stage, and he would not risk losing all of those lucrative U.S. contacts because of a plot in Washington to change the way their military establishment was funded. Old alliances had to be constantly weighed on the scales of current and future value. Gates would be angry, but they would still work together in the future no matter how this single incident turned out. Gates would have no choice. There was a bigger game. Rassad could not allow the kidnapping to convince the American government to pick someone else to be George Washington.

Rassad asked his aide, "Have you acted on this instruction from the Americans to have our friends in Syria execute the Marine general?"

"Yes. I made the contact within this past hour. They will gather the needed video equipment overnight and record his beheading tomorrow morning." He bowed slightly, expecting praise for a well-done job.

The Rebel Sheikh puffed out his cheeks, then ran a finger across his dry lips. "Send this new order. Do *not* kill him. Dispatch my plane to Syria at first light and fetch the general down here to me. Dispose of the two American mercenaries who deliver him."

"As you direct." The assistant bowed and left the office.

Rassad had not decided what to do with Middleton. He might yet kill him, or give him back to the Americans and appear to have negotiated his release. What had hardened in his thinking was that he would be the one to make the decision, not the American power brokers.

CHAPTER 29

THE SMALL U.S. AIR FORCE C-20 executive jet sped across the Atlantic, bucking through pockets of rough air that were being pushed east by a storm front. Colonel Ralph Sims, the only passenger aboard, was strapped tightly into a wide, comfortable seat. This rough, bucking ride might be a mild flight compared to what awaited him when he landed.

An Air Force staff sergeant came back to check on Sims, and perched on the armrest of the seat across from him. She was an attractive brunette, with her hair cut short to frame her face and flawless makeup. Slender and with long legs that were close enough for him to touch when she crossed them. She was barefoot, and had replaced her uniform jacket with a small dark blue apron. Her perfect breasts swayed with the motion of the aircraft, threatening to break free of the little buttons on her shirt. The staff sergeant obviously had been chosen as a hostess for VIP flights because of the sum total of all of her assets, and she was given custom-tailored uniforms and had her hair done professionally at a pricy salon, courtesy of Uncle Sam.

"How are things back here, Colonel?" she asked. The accent was uniquely regional to her native West Virginia, and added to the package of charm.

"Bumpy." Sims had larger things on his mind than this girl's sexuality, but damn, she looked good.

"It does get that way sometimes, but the pilot is going to take us up higher and bend a little to the south to pick our way through this muck." She waggled her foot up and down.

"No shoes today, Staff Sergeant?"

"I'm from the coal fields, sir. Didn't even *have* shoes until I joined the Air Force and the government gave me some," she laughed. "That's a lie, but unlike most women, I hate shoes, and kick 'em off after everyone is aboard and we're off the ground. Easier to work barefoot." She waved her right arm at the otherwise empty cabin. "Can you imagine trying to carry a tray while walking on high heels during a storm like this? Some gay designer who hates women created high heels, that's what I think."

Sims smiled. "Well, I guess none of your passengers tonight will complain."

"Nobody has yet, sir. We were going to be flying back empty tonight, but got a last-minute call to hold and wait for you." She enjoyed only having to deal with just one person. "It's dark outside and we're flying into time, so maybe you want to get some rest? Nothing you can do to hurry us along."

He thought about the valuable hours that were falling from the clock, never to be recovered. Double-Oh and the Sergeants' Network had done a great job on logistics, for his departure had to look normal, which meant the staff had to be given an opportunity to prepare the PowerPoint slide show and a set of briefing papers. He spent the interval finishing the hardest part of his job as the commander of an elite unit, writing letters to the families of the Marines who were killed on the raid, personal notes that said how proud he was to have served with them. The letters would console some of the heartbroken recipients who would cherish the letter and read it out loud on birthdays, holidays, and special occasions. For others, his message would only fuel the deep personal hurt of losing a loved one, and he would be blamed. He had finished the last one just before going on deck for the evening memorial service for the fallen Marines, HIS Marines!

A helo carted him from the *Blue Ridge* to the battle group carrier in time for the last COD run of the day to Aviano. He boarded the awkward plane carrying a large briefcase that contained the mystery letter amid the other papers, and wore the grim look of a dejected officer going to a balls-cutting session. Rumor spread that he was being called back to CENTCOM to explain the fuckup in the desert. At Aviano, the sleek C-20 had been waiting with its engines buzzing quietly and the beautiful staff sergeant at the bottom of the small, carpeted staircase.

"What time is it?" he asked. He had crossed several time zones since leaving the boat.

She turned and looked at three small clocks in gleaming brass holders on the rear bulkhead. One gave Greenwich Mean Time, one read Washington time, and one was set to the aircraft's current zone. "Right now, in our itty-bitty piece of sky, it is exactly twenty-two hundred hours and, uh, forty-three minutes and, uh, fifty-eight seconds. We are right in the Greenwich zone."

He had not realized the clocks were right behind him. Almost 2300 GMT, an hour before midnight. Subtracting five hours meant it was 1800 at both CENTCOM in Tampa and the Pentagon in Washington. No matter how fast the little bird flew, it was unlikely that there would be any meeting with General Turner today.

"Tell you what, Sergeant. I'm a bit wound up, but maybe if you bring me a Jack Daniel's Black, ice, no water, it will help. After I work on these papers a little longer, I'll try to get some shuteye."

She smiled again. White, white teeth. "Yes, sir. One Black Jack coming up. How about I make that a double, and then tuck you in beddy-bye? You could get shitfaced, knee-walking drunk tonight and still be sober enough to finish your papers by the time we get to Tampa."

The telephone beside him buzzed. "Your language needs work, Staff Sergeant."

"Yes, sir! That's what they tell me." The girl laughed and padded away to the forward galley. She had long ago become a member of the Mile High Club, and this colonel was sort of cute, in a dumb brute kind of way, kind of like a big German shepherd that needed to be cuddled. Possibilities loomed.

The colonel answered his encrypted STU-III satellite telephone. "Sims."

"Double-Oh here, sir. Your pilot is going to be getting the course-change message from Tampa to Andrews in about an hour, but there's a problem."

Sims gripped the telephone tightly. "What?"

"General Turner has left the Pentagon. He won't be there when you get to Washington."

"Damn, Double-Oh. Where is he?"

"The general is on his way to China, sir, some kind of emergency defense committee meeting about the new round of North Korean missile tests."

"Oh, fuck me," said Sims, closing his eyes.

"Not to worry, Colonel. I got the Network on it. His plane lands at Elmendorf in Alaska to refuel before jumping the Pacific by the polar route. A mechanical problem will keep him on the ground until you get there."

"He will just take another plane."

"Yessir, that's probably exactly what he will try to do. Then that one will also have a malfunction. Airplanes are tricky things, particularly up there in all that extremely cold weather. You just keep going, Colonel. We will have another C-20 waiting at Andrews. Keep closing the gap, sir. He's got to stop. You don't."

"But he's got a half-a-world head start!" Sims replied. "Okay. Do your thing. Keep me posted." He turned off the phone, tossed it onto the seat beside the briefcase, and shook his head. "China. Oh, fuck me, fuck me, fuck me," he whispered.

"Ooooh, high-altitude sex. I think that can be arranged, Colonel Sims," the soft voice with a West Virginia twang purred. The staff sergeant was kneeling at his side with a glass of whiskey and two buttons undone on her blouse. "Drink up while I lock the door, turn on some music, and dim the lights. By the way, my name isn't Staff Sergeant, it's Mandi."

CHAPTER 30

DARKNESS CAME SLOWLY, A gauzy haze of dust-laden, fading light streaks. Even when the final fiery edge of the sun disappeared, the temperatures stayed stuck in the nineties. Within a few hours, Swanson would be freezing his butt off. It would not really be cold by the thermometer, but a thirty-degree drop after sweltering in 110-plus heat would bring a good dose of the chills. When the sun took away its warmth, the sweat that had oozed from him all day and drenched his clothes would feel like ice when the nightly winds blew. The mission was to have been a quick in-and-out, so he had only the clothes on his back. Fuck it. Nothing he could do, and that missing sun was his clock.

It had to shift away and benignly bathe places like the south of France and Miami Beach and Waikiki and Bondi Beach before returning to Syria, but it would not really be gone very long. The sniper had to be out of the hide, do his job, and be long gone before that orange beast once again started to eat this chunk of sky.

He had finished the logbook, done the surveillance, eaten some more crackers and water, and pissed into a hole in the dirt beneath him. A Syrian army contingent had shown up at the helo crash site, done some cursory investigation, loaded up the bodies, and taken them away. Swanson felt pangs of guilt while he watched. What were they going to do with the bodies? Give them back? Deep in his gut, he had a sense of failure and was angry with himself. The saying that Marines don't leave their own casualties behind was not just a catch-phrase. Dead or alive, everybody comes home.

Then reason took over. He did not have the resources to change this situation, and if he survived, he could report what had happened. And importantly, there was still one Marine who was alive and needed his attention, so all Swanson could do was bid a silent goodbye to the dead rescue team of Marines and hope the pinheads in Washington fought to bring them back.

The wrecked helicopters, stripped of all value, were left where they fell, just more bones in the desert, a macabre tourist attraction for snooping American satellites to photograph from space. Two new soldiers were dropped off to replace the guard post sentries Swanson had killed, and the army convoy left.

Swanson waited without anxiety as life began to slow down with the approach of action. His focus would narrow and he would see things differently, at a slower speed, more of a black-and-white film in a neighborhood theater than as a jerky, quick-cut television story. The metamorphosis would continue, like he was changing into someone new, and the sounds would amplify, the smells would become more intense, his eyesight would sharpen, and his reactions would quicken. Each breath would be slow. He had been an observer all day. Now he was becoming a sniper.

The village activity settled into an easier pace for the evening prayers and meal. Stores closed and the streets emptied. One by one the lights blinked out in the little windows because after a hard day of toil, working people wanted their rest. Some would make love, some would smoke a cigarette, some would dream of better times, and some were going to die by Kyle Swanson's hand. That was a fact.

He used the final hour to finish settling into his zone, almost physically filing things away in mental drawers and cabinets and closing them tight. Shari was in a special compartment, with a tight lock on it. Whoever started all this mess back in Washington was in another. His family, friends, even the Marine Corps were banished from his thoughts, and as time slowed down, Swanson felt that familiar presence of another Kyle Swanson, someone outside himself who would help him through the night, guiding and watching and planning and whispering in his head. Kyle knew a psychiatrist would love to get hold of him someday, at first for a long talk, and then maybe to saw open his skull, shake out his brain, and try to find what made it work. Swanson was curious about that, too, but did not question that other voice in his head. It was part of his natural progression into his lone gunman battle mode, and he trusted it. The voice had been a big help in other tight places, when he was kicking in doors and crawling through swamps. A bit of paranoia was a good thing when you were really in danger. It was not fright, just instinct, a sixth sense sharpened over the years, a total awareness of his environment that almost let him know what was around a corner.

Turning to Excalibur, he checked the ammo load. He pulled the bolt back enough to slide a fingertip into the raceway and tap the brass bottom of the big .50-caliber round seated in the chamber, then pushed the bolt home again. Four more rounds rested in the magazine below.

Another hour passed and he hardly moved at all, just waiting. Black dark now. Dark as sin. It was time to roll.

The first thing he planned to do was tweak the single guard on the Zeus, apparently the only person still awake in the entire village. Swanson checked the logbook for the range, 547 yards, then brought Excalibur's cool epoxy stock to his cheek, stared down the scope, and saw the figure standing motionless, probably leaning against a tire, with an AK-47 drooped across a shoulder. He was obviously having a hard time staying awake at one o'clock in the morning. The advanced night-vision ability of Excalibur showed every possible detail, not just a green shape, and Swanson fine-tuned the focus ring. He clicked the button to lock onto the target, and again to confirm the range. The GPS, the gyrostabilizer, and the laser communicated, and numbers flashed in the scope as the built-in computer continued to enhance and clear the picture and figure out the range, windage, and barometric pressure. When all was ready, the azure stripe flashed on the edge of the scope. It could just as well have been a neon sign spelling out, "This dude is history." This was just target shooting and almost unfair. Almost.

The guard's figure almost filled the scope and Kyle could see the young, bored, sleepy face. Adjusting to the final numbers, he dropped the sight to an inch above the center of the chest. Roy Rogers and John Wayne might shoot guns out of a bad guy's hand, but professionals went for center mass, the sure hit. Swanson slowed his breathing even more, and the heartbeat followed suit, and the crosshairs of Excalibur did not wiggle.

It was unfortunate that this young man had been so low on the totem pole that he drew the midwatch guard duty. He had been on post for only ten minutes, since one o'clock, and Kyle had watched as the boy relieved the earlier guard. They stood four-hour shifts. Nobody would miss this fellow until at least 0500. Swanson exhaled a half-breath and started the easy trigger pull as his muscle memory kicked in—time to work—slow and smooth and straight and steady and squeeze. The rifle seemed to fire on its own, and although Kyle felt the recoil buck against his shoulder, there was no sound other than a quiet cough as the silencer killed the noise. In the scope, Swanson watched the big bullet slam into the guy's chest and explode inside him, ripping his muscles and guts to pieces. The location, speed, and power of the shot did not give the guard time to cry out or even look surprised. He crumbled to the dirt beside the big antiaircraft gun, dead before he hit the ground. The front of his shirt was soaked in blood. Swanson used his thumb and two fingers to jack a fresh round into the chamber and swept the scope around the village. He heard a goat bawl and a dog bark twice, but nothing indicated anyone had heard his shot.

He moved from the hide on his elbows and knees, the other voice talking now, whispering, *Slow is smooth, smooth is fast.* He squelched the natural urge to get up and run to the downed soldier, and instead began crawling, fast but quietly, with the easy grace of a night predator.

CHAPTER 31

SEARCH. EVALUATE. LISTEN. The game had begun. Swanson had to cover about the length of one and a half football fields, and while speed was important, doing it right was more important. He was out in the open for God and everybody to see, slithering forward, his heartbeat slow and his eyes constantly moving.

Just because the village was quiet did not mean that no one would be up and around. It could all change in an instant, but for now the only sounds were the scuffling of animals within the walls around the houses. Rocks slid beneath him as he crawled, and the weight of his pack pressed him down. The M-16 was cradled in his arms, and Excalibur was in its drag bag, sliding along behind him, attached to a D-ring on his web gear.

It took twelve minutes to cross the open space and reach the body, where he stopped to take a careful look around, checking likely places where danger might hide, points from which a threat might emerge. He had to be lucky every time he moved. The enemy only had to be lucky once to detect him. He was burning minutes, but not wasting them.

The glazed eyes of the guard pointed up at the night sky, but Swanson checked the pulse anyway and found none. It was a boy, no more than sixteen, probably a product of the radical religious schools who had joined the war for his true faith and paid with his short life, the end coming so fast that he had not even felt the shock. *Tough shit, kid.* Kyle jerked the corpse into a sitting position, stood, and pulled the guard upright against the side of the Zeus.

Propping him up with one hand, he peeled off the long strips of duct tape pressed along his uniform and secured the body to the hooks, rails, and protrusions on the big weapon. A belt of tape went around the waist and was tied to a heavy ammunition box. With the tape taking the weight, he crossed the ankles and taped them in place, crossed the dangling arms, and tied them at wrists. Swanson draped the AK-47 over the boy's shoulders. The head lolled forward, which was fine, and he made a few adjustments to the clothes so as to obscure the bloodstains. Swanson took two steps back. To any distant passerby, the kid would appear to be dozing on the job, standing but sleeping.

The sniper checked the area again. Still cool. He knelt on the ground, reached into his pack, and pulled out a claymore mine, then carefully broke it open to get at the small ball bearings packed inside. He gathered a handful and rolled them, one by one, down a barrel of the Zeus, repeating the procedure until all four barrels were packed with dozens of tiny steel balls. Then he inserted the little rolls of C-4 explosive he had molded earlier. Each roll had a detonator. He opened the butt of his M-16 and took out the four-piece cleaning rod, which he twisted together into a single long, thin shaft that he thrust into each barrel to compact the mixture.

Time. Time. Tick-tock. Keep going. The voice was insistent. Swanson's senses were honed to the rhythms of the sleeping village. This was their everyday life. Nothing was supposed to happen here, particularly at night. It was like a base camp for the jihad fighters, and routine gave them an illusion of safety. Many people had washed their clothes to get rid of the day's dirt, and now the various shapes of cloth hung on lines behind the houses to dry overnight, shifting slowly in the low breeze and providing Swanson with an extra shield from sight.

He moved into the village, to the little store he had watched throughout the day. A low wall surrounded most of the two-story building, with a rollaway gate locked across the front. When open for business, the gate was pushed back to allow customers to wander in and out. The owners lived upstairs.

Kyle went over the rear wall and dropped into a crouch, pausing long enough to drop his pack and rifles inside the yard. From a lightweight vinyl holster near his left shoulder, he pulled a silenced match-grade .45-caliber pistol with an infrared laser scope, a competition-class weapon that carried an expanded magazine of fifteen rounds.

The front door of the store was locked, but a side window stood open to catch the night coolness. Swanson looked inside with his night vision goggles to avoid kicking anything, and then went over the windowsill. The pungent smell of spices was overwhelming. He did a 360-degree check of the room, holding his pistol in a firing position. Shelves, crates, a table with two chairs, a cooler in the corner, where an electric motor hummed. A stove was along the back wall beside a big cutting board on some cabinets. A carcass hung from a hook, waiting to be butchered. Cans were stacked in neat rows.

A plate of small cakes sat in a bowl on the main counter and Swanson wolfed some down, and it was the best food in the world, although he had no idea what it was. Taking a chance, he moved to the cooler and lifted the lid only a millimeter at a time to avoid making it creak, and a wave of chilly air rose into his face. Bottles of juice, water, and soft drinks were lined up like little soldiers and he pulled one out. The cold water went down better than the cakes, and he drank until he was ready to puke. After hydrating himself, he topped off his canteens. Water came first. He could not live without it. Then he grabbed an orange juice drink and gulped it down for the electrolytes, vitamins, and nutrients. *It ain't Florida OJ, but it's better than nothing.*

With his thirst slaked, he checked the available food, still able to read labels in the crisp green light of the night vision glasses. The shopping list was short but definite, and he fought the urge to belly-up on food. He had a roll of Ziploc bags in a pocket and loaded them with things that were small, easy to carry, and required no preparation. Dried figs and dates were in trays, in measured little plastic bags with twist ties, and he stuffed some into his Ziplocs, the sides of which had been strengthened with duct tape. He hated dates, but fruit was fuel. Flat cakes of day-old pita bread were taken for their starch, along with the peculiarly Middle East favorite, the ever-present Mars bars, with chocolate to provide sugar and energy. Finally, he grabbed a few boxes of unscented baby wipe tissues, one of the best things going for desert hygiene. One more look around and he decided that was enough. *I'm not packing for a vacation, for cryin' out loud.*

The luminous dial of his watch showed that eleven more minutes had elapsed, so he packed his goodies and went back out through the window. He gathered the rest of his gear and scaled the wall. *Slow*, warned the voice. *But go!*

Swanson reassembled everything, took some deep breaths, and turned the NVGs to his next target, the house where the fighters nested. Nothing stirred, not even a fucking mouse.

He crossed the street and stalked completely around the wall of the house, peering over the wall and into the shadows. Nothing. He hoisted himself onto the barrier and spider-dropped down the other side into the space between the wall and the right side of the house. A window was open, and he could hear the grunts of sleeping men. At least two were snoring. He had counted at least eight men going into the house, and guessed there were probably a few more, each having a gun within reach, and he planned to kill them all.

His first move was to check the inner perimeter, and he again stashed the pack and took out the pistol. Holding it in his right hand, Swanson flattened against the wall of the house and slid in a sidestep to the first corner on his right. He did a quick peek around and saw the dark backyard, criss-crossed by clotheslines laden with tunics and robes. With careful strides, he turned that corner and stepped along the rear wall to the next one, where he again stopped and slowly leaned his face around the edge.

A guard with an AK-47 on a shoulder strap, who had been obscured by the drying clothes when Kyle had studied the place, was staring straight back at him, face-to-face, within a foot of each other. The guard's eyes went wide with surprise at the goggle-eyed creature that had appeared before him out of the night. He had one hand on the stock of his AK-47 and started to raise it at the same time Kyle brought up his pistol and pulled the trigger. The gunfire sounded like the explosion of an ammunition dump to Swanson, and he felt and smelled the heavy warmth of blood wash on his head and chest, and pieces of flesh and bone plaster his arms and face. *I'm hit! It's over! I failed!* Kyle Swanson staggered backward and fell to the ground.

CHAPTER 32

LIEUTENANT COMMANDER SHARI Towne spent a long time in the restroom preparing for the afternoon meeting of the National Security Council. She peered into the mirror and thought she looked horrible, but her magic bag of makeup, with careful application, helped hide the lines of worry and the darkness beneath her eyes. She put on a fresh white uniform and brushed her short hair one final time. Still horrible, but it would get her through the meeting. Through every source of effort she could summon, she donned the professional, no-nonsense mask of a neutral expert.

She just wanted this over with, and to go home to her little brick condo in Alexandria, pour a stiff shot of ice-cold Boodles gin with a lemon twist, follow that with a scalding shower, a warm cup of Celestial Seasonings Tension Tamer tea, and a little oval white tablet, 10 milligrams of Ambien. That combination cocktail would go a long way toward putting her down for the night, and at least allow her body to get some rest, but she did not expect much sleep. Her mind was still on Kyle, and tears were only a couple of blinks away.

Doing her duty, making automatic responses to familiar sights and sounds and questions, had propelled her through the personal sorrow so far, and she would be back on the job tomorrow, because what was happening in Syria was much bigger than any one individual, even bigger than two people in love. When it was all done, she intended to call Jeff and Pat and get back out on that yacht and forget everything, particularly this job. The damned Middle East was her desk, and bad things were always happening there. There would be another crisis next week, and the week after that, and the week after that, and plenty of work would always be coming her way. She knew from watching other people go through grief that the mind-numbing work would help her start getting over what had happened to Kyle, one day at a time, never forgetting the death, but learning to accept it. She already missed his crooked grin, and longed to be able to go home tonight and find shelter in his strong arms.

Shari made a final mirror check and grimaced at what she saw, and five minutes later she entered the Situation Room to take her seat along the wall behind Gerald Buchanan, beside Sam Shafer.

She neither liked nor trusted Shafer, who was smart, slim, and handsome, with thick black hair slicked straight back. He was nothing more than Buchanan's slavish go-to guy for shortcuts on things that might stray over the foul line. Shafer was always flirting with her, eyeing her with open desire and working sexual innuendoes into almost every conversation.

He turned as she sat down and handed her a brown folder with a red stripe running diagonally across the front. "Here's a new file on the helo crash. Crazy stuff. Turns out that Gates Global had a couple of operators near the village, looking for the general on their own. They made it to the crash site and brought back these images of the victims."

Shari looked at him. "Gates Global? The private security company? What were they doing there?"

"God knows how they did it. It's really making us look bad—not only did the rescue mission fail, but a PSC team infiltrated and got these photos. Buchanan received the file from Gates himself. Now the boss wants somebody in this meeting to explain how a private company could do something we could not."

"Good question." Shari hesitated before accepting the

folder. If these were the dead Marines, then she surely would see Kyle's body. But she wanted to do it, for maybe photographic proof would finally erase any lingering hope that somehow the man she loved actually had survived.

"I've got to back up Buchanan during the meeting, so could you take a look at it and let us know if everything is in order? Brace yourself, because it's awfully graphic, Shari, but you have the best eyes for detail of anyone at this table. We need to match up the Gates Global data with the names of those actually on the mission. The roster is in there."

She nodded and put the folder in her lap, then looked around the table. So much power. The Vice-President. The Attorney General, the Secretary of State and several cabinet members, the American representative to the United Nations, and military leaders. Buchanan, quiet and arrogant, sat directly across the table from the President. Many considered him a peculiar hybrid of Henry Kissinger's showboating, Colin Powell's confident manner, and John Poindexter's sneakiness, a man who placed himself above his position and somehow got other powerful people to recognize that self-created authority. Shari was part of his staff, but she wouldn't trust Gerald Buchanan to paint a fencepost. It was impossible to ever determine what the man really wanted.

She tuned one ear to the conversation and reluctantly opened the folder, then snapped it closed again, her heart beating hard. The first photo was of a charred corpse, the skin of a blackened skull dried out and pulled back so tight by the heat that it was set into a horrible grin. Shari felt a nudge from Shafer, who whispered, "You okay?"

She nodded again, and listened for a few minutes to comments of the NSC principals. Buchanan railed about the Gates Global identifications, letting unspoken accusations of Pentagon incompetence hang in the air like invisible vultures. The Syrian government was outraged, but there had been no major troop movements. U.N. and SecState both believed the biggest danger now was a possible Syrian or Hezbollah missile strike against Israel for allowing the Americans to fly through Israeli airspace. The Israelis were saying they would respond to any rocket attack. Shari tuned them out. The eternal Middle East waltz. *So what's new?*

With a deep breath, she turned her attention to the folder again and steeled herself against the ghastly images. The names of the dead Marines were on a separate page that she removed, and found "Swanson, Kyle M., Gunnery Sergeant" listed close to the alphabetical bottom. An asterisk beside the name of "McDowell, Harold H., Lance Corporal," indicated that he was missing.

She turned the pages slowly, one by one. Each photo had the matching dog tag image superimposed in the lower left-hand corner. Shari mentally checked off the names against the complete flight manifest. The names were seared into her brain. Three-quarters of the way through, she paused, knowing the next photo in alphabetical order would be that of Kyle. She bit her lower lip and turned to the picture, keeping her mental defenses firm and letting her analyst training guide her eyes and thoughts.

Her fingers grew white with a tight grip at the sight of the broken and burned body. No facial identification was possible because of the fire, but the size and shape of the torso seemed about right for Kyle's dimensions. She felt wetness at the edges of her eyes as she studied the picture, read the dog tag, and examined the photo in detail. *Something isn't right.* The dog tags were authentic and accurate, but an anomaly she could not pinpoint chewed at her. Instead of looking at the grisly picture as an entirety, she studied it a square inch at a time. Left to right. Top to bottom. Shadows and light. Pixels. Uniform and flesh. A dead Marine. A destroyed human body. *There!* She stared in disbelief, trying to persuade herself that she was wrong while knowing she was not.

"Oh my God!" she whispered loud enough for Shafer to hear. The folder spilled from her lap and onto the carpeted floor of the Situation Room as she grabbed the single picture with both hands and stared at it. Buchanan spun in his chair and gave her an angry stare as the most powerful people in the United States government turned to watch her gather the papers.

"Sorry," she said, shuffling the papers and photos back into the folder. Using every ounce of her considerable willpower, she sat motionless through the rest of the meeting, letting her mind work the problem. A slight smile played over her lips and a new brightness shone in her eyes.

CHAPTER 33

KYLE SNAPPED BACK INTO consciousness, flat on his back. He took a deep breath, surprised that he wasn't dead. The air he pulled into his lungs was fresh and cool and reviving, and he lay still as his brain stitched together wisps of memories about what the hell had just happened. Being right-handed saved his life.

The brief, deadly confrontation was nothing but a quick-draw contest. The guard had been holding the stock of the AK-47, but not with his finger on the trigger, and hesitated for a heartbeat before trying to bring it to bear on Swanson. Professionals do not hesitate, and Kyle put the barrel of his pistol right against the man's eye and double-tapped him. Two big bullets at point-blank range totally destroyed the head.

Swanson roamed his hands across his own body and felt no pain, no wounds. The gore covering his face and chest was the blood, brains, and bone fragments of the other man, whose skull had exploded, and the unexpected concussion had scrambled Kyle's senses for a few seconds. He pushed onto his elbows and wiped his face. The guard lay dead at his feet.

Where are the others? The whole village had to be awakened by those explosions! He grabbed the pistol that had fallen by his side while his befuddled mind realized the guard had not shouted, had not fired his rifle, and Kyle's own silenced pistol had spoken with only two burps, quick and quiet except for the weapon recycling. There had been no detonations at all, and the great sounds he imagined that had been heard by everyone were only his gun firing almost next to his ear. He and the guard had both fallen where they stood, but everyone else slept on. He wiped his eyes with his sleeve, and poured water from a canteen over his face for a quick cleaning while he caught his breath.

Enough of this recovering shit! Get back to work! The inner voice, immune from physical hurt, was pissed, and the minutes were slipping by like desert sand.

The shadow of the house loomed like a big castle, and Swanson dropped the pack and stuffed eight blocks of C-4 into his pockets. He had guessed right back at the helicopter crash by topping off with C-4. Before the night was over, he would need a lot of explosives to help him survive.

He found a handful of pencil-thin detonators that had small timers like a digital watch and spent a moment activating them all to blow at exactly the same time. He needed at least an hour, with extra time for unforeseen circumstances, but he wanted to keep as much darkness as possible to help his escape. He set all of the timers to go off at exactly 0300.

He attached the first of the six-inch-long blocks of gummy explosive to the corner of the house where he had had the shootout, pushing the clay tight, like a kid playing with Silly Putty, and sticking in two of the detonators, just to be sure. The second block was placed just below the single window on the left side of the house, and he repeated the pattern all the way around until C-4 was in place on each corner and in the middle of each wall, all molded to force the explosions inward. The detonators blinked silently, and Kyle was sweating hard by the time he was finished, drops of water falling into his eyes. He struggled back into his pack, gathered his weapons, and stole enough laundry from the clothesline to outfit himself and the general.

This was going to be overkill. The simultaneous explosions

would destroy the supports of the house and collapse it on the sleeping men, then the surrounding outer wall would bounce the concussion wave right back toward the house instead of letting the blast effect roll away. It was time-consuming, but the house was the roost of his biggest source of potential opposition, the jihadists, and to wipe them out in a single attack was worth the risk of time.

It would also be a hell of a diversion, and Swanson had to be gone before the place lit up like a space shuttle launch.

It had taken him another eight minutes to plant the C-4, and he was at the wall at 0153. That left only another hour and seven minutes to do what he had to do and get the hell out of Dodge, including the ten minutes he had built into the timetable for the inevitable visit by that black cloud asshole Mr. Murphy. He ran through a mental checklist: *The guard. The Zeus. The groceries. The fighters. Time to go.*

He pulled himself onto the wall, rolled over, and almost landed on a goat. It jumped back, then stood facing him, shaggy and white, big ears, the lower jaw chewing something and the dark eyes staring without curiosity or fright. Two stubby horns had been cut off. Behind it was another goat that looked exactly the same. If they panicked, they might awaken somebody, and he couldn't shoot both of them at the same time. Swanson stood stone still and let the animals take a good look at him. They walked away.

Kyle headed the other way, down the street, sticking close to the walls. Time to *parlez-vous* with a Frenchman.

CHAPTER 34

DOUBLE-OH WAS EMOTIONALLY exhausted after working the Sergeants' Network most of the night and stood at a rail of the USS *Blue Ridge,* letting the sea wind revive him with its chill. His Air Force and Marine contacts in Washington were unable to rustle up another spare C-20 for him, and even the Army guys down at CENTCOM couldn't find anything appropriate that they could spring loose. So as far as he knew, Colonel Sims would be landing on a bare runway at Andrews, but he was confident that the sergeants would turn up at least some sort of rust bucket with wings so Sims could continue chasing the chairman of the Joint Chiefs.

"Since this is about those boys who died out yonder in the desert, we'll come up with somethin'," promised a flyboy master sergeant who had a thick Southern drawl. "Just won't be no C-20. But I got me an idea. Lemme make a couple of calls." It was, Double-Oh thought, a hell of a way to run an airline.

Weariness and tension had crept into his bones, and he was ready to go below to his quarters, one of the six racks in a small squad bay reserved for chief petty officer ranks. Privacy was not a high priority on a ship, and the bunks were arranged in two stacks of three each. With the combined farts, snoring, and belching of six middle-aged men at night, sometimes the flight deck was more quiet, and never mind the smell.

Once he entered that steel-walled room, there would be no cell phone reception, so he made one last check of his messages before putting the phone away until morning. He would be able to catch an hour or so of sleep before Sims changed planes at Andrews, if the air force types came through. He pressed a button on his Nokia and the screen showed that two calls had come in while he was busy, both from the same number in Washington, both from Shari Towne. Each flashed a red exclamation point icon that meant "urgent." He hit the automatic dial and heard the beeps and squawks of an international commercial call, then the phone was answered after the first ring.

"Shari? What's happening?"

"Thank God you called back, Orville. Something is going on here that I don't understand . . . about the mission." Her voice was agitated, unusual for Shari. "Have you heard anymore about Kyle?"

Double-Oh's thoughts begin to race. She worked for Buchanan at the NSC. Had she found out about the letter? "No, we haven't. It's tough to accept, Shari, but he probably died in the crash. I know you're hurting, girl. Me, too."

"No, no, no. Listen," she said rapidly. "I apologize for bringing you into this, but just listen. I've got what may sound like a silly question, but it's very important."

"Okay. Shoot."

"Did Kyle get a tattoo before he left the boat?"

"What?" Double-Oh was rocked by the question. "Hell, no. First, there is no place to get a tattoo around here because we are at sea. Anyway, you know how he feels about that stuff. No markings for a sniper. Ever. No way would he put any distinguishing marks on his body." If a sniper was captured, he did not want the enemy to know his job.

Shari exhaled, and Double-Oh heard the breath from thousands of miles away. "Well, then. He's alive."

There was silence for a moment. "What makes you think that?" Double-Oh was suddenly wide awake again.

"They gave me the official file on the crash to examine, and it contained horrible photographs of each of the Marines who were killed."

"Photographs? How the hell did you get individual pictures?"

"That's just one of several weird things. They came to Buchanan through Gordon Gates. Seems a couple of his PSC guys were near the village and able to get into the crash site. We have no idea how. Anyway, each photo included a close-up of the dog tags for identification. Double-Oh, the picture that was supposed to be of Kyle was of someone burned beyond recognition about the face, but the dog tags were clearly readable. They had not even been charred and the rubber ring was still intact. How can a torso and face be destroyed by fire, but the dog tags around the neck remain untouched by heat? The tag laced into his boot was identical. No doubt that those were Kyle's tags."

The big sergeant was holding tight control of his voice. He was not going to jump to conclusions. A couple of mercs were at the scene? "Maybe they made a mistake, screwed up with the wrong dog tags."

"Doesn't matter, Orville. It was the left forearm that really caught my attention. It was visible and in pretty good shape, with DEATH BEFORE DISHONOR lettering around a good-size USMC tattoo of the eagle, globe, and anchor. I think Kyle was betting that you or I would see the report, and would pick up on it."

Double-Oh rubbed his face. *Good God!* "I don't know, Shari. Maybe he got a tattoo somehow that I just didn't notice because I wasn't looking for one. Anyway, he was sleeves-down when he left the boat. We can't get into wishful thinking."

Shari paused, then said, "Okay. Try this. They report one Marine is missing and presumed alive; a young radioman with no combat experience. So far, this kid is out there on his own and has not only managed to escape the crash site without being spotted, but has evaded the Syrian army, dodged all of the civilians and any Bedouins in the area, and has not even been spotted by our own satellites. You tell me, Double-Oh. How many men on the mission could do that? Not some dial-spinner, that's for sure. So who would it be?"

"Jesus." There was a moment of silence, then Double-Oh agreed softly. "Gotta be Kyle. He's alive."

"Yes. He is. I just needed to confirm my conclusions with you before I did anything. We have to go get him. I'm going to talk to my boss and get things moving from this end right away."

"No!" Double-Oh's voice changed from wavering uncertainty to parade-ground intensity. "You can't do that, Shari."

"Why?"

"Are you calling from your office?"

"Unh-uh. I'm on my cell outside of Starbucks. I took a walk after the meeting to clear my mind and call you to confirm my thoughts about the tattoo."

"Okay. Listen up. I've got to bring you up to speed on something that's going on. My boss, Colonel Sims of the Thirty-Third MEU, is heading your way." He outlined the letter Kyle had received from Gerald Buchanan's courier, how Kyle had refused the assassination order, and that Sims was flying under covert conditions to deliver the copy of the letter to someone higher up. "It seems like Buchanan is involved in some borderline treason, Shari," he said. "If Kyle brings General Middleton out safe, there is going to be some big trouble when this thing blows up in public."

"Tell me about the courier." She dropped the cardboard cup of coffee in a trash can. Down the street she could see the White House, the black fence in front of it, and the broad open plaza. Protesters, cops, and tourists mingled. Buchanan secretly sending a Marine sniper in to kill the general instead of rescuing him was illegal. No wonder there had been no memo about it, not even Top Secret. "The man who came out there to meet with Kyle. What did he look like?"

"Civilian dude, playing at being a spook. He admitted later being from the White House. He was slim and tall, with a big mop of black hair that was slicked back like he was a singer for some doo-wop quartet. I never caught his real name, but he was a real cocky asshole."

Shari sighed. "That's Sam Shafer. He's Buchanan's right-hand man."

Double-Oh said, "Look, Shari. This is spinning off the deep end fast. Did you tell Buchanan and Shafer what you were thinking about Kyle?"

"Not yet. Like I said, I wanted to call you first and make sure."

"You can't trust those two. If they are suspicious about why you acted strangely at the meeting, they are going to force you to give up the information."

"What do you want me to do, Double-Oh? I can't just sit here while Kyle is in big trouble!"

"Don't worry about Kyle right now. He can take care of himself. I'm more worried about you calling me on an open circuit. Shari, my special ops nerves are shaking like leaves on this. Those two guys will do anything they have to in order to keep that letter secret, because if they don't, it will mean prison for them." His voice went softer. "That includes getting rid of everybody who may know about it. That means Kyle. It means me. Now it means you, too."

"Me?"

"Yes. You can't go back to work until this thing is settled. And when you don't show up, they are going to pull out all stops to find you and get what you know. Guaranteed they will discover your relationship with Kyle. We have to assume that Buchanan, with all of his intel assets, will have the NSA recording this call."

"They won't bother me. I'm a serving naval officer."

"That will be no protection whatsoever. Trust me on that. You and I both have to disappear before Buchanan can get his hands on us, Shari. Hang up this phone and dump it, then get to somewhere safe. Not your apartment."

"Orville, I can't just leave! If I don't show up for work, it will be an unauthorized absence."

"Take it from me, honey," said Double-Oh. "Right now,

that is the least of your worries. When the house is burning down, your first job is to save yourself, then worry about the house. You get out to Quantico right now and contact the duty NCO, and he will stash you in the VIP lodgings . . . until I can contact you on an *encrypted* line." He emphasized the word.

Shari almost dropped the phone when she realized that Dawkins was right. The NSA would be listening to her call, particularly since it was being made within an invisible listening cone that surrounded the White House. "Right. The duty NCO at Quantico will be expecting me."

"We'll talk soon." Double-Oh broke the connection and threw his cell phone overboard, watching until it splashed into the Mediterranean Sea. There would be no sleep for him tonight.

In Washington, Shari Towne moved quickly. She put her phone into the same trash can as her coffee, stepped to the curb, and hailed a taxi.

By the time the cab drove away, a supercomputer at the National Security Agency had recorded the call and traced it from Lieutenant Commander Towne to a number assigned to Marine Master Sergeant Orville Oliver Dawkins.

Instead of racing down to Quantico, Shari Towne had the cab driver turn right and head toward the Hashemite Kingdom.

CHAPTER 35

GERALD BUCHANAN AND THE secretary of state had a private meeting with the President following the NSC session, but as soon as he returned to his office, he called for Sam Shafer. "What the HELL was that all about with Towne? The world is coming apart and one of my staff members interrupts an important meeting by dropping her schoolbooks? In front of the President of the United States? For God's sake!"

"Commander Towne has been under a lot of pressure, sir. She was the one we brought back from leave to work on the crisis."

"The woman is supposed to be a professional!" He spun his chair around to stare out the window. "Her action today reflected directly on me. Everybody will think I hire morons who can't take the pressure."

Shafer ran a hand through the hair, a finger comb. "I don't think that's what happened."

Buchanan turned back around, his anger replaced by curiosity. "Talk to me, Sam."

"I've worked with Shari Towne for a long time, sir, and nobody has a cooler head in a crisis. That damned brain of hers goes so fast it throws off sparks, and I have never seen her rattled. If a situation is really going to hell, she might squint an eye in thought. Nothing more."

"So why was she dropping Top Secret files all over the President's expensive rug?"

"She saw something in that folder of the dead Marines, sir. I gave it to her to review while I took notes on the meeting. She was going through the meat shots when it happened. I thought at first that it might be because the pictures are pretty gruesome."

"So what? Pictures of dead people usually are."

"I agree. She had not yet reached the pages of text, so all she had seen were the photographs. Right before she dropped the file, she was looking at the picture of one of those poor faceless bastards. More than looking at it, she was studying it hard, almost breaking it down into pixels. When everything else hit the floor, she held that picture so tightly her knuckles were turning white."

Buchanan shook his head. *So what?* "Several people, including me, have looked at the file and none of us had that kind of reaction."

"That's just my point, sir. But how many of us who examined it were trained intelligence eyes? Shari Towne is one of the best analysts in the building, and she doesn't work here because she misses things. No one else apparently picked up on whatever it was she spotted. It's not the first time she's done that. Remember how she pegged the Libyan missiles that Gadhafi claimed he had destroyed?"

"So she saw something." Buchanan had found the file to be exactly what he had expected. Bunch of dead guys. It was supposed to be nothing more than an impressive visual prop to demonstrate the abilities of the Gates Global operators. He did not like the idea that Towne had picked up a detail he had missed, something that might be important.

Shafer crossed his arms. "Whatever was in there made the stone-cold lieutenant commander lose her cool, for maybe the first time in her life, outside of an orgasm."

"Wait a minute, Sam. She didn't tell you what it was after the meeting?" Buchanan leaned forward, elbows on the desk blotter. "Get her ass in here. Right now!"

"Can't do it, sir. She grabbed her purse and left the building. Told a secretary she was going for a walk and hasn't come back." Shafer glanced at his watch. Seven o'clock. "She left about thirty minutes ago. I called her cell phone. No answer."

"The bitch is keeping a secret from me?" Buchanan's anger flared so hard that he broke his pencil.

"It gets worse, sir. I had the White House operator call Towne's secure beeper ten minutes ago. All White House staff must answer such a page immediately, without exception. Nothing. For whatever reason, the commander is choosing not to communicate."

"Damn! We have to find her, Sam." Buchanan's mind churned. "Meanwhile, put some of our other intel people on the file and see what they can get. And I want to know more about Miz Towne. Put the bitch under a microscope."

"Just here in the office?"

"No. I don't think she's coming back," said Buchanan, making a guess, then a decision. "Do the full package. FBI, CIA, Homeland Security, and the National Intelligence Center. Pull her Secret Service background check. Yank the computer hard drive from her office and have the NSA crack it. Wiretaps, computer scans, the full audio-video surveillance package, pictures, financial information, the whole nine yards, including interviews with people who know her. I want to know everything she does, everybody she knows, where she buys her damned groceries, who she is screwing, and the name of her third-grade teacher's pet canary. Everything!"

"Warrants?"

The National Security Advisor leaned back and dodged the question. It had been proven too many times that White House walls have ears. "Sam, as I recall, isn't Lieutenant Commander Towne of Middle Eastern extraction?"

"Her mother is Jordanian, father was an American diplomat. He died in a plane crash when she was a child."

"An Arab, then. So considering the seriousness of her withholding vital security information during an international crisis, I must direct that Lieutenant Commander Towne be considered a terrorist mole who somehow infiltrated the White House. She may be aiding our enemies."

Shafer broke into a big grin. Buchanan amazed him. Nothing was beyond the man. "Yes, sir. A possible al Qaeda connection would be a very serious matter. I'll get the file."

"And Sam?"

"Sir?"

"Have Towne in custody before dawn."

CHAPTER 36

COLONEL RALPH SIMS DEPLANED from the luxurious C-20 executive jet at Andrews Air Force Base in Maryland with some reluctance. He was freshly shaved, in a pressed uniform with shined shoes, and although somewhat tired from the long journey, he felt like a million bucks. Staff Sergeant Foster, Marcia L., who had turned the routine puddle-jump flight into a cruise among the stars for him, stood at attention at the foot of the small stairs, saluting smartly as Sims stepped to the ground.

"Call me," she said with a wink, passing a card with her telephone number to him. She hurried back into the plane, pulled up the stairs, and closed the door, and the sleek C-20 followed a Jeep with a rack of lights down a long, empty approach runway.

Sims had expected to be deposited in front of a terminal, with another C-20 waiting for him, but instead there was nothing around but darkness. A tall cyclone fence was set back at the edge of the field, and no blue lights marking the runway reached into this far corner. Low bushes and scrubland fell away from the tarmac and into the field bordering the fence, and he could barely make out the big control tower outlined by lights several miles away. A breeze carried the salty scent of the Chesapeake Bay, and he could hear the hum of distant traffic. It seemed that he had been dropped off in the middle of nowhere.

"Where the hell is everybody?" he said into the emptiness.

"Right here, sir." One of the bushes stood up, a Marine in a full ghillie suit with a long rifle in his hands. "Staff Sergeant Gonzales, USMC scout sniper, sir. May I see your identification, please?"

Sims was aware that several other bushes were also moving around behind him as he handed over his laminated military identification card. The staff sergeant checked it in the briefly seen red beam of a flashlight. "Right. Thank you, sir." He turned and called into the darkness, "Mr. Dillon, you may come forward."

Footsteps in the darkness on the far side of the runway came closer and Sims made out the shape of a small man who extended his hand. "Billy Dillon, colonel, United States Air Force, retired. Glad to meet you." Sims's eyes had adjusted to the night surroundings, and he saw that Dillon was dressed in a ribbed and pressurized black flight suit.

"What's going on, Staff Sergeant? Why is your team out here, and what is Mr. Dillon, a civilian, doing in a restricted area?"

Dillon handed Sims a flight suit like the one he wore. "We will explain while you get dressed. You can't fly with me without it. The boys will tuck your uniform into the Val Pak and we'll carry it in a storage space. Hurry, please, Colonel. Time is of the essence."

Staff Sergeant Gonzales made some hand motions and his men went prone again, facing outward. "We're a Force Recon team, Colonel, out of Camp Lejeune. We're just doing a routine drill here tonight," Gonzales said with a grin of white teeth against his grease-darkened face. "I will say that a couple of unexpected telephone calls had something to do with this assignment. In fact, my Top threatened to feed my ass to the buzzards if I didn't move fast enough to get here before you did."

Sims stripped to his underwear and was struggling into

the tight flight suit, which looked like the skin of some pre-historic alligator. "I got a call, too," said Dillon. "Bit of personal history first. I was flying an Air Force F-16 several years ago somewhere that we weren't supposed to be and the bad guys got lucky with a missile. My radar intercept officer was killed, but I got out with just some broken bones. A Marine Special Ops team came and fetched me home, along with the body of my RIO." He helped Sims zip up. "After rehab, I couldn't fly military anymore, so I got another gig. I owe the Force Recon boys big-time, and I always pay my debts."

Gonzales was no longer smiling, and his eyes burned with anger. "All we really know, sir, is that you have something to do with settling the score for what happened over there in Syria. We're here to help. Those were our brothers."

"Let's go," said Dillon, handing Sims a black flight helmet.

"Go where? There's a plane here?"

"Right there. A hundred yards straight in front of us." He started walking and Sims followed.

As they closed in on the spot, Sims saw a ground crew dressed in black working on a shape beneath a big camouflage net. At a signal from Dillon, they pulled it away.

"And just what the fuck is this, Mr. Dillon?" The plane was almost invisible, with flat black paint, no sharp surfaces, and standing high on a tripod of wheels. He touched the surface, which was as smooth as a mirror.

"Call me Billy, please, Colonel." He led Sims around the strange aircraft and pointed to the small white acronym lettering the tail fin. "Meet the X43-D scramjet, the latest in the Hyper-X series. We're trying to make a reusable space vehicle. You're flying courtesy of NASA tonight, Colonel. I have to get this bird out to Edwards Air Force Base in California before dawn, so we arranged a little side trip to Alaska for you. It will get both of us where we need to be in plenty of time. Up you go into the rear seat." He patted a footstep in the hull.

"You're going to make it from Washington to Alaska and back to southern California in a couple of hours?"

"Yep. The old SR-71 Blackbird used to be the fastest thing in the sky and it only did Mach three, three times the speed of sound. Tonight, you and I are going to climb about sixty miles up, just under the edge of space, and you'll be able to see stars like you cannot believe. There will be some weightlessness. Then I level off, kick her into high gear, and peg the speedometer at about Mach eight. When we start the descent, we'll be going like a bat out of hell. A ceramic covering more advanced than that on the space shuttle will protect us against the heat of reentry."

"No shit?"

"No shit. It will be the ride of your life. Now let's buckle you in."

"Colonel?"

Sims looked over his shoulder. Gonzales was still standing there. "You have something to say, Staff Sergeant?"

"Get the motherfuckers, sir."

"Bet your ass on that, Staff Sergeant." Sims climbed into the rear seat of a cockpit unlike anything he had ever seen, and ground crewmen reached around him to hook up the hoses and belts.

"Ready back there?" Dillon asked, face-to-face over the televised intercom.

"Let's do it, Billy. I'll see if you're lying about the speed."

The cockpit hummed down and locked into place, the instrument panel glowed green and red, there was the hiss of cool oxygen into the mask, and the radio came to life in his ears. "Hold on, then. We don't call her 'Greased Lightning' for nothing."

CHAPTER 37

KYLE SWANSON DROPPED HIS pack as softly as a mouse's footstep, and moved to the side of the bed. His night-vision glasses gave a clear, green view of the bearded man sound asleep beneath a cotton sheet, and Swanson brought his big pistol down hard on the crown of the man's head. He needed a few moments to set up, so the guy had to stay asleep.

He ripped off a strip of duct tape and pasted it across the man's mouth. A broom leaning against a corner went behind the shoulders, and he secured the wrists to it with flexicuffs and duct tape. He cinched the ankles and the knees together with more tape. Duct tape had many uses. He wound more of it all the way around the bed and secured the torso and legs. Almost ready. He clicked on a single bedside lamp and covered the shade with a towel to cut down on the glow. It would be important that the Frenchman be able to see what was about to happen.

Moving to the stove, he lit a propane flame and propped the largest spoon he could find to roast over it.

Back at the bed, Kyle hauled the sheet up to the man's neck and straddled the chest, his weight pinning the edges of the sheet to the bed like a giant sleeve. With one hand, he poured a cup of cold water on the man's face, while the other hand kept the pistol right between the eyes. Hell of a way to wake up.

The eyes flew wide open in surprise. Kyle said nothing. He knew the value of silence to an interrogator and wanted to establish the parameters of the session before the man even started to think he might have a vote in what was happening to him.

Kyle returned the pistol to the shoulder rig and withdrew his long, sharp knife. He grabbed the left hand secured to the broomstick, and took his time sawing off the thumb. The victim yowled behind the tape as blood spurted out in a dark stream. Swanson got off the guy and brought over the large spoon from the kitchen, holding it up so the Frenchman could see it glowing with heat. Tears of pain and shock and fear spilled from the eyes. Then the spoon went against the bleeding stump, where it sizzled, and the muzzled man screamed again.

When he calmed down, Kyle said, "*Bonjour,* asshole."

He pulled up a chair and looked the man in the face. "That was just to save us some time. We're both professionals, so let's make this as painless for you as possible." He wiped the blood from the knife on the man's hair, pressing the flat of the blade against the skull. "Still going to hurt, though. You decide how much."

Swanson held up the small photograph he had received during the pre-mission briefing. "Recognize this dude? Oh my God, it's you! How about that for a coincidence? Your name is Pierre Dominique Falais, an ex-Legionnaire who is now an intelligence snitch for whoever will pay you. You speak Arabic, French, English, and German, so don't insult me by saying you do not understand what I am saying." It was easier to break a prisoner early in the interrogation if he thought the questioner already knew everything. Falais had no idea that the French had given up his entire record.

He mumbled.

"Ummmm," said Kyle, sniffing. "Smell that? The unmistakable odor of burning flesh. I smelled it only a few hours ago when I got out of that fucking helicopter. A lot of Marines who were my friends were killed out there, and were burned worse than you." He leaned across and laid the razor-sharp knife blade on the pinkie of the mutilated left hand and cut that off, too, then took his time reheating the spoon before stanching the flow of blood with it. Another scream.

"Okay. You have eight fingers left, ten toes, a nose, two ears, two eyes, lips, legs, arms, and of course your dick and balls, which will go into your mouth or up your ass, I haven't made up my mind yet. But that would be a lot of work, and you would experience some discomfort. So you answer my questions and I won't chop you up like frog legs. I'm going to remove the gag now, and if you try to shout, I will ram this big knife through your cheeks and knock out a few teeth. Then the questioning will resume. Understood?" The man nodded a vigorous yes. Kyle tore the tape off so that it clung to one cheek in case he needed it in a hurry.

The Frenchman sucked in some deep breaths. "Who are you?"

"I ask the questions. Where is General Middleton?"

"You're an American," he protested. "Americans don't torture prisoners."

Kyle felt a wave of revulsion when he decided to hurt the man to get the information, but steeled himself for the job by reasoning that it would take hours to make him talk any other way. He did not have hours to spare, so he slapped the tape across the mouth again. "I can do whatever the fuck I want, Dominique. Not because international laws might be bent enough to allow it, but because, thanks to you, I'm dead. I don't exist." The knife flashed and he sliced deeply through the left ear. The ear is a bleeder, and a crimson pool spread out beneath the man's head, the warm wetness scaring him more than the cut.

After the expected scream, Swanson tore off the tape again and let it dangle.

"The next 'procedure' is something you will recognize, because I learned it while I was on assignment with the Foreign Legion myself. A deep cut down the underside length of a finger all the way to the palm, severing all those nerves on the way." He leaned forward, almost nose to nose. "So once again, asshole. Where the fuck is General Middleton?"

Falais gave up and answered through gritted teeth, "In the house of the Americans."

The mercs! "Well done, Pierre. Now, who are they?"

"There are two of them. Victor Logan is the biggest, and he is crazy dangerous, a former SEAL in your navy. The other man is Collins, ex-army, but really just an extra set of hands for Victor. They work for Gates Global, which also hired me."

When Kyle did not reply, Falais panicked. "Wait! I have money. Lots of money! I will give it to you!"

"No. I'm not in this for cash." Kyle jammed his left forearm into Falais's mouth hard and slapped him on the wounded ear.

The scream was muffled. *"Merde!"* The Frenchman groaned with the searing pain. "Look. I can help. *I can help you!* I will take you to them."

"Where is the general kept in their house?"

"A small room in the right rear corner, handcuffed to a bed. They have not harmed him greatly, although Victor really wants to. Victor is a killer." The dark eyes studied Kyle's face, seeing if a deal was possible. "You will have to hurry because the jihadists are to behead your general in the morning."

"What kind of security do the Americans keep?"

"None. Everybody here is afraid of Victor, and they have plenty of guns. No one bothers them. Again, let me help."

"How?"

Pierre Falais detected a faint opening, a chance. "I will take you over there and distract the Americans while you attack. We kill them, get the general, and I will guide you safely to Israel. People in the villages know me and will help. I'm the one person around here who can get you out." He was breathing heavily.

"What do you want in return?"

"You let me live," the Frenchman said. "Then I am sure the American government would be generous with a reward. We will not mention what you have done here."

Kyle nodded. "Not bad. I guess you might have some

value after all, Pierre. I promise not to filet you anymore."
He took a rolled-up towel and pressed it against the bleeding
ear, then suddenly reached over with his knife and cut off the
small finger of the other hand. "Do you think I'm a fool?" he
hissed. "I told you I'm not playing around and I am damned
sure not going to let you walk me into an ambush. Tell me
what else you know. Tell me everything. Right now, or I cut
you some more!"

The French spy broke and started to cry. "That's all I
know! What else do you want? I won't ambush you. I'll tell
you whatever you want! Just tell me what you need!"

Swanson stepped back, wiped off the knife, and put it
away as he looked hard at the bleeding man strapped on the
bed. The guy was not holding back now, and further mutila-
tion would be counterproductive. The prisoner had reached
the point where he would say whatever he could guess the
interrogator wanted him to say. True or false didn't matter,
because he only wanted to stop the pain.

"Okay. I believe you." He opened a little box from his
medical kit. "I'm going to give you a shot of morphine now
to take away the pain. While you sleep for another hour, I'll
patch you up, and when you come around, we'll have something to eat and think this over." He injected the fluid into the
Frenchman's left arm, and within a couple of heartbeats
Falais's eyes fluttered and rolled back.

When the Frenchman was unconscious, Kyle undressed,
put on the Arab clothes he had stolen, and doused the light.
He put on his night-vision goggles again, checked outside,
and quietly loaded his pack, web gear, and rifles into the bed
of the pickup truck.

Back in the house, he reduced the single burner of the little propane gas stove to low, blew out the flame, then placed
a block of C-4 beside the stove, armed with a ticking detonator that would go off thirty minutes after the other house
exploded, causing still another diversion.

The Frenchman would not feel a thing. Swanson had not
wanted to torture him, but having done so, he would allow
the man a quiet, easy death. Falais was still asleep when

Kyle injected him with two more full Syrettes of morphine, and with each heartbeat, the narcotic overwhelmed his system. The man would never awaken. When the detonator ignited the C-4, the explosion would instantly set off the growing bubble of gas in the enclosed house and the place would blow up, taking the body of Pierre Falais with it. "I don't make deals with terrorists, particularly terrorists who have killed Marines," he whispered to the dying man.

Kyle Swanson turned off the bedside lamp, locked the door, went back over the wall, and was approaching the truck when he heard the grumble of heavy engines. He hit the ground and rolled under the Toyota just as a pair of BTR-80 armored personnel carriers of the Syrian Army roared past, their headlights flashing along the walls, seeming to search for him.

How did they get on my trail? Oh, fuck, Murphy's Law has screwed me again.

The huge vehicles continued down the street for a few more blocks and stopped at the house of the Americans. Soldiers jumped from the vehicles and spread into a perimeter around it, facing outward like guards, not inward like attackers.

CHAPTER 38

SWANSON WIGGLED FROM beneath the truck and rolled into the flatbed, unzipped the dragbag, rested Excalibur on the rear gate, and brought the scope to his eye. *Good as fuckin' daylight.*

He recognized the telltale four big wheels on each side of the vehicles, and the BPU-1 turret machine gun mounts. The Russians had been selling these relics all over the world for years, but the old dogs still had a lot of bite. His mind turned up the information on the weapons systems faster than a Google search: each carried a 14.5 mm KPTV heavy machine gun with five hundred rounds and a range of two kilometers, and a smaller 7.62 mm PKT machine gun with 2,000 rounds that could reach one and a half kilometers. Smoke grenade launchers were mounted on either side of the turret, and their beefy engines could shove them along at speeds of up to about 50 miles per hour. The lead vehicle bristled with the antennas that indicated a battalion commander might be leading the mission. *Is a whole damned battalion on the way?*

An officer climbed from the command vehicle, walked directly to the front door, and pounded hard. Lights came on, the door was thrown open, and the hulking Victor Logan stood there, wearing only a T-shirt and boxer shorts but carrying a pistol in his right hand. The Syrian was about half

Logan's size, but had an air of authority that made him immune from threat. They spoke for a few minutes, and Kyle
saw Logan nod in agreement, go back into the house, and return moments later, fully dressed. He climbed aboard the
lead BTR-80.

The officer waved his hand and sergeants barked orders.
Logan climbed awkwardly into the front vehicle with the officer and the other soldiers hustled back aboard. A single
man was left behind as a sentry and the BTRs pulled out,
heading toward the crash site.

The soldier stood at attention beside the front door of the
house, his AK-47 at the ready, as the carriers growled off into
the darkness. Swanson held his breath as they went past the
Zeus and the apparently dozing guard taped to it, but they did
not slow down.

The lights in the house were turned off and the soldier by
the door relaxed. He unslung the automatic rifle and rested it
against the wall, then sat on a wooden crate, leaned back,
and made himself comfortable, arms on knees. Through the
scope, Kyle watched the man reach into a chest pocket and
get a cigarette. A match flared.

As the soldier inhaled the first puff deeply, Swanson
lasered the range, and when the man exhaled, Kyle shot him
beneath the left arm. The bullet tore out the heart. There was
only a slight twitch of the body on impact; then it toppled
from the crate onto the dirt. Kyle put a second bullet through
the head to be sure he could not cry out a warning.

Swanson had to move fast because those BTRs would be
coming back. He returned Excalibur to its bag, climbed from
the truck bed, and transferred his primary weapons to the
passenger compartment. Then he slid behind the steering
wheel and cranked the Toyota, which started with a reliable,
deep rumble.

He did not have to disguise it, because that was the
essence of this "announced attack." By imitating the previous incident, and with the familiar sound of the Toyota in the
neighborhood, people would think that he was either the

Frenchman or somehow related to the arrival of the army unit. With any luck, Jimbo Collins would be trying to get back to sleep, not alert.

Kyle stopped in front of the house and, mirroring the actions of the Syrian officer, marched directly to the front door and pounded on it with his left fist as he pulled out his pistol with his right hand. Inside, the lamp snapped on again. He heard Collins curse aloud, "Oh, what the fuck do they want now?"

When the door opened, Kyle extended the big pistol and put one round right in Jimbo Collins's chest, knocking him backward, and fired another into his surprised face. He gave the collapsing body a hard shove so that it fell away from the door and did not block the exit. He stepped fast into the room with his pistol held straight out with both hands to scan for targets. There were none, and he closed the door.

There were two more doors in the rear and he chose the one on the left, stood with his back to the wall, and pushed it open with his left hand, the pistol pointing inward. No reaction, but there was a horrible stench, and enough light for him to see the defiled body of a young girl tied to a bed. *Sick bastards!* He did not have to feel for a pulse.

Swanson spun and kicked in the second door. A man wearing only boxer shorts lay handcuffed to a filthy bunk. He was unshaven, and the room stank. The man blinked in disbelief. All he saw was a silhouette until Kyle flipped a switch that turned on the bulb hanging from the ceiling.

"Hello, General," Swanson said, moving around the room, searching for unseen dangers, the pistol out, ready to shoot.

"What?" The voice was firm but raspy. Only moments ago, Bradley Middleton was thinking about having his head chopped off by lunatics, and now an escape was possible? "Who are you?"

"Take it easy, sir. It's Gunny Swanson."

"Swanson? Two hundred thousand Marines on active duty, and *you* are the first asshole through the door? They sent *you* to rescue *me*?"

The silenced pistol waved loosely between them. "Well, that's not exactly accurate, General," replied Kyle. "Actually, they sent me to kill you. Orders are orders, and a good Marine always follows orders."

CHAPTER 39

FOREIGN GOVERNMENTS THROW parties, receptions, or formal dinners every night in Washington to promote good-will and develop Beltway contacts. Tonight the Embassy of the Hashemite Kingdom of Jordan was honoring a young filmmaker who was creating a stir in Hollywood with his lat-est effort, *The Arab Street*. Some of the invited guests ar-rived at the embassy's ornate gates at 3504 International Drive NW in limousines, while others, mostly staff mem-bers from Capitol Hill, came by subway or walked, intend-ing to let the Jordanians feed them. Invitations to such parties saved on their food bills.

Shari Towne found a guard at the front gate and asked him to page the head of the public relations department. Within five minutes, a slim and elegant woman walked down a sculpted path toward the guard post. A snowy-soft Chanel blouse contrasted perfectly with the black pantsuit and the full dark hair that was cut to frame her face. A loose scarf of white Belgian lace wrapped her shoulders, and her long legs were accentuated by sharp Roger Vivier heels.

"Shari? Darling!" the woman exclaimed in a burst of sur-prise, opening her arms and wrapping her in a hug. "I didn't expect you come to our vapid little event tonight. Why didn't you call?"

"Hi, Mom," Shari responded, and tightly hugged her mother.

Layla Mahfouz Towne whispered, "This little movie director is simply awful, but he's signed a deal with Paramount, which gives us an excuse to throw another 'We're Not All Terrorists!' party." She detected the strain coursing through Shari. Her daughter seemed to be a brittle piece of glass that was about to shatter. "What?"

"I'm in trouble," Shari whispered back. "Can we go inside?"

Layla lifted an eyebrow, then told the guard, "She's with me." He nodded, looked at Shari's U.S. Navy uniform and identification card, and wrote out a pass. He thought they almost looked like twins. Very attractive twins.

Her mother led the way through the swirl of people who were washing down tiny pieces of food with liquor from an open bar, as a Jordanian-American oud player easily plucked the stringed instrument to provide classical Arabic music in the background. Layla said hello here and patted a shoulder there as she smiled a path through the crowd. Shari, although in a crisp white uniform, felt positively early Banana Republic beside her. Women usually felt frumpy in Layla's manicured presence. They went into her private office on the second floor.

As soon as the door was closed, Shari collapsed onto a big, soft sofa and stared at her mother and tears welled in her eyes. She began to cry, angry at herself for doing so. "I'm sorry, Mom. I'm really sorry for barging in like this."

Her mother kicked off her high heels and put an arm around Shari, rocking her back and forth, smoothing her hair and dabbing at the tears with a tissue. In Arabic, she said, "What's going on, Little One?"

The gestures were as comforting to Shari as they had been years ago when her father died in a plane crash. "Something big and complex and dangerous is going on and Kyle and I somehow got dragged into the middle of it," Shari sobbed. "I have to hide for a while, which is why I rushed over still dressed like this. The embassy, thank God, is foreign soil. This is Jordan. They can't touch me here."

"Who can't?"

"The United States government."

Layla gave her another little squeeze, and then put on her high heels again. "My, oh my, Little One. Just like your father, bless him. You never do things by half-measures, do you? I'd better go get the ambassador," she said. "He's an old Rolling Stones fan, and will welcome the chance to avoid having to listen to any more oud music. You, my dear, don't leave this room until I get back."

CHAPTER 40

HOW FRESH IS THIS MATERIAL?" National Security Advisor Gerald Buchanan asked as he scanned the computer-generated transcript of the conversation between Shari Towne and Master Sergeant Dawkins.

"Almost real-time," said Sam Shafer. "Thirty minutes max."

"Fast," said Buchanan with a nod of approval. He loved, and *love* was not too strong a word, to see the giant security apparatus of the United States bend to his will like a whipped puppy. The sheets of paper before him proved his reach and his power. He held a big whip.

"It's a pretty easy catch on the intercepts when the NSA has exact names and numbers, like her cell phones. She was near the White House when her call pinged the system. The computers automatically translated the audio into printed text."

Buchanan read the conversation again. Kyle Swanson was alive. The man he had sent to make sure Middleton died had almost been picked out of a damned hat, and not only had he turned on them, he had also had a link into this office! "So now we know what she saw, and the sniper is alive out there. What is this relationship between Towne and Swanson? Why should we care?"

"According to the gals in the secretarial pool, Commander Towne has kept it under wraps because she is an officer and he is an enlisted man. That kind of fraternization is against military regulations, although it is violated all the time."

"Ahhhhh!" Buchanan gave a grim smile. "One and one finally equal two. She had thought him to be dead, but the photos proved that he is not. She calls a mutual friend and realizes she has stepped in shit. Right?" He smiled with tight lips. "You have a chat with the secretaries?"

"Yes, sir. The ones whom we identified as her friends, or worked with her. Took them all to the safe house in Falls Church in a darkened van, had agents perform cavity searches to break their spirit, then put them one by one under the kleig lights, just like in the movies. They were most cooperative once I explained that it was a matter of national security and they would be held incommunicado under the Anti-Terrorism Provisos until we cleared this thing up. I pointed out that Section C states that if a White House employee is found to be an accomplice, that employee would face a secret military tribunal. They gave up everything. We also searched their desks, and the whole thing took less than an hour."

"There's no such Anti-Terrorism Provisos," said Buchanan.

"They didn't know that." Shafer wore a look of satisfaction.

Buchanan grunted a small laugh. "Where are they now? I noticed some new faces out there."

"Still up in Falls Church. Can't let them go until it's done. You know women can't keep secrets, and one of them would most likely confide in their husband, boyfriend, or particularly with a close girlfriend. Actually, I believe they feel kind of important right now, helping catch a possible terrorist. They were already whispering together about Commander Towne when I left. Probably guessing who will play who in the movie."

"So no one was hurt?"

"No. Just threw a scare into them is all. Time is of the essence."

Buchanan made a note. "When they come back to work, I'll put a confidential 'Attagirl' letter into each of their files and have it signed by the director of Homeland Security."

"Yes, sir," replied Shafer. "I pulled the Marine personnel jacket on Gunnery Sergeant Swanson and confirmed he has no identifying tattoos."

"So she called this other guy, who must be a close friend because they are on a first-name basis, and they agree that Swanson escaped the crash." Buchanan steepled his fingers beneath his chin as he thought out loud. "This Sergeant Dawkins also saw my letter and gave it to his commanding officer, a Colonel Sims." He hunched his fat shoulders and stared hard at his aide. "That is not good. You told me you destroyed the letter, did you not, Sam?"

"Absolutely, sir. After having Swanson open and read it, I then personally read, burned, and flushed it. Somehow while this big guy Dawkins was pulling me around the carrier on a wild goose chase, Swanson must have gotten to a copying machine. He's a resourceful son of a bitch."

"Not good. Not good at all. We must contain this circle of knowledge to only those four people. Where's Swanson?"

Shafer shook his head. "We don't know. In Syria somewhere, disobeying your order and apparently on a one-man raid to pull out General Middleton. He has shut down all electronic contact."

"And Lieutenant Commander Towne. Why do we not have her in custody?"

"Can't find her. Her apartment was locked, no lights or music on. The cell phone and her beeper were in a garbage can outside Starbucks. The gate log shows she never showed up at Quantico."

"At least the master sergeant is confined to a boat in the middle of the Mediterranean, so I can safely assume that Dawkins is now in the brig?"

Shafer was clearly uncomfortable as Buchanan led him on, pounding with question by question like a criminal prosecutor, knowing the answers before he asked. "No, sir. He's still on the carrier, we think, but the Naval Criminal Investigative Service agents have not found him yet. Dawkins is another one of those Special Ops types, and if he does not want to be found, we won't find him. Plus he has a lot of friends on that ship who probably are helping him stay hidden. And it's a really big boat."

Buchanan doodled on a white legal pad. "Send an instruction to the *Blue Ridge* captain to make a shipwide announcement ordering Dawkins to report the bridge. He won't disobey a direct order."

"Good idea, sir," Shafer responded. "But I think he will stay hidden if he considers the order to be illegal. Sooner or later, we're bound to find him."

"So that leaves us with Colonel Sims, the one carrying the letter itself."

"Another blank, sir. We have him arriving at Andrews Air Force Base a few hours ago, but then it's like he fell off the planet. The aircraft crew dropped him off at the dark end of the runway, didn't see anything, and assumed it was part of a clandestine operation. No records in the tower of any military or civilian planes taking off from Andrews at that time. The only thing that left was an experimental NASA scramjet headed for California on a test flight. So we can assume Sims is still around Washington trying to contact somebody at the Pentagon. The phone call mentioned that he would deliver the letter to 'someone higher up.'"

"Very well, Sam. Keep pulling out all the stops, on my authority. All four of them are now to be treated as national security risks. I want that letter back before the circle expands." Buchanan waved his hand and Shafer took the hint to leave. "Don't fail me, Sam. Understand?"

"Yes, sir. I'll get them." Shafer left the office feeling small saddlebags of sweat growing in his armpits. A White House assignment was always a prestigious stop on the career path and usually paid off with a lucrative K Street lobbying position, but his job was falling apart. *Damn that fucking Marine to hell!*

After his aide closed the door, Buchanan went to the wall safe and opened it. A hundred thousand dollars was in a padded envelope along with a valid Canadian passport, birth certificate, international driver's license, and authenticated work history under a false name, and several one-way airline tickets abroad with the flight dates left open. After making sure all was in order, he put the big envelope into his briefcase to keep it close for the next few days. He had no intention of letting these four small people ruin his lifetime plan to become the most powerful man in the American government, a strong Caesar needed for troubled times. Lock up Shari Towne, Swanson, Dawkins, and Sims in four prison cells, with no charges or trials or lawyers, and it would all be over. At least Gordon's people still had Middleton and he would be killed and done with. That led him to another idea: *Can I have them all executed, or killed while resisting arrest? Something to look into.* It was comforting to know that his documents and the cash were at hand.

Back at his desk, he punched a button on a red telephone, an encrypted line, and automatically dialed the private number of Gordon Gates. It was time to get some help.

"Yes, Gerald," Gates said in a calm voice, personally picking up the receiver after reading the identification number of the caller.

Without preamble and keeping his own voice as smooth as possible, Buchanan reported, "Gordon, it seems that we might have encountered some difficulty."

CHAPTER 41

SWANSON CONTINUED TO SCAN the dirty room with a careful visual search. Although the space was small enough to be taken in with a single glance, he always assumed the worst in a combat situation. Death could be waiting in a closet or a corner, behind a door or curtain, in a shadow, and he had learned from experience that the little bastard can hide anywhere. Only after he was sure no one else was present did he approach Middleton and said gruffly, "However, as you so often told anybody who would listen, I'm not really a very good Marine. So I'm going to disobey a direct order from the White House and get you out of here." Then he smiled. "Let's go home, General Middleton."

He examined the handcuffs. "One of the Americans put these on you? They're Smith and Wesson."

Middleton nodded, still numb from the sudden appearance of Gunny Kyle Swanson, the man he had considered too much of a weak link to be effective in special ops. True, he was good enough as a scout sniper, but he was not a team player at all, and Middleton had on several occasions witnessed the troubling sight of Swanson almost having a nervous breakdown after a battle. Those post-traumatic stress disorders following intense combat came on like thunderstorms, then disappeared just as fast and he would again be normal. Until the next time. The bottom line for Middleton was that he now had to put his life in the hands of an operator he did not really trust.

Kyle handed his pistol to the general, then rummaged through the butt pack on his web gear to get the survival kit, and from among the fishhooks, water purification tablets, bandages, and other items, he picked out a small plastic bag and opened it. "Standard issue. A Smith and Wesson universal key." He unlocked the handcuff with a single, smooth click. A red, blistered welt had been ground around the general's wrist.

"That feels good," Middleton said in a croaking voice, rubbing his sore arm to restore some feeling and blood flow. He handed the pistol back, levered himself into a sitting position on the bunk and groaned. "They busted at least one of my ribs, Gunny, but I can get around. Let's get out of here."

Kyle held up his palm, then put a finger to his lips. "Keep the noise down, sir. I don't think anybody is around to hear at this time of night, but we can't take the chance. Anyway, it's not quite time to leave yet." Kyle handed Middleton a full bottle of water. "Drink this. All of it, to hydrate." He unscrewed another bottle and drank it himself.

Middleton felt slightly better after the long drink, but when he tried to stand up, he was wobbly. Swanson steadied him until he regained his equilibrium.

"I'll tape your ribs, then get you into these fresh robes." He pulled out the clothes he had stolen and tossed them on the bed.

Every movement seemed to aggravate Middleton's broken rib, as if he were being prodded in his guts by a big needle. "Are you the only one here?" he asked.

"We sent in a Force Recon team to get you, but the helos somehow tangled up and crashed not far from here. I was thrown out through a hatch. Hold your arms out so I can wind this around you." Swanson spun the duct tape tightly around Middleton's stomach and lower chest. "I figured out later that we were flying into an ambush."

"Jesus, that smarts!" Middleton hissed through clenched

teeth, wincing in pain as the tape cinched tight. "Yeah, you were. I heard them talking about it."

"Sorry, sir. I'm not a medic and we just need to get you mobile. Broken rib hurts like hell, but it won't kill you." Kyle tore off an end of the tape, then ripped off a smaller piece and untied the strip of cloth binding the broken finger. Tied it more securely with tape. "How'd that happen?"

"I had a disagreement with one of the mercs. He was beating up on a woman in the next room."

"Yeah. I saw her before I came in here. Young teenager. He really worked her over before she died." Swanson shoved the remainder of the roll back into his pack. "You need help getting the clothes on?"

The general cursed Logan. "I figured he had killed her. Poor kid."

Swanson did not want Middleton to dwell on anything but their escape, so he held out the baggy pants and the general worked his legs in and tied them off with a loose belt, and they pulled the long shirt down over his torso. He found a pair of sandals and the general put them on. "Okay. Let's get you out to the front room."

Middleton took a shuffling step, and the next one came easier. By the time he reached a chair beside the table in the outer room, he was feeling stronger, and he sat down while Swanson gathered his gear. Jimbo Collins lay dead nearby, blood caking his face and chest. "The other guy, name of Vic Logan, will be back soon," he said.

"We'll be gone by then, sir. He headed out to the crash site with a bunch of Syrian Army types. We have a small cushion of time, but not much. Do you think you can fire a weapon?"

"Sure. Give me some more water, will you?"

Swanson handed him another bottle, then put some pita bread, orange juice, figs, and a Mars bar on the table. "Eat up, sir. We've got to wait a few more minutes before we take off."

The general did not question why. He gulped down the food and liquid, feeling strength surging back to him. "What did you do, Gunny, stop by Wal-Mart on the way over?"

Kyle had spotted the AK-47 on pegs above the front door when he searched the house, and took it down. Loaded and clean. He laid it on the table. "Something like that. Now here's what is going to happen. I planted bricks of C-4 around a house near here where a bunch of raghead fighters are sleeping. It's timed to go off in about sixty seconds. Right after that, you and I are through the front door and into a white Toyota pickup waiting outside, you in the shotgun seat with the AK. The moving will hurt, but you have to force yourself to get in quickly."

He rummaged through the room as he spoke, and ripped a good map off the wall and rolled it up. With the butt of his pistol, he smashed the satellite telephone, but when he started to wreck the two laptop computers, the general stopped him. "Wait! Take them along," said Middleton. "They are probably loaded with intel and e-mails about this whole operation."

Swanson stuffed the map and the laptops into his bulging pack and put it on. "Okay, here we go. Stand with your back against the wall beside the door. Keep the AK ready. I'll do the same thing over here."

Middleton hesitated, but got to his feet. "Watch your tone, Gunnery Sergeant."

"General Middleton, let's get this straight right now. Until we get out of this shithole, I'm in charge. You're my passenger and you do what you are told. Now get your fucking back up against that wall!"

Middleton moved, but with a frown. It felt good to have a weapon in his hands and no longer be helpless. He thought about the poor dead girl in the other room, and about the Marine and Saudi guards and his aide who were murdered in the ambush. He wished Vic Logan would walk through the door right now.

The explosion came with unexpected violence, and the concussion rocked the area. Swanson and Middleton felt the wall shake with the pounding stress, and the falling debris sounded like a hailstorm as the blast wave rolled over the village.

"NOW!" Swanson barked. "Go, go, go!" He led the way

out with his M-16 ready and ran to the driver's side of the truck, throwing his big pack and Excalibur into the bed as he jumped inside. Middleton limped behind him and clawed into the passenger seat. The night had changed to bright, dancing light and shadows as fire mushroomed upward from the destroyed structure, where secondary explosions from ammunition stored inside the house joined the carnage.

Kyle propped the M-16 beside him and turned the key, and the little truck's engine roared to life as people rushed out of their homes and into the streets. "You in?" he called over to the general as he pulled his night-vision goggles into place.

"Yeah. Let's go," replied Middleton. "Floor it."

The figure of a man with a weapon appeared in the road ahead and Swanson knocked him down, gaining speed, heading out of town. Middleton fired several bursts at other figures running toward the truck.

Swanson jammed the transmission into second gear, the four big tires dug hard, and the truck lurched ahead as if it was a racehorse. Kyle blessed the care the Frenchman had lavished on the vehicle, keeping it unremarkable on the outside but with powerful mechanical guts. He could feel the strength of the machine through the steering wheel. This was no standard Toyota engine. As he shifted into third as they swung past the big Zeus, they spotted a man climbing into the gunner's seat. With the accelerator on the floor, he sped away into the world painted green by the NVGs.

"Somebody's on the Zeus!" shouted Middleton, raking the area with an automatic burst.

"He's not a problem. I rigged it to blow up when the trigger is pulled."

Middleton pulled his AK-47 back inside and took some deep breaths. He was free! *Goddam!* "So what's the escape plan, Gunny?" he asked.

"We just did it, General," said Swanson. "From here, I got no fucking idea."

CHAPTER 42

MAJOR YOUSIF AL-SHOUM walked slowly around the remains of the crashed helicopters saying nothing, his eyes taking inventory. He was a small, quiet man whose frail physique belied his importance. It was his brain, not his physical strength, that had won him attention and respect within the Security Directorate in Damascus. He had graduated at the top of his class from the Military Academy at Homs, had advanced training in the old Soviet Union, and won both the Medal of Military Honor and the Order of Umayyads during his extended work in Lebanon and Iraq. Later, as military attaché at Syrian embassies in London and at the United Nations, he developed flawless English. Al-Shoum was a loner with a secret passion for American mystery stories. He conducted his investigations like a slow, plodding, methodical Los Angeles private detective.

He had been assigned to head a special investigation into the American raid and recommend what his government should do with the captive American general. Damascus had known about the abduction from the start, but never officially sanctioned the kidnapping. By turning a blind eye toward the operation, they gained a favor from the Rebel Sheikh down in Basra and several hundred thousand U.S. dollars in military credits from Gates Global. Now the abduction had become a diplomatic problem and Yousif Al-Shoum was to gather the facts and make a recommendation.

He originally planned to drive over to Sa'ahn on his own, but when word came that the Iraqi hotheads were planning to decapitate the American, Al-Shoum decided to bring the extra guns. He got them without difficulty because he was not really a major, but a general, and head of operations for the Security Directorate. Al-Shoum had chosen to use a lower rank because ordinary people became nervous around generals, and he might want to ask some important questions of the citizens. His security team knew his true identity because it was made up exclusively of soldiers chosen because they were loyal to him. After examining the attack area, he would take custody of the American Marine general. His country was not willing to get sucked into a war over this incident, which had not gone as smoothly as promised.

"You examined this site carefully, correct? And you determined that someone lived through the crash and escaped on a motorcycle." He spoke softly to the large American trailing him, who seemed elephantine in both body and mind.

"Yeah," said Victor Logan, drawing a sharp look for his discourteous manner. "Whoever it was headed west, toward the Israeli border. That's when he blew through those two idiots at the roadblock."

The little officer stroked his thick mustache and continued his circular stroll. He knelt and let a handful of dirt trickle through his fingers. Easy to leave tracks in this loose sand. *The Case of the Missing Marine.* "And you identified him."

"Not me, but our people did. Absolutely. Pictures and dog tags. Doesn't get any better than that."

"Actually, it can, Mr. Logan. Photographs can lie. Identification tags can be misleading." Al-Shoum turned to face the big man, rocking on his heels, looking up at him and motioning toward the horizon with a slow sweep of his right arm. "This land is filled with the bones of foreign soldiers who were never properly identified." He looked up at Logan. "I think you made a mistake."

"What?" Logan almost laughed in the midget's face. "This was a no-brainer, major."

"Suppose we postulate a new theory, Mr. Logan—that whoever got away wanted you to believe that he was someone else. Would he have had time to switch the dog tags?"

"Hell, no! These birds collided, fell down, and everybody died but one. End of story."

"I understand that. But in the very moments immediately after the accident, time stands still. The normal tendency of spectators to a disaster watching is to freeze where they stand, giving time for brain and body to cooperate, and even more time passed before people approached because the ammunition and fuel were exploding and burning hot. That is the reaction of a normal person, not a highly trained military professional. Several minutes passed, time enough for such a soldier to accomplish any number of things, and smoke and fire covered his escape. Therefore, your conclusion was only an educated guess, not much more than an assumption. Am I correct?"

"Then it was a damned good guess, Major. Sometimes things are exactly as simple as they appear. He was a young guy who took off, looking for safety."

"I disagree. Our helicopters and trucks have thoroughly combed the area between here and the Israeli border. Beyond the assault at the checkpoint, they have not found a trace of the man, nor of his motorcycle. Not even tracks."

"So he got lost in the desert. Big deal. He's dead no matter how you cut it."

They walked back toward the waiting armored personnel carriers. "I should have wanted more proof before reaching such a conclusion myself."

"Yeah. Right. So, then, what's your idea?"

Al-Shoum grimaced. "Bluntly put, Mr. Logan, you fucked up. You were the experienced military advisor on the scene and everything depended on your assessment. I think this Marine wanted everyone to believe he was a youthful radioman so they would consider him rather harmless, just as you have done, and not look too hard for him. I agree that we are facing only one man, but in my judgment, he obviously is a rather formidable opponent who has played you for a fool."

Logan wanted to pound the little Syrian Army officer on the head, grind the little shrimp beneath his boots. But he did nothing because they were surrounded by armed soldiers who were watching him closely. "Then who is he, and where is he?"

Before Logan could answer, a tremendous detonation rocked the village of Sa'ahn behind them as the house of the jihadists exploded. A column of fire shot into the black sky. The concussion rolled across the desert and shook the heavy BTR carriers on their tires. Everyone turned to watch, fascinated, frozen in place.

Al-Shoum recovered and sighed aloud. "I do not yet know the name of the Marine who escaped this crash, sir, for it is not the one you reported. But I do know where he is. He is right over there." The major pointed toward the fire and moved back toward his command vehicle.

"We will return to the village now, Mr. Logan. Unless I am gravely mistaken, you will find that your prisoner is gone. My country has been placed in a quite uncomfortable diplomatic position due to your stupidity and arrogance. Consider yourself under arrest." He motioned to his soldiers. "Take his weapons."

Victor Logan knew he was in shit up to his eyeballs. If he remained in custody, Gates Global would toss him to the wolves because the kidnapping had gone sideways. The little Syrian asshole was right; Vic had been in charge all the way. He and Jimbo would be disappeared, and he would never touch that pot of gold waiting for them.

The Syrians searched him thoroughly and stripped off all of his weapons, including the hidden boot knife. They had been well trained in that little science, which indicated that they were not common enlisted men, and he could expect them to be just as professional in other things, such as shooting a prisoner who tried to run away.

The best time to escape would be within the first few minutes, before the captors could lock him up tight and establish total control. But that damned explosion had heightened their alertness. They roughly pushed him aboard the carrier, leaving him untied so he could crawl inside. Which meant his hands would still be free when he got out. He still had a chance. An opportunity popped into his mind.

But even if he escaped from these dudes, where would he go and how would he get there? *One thing at a time, Vic. Get out of this mess first.*

He was jerked back against the small seat as the big vehicle lurched forward and turned around to head to the village. Logan kept his hands clasped in his lap, a picture of cooperation, the temporary victim of a misunderstanding between friends.

"Say there, Major?" he shouted over the sound of the engine.

Yousif Al-Shoum looked back at him from a front seat. Said nothing.

"My computer, back at the house. I think you'll be interested in some of the things I can do for you."

"Such as what, Mr. Logan? I can access as many computers as I need."

"But mine can get real-time American satellite imagery. I make a call on my sat phone, we're uplinked in half an hour. How's that?"

The major nodded his head and turned around again. "Hmmm," he said.

Logan did not really have access to those satellites, which were so deep within U.S. government security that they were well beyond even the reach of Gordon Gates. But the major did not have to know that, and Logan believed that by tossing out the satellite idea as bait, he had bought a few more minutes. The inference was that Logan had to be kept alive in order to obtain this help, thus bringing value to his life. They would keep his hands free if he had to work on the keyboard.

So when they walked through the door of the small house, it would be normal to have his hands raised slightly above his head, as if in surrender. He would grab the loaded AK-47 hidden above the door, spray the guards, and hope that Collins would be able to take down a few. Or they could at least force a standoff, with the soldiers still outside the house but with the little major inside as a hostage, with a rifle in his ear. Then Vic could deal on better terms. It is always better to negotiate from strength.

Then a second huge explosion flashed. The gunner on the Zeus had opened fire on the fleeing white truck, and the booby-trapped big gun blew to pieces when the bullets hit the C-4 explosives Kyle had stuffed down the barrels. Cases of ammunition then detonated around it with mighty stutters and new flames billowed up. Logan did not know what this one was, either, and the surprise was plain on his face. The little major turned again and stared at him with total disgust.

CHAPTER 43

SOME DIFFICULTY? GERALD, we have quite a bit more than that," Gordon Gates said after Buchanan briefed him. "You have let things go astray. I would have thought better of you."

"It will be brought under control soon, Gordon," Buchanan promised stiffly, feeling the back of his neck redden in embarrassment and anger. "I just wanted to keep you abreast of what was happening." He did not like being insulted, and did not miss the careful wording from Gates that this was a problem created by *Gerald Buchanan*. They were in this together! Was Gates distancing himself and his company from the national security advisor?

Buchanan took a deep breath to keep his voice calm, as if they were talking about the weather in Aspen rather than creating a constitutional crisis. "I think it would be good if you and I and Senator Reed meet and discuss our options."

Gordon Gates laughed, a cold sound that disturbed Buchanan's false calm. "Out of the question. You tell me you have things under control, so I shall accept your statement as fact. When you resolve your little 'problem,' Gerald, then we will get together."

Buchanan rocked back against his chair. "But, Gordon, I need your help!"

"Don't be a stupid ass. You are putting thousands of your

Junior G-Men all over this situation and there is no telling what they are going to do or uncover in their zest for carrying out your orders. If some eager beaver government cop stumbles onto the truth, *then* we will have a real problem. Isolate these people, Gerald, and take care of them. You've got Patriot Act IV, that Homeland Security Department, and every imaginable legal power you need. Damn, the attorney general would give you retroactive authority if you ask. You are *above* the law! How much more do you fucking need?"

"You won't help?"

"You do not need to know what I will or will not do." There was another long pause.

Buchanan could almost envision the lean face of Gordon Gates concentrating in thought. It was not the face of a businessman, but that of a killer.

Gates spoke. "You must convince the President to increase the threat level up to Red immediately. Make up some excuse tied to the Syrian situation or better yet, change the conditions of the entire argument. North Korea plans another nuclear test. Iran is gathering forces on the border of Iraq. Maybe a rogue Mexican Army unit plans to tear down part of the border fence. Use your imagination. Something international to make everyone look the other way and give us more cover. I give us no more than twenty-four hours."

"Twenty-four hours?"

"Yes. If that sniper brings General Middleton out of Syria alive, this whole thing will blow up in our faces. Middleton must be stopped, as well as all four of the other people who know about your order. You *must* get to them. Understand this, Gerald, everything is at risk here. Everything!"

"I can do it. I already have the machinery moving," Buchanan said.

Gates was thinking far ahead of him. "We're almost out of time. Once you get the red alert in full force, and homeland protection is at its maximum, I will signal my Shark Teams to prepare Operation Premier with terrorist attacks on multiplex theaters in Houston, Kansas City, Atlanta, and San Diego. They will be in position for simultaneous strikes within two days. Then some schools will be hit during the following week, and the shopping malls. Every day there will be something new until this country finally wakes up and realizes the military and police services and the civilian leadership, as currently constructed, are unable to protect them. Sad, but true."

"I see. Can we avoid significant casualties?"

Gates exhaled in frustration. "Don't be thick, Gerald. It is only when we sustain major civilian losses that this country will finally turn in the direction it needs to go. It cannot move that way now because of that old piece of paper called the Constitution. When television sets across the land show horrific pictures of thousands of dead Americans—many more than 9/11—including a lot of kids, for hour after hour, day after day, you just make sure you have the Declaration of Martial Law ready, as well as your new draft constitution."

"Very well." Buchanan was sweating.

"Now buck up, Gerald, old boy. Do your job and you will be running the United States of America in a couple of weeks. The clock is ticking. I look forward to talking with you after you have sewed up these loose ends. Meanwhile, you give me every scrap of information you have on those people. Maybe there are some ways I can help after all." He terminated the call.

Only then did Gordon Gates let his anger show. He threw a delicate bowl of blue glass made in Venice against a wall. It shattered, and he yelled aloud, "Buchanan, you goddam fuckup!" Buchanan didn't have the balls or the smarts to take out those four people, because he had never lived in the dark world of spies and special operators. *I have to clean up your shit! You are weak!* Gates poured a stiff Scotch and took a deep drink as he stared out the window at the lake behind his home. Then he activated a special communications device on his desk and prepared to send encrypted messages to some of the Shark Teams. Some would independently be sent to hunt down the four people who had become threats.

He had come too far, planned too much, and spent too much money to let an incompetent bureaucrat like Buchanan screw things up. Operation Premier would go forward, and faceless terrorists would be blamed for the tragic attacks.

He knew the idea of staging false attacks was not original. The Pentagon had seriously considered the tactic back in the 1960s to whip up a frenzy for an invasion of Cuba—shooting down a moon rocket and an airliner, hitting some civilian targets, and killing important officials, blaming it all on Castro. But President Kennedy intervened and trashed those plans. Gates had studied the scheme in detail at the War College, and thought it might have merit in the modern world. This time, he would run it privately so no governmental leadership could block the attacks.

The United States would cry out for someone who could stop the fighting and erase the fear but still guarantee rights for a free people, within reason. Who better to step in and bring order out of chaos than a decorated war hero, a proven patriot, who was at the helm of the world's largest private security company?

First, he had to clean up Buchanan's mess, including that sniper in Syria.

CHAPTER 44

AS SOON AS KYLE SWANSON saw the headlights of the troop carriers begin to move away from the crash scene, he swerved the pickup truck off the road to the right and down into a wadi that spread into a cultivated field. He stopped beside a thick stand of trees and brush and turned off the motor. The dust the truck had kicked up settled to the road, leaving no trace of their passing.

General Middleton whispered, "What are you doing? Get the hell out of here."

Swanson held up a finger to silence him. Within thirty seconds, the two big armored personnel carriers roared past, heading back to the village where ammo was still crackling in the two separate fires.

Kyle jumped out, dug through his pack, and grabbed a claymore mine bandoleer. Middleton still wanted to move out. "What are you going to do now? Get back behind the wheel! Let's go!"

"I'm going to plant a claymore out on the road," Swanson said as he swung the bandoleer over his shoulder.

"A claymore won't destroy a BTR-80, Gunnery Sergeant Swanson."

"No shit, Brigadier General Middleton," Swanson shot back. "But the next vehicle moving down the road will probably be one of those BTRs coming after us. With any luck the claymore can puncture the tires, maybe even the gas tank, and also take out whoever has their heads above the armor. The other BTR will stop because they will be worried about an ambush or another booby trap."

"Think, Swanson! It's a waste of time. The other one will just swing around the wreck and keep going."

"No, dammit, *you* think! It will take me three minutes to plant this thing, with the trip wire. When the first BTR is hit, even if it is not disabled, they will stop to sort things out. That will mean at least a ten-minute delay. Do the math, general. We get a net gain of at least seven extra minutes . . . that is, if you will shut the fuck up and let me get on with my job."

Kyle scrambled up the incline of the wadi and opened the claymore kit bandoleer. He loved these things, and his fingers worked fast as he checked off the familiar equipment— the powerful M18A1 mine, the M57 firing device, the M40 test set, the spool with a hundred feet of firing wire, the electrical blasting cap, insulation tape, and two wooden stakes. The whole deadly thing in a single handy package.

The Germans in World War II had invented the concept of a mine with a concave surface that would be capable of slinging a solid slab of steel through the armor of an enemy tank. By Vietnam, almost every American infantryman carried the modern lightweight version of the claymore, which was an inch and a half thick and packed with C-4 explosive and 700 steel balls that could devastate enemy personnel and take out thin-skinned vehicles. Swanson considered it the perfect ambush and perimeter defense tool. The trick was to remember how to place it correctly. It had not been named the claymore for nothing, because like its namesake. the ancient Scottish broadsword, it could cut both ways. The soldier setting it off with the clacker had to be at least about twenty yards behind it and under cover because of the backblast. Embossed on the lethal side of the olive-drab casing was the reminder, FRONT TOWARD ENEMY.

Swanson braced the mine solidly into the dirt with its built-in spikes, stretched the trip wire low across the road, about four inches above the surface, and tied it off to one of the stakes. He ran a quick circuit test and stacked some brush and twigs over the mine. He was counting on the darkness, and the Syrians not expecting to be hit. When the BTR ran over the trip wire, those hundreds of steel balls would blow out up to a height of six feet and in a 60-degree arc, with a casualty reach of up to 330 feet.

He hurried back to the pickup, restarted it, and threw it into low gear. They crashed through the brush and up the side of the wadi, back to the road on the far side of the mine.

"What if a civilian vehicle comes along first?" asked Middleton.

"Jesus, you're a worrywart," snapped Swanson. "You want me to go back and put up a warning sign? With so much stuff going on, the civilians are staying put. And if it happens, it happens. But it won't." He was already tired of Middleton and they had a hundred miles to go.

They sped along in silence with the lights off, and Kyle eyed the familiar surroundings through his NVGs.

Middleton seemed to relax a bit. "They still call you 'Shake'?"

"Don't start that shit on me now, General. We can argue later. Right now, I'm sort of busy." Swanson removed his foot from the accelerator and let the truck coast to a stop without touching the brake.

"Now what?" Middleton shifted in his seat, picking up the Kalashnikov.

"There's a checkpoint up ahead, about a kilometer."

"How do you know? Can you see it from here?"

"No, but I've already taken it out once," Swanson said. "On the way in." He climbed into the bed of the truck.

"So we're going to do it again?" the general asked through the small window behind the passenger compartment. "How?"

"With Excalibur." He unfastened the protective drag bag and removed the long sniper rifle.

"It's too dark and too far away," Middleton protested. "You can't hit them from here no matter how good you think you are. All you're going to do is alert them and give them time to radio for help."

Kyle adjusted Excalibur and racked a round into the firing chamber, then threw his pack on the cab of the truck and pressed a groove in it to use it as a steady platform. He took off the NVGs and clicked on the scope, dialing it to night vision. The scene lit up almost like daylight as the sensors grabbed every available source of light and heat and amplified them, and then the computer enhanced the forms it saw.

One guard was seated atop the checkpoint shack, smoking a cigarette. The other was standing to one side. Both had rifles and were looking at the glow from the village, watching the distant fiery show instead of looking for intruders. Kyle put the crosshairs on the standing man and let the scope do the math and automatically make the adjustments while he took up slack on the trigger. The blue strip flashed and he squeezed the trigger to complete the shot.

The soldier was caught center mass and the big bullet tore through him as it slammed him back against a pile of sandbags. As Kyle racked in a new round, the other guard, apparently thinking his partner had tripped and fallen, stood and looked over the edge to see what had happened. Only two seconds passed before Kyle got the blue stripe again. He fired. At that last moment, the target moved, and the bullet meant for the chest went in above his ear and took off most of his head.

Swanson returned Excalibur to its sheath, dumped his pack into the bed of the truck, and climbed back into the driver's seat. "There. That was easy, wasn't it?" He put the NVGs on, gunned the engine, and took off.

As they maneuvered through the roadblock, Middleton saw that both guards were dead, and the skull of one had been crushed by the force of the bullet. *Shake made a head shot in the middle of the night, while standing in the back of a pickup truck from a klick away, and thought it was easy?*

"Umph," the general said in reluctant approval. "You hit him in the head."

Swanson just drove.

CHAPTER 45

YOUSIF AL-SHOUM, STANDING in the hatch of his BMR, saw the smoking ruin of the quad-barrel Zeus as they entered the village. Clumps of junk littered the street in front of the Americans' house, debris blown over from the demolished building of the jihad fighters, which burned with fury. The door to the Americans' place had been splintered by the force of the blast and was hanging on a single hinge. The body of the soldier he had left on guard was sprawled dead beside the steps. He ordered both vehicles to a stop, and his men formed a perimeter.

"Mr. Logan, you come with me." Logan wiggled from the hatch behind him and a soldier followed with a pistol at Logan's back. "Call out to your friend," Al-Shoum ordered.

"Hey, Collins! Jimbo! You in there? It's me, Vic. Put down your weapon. We're coming in." Logan stepped to the doorway, but the officer cut in front of him with his pistol out.

"I will enter first." He stepped around the sagging door and into the room. The body of Jimbo Collins was sprawled in a corner. Al-Shoum moved toward the back of the house.

Logan kept his hands above shoulder level as he went up the steps with the guard at his heels. It was now or never. Get the AK, spray the guard, and take the smarmy little officer as a hostage. When he cleared the doorway, Logan back-kicked the guard and sent him reeling. He reached up to snatch the AK-47 waiting above the door, but his hands closed on thin air and his palms slapped the empty wall. He looked up. The gun was gone. NOTHING! He lowered his hands.

The major spotted the pegs. "A weapon was hidden up there, wasn't it, Mr. Logan? For emergencies . . . like this." Al-Shoum smacked Logan's head with the butt of his pistol and Vic staggered, seeing stars. "You were going to try to escape, and maybe shoot me in the process." Two soldiers ran in, grabbing and punching Logan. "Try something like that again, and you will be as dead as your friend in the corner. Now where is the general?"

"Over there, that room behind that door." Logan pointed. "Handcuffed to the bed."

Al-Shoum opened the door, took a look, and stepped right back out. "No one is there. It seems that you have lost your most prized possession. So what about this magic computer? Where is it?"

Logan looked at the table where the laptop usually rested beside the secure telephone. The phone had been crushed, and both computers were gone. He began walking around the room, looking for a place where Jimbo might have hidden them. "It has to be here somewhere. When I find it, I'll show you what we can do. Gates Global has a fantastic network." He rummaged through the kitchen area and the meager belongings in the living quarters, his mind working fast. The damn things were obviously gone.

"And what is this!" The Syrian officer had opened the door to the second bedroom and seen the naked and tortured body of a young girl exposed on the bed, with flies feasting on the dried blood and cuts. Her wide, lifeless eyes stared toward the door and a wide strip of tape was on her mouth.

Logan pushed past him, ran into the room, and came to a stop beside the body. It was time for the performance of his life, or he was breathing his last breaths. He thought of Charles Bronson, but he needed emotion, some heavy Clint Eastwood. "Ohhh. Nooo! Jimbo, you fucking bastard!" he howled in mock outrage. He stormed back to the body of Jimbo Collins and kicked it hard in the ribs. Again. "You sick fucking bastard! Couldn't keep your hands off her! I hope you rot in hell!"

Logan turned to the officer, panting and trying to appear shocked. "She was our cleaning girl, and Jimbo was always giving her the eye, saying what he wanted to do with the kid. He was a sick fuck with a record of sex crimes that got him thrown out of the army. I made him leave her alone because we were here to run an operation, not get involved with his sex fantasies. The sick asshole probably raped her this afternoon, and I didn't know because I came in late. I didn't even know she was in there!"

"A young Muslim woman has been defiled and murdered by you infidels," the major said with stone in his voice. "You tried to find a hidden weapon, your computer has apparently been taken along with the missing general, and somebody is waging a one-man war out there." He buried the barrel of his pistol into Victor Logan's stomach, then pushed it up his chest and beneath his chin. "I have run out of reasons to keep you alive, Mr. Logan, other than to let the villagers kill you slowly for the death of that child. I'm sure they would be quite imaginative in the punishment. I will suggest that long knives play a part."

For one of the few times in his life, Victor Logan felt fear. "I didn't have anything to do with the girl!" he protested, now Charlie Sheen earnest, like in the movie when he was pitching for the Cleveland Indians. "I didn't touch her. I swear, Major. Jimbo wanted her!"

"Stop lying!" The major cracked him with the pistol butt again. "We can smell the body rotting from out here. You did it yourself, or you let it happen. You are nothing but a piece of filthy trash. Either way, under our laws, you will be put to death. I can give you a bullet in the head right now, but I would prefer that you be gutted in public."

Logan was sweating hard. "Come on, man. Don't even think like that. You know that through Gates Global, I got a lot of resources. Let's just get another computer and I can try to link up with my passwords. I'll give you anything you want to know." He was bartering for time again. Having both computers suddenly go missing had worked to his advantage because he did not have to deliver on his promise yet. And he didn't think the officer was really all that upset over the whore. He had seen how Arabs treated women.

"That will take some time," the Syrian replied. "There probably are no more computers in the entire village."

"Yes, there is. I know of one," Logan said, a desperate idea bouncing into his head. "There's a Frenchman who was helping us. He lives just a few blocks away. I know that he uses a laptop for his business, and has wireless reception. Maybe I can rig that up to do the job." He could always make it *not* work, and blame it on sand or poor construction, or some other problem. Anything to stop this little shit from killing him for a few more minutes.

"Really? In my opinion, we are wasting time. I want to go find your escaped general now."

"Look, Major, I know you think I'm a fuckup, but there are other ways that I can still help you get him. Really, I can. The Marine who snatched the general has to be some sort of special ops dude, which means that he and I went through all of the same schools and training in the States, because I used to be a Navy SEAL. *I can think like him!* I know his limitations and his strengths and what his choices will be. I can help you find them." Logan was just treading water now, grabbing at straws to stay afloat, to stay alive.

"We have plenty of people trained in special forces techniques. I don't need you."

"Are they right here? Right now? How many of them went to U.S. spec ops courses? I guarantee this guy would run rings around any of them."

"Like in the mystery books, Logan? It takes a thief to catch a thief?"

"You got it. And I want this guy as badly as you do. I know that you will pop me if I don't catch him. He's my ticket out of here, right?"

"Maybe." Al-Shoum told a couple of soldiers to go to the

Frenchman's house and fetch his computer. He had known Pierre Falais for a number of years and considered him one of the better sources of information from the outlying territories, although he played all sides of the street. But Falais obviously had not reported everything he knew about the kidnapping of the American. He made a mental note to have a talk with him a little later.

Al-Shoum dialed a number on his cell phone and got his office in command in Damascus, reporting in rapid Arabic that the Marine general had escaped, apparently with the assistance of a skilled American special forces operator. He paused, listening, and wrote in a notebook. He replied with some questions and listened to the answer with a frown, then closed the telephone.

"Our intelligence sources have come up with the name of the man behind all this," he told Logan. "He is a U.S. Marine sniper named Kyle Swanson. Apparently he is very good, and sometimes does special work for the CIA. The bad news is that Damascus is pressing me to decide what our government should do."

"You get to make that kind of decision?" Logan asked.

"I work in the Security Directorate as the director of operations, and rank is meaningless, because I have the authority to do anything I need to do. That means that I can have you killed at any time and no one will question it. Are we clear?"

Victor Logan nodded vigorously. *Jesus H. Christ! Their top spook!*

Al-Shoum turned on his heel, heading for the door. "I'm going to let you live a while longer, Logan. You will be my hound going after this fox. And you had better prove that you are very, very good at the job."

Logan kept his face iron-straight. "Not to worry, General. I'll get 'em back."

Another thunderous roar shook the village when the booby-trapped home of the Frenchman blew up three blocks away. Al-Shoum was flung against a wall, and a sharp piece of flying glass sliced the arm he threw up over his face to protect his eyes. Logan was tumbled to the floor and the table collapsed on top of him. Dirt poured from the ceiling, and windowpanes crinkled the floor with glass shards. The men looked at each other.

"Let me guess. The Marine visited the Frenchman's house, too." Al-Shoum got up and brushed himself off, casually pulling the fragment of glass from his arm, then stomped outside and watched the latest fire. A soldier rushed up to bandage the wound. "You are one pathetic operator, Logan."

Behind him, Victor Logan suppressed a grin. There went that computer, too.

CHAPTER 46

AMBASSADOR SAMIR ABU-ADWAN of Jordan picked at his dark mustache as Shari Towne told her story. Her mother, his good friend Layla Mahfouz Towne, sat beside Shari, gently holding her hands. Layla had given him a synopsis, and he now listened to Shari himself with growing shock and indignation. Abu-Adwan knew the President of the United States would never order the assassination of a kidnapped Marine general. If such an order came from the White House, it certainly had not come from the President. Shari Towne's superior was running amok and creating an international crisis.

"You do not have a copy of this letter yourself, Shari?" he asked in a smooth baritone voice that showed sincere sympathy. As a veteran diplomat, he had many voices for different situations, but he knew that if he tried any disguise now, Layla would see right through it. Better to be honest.

"No, Mr. Ambassador. I don't."

"And you have never even seen a copy of it, either, am I correct?"

"That's right."

The ambassador entwined his fingers and rested his chin on them. "Gerald Buchanan is a shifty weasel," he said. "Such a thing is not beyond him. I sincerely doubt that the

President knows anything about this. Your information adds significantly to the new situation."

Layla blinked. "What situation?"

"One reason that I am being such a bad host and ignoring my guests is that something urgent has come up. The Department of Homeland Security has increased the terror alert status to Red, the highest level, and television networks are reporting that American intelligence agencies have picked up credible evidence of a possible terrorist strike against the United States. I think our party downstairs will be breaking up very soon as people learn that. From what you have told me, this alert also bears Buchanan's fingerprints."

"There was no such terrorist chatter mentioned just a few hours ago when I was at the National Security Council meeting," Shari said, shredding the tissue clutched in her hands. "In fact, everything was focused on Syria and General Middleton. Usually these things take time to build up enough to get our attention. Since the Middle East was my desk, I certainly would have heard something, and I haven't."

"That brings me to the other matter," said Abu-Adwan. "We have received notification from the State Department that U.S. military action is now being contemplated against Syria."

"But why?" Shari was on her feet now, pacing the elaborate burgundy carpet, the tears gone and her mind again at work, picking at the puzzle. "We have no true evidence of Syrian involvement, at least officially. The general was kidnapped in Saudi Arabia, not Syria! Why would they take him back to their country and make a big announcement about it, then allow some terrorist group to threaten a public beheading, which would be a hostile act guaranteed to inflame the United States, just as it is happening right now?"

"Why indeed?" replied the ambassador. "That is why you and I and your mother are going over to State right now to ask these same questions. Before I came to see you, based on Layla's comments, I made some telephone calls and arranged a meeting with Undersecretary James Dalton and the ambassadors from Syria, Israel, and Lebanon to try to make sense of what is going on. Amman has advised me to relay the great concern of King Abdullah and our government about this situation. I asked to include you in our meeting. Mr. Dalton told me that you are a fugitive from justice."

That hit Shari hard, and she took a deep breath. "It's not a good feeling to be considered a traitor to my country."

"I know, Shari. You've done the right thing, and we will smooth it all over after we douse this crisis. For your information, our Syrian neighbors disclaim any active participation in the kidnapping. Didn't even know it had happened until General Middleton showed up in their backyard. They also are distancing themselves from the Rebel Sheikh in Iraq, who is getting too strong and influential for the tastes of many of us. They think that despite what he claims, the sheikh arranged to place Middleton in Syria to embarrass Damascus and cover his own involvement."

"Can we believe the Syrians?" Shari looked at him hard.

The ambassador nodded. "They don't mind plucking a tail feather out of the American eagle every once in a while, but this incident is spinning far beyond anything they had bargained for. They definitely do not want to bring a hail of cruise missiles down on their heads." He stood up and adjusted his impeccable suit.

"Now, Shari, I think I have a bit of good news for you. There are some reliable reports from Syria that General Middleton is no longer in captivity, and that he escaped with the help of an American Marine who survived the tragic helicopter crash. It seems like your friend Kyle Swanson and General Middleton are on the loose."

Shari sat down beside her mother. "Thank God! They're both safe?"

"Apparently for the moment, but Syrian army units are in pursuit. Let's hope we can settle this mess diplomatically before there is a confrontation," the ambassador responded. "Shall we go?"

Shari balked. "They will arrest me."

"Shari, you must turn yourself in. I will deliver you personally to the undersecretary at the Department of State, and you will tell him your story. There is a high probability that you will never be taken into custody. In addition, the presence of your mother, myself, and the other ambassadors will guarantee an unpleasant diplomatic incident if Mr. Buchanan tries to take any hasty action."

"You don't know Buchanan, Mr. Ambassador. He can do anything he wants to do. If I give myself up, I may be spending the next few years in some dark prison in the middle of nowhere."

The ambassador lowered his voice. "I do not intend to let you out of my sight until this matter is resolved. I promise that you won't get lost in the system. Undersecretary Dalton is an old friend and an honorable man, and the information you possess is of such value that you were right to seek our protection. Turning yourself in will demonstrate that you were simply trying to stay alive long enough to get the truth out. In fact, I think your government will probably want you to be a witness against Mr. Buchanan in a courtroom. They also will be very appreciative that you did not go to the media with this."

Ten minutes later, Shari was in the front seat of a black Mercedes, beside a handsome Jordanian soldier who served as a combination driver and bodyguard. Her mother sat in back with the ambassador, who was talking on his cell phone.

The ambassador had been correct, and the embassy party had emptied quickly as word spread of the unexpected increase in the terror alert, everyone forsaking the food and drink tables to rush back to their offices to cope with whatever was happening. Taxis sailed about and traffic was heavier than normal for the hour.

The Mercedes with diplomatic license plates drove easily through the streets of Embassy Row and Shari drew comfort from the familiar monuments and squares of Washington, which was aglow in the early night. People had gotten off work and were packed into the bars and restaurants, and the nightlife was beginning to throb. The driver edged around a bicycle messenger with a flashing taillight. Even at night, those bikers were an effective way to get important documents from one federal department to another, or to bureaucrats from the K Street lobbyists, and the government never really slept.

The car stopped at a red traffic signal, third in line, and Shari knew the State Department was only about five blocks away. Maybe they could stop this madness. And she could not help but be happy that Kyle was alive. If he had Middleton and they were escaping, Kyle was in his element and would use every trick in the book to elude pursuit. Soon they would be together again.

She was startled by a tap on her window, and the bike messenger smiled and made a hand motion to roll the glass down. Beneath the visor of his black helmet, she saw that he had a lean face, with a neat beard and bright teeth. He probably wanted directions. As the driver looked over at the noise, another bike rolled up on his side, and its rider slammed a small sledgehammer into the window, stuck a SIG-Sauer pistol into the jagged hole, and fired four bullets into the distracted young driver. Shari screamed and covered her face with her hands as the man's blood and brain matter splattered her. Restrained by her seatbelt, she could barely move.

The biker on her side then used a hammer of his own to smash through her window, and Shari felt glass shards cut into her, sharp pins and knifelike slashes chewing at her skin. In the back seat, Layla screamed, and leaned forward to try to reach Shari while Ambassador Abu-Adwan scrambled to grab a pistol secreted in the armrest. Both bikers now had their pistols inside the car and sprayed full clips at all of the passengers while shouting *"Allahu Akbar,"* the familiar "God is great" war cry often used by terrorists.

They remounted the bikes and sped away through a park, lights off, cutting sharp corners and disappearing into the darkness in moments. Two hand grenades they left behind detonated inside the Mercedes, setting the big car afire as stunned pedestrians and other drivers who had moved forward quickly backed away.

The bikers rode up a platform into the rear of a waiting panel truck bearing the logo of a plumbing company that was parked in a loading zone outside a restaurant. The doors were shut behind them and the blue truck moved out into traffic, heading for a garage in a run-down area of suburban Maryland.

In Alexandria, Virginia, Gordon Gates watched the entire attack unfold on a television screen through streaming video transmitted live by small cameras mounted on the bike helmets of the Shark Team. Buchanan had fed him the information intercepted from the Jordanian Embassy after the NSA computers picked up the name of Shari Towne. Gates assigned the job to his closest sharks, and they did well, he thought. One down.

CHAPTER 47

ARE YOU GOING TO HAVE ONE of your little mental earth-quakes now?" General Bradley Middleton did not take his hand from the AK-47 or stop scanning the darkness moving around the truck.

"You better hope I don't." Swanson kept his eyes on the road, watching a landscape painted green and black in his NVGs. He maneuvered around potholes, driving as fast as he dared without lights. "You know what I like best about being a sniper?"

"What?"

"I get to pick my partner, so at least I'm with someone I like. Unlike now."

The two men settled into an uncomfortable silence as Swanson drove due west. Every kilometer they covered added to what he considered a growing debt of good luck that would not last forever. They were about six klicks out of Sa'ahn, had seen no other vehicles, and the truck was run-ning smooth.

"There's a McDonald's up the road a couple of miles," he told the general. Swanson was extending an olive branch be-cause they had to work together. In this kind of situation, there should be only one enemy. "We can stop and get coffee and a Big Mac."

Middleton actually grunted what might have been a laugh under other circumstances. He wanted to back off, too. "I prefer Burger King. Double Whopper with cheese. Flame-broiled."

"Of course you would. You argue about everything?" Kyle asked.

"Yep. I'm what they call a contrarian." Middleton sucked in a sharp breath, and his words were hoarse.

"I was lying about the Mickey D's." He handed the general a canteen of water. "We'll be able to eat in a little while. How you feeling?"

"Been better. Been worse." Middleton paused, and seemed lost in thought and more focused. He said, "Who sent you to kill me?"

Swanson slowed and steered off the road to avoid a ragged, deep hole. A sharp bump like that might make the broken rib puncture Middleton's lung. "Gerald Buchanan, the national security advisor, wrote the order directly to me on official White House stationery. He didn't give a reason, just the assignment. If the mission to rescue you failed, I was to shoot you."

"He can't do that."

"Well, he did." Kyle pushed the accelerator back down to regain his speed, and another kilometer passed beneath their wheels. "He bypassed the military chain of command by handling it through the CIA, which has used me once in a while. It was handed to me by a guy from his office."

"Why would he want me killed?" Middleton asked.

"Beats the hell out of me, General. But you do tend to piss people off. Why were those American mercs involved?"

"They worked for Gates Global. That's who organized the kidnapping, I think, because of my opposition to the military privatization bill. They were going to let the damned jihadists chop off my head anyway, so why would Buchanan send you out to do the same job, other than as an insurance policy in case that plan failed? There must be a direct link between Gates and Buchanan." He sucked in another breath with a grimace.

Kyle removed his night-vision goggles. The black sky was showing the first signs of the new day, and he could make out shapes along the road. "General, keep in mind that our whole rescue mission was a setup. We were flying into an ambush. We were never supposed to succeed. I might not have even gotten through. Only somebody pretty high up could have gotten that information to the mercs. Buchanan would have been in the loop somewhere."

"Damn. I need to think about this for a while." Middleton fell silent.

Pinpoints of headlights crossing the road far ahead were easily visible in the remaining night. "Those have to be trucks on the main highway between Damascus and Amman," Kyle said. "End of the road for us."

Middleton watched the busy traffic, drivers hurrying with their loads to reach their destination before the sun rose and the heat of the day baked the roadways. "So we wait for a break and just scoot across. The Golan Heights are what, about thirty or forty klicks straight west?"

"We're not going that way," Swanson answered.

"But the Israeli army is all over those hills," Middleton shot back. "It's the quickest way out of here, and solid protection when we reach them."

"There are just as many Syrian soldiers on this side of the border, General, and they all will be looking for us. Hold on." Kyle found a narrow, paved frontage road that paralleled the main distant highway and skidded onto it with a sharp right turn that took them off the pavement. He intentionally clipped a traffic sign, crushed roadside brush, and shifted into a lower gear to dig deep ruts, leaving a clear trail before entering the northbound road.

The general was shoved against the door by the force of the turn and yelped in pain. "You're going north? Toward Damascus?"

"Of course not." Kyle stopped the truck and did a three-point turn to head back the way they had come, careful to stay on the pavement. He jumped out and used a small bush as a broom to erase marks of his reversed turn. The bush went into the truck bed and he headed east again.

"We'll double back for a couple of klicks. The stuff I did back in the village and the claymore ambush worked better than we thought. It slowed them down so much that I haven't seen the BTRs or anybody else on our tail. There are no headlights coming this way, so I think they stopped to regroup and call for help." He mashed the accelerator, tearing along the quiet road.

"There's a little road back here that heads south. We'll get on it for a little while, then hole up for the day. They're going to have a lot more choppers up as soon as daylight comes, so we can't run in the morning hours. Both of us need rest, too. I haven't slept in two days and you're hurt."

Middleton leaned back against the seat. "Not the way I'd do it, Gunny."

"I know. It's hard to stay still when the natural inclination is to haul ass, but this is how to best exfiltrate enemy territory and get out of here alive. Right now, they don't know where we are, and probably will conclude that we are heading straight for Israel. So we have to do something else, and going north to Lebanon isn't an option."

The countryside rolled by as the sky lightened to a warm gray, and as the very edge of the fiery sun showed above the horizon and into his eyes, he found the road and turned right. The Syrians would try to cordon off all of the escape possibilities. Swanson felt exposed and vulnerable with morning coming on so rapidly, the sun seeming to point at him, giving away their position. There was nowhere to hide.

CHAPTER 48

HELLO, RALPH. AREN'T YOU supposed to be on the other side of the world?" General Hank Turner returned Colonel Ralph Sims's salute and shook his hand. Turner introduced Sims to a three-star air force general with short silver hair who sat behind a huge desk in a spacious office where pictures of airplanes covered the walls.

Lieutenant General Peter Brady, commander of the 11th Air Force, also shook Sims's hand, and his dark eyes examined the disheveled appearance of the commander of the 33rd Marine Expeditionary Unit. "You look a little worse for wear, Colonel. Have a chair. Coffee?"

"Thank you, sir, I will. I just came in on a meteor, that NASA X43-D scramjet." Sims was wearing a borrowed air force jacket over his short-sleeved summer uniform. What was appropriate wear in the warmth of the Med offered little comfort at Elmendorf Air Force Base outside Anchorage, Alaska. Only a few hours earlier, his uniform had been crisp and starched, and now it was a mass of deep wrinkles.

General Brady's eyes narrowed. "Colonel, there is no such aircraft, but I would like to know how the hell you were riding in it."

"Yes, sir, I understand. I've never heard of such a plane either, and I'm not quite sure how I ended up in the back seat.

The pilot told me to get in, and I did." He sat down, wrapping his palms around a warm mug. "Forgive my appearance. I barely had time to change out of the flight suit before your command sergeant major hustled me over here."

General Turner refilled his own cup. "I heard you were on the way with something special, so I sat here while my plane kept being repaired over and over. I heard that the Sergeants' Network has been busy, so a lot of pretty smart people must think your news is important enough to hold the chairman of the Joint Chiefs on the ground. I am curious." He sat in a big leather chair and crossed his legs. "Let's have it, Ralph."

Sims took a long drink of coffee and felt the warmth go all the way to his stomach. "No disrespect to General Brady, sir, but I believe you should have this on an 'ears only' basis."

Turner waved his hand. "Pete Brady and I go back more than twenty years. I value his counsel. He can listen to whatever you have. Proceed."

"Yes, sir. I'll give you the short version, then answer any questions that I can." He handed the plastic-enclosed envelope and note to Turner and stood by silently while the two generals passed the order between them.

"This was delivered personally to Gunnery Sergeant Kyle Swanson by the senior military aide of National Security Advisor Buchanan," the colonel told them. "It was to be destroyed as per instructions from Buchanan, but the Gunny managed to sneak a copy, which was what the aide unknowingly burned. This is the original," Sims explained. "Then Swanson went in with the Force Recon team on the Middleton mission as scheduled, but did not plan to obey the order. When the choppers crashed and it was assumed Swanson was dead, my Top brought that letter to me. Swanson had planned to bring General Middleton out of there safely."

Brady slid the letter back into its envelope. "So you flew halfway around the world to hand-deliver this to Hank?"

"Yes, sir. It was too hot for a messenger and I intentionally bypassed a couple of layers in the chain of command. This is way above my pay grade, General, but I think it has to be illegal for a civilian bureaucrat who has never been elected to anything to use the clout of the White House to order the assassination of a kidnapped American general."

Turner had uncapped an elegant old-style fountain pen and made some notes in a little book. "Bet your ass it is. Does Buchanan know that you were coming to see me?"

"I don't see how, sir," said Sims, taking another sip of coffee. "The only people who knew about the letter, other than Buchanan and his aide, were Swanson, Top Dawkins, and me. Now Swanson is dead. Since Buchanan believes the letter was destroyed, he would see no loose ends."

General Pete Brady glanced out of the window. It was dark outside. Rain scratched at the glass. "He figured it out, Colonel."

"Sir?" Sims asked.

"About an hour ago, Homeland Security jacked the terrorist warning level all the way up to Red, and an attack in Washington killed the Jordanian ambassador." He handed Sims a news story downloaded from the Internet. "Not that we have much to worry about up here in Alaska, but it certainly got our attention."

"I received a separate message, ultra-encrypted, from the National Command Center, authorized by none other than Gerald Buchanan," said General Turner, beginning to pace around the office. "You are to be arrested on sight, on a charge of treason, no less. You are to be held here until Homeland Security personnel can pick you up for questioning. There's a cheery thought. How do you reckon he knew to send that message about you, who are supposed to be in the Med, to me, who is stuck up here in Alaska?"

Ralph Sims bit his lip. Arrested?

General Brady reread the order. "We couldn't figure why he would want you in custody so bad. Now we know. The alert level should have nothing to do with you being tagged as a bad guy, nor with the strange message direct to Hank, but I don't believe in coincidences."

"Our question now becomes whether Buchanan is acting on his own." Turner moved to a wall map. "The President was on the campaign trail tonight out in San Diego, one of those thousand-bucks-a-plate things. He was glad-handing the faithful when he got word of the attack in Washington and authorized raising the alert level. He skipped the speech and got back aboard Air Force One. They're already in the air." He tapped the map. "We're up here outside of Anchorage, and before the sergeants intervened, I was en route to Beijing for a meeting that has been six months in the planning. Naturally, I've cancelled the China trip. Instead, I'm going to rendezvous with Air Force One when it lands at Andrews. You're coming with me, Ralph."

"I just left there," Sims said with a groan.

"Quit whining, Colonel. I hate air force weenies to see a Special Ops CO whimper like a little girl. Anyway, you can sleep on the way back, and I've got some good news for you. Seems that your Gunny Swanson lived through the crash after all, and that General Middleton has gone missing from his captives in Syria. Swanson apparently busted him free and has been raising holy hell in the town where he was held. They're on the run, with the Syrians hot on their tails. Things are getting interestinger and interestinger."

Brady turned to his computer terminal and called up a program to show the weather. "This rain squall is just passing through, and the sergeants have assured me that all of our aircraft are suddenly ready to fly again. They're warming up my Gulfstream II/SP even as we speak. I say let's go meet the Boss." The 11th Air Force commander went to a closet, took out a flight suit, stripped to his underwear, and pulled it on.

"We'll go back with Pete aboard his Gulfstream," said Turner. "I could use my own big-ass plane that was going to haul me over the Pole to China, but Pete's toy is a lot more comfortable," Turner said. He looked at a big clock on the wall. "Matter of fact, the big bird will be taking off in a few minutes. Bet we beat them to Washington."

"Am I under arrest?" asked Sims.

"Oh, hell, no," snapped Turner. "We don't take orders

from that overblown asshole. Buchanan's up to no good, it
has something to do with our Marines getting killed, and I'm
going to get to the bottom of it."

Sims read the news report about the terrorist attack in
Washington while the two generals finished getting ready.
"Oh, shit!" he exclaimed.

"What 'Oh, shit'?" asked Turner.

"This story, sir! The four people killed by the terrorists in
Washington: the ambassador, his driver, another embassy
official, and a U.S. Navy officer, Lieutenant Commander
Shari Towne." Sims's face had gone red with anger.

"Come on, Colonel. Talk to me."

"General Turner, it's an open secret that Lieutenant Commander Towne and our sniper, Gunny Swanson, have been
together for a long time. One of those don't ask, don't tell
things, so nobody officially knew about it. They're almost
engaged, from what I hear. That direct link between her and
Swanson is only point one. Point two is that she ran the Middle East desk on Buchanan's staff in the White House."

The generals looked at each other. "Goddam, Hank.
Those bastards weren't after the ambassador at all!" said
Brady. "They were after the girl!"

Turner, Brady, and Sims walked outside toward the flight
line, where the beautiful Gulfstream was warming up in a
circle of bright light. Plumes of jet exhaust streamed away in
the cold air, and the light rain glistened on its polished skin.
Brady asked Sims, "Do you think this Gunny Swanson can
get Middleton out of there alive?"

Sims nodded his head in the affirmative. "Sir, I'm beginning to believe that Gunny Swanson can walk on water.
Don't bet against him."

A great bellow of noise rolled across from the main runway as a Boeing 707 painted in the distinctive sky-blue-and-
white pattern of a VIP of the U.S. government raced past
them and gathered speed for takeoff. "There goes my plane.
Sort of a shame it's flying empty," said Turner.

Brady added, "The crew is happier to be going home than
to China."

They watched it lift smoothly into the air. A spark of bright light flashed on the ground in the distance, and a bright dot streaked higher and higher, gaining momentum and altitude at a dizzying rate. The Stinger shoulder-fired missile rammed into one of the hot engines on the Boeing and detonated, and in a fraction of a second the dark sky seemed filled by a ball of fire that consumed the plane even before it hit the ground.

Ralph Sims grabbed both generals and threw them to the paved runway, sprawling across them. "Jesus Christ, General Turner, you were supposed to be on that plane!"

"Go to Alert One! Scramble the fighters!" Brady yelled to a nearby security guard, who grabbed his radio and relayed the order to the Elmendorf command center. Sirens wailed as ambulances and fire trucks burst from their garages and raced down the runway.

A whine buzzed in the sky, and an explosion shook the ground when a mortar round arced in from the darkness beyond the wire. A second round was on the way before the first one struck and landed closer to a big hangar; then a third mortar round landed right on the building that was filled with volatile fluids and ammunition. It erupted like a volcano. Three fighter-bombers undergoing maintenance inside, out of the weather, were blown apart, and the maintenance crews were incinerated. When Sims saw that the mortars were not coming their way, he got the generals to their feet and they all ran for cover.

Air Force security police surged toward the wire as three more mortar rounds rained down, two of them chewing holes into the main runway. The last one grazed the big control tower and exploded on a parked truck, which set fire to everything around it.

The Shark Team was gone by the time police found the empty launching tubes. Both men had been members of the Security Police and nearing retirement when they were corrupted by the big bucks offered by Gordon Gates to join the Sharks. Weapons had been stashed in an off-base apartment for months just in case they were needed. They also had new identities, new passports, and thick bank accounts and were flying first class to Seattle before it was even discovered that they were missing.

When ground troops had cleared the flight path beyond the fenceline, the Gulfstream piloted by General Brady zipped from the runway, with Turner and Sims strapped into the leather seats. Rolling next were a pair of F-16 escorts, armed to the teeth, which took station off the wingtips.

In the calm skies above the Arizona desert, the President of the United States was briefed about the deadly strike at Elmendorf. Four more F-16s sped out to sandwich over and around Air Force One. The President had no doubt that the terror alert was right at the level it should be. His country was once again under attack.

CHAPTER 49

GORDON GATES BROUGHT up a secure e-mail from the Sharks who had hit Elmendorf, read it, and then electronically shredded the message through the Magneto program. It vanished as if it had never been sent. They had done an extraordinary amount of damage and gotten away clean. Gates had long ago discovered the truth of the old question, "Who guards the guards?" and had spent a lot of time and money penetrating the security forces of many military bases. Surprisingly, it was not difficult at all to find otherwise good soldiers ready to sell their services to a high bidder.

Buchanan's security net had tracked Colonel Sims to Elmendorf, where he was likely to link up with General Turner, the chairman of the Joint Chiefs, who had been delayed there on a trip to China. Sims would have given Turner the message. So bringing down the Boeing with a Stinger missile meant that Turner and Sims were dead, and the assassination letter would have burned in the crash. Perfect. The mortar rounds were thrown in as icing on the cake to embellish the terrorist possibilities.

Gates considered the situation at this new point. Shari Towne had been taken out in the attack on the Jordanian ambassador's car. He would like to have had visual confirmation on Sims and Turner, but he had seen a lot of plane crashes and the odds were overwhelming that they were both cooked. Nothing had been heard from them since the shootdown. So three of the people who had learned about the letter were dead, which left three elusive Marines—Swanson, Dawkins, and Middleton.

The master sergeant aboard the ship was proving to be invisible, which won an approving smile from Gates for the Spec Ops veteran. It would take some luck to dig him out, particularly if he had the assistance of other people on the boat, but sooner or later he would be discovered. Gates just had to leave that in the hands of the NCIS people for the time being. Dawkins had no proof of whatever he might claim, so he was relatively harmless and totally isolated at sea.

He turned to the problem of General Middleton and Gunnery Sergeant Kyle Swanson, who apparently had been on a rampage in Syria. The stakes for catching those two were enormous. The whole plan hung on finding them. One of his Sharks in Syria was dead, and the second was in the custody of the Syrian army, but alive and helping track Swanson. That didn't worry Gates, because all Sharks were expendable. The risk was part of the big pay and benefits package.

But Swanson had freed General Middleton and had so far eluded the Sharks and the Syrian army. Gates had sent a message to the Rebel Sheikh requesting more jihadists to augment the search, because the more eyes they had looking, the better. It was best not to count too heavily on the Basra cleric, however. He was a slippery devil.

Gates went to a bar built into a wall of his office, where he kept a bottle of Absolut vodka in the freezer. He poured some into a tall glass and added ice cubes, club soda, and a slice of lime. He stirred and drank, letting his thoughts roam.

Google Earth was an excellent map program that could be used without pinging the military system. He called up the image of lower Syria and projected it on a large plasma screen. The southern area of the country jumped into view and he worked the mouse to increase magnification and tilt the image.

Not much there, he thought. Mostly flat and brown, with some stretches of cultivation. He put his mind in Spec Ops mode, placed the cursor on the village of Sa'ahn, and used the pointer tool to trace and measure possible routes of evasion. He had plenty of time, because the sniper and the general would be hiding in the daylight hours.

Swanson would avoid populated areas. The Syrians had helos in the air, but they had to cover a search area of several hundred square miles and probably would not see him. With so many helicopters searching, Swanson and Middleton had to keep their heads down during the day. If Gates were in the sniper's boots, he would head south tonight and make a dash to the Jordanian border tomorrow at first light.

He sipped his icy vodka and tonic. Then he minimized the Google Earth map and brought up the digitalized copy of Swanson's military jacket. Quite the package: a real war fighter and a gold-plated pain in the ass. Buchanan had screwed up by picking him for the job. Gates thought the man would be a terrific Shark Team leader, but would never flip for money.

He had to be stopped. Both Swanson and Middleton had to be killed. First they had to be found, and who better to look for Spec Ops types than Shark Teams who knew all of the tricks of that dark art? Victor Logan, a violent cretin in many ways, was one of the best, but Gates decided to lend the Syrians some more specialized assistance.

He tapped into his private database to see what was available. There was an unmanned aerial vehicle, a pilotless UAV with a video link, on the ground in Jordan, and he sent instructions to get it into the air. It would be one more thing from which Swanson would have to hide. Gates added the Shark Team that was helping to train Hezbollah fighters in a remote part of Lebanon. That team had a serviceable UH-1E Huey helicopter with miniguns slung on the sides. He also sent in another team from Israel, where the two Sharks were acting as counterinsurgency advisors with the Israelis on how to trap Hezbollah guerrillas. They would drive over in their armored Humvee. He sent a coded message through a Syrian contact to the search team in the desert. Five well-trained Sharks brought a lot of expertise to the operation. Plus the new Iraqi jihadists. A lot of eyes.

Gates studied the Marine's personnel jacket some more, looking for anything that might help. This sniper had already proven to be very aggressive, so Middleton and Swanson would be watching for the watchers. Middleton probably would have the strong binos, while Swanson would use the powerful Unertl telescope on his SASR, the big. 50-caliber M82 Special Applications Scope Rifle. That was a hog of a weapon, a real bone-breaker that Gates knew well from lugging one himself. That would slow Swanson down even more when it came time to run.

Every pound Swanson carried would weigh him down a fraction, and the SASR was 37 pounds even before adding the ammo. The sniper had to be carrying a big pack, more weapons, and maybe some other gear, too. He would start to shed the unneeded items, but in the current time frame, he was losing the speed contest. This was the moment to catch them, while they were at rest and before they could start moving again.

Gordon Gates slammed his drink down onto the thick glass top of his desk. *The rifle!* Of course! He scrolled down through Swanson's jacket to read about Swanson's recent assignment to Sir Jeff Cornwell's company, advising in the development of a new generation of sniper rifle. Vague stories had been carried in the gun magazines about the experimental weapon with the magical, highly comput-erized scope, and Cornwell had garnered the venture money needed to take it into production. Gates did a web search for the rifle through "sniper" Web sites until he found the name of the weapon: the Excalibur. He waded through a bunch of sites about King Arthur's sword before coming up with some of the specs on Cornwell's futuristic gizmo. It was lighter than the SASR by far, so maybe Swanson had this thing along, the Excalibur, and if he did, he might save on weight, but there was a potential weakness. *Gotcha!*

Gates opened his private electronic Rolodex and found an overseas telephone number. London. A quiet British voice answered.

CHAPTER 50

YOUSIF AL-SHOUM WAS BIDING his time. Logan had been correct, that the sniper would go to ground during the daylight hours, so moving fast was neither necessary nor wise. Al-Shoum rested in a large tent that had been set up beside the road near the village and watched his soldiers probe up the road for more mines and booby traps. Not far from the tent was the burned and blackened hulk of the BTR-80 troop carrier that had triggered the mine. The two men whose heads were above the armor were decapitated by the blast, and the fuel tank ruptured and exploded, which took out three more men. Al-Shoum was alive only because he had stayed behind with the second BTR to communicate with Damascus. Otherwise his own head would have been sticking out of the forward hatch of the lead vehicle.

The Syrian intelligence officer had had his fill of surprises for one day. Five of his men had died in the BTR ambush. Another was killed at the front door of the house in the village, along with one of the American mercenaries. The house with eleven jihadist fighters from Iraq was blown to pieces and they were all dead. Parts of the Frenchman who was everybody's intelligence contact were found in the smoking ruins of his demolished home. The guard who was taped to the Zeus and the gunner who tried to fire it were dead. Two pairs of sentries at the checkpoint down the road had been slain. Two pair! The Marine general was gone. Enough was enough.

Al-Shoum would coordinate the search from this tent and be the spider at the center of the search web. While he waited for more troops and helicopters, he sent a squad back into the village to conduct a house-to-house search to be sure the American troublemaker had not taken shelter back there where he was least expected.

A big map was spread on a table before him, along with two radio sets, a Thermos of tea, water, and some food on clean white plates. Al-Shoum munched bread and cheese. "Well, Mr. Logan. Where did he go?"

Victor Logan had been impressed by the wreckage of the BTR, which still wore big stripes of dried blood and guts. The undamaged armored personnel carrier remained parked nearby, almost as if cowering until the minesweepers pronounced the area clear. This sniper knew what he was doing. Logan wiped his palm across the lower half of the map. "South. Toward Jordan."

"Our scouts report some damage to a road sign at an intersection to the west, several kilometers from here, big truck tires digging around a sharp corner that would lead them north, toward Lebanon."

Logan shook his head, a statue with his beefy arms crossed across his chest, thinking hard. "It's a bullshit play to draw you that way. He's not going there."

"I agree," said Al-Shoum. Still, he had to devote some search assets to the area, because from what this American Marine had done so far, he was not beyond leaving a false trail, doubling back on it and then doubling back still again. The Syrian remembered reading about that trick in a detective story about how a serial killer trapped a never-give-up New York cop and his beautiful FBI partner . . . he snapped his mind back to the present. "One would think he would take the general due west, as fast as possible, toward Israel." He glanced at Logan. "Why not?"

"He's made the same deductions that we are doing now.

Getting to Israel would be the most logical and quickest route to safety, so he knows your troops will flood the area. Therefore he won't use it, and he cannot head the opposite direction, to the east, into territory that is just as dangerous. To the south is Jordan, which is friendly with the United States. That's where I would go. It's where he will go."

Again al-Shoum agreed, and scratched his head. Logan could afford to guess, but he had to cover all possibilities, and there were many. He could not rule out the dash to Israel, and he had sent search teams toward the Zionist border, further depleting his force.

Then there was the problem of the vehicle itself. The Marine had stolen an old white Toyota pickup truck, which was the most common vehicle in Syria, if not in the entire region. There were hundreds of white Toyota pickups on the roads, going in every direction, in and out of every population center, all day long. The escapees could be in any of them.

In a professional sense, al-Shoum held a grudging respect for his opponent for sticking with his job after the helicopter crash, coming into the village and rekidnapping the general. It did not matter. His job was now to catch them both, and that was what he would do. Afterward, he looked forward to dealing with Victor Logan for the murder of that girl.

He stood and turned when a soldier called out to him and pointed. A dark blue Land Rover came sailing toward them from the village, the tinted windows sealing in the air conditioning as the tires threw plumes of dust into the air behind it. A man with a gray beard and thick eyelashes, wearing clean white robes and head covering, got out of the back seat when the vehicle stopped beside the tent.

"General al-Shoum," the visitor said. "My dear friend."

Al-Shoum bowed with respect, then embraced the senior imam from a mosque in Damascus. He helped the cleric to a chair at the table, and poured tea. A guard moved Logan out of earshot.

"I am always delighted to see you, my friend, for you have the peace of Allah with you. But what brings you to this desolate place?" al-Shoum asked. "A man of the Book need not trouble himself in this routine business."

The old man sipped his tea and spent about five minutes exchanging pleasantries. The children, of course, and the crops and the animals, and also the wife. Al-Shoum grew more impatient by the minute. This imam did not leave his mosque to drop by as a curious tourist. He might have been sent from the government to report on al-Shoum's work.

"Please forgive me for keeping my radios tuned so loudly," he said. "I am conducting a wide search for the missing Americans." *Take the hint, old man.*

"That is part of why I am here, beyond learning the joyous news of your family. I am doing a favor for my fellow cleric and our important ally, Sheikh Ali Shalal Rassad in Iraq, a very respected man in the service of the Prophet, whose name be praised."

"Praised be the name," al-Shoum parroted. "Anything I can do to assist your mission, I shall do." The Rebel Sheikh was sending a message through a messenger of such high pedigree that there could be no doubt about its validity and importance.

"Our friend is most disturbed. He dispatched an airplane early this morning to transfer the American general safely to his hospitality in Iraq. He knows our own nation had nothing to do with the kidnapping, and it appears that many things have changed since the man was taken. Matters have gone to the highest levels."

Al-Shoum said, "Which is why I am present here."

The imam continued without pause. "Our friend, of course, was unaware that you had been sent by Damascus, and offers his most sincere apologies for the misunderstanding. He meant no offense to you or to your abilities. He was only attempting to salvage the situation and help our nation."

Al-Shoum put his hands flat on the table, eyes downcast, humble, obedient as a sheep. *And what's your damned point?*

"But you can only imagine our friend's surprise when he learned that not only has the American general escaped with the help of another American, but that all of the Sheikh's holy warriors who had been guarding him have been martyred. All of them!"

"That is true. His Iraqis apparently were too careless in posting guards." Al-Shoum's tone was a sneer at their carelessness.

The old man stroked his beard, the dark eyes stronger than the frail body. "Something insulting has happened. The American infidel Gordon Gates actually ordered our friend to dispatch even more fighters, a large number of them, up here to join your search. *He ordered a man of the Book to do so!* It is an outrage! So our brother has decided to do what is best for us all."

"Of course. And what was his decision?"

"Naturally, he would never intrude into your operation, brother. He expresses full confidence that you will resolve this situation, and his attention is demanded elsewhere, on more fruitful things." Having delivered his message, the old man rose and gave the Syrian intelligence officer a final hug. "*Inshallah,* the will of Allah be done," said the imam. He bestowed blessings for al-Shoum's sons to grow strong in the service of the Prophet, got back into the Land Rover, and was driven serenely away.

Al-Shoum watched the blue SUV vanish back the way it had come. *Shit!* First that Iraqi pig had tried to sneak in and steal the American general right from under al-Shoum's nose, and now he was abandoning the search. That would leave al-Shoum alone to take any blame if they escaped.

"What was that all about?" asked Logan, ducking back beneath the tent.

"Nothing," said al-Shoum. "An old friend who happened to be in the area and wondered what was going on." Ali Shalal Rassad, who had already lied to the world that his organization, the Holy Scimitar of Allah, was not involved, was washing his hands of the whole mess. The old imam who brought the message was often employed as an unofficial emissary by the Syrian government, which would now be considering doing the same thing to ease international tensions. While al-Shoum sat beneath this tent in the middle of nowhere, the distance from Damascus hung around his neck like an albatross, for he realized that being stuck out here meant that he would not be privy in the final decision-making. Damascus had changed his mission. Instead of making a decision himself, he had been sent off running after a couple of Marines. If a scapegoat was needed, he might be chosen as the sacrifice.

He looked at the sky, where the sun had risen higher. No helicopters in the area. He increased the volume on the radio net. The sooner he captured those Americans, the better, because then he would be on the next chopper back to Damascus, possibly entering the city as a hero. He spun to face the American mercenary, whose help he now needed much more than he had only ten minutes ago. "We are wasting time, Logan."

CHAPTER 51

THE DESOLATE ROAD LED BACK into a countryside that was green with agriculture rather than the normal desert brown, with ditches on each side to help with the irrigation of crops in a dry climate. Small canals with gates separated the larger tracts of land in a crossing pattern, to feed water from one area to another in a rotating schedule. As the sun crested totally above the horizon, a shining torch that removed the protecting darkness, Swanson found a major canal that apparently spilled into much of the region, with a low level of water. He dropped the truck into four-wheel drive, cut onto a cart path, and bounced down into the big trench.

Middleton grimaced in agony as he was tossed around in the cab, but Kyle kept going until all four wheels were in the water. He plunged ahead into a large concrete culvert that served both as a waterway and an opening through which farm machinery could transit from crops on one side of the road to the other. With a high clearance and only about a foot of water, the truck fit easily beneath the shelter, with both ends deep in shadow. He stopped and turned off the engine, and silence engulfed them. "This is it for the day. No choice."

Middleton adjusted himself in the seat, eyeing the broad openings in front of and behind them. "Pretty exposed." Kyle started to respond, but Middleton added, "You're right. Nothing else was around."

Swanson opened his door and stepped into stale water. "The truck sits up high enough for the water not to be a problem. I'll go brush over our tracks." He waded away, back into the daylight, and spent ten minutes covering their tracks from the road into the culvert ditch, then used his binos to examine the fields all around them. Quiet, with no workers, even in relatively cool morning. He returned to the truck and climbed into the back.

Middleton was standing there cradling the AK-47. "Anything out there?"

"Nope. We're okay for now. If they are not working the crops at this time of day, maybe these fields are just being watered. We might get lucky and not have to deal with any farmers coming through. Let's look at the map."

They unrolled it on the roof of the cab, each holding down an edge. "The place where you were being held is called Sa'ahn, over here." Kyle pointed to a small symbol that denoted a village of fewer than a thousand people, and dragged his finger along a dark line. "We drove all the way over here to where that big highway goes up to Damascus, and then doubled back. I estimate that we are about right here, close to midway between these two big population centers, As Suwayda to the east and Dar'a to our west."

He stopped talking and both grabbed their weapons when they heard a truck engine. Kyle motioned for the general to watch one end of the culvert while he covered the other. The truck came closer and closer, then rumbled across the bridged culvert and pushed on down the road. "We'll probably be getting more of that during the day. Farm traffic."

"So how far are we from anywhere?" Middleton squinted at the map.

Swanson found a scale of kilometers printed on the bottom and measured with his finger. "This road runs into As Suwayda in about forty-four kilometers. About a mile away from where we are now is another small road that goes due south for, let's see, about seventeen klicks."

"Doesn't reach all the way to the Jordanian border," Middleton observed. "Dead-ends at the next crossing. But it looks like a straight shot from there."

"I figure that we are about twenty-one miles, more or less, from Jordan," Kyle estimated. "We can drive closer and hump it tonight if we have to. Just have to get close."

"Should we get rid of the truck?"

"No. It's a hard worker and blends right in. Anyway, if we take another one, we alert more people."

Middleton looked over at Swanson. "What do you mean that we only have to get close?"

Kyle dug into his pack and pulled out the battery-powered satellite telephone he had taken from the dead pilot in the crash. "In a few hours, about noon, we break radio silence and call our guys in the fleet for help. They might not risk coming in just to get me, but they sure as hell will come in to get you!"

"Rank has its privileges, Gunny. Why not call right now and get it over with?"

Kyle sat down and propped his weapon beside him. "When we light up that phone, we expose our position. The Syrians and Washington will be listening, so we want to burn off a few daylight hours to cut into the available search time, but still give the MEU enough of a window to execute a pickup."

Middleton eased himself into a sitting position, holding his ribs. "You mentioned Washington. Made me think of something. Did anything really unusual or important happen while I was being held?"

"No, sir. I don't think so," said Kyle. "I was out of the country and wasn't watching the news before things started happening pretty fast."

"Think hard, Gunny. Anything that impacted the military services?"

Swanson lay down, resting his head on his pack. "Nothing comes to mind. I got to get some zs, General, so let's take two-hour shifts. You wake me up and then you get some sleep. I'm about to fall over." He pulled his boonie cap over his eyes, then lifted it again. "Yeah, wait. There was this one thing. Senator Miller, the old airborne guy, died of a heart attack while campaigning."

"Miller? The head of the Senate Armed Services Committee?"

"Yes, sir. Apparently keeled over in his hotel room after a speech."

"Be damned!" Middleton let out a low whistle, feeling the pieces click together. "Tom Miller was the one person in the government who was more opposed than me to privatizing the U.S. military. We had been working together so that my testimony before his committee next week would block the legislation by turning a bright light on its ugly side."

"So with Senator Miller dead and you held captive and maybe also dead, what would happen?" Kyle pushed back his hat.

"Not good, Gunny. Not good at all. The hearing would probably go forward as scheduled, only with Senator Ruth Hazel Reed succeeding Miller as head of the committee."

"Does that change things?" Kyle cocked his ear and sat back up.

"Yeah. In a big way. Rambo Reed was the one who wrote the damned privatization bill. If major parts of the military are given to the lowest bidder, it will still involve billions of dollars and an immense amount of political power. Worse, it will set the pattern for other parts of the federal government to be sold off." The general rubbed his eyes with the heels of his hands. "I kid you not, Gunny, this thing threatens America as much as any terrorist group. So Gates has some of his mercs kidnap me. They plan an ambush to create a military fiasco, but the choppers crash, doing the job for them. Buchanan has sent you in to make absolutely sure I don't come back. Rambo Reed takes over the committee and pushes the bill through. They're all in this together. Jesus, Gunny, I've got to get back there."

"Listen!"

The thump of helicopter blades was heard in the distance, but coming nearer.

CHAPTER 52

EACH TIME YOUSIF AL-SHOUM received another report of a white pickup truck being spotted, the position was plotted on the plastic overlay of his map with a red thumbtack pushed into the corkboard backing. After a few hours, the map was littered with the little pins, each a sharp point of failure in his massive search. Several dozen white Toyota trucks had been stopped at checkpoints or by search teams, but all were legitimate, except for one fool who had been trying to steal the vehicle when he was apprehended. It was almost noon when he decided to abandon all efforts to the north and toward Lebanon, peel away some of the strength watching the routes to the Israeli border, and take Victor Logan's advice. He would saturate the southern region all the way down to Jordan.

With a black marker, he slashed a boundary line from the southernmost point of the border with Israel, curving over to Dar'a, then northeast to As Suwayda and back down through El Adnata to Jordan. It was a kill box that had the look of an inverted cup. They had to be in there somewhere, and he would construct a net of roving search parties and scour the area like a broom.

Members of his staff had arrived from Damascus and he told them what he wanted, leaving it up to them to draw up the grids and issue the necessary orders. One by one, the helicopters and the road units would be reassigned and move into southern Syria. Al-Shoum had never failed, and was absolutely determined to find the elusive sniper. The chase had become a challenge to his pride and his ability, while back in the capital, competitors probably were already measuring his office for their own desks. If the Marines got away, they might be taking his career along with them. That could not be allowed to happen.

The heat was growing. Even beneath the tent, the air was thick and stale and unmoving. He put on his beret and sunglasses and stepped into the sun to have a word with Victor Logan and two mercenaries who had come down from Lebanon aboard a Huey that was parked in the distance with its rotors pegged tight. Logan had told him in advance that the tall man with the dark tan was from South Africa, and that the pilot was a former Russian Spetsnaz commando with big arms that bulged from a skintight muscle shirt.

Al-Shoum paid no attention to their names when Logan introduced them. The mercenary added, "We have two more men driving over from Israel. They should be arriving in about an hour."

"Good," said al-Shoum. "Will you be in charge, or do I have to talk to someone else?"

"Anything doing with Gates Global still comes through me," Logan said, careful not to appear impolite. He had not forgotten to whom he was speaking, and had warned the new men to watch their mouths or they would all end up in a Syrian jail.

Al-Shoum explained the changing search patterns. "There is no need for you to be out flying without a target. It would only waste your fuel and time, for your expertise will be needed soon enough. Brief your team and be ready to move as soon as somebody spots the Americans. When they start to run, as I anticipate, you will go get them."

Logan shifted the strap of his rifle. "Good plan, sir. We'll be ready."

"Very well," al-Shoum said. "I'll call you when something

turns up." He turned on his heel and went back to the tent, where more pins had been stuck in the map overlay. He issued a new order: Every Toyota pickup in the new search area would be halted and immobilized until the Marines were found. There was no use counting the same ones twice. The pins seemed to mock him.

"Sir! I've got something here!" A sailor at a communications console inside the Combat Command Center of the *Blue Ridge* remained calm, although it took everything he had to keep from standing up and shouting. The chief petty officer in charge and the CCC officer of the watch moved to the console and plugged in their headsets.

"What's up, Armstrong?" asked the lieutenant.

"We're picking up a repeater sat phone signal, sir. Call sign is Long Rifle."

The bosun tapped a computer to scroll a list of recent call signs. "That's Gunny Swanson from the rescue mission!"

"I've got it." Lieutenant David Garvey immediately depressed his TALK key. "Long Rifle . . . *Blue Ridge* . . . Do you copy?"

Kyle Swanson gave a thumbs-up sign to General Middleton. "Loud and clear," he responded. "I have a package and need a FedEx pickup."

"What is your address, Long Rifle?" The call was encrypted but was still over an open frequency, which required both parties to use code whenever possible.

"Simple Shackle," Swanson said, then read off a line of numbers in an encoded format specified in the operational orders. The Simple Shackle was a 1-to-10 box grid, horizontal and vertical, that could be interpreted only if the recipient had a similar code sheet. The little code in 100 squares repeats hashed versions of the alphabet. Any specific letter might appear in three or four different boxes that are used at random. "THE" might read 1-12-16 on first use, but 36-98-53 the next time. As an added safeguard, it would change at specified times. Even computers as powerful as those at the National Security Agency would have to put in some time to break it.

"How long can our driver expect you to remain at that address?"

"No more than a few hours, then we are going to see *March of the Penguins*." The brevity code, also from the original ops order, specified that "penguins" meant south.

"Roger on the *March*. Come back in sixty mikes to confirm pickup time." Garvey unplugged. "Chief, I'm going up to see the captain. Keep two men on that frequency at all times."

"Aye, aye, sir." Chief Petty Officer Dwight Marshall made the personnel arrangements. When Garvey was gone, he switched to a private internal net.

A wall telephone rang deep in the stern of the ship. "Yes?" answered a deep voice.

"Double-Oh. We just picked up traffic from your boy Gunny Swanson. He's coming out with a package. I think you need to be in on this. I'll pass the word for a five-man protective detail to bring you up to meet with the MEU XO." Marshall clicked off, found a Marine, and passed along the instructions. A team saddled up in full combat gear, locked and loaded, and headed down the ladders to escort Dawkins to the CCC. The executive officer of the Marine Expeditionary United would want his top hand in on planning whatever happened next, and no NCIS civilian investigators would be allowed to interfere.

Dawkins pulled on his boots. He had been comfortably whiling away the hours in a secluded area carved out deep belowdecks by creative sailors. It had a locked door, a television set with a lot of interesting videos, access to a nearby head with a toilet and a shower, a comfortable bunk, a tattered easy chair, a bunch of books and magazines ranging from *Playboy* to *Sports Illustrated* to *Vogue,* and shelves holding clean sheets. On a table was a bowl with fruit and candy bars gathered from the mess tables and the ship's store. He had taken refuge in perhaps the most pleasant place on the entire ship, a hidden love nest to which boy and girl sailors could retreat, grossly violate naval regulations, and fuck like rabbits.

CHAPTER 53

JACK SHEPHERD OF CNN WAS having an early pint of beer in a Fleet Street pub with a leggy intern from the London office of the Cable News Network. Chrissie Rogers was blond and busty, a twenty-two-year-old journalism school graduate from Nebraska, and she was enchanted with every word the rugged, veteran foreign correspondent bestowed on her in the privacy of a small booth. He was wondering whether to get her in bed before or after an expense-account dinner. The cell phone clipped to his belt chimed and vibrated. He reluctantly answered: "Shepherd."

"Ah, my friend Jack Shepherd of CNN. This is your friend from Basra." The unmistakable voice of the Rebel Sheikh was smooth. Jack slid out of the booth and walked outside for privacy.

"Good afternoon, sir. How may I help you?" No use wasting time with idle chatter. If the Rebel Sheikh called, it was for a reason.

"I am sorry to interrupt your afternoon, but I have something for you." There was a pause. "This is on deep background, of course. My name and position cannot be used."

"No problem, sir, and you're not interrupting. I'm always on duty. What are we talking about?"

A gentle laugh. "Impatient Americans. Well, the kidnapped General Middleton of the Marine Corps has escaped his captors, with the assistance of a Marine sniper who survived the crash of the helicopters, a man named Kyle Swanson. The Syrian Army and intelligence forces have launched a wide search to find both of them."

"Can I go with this, sir?"

"Oh, absolutely, Jack, providing you leave me out of your report. I just received a briefing from Syria. The manhunt is going on even as we are speaking, so you should hurry and get this on the air. Come see me again sometime, Jack." The Rebel Sheikh gave that little laugh again. "And I really do apologize for interrupting your meeting with the lovely Ms. Rogers."

By using Chrissie's name, the Rebel Sheikh was telling the correspondent that he was being watched. Jack Shepherd didn't care. He wasn't in the television news business to be invisible. He returned to the table, tossed down the rest of his pint, and laid down some money for the drinks. "Come on, Chrissie. Back to the office. Time to do some work."

A woman in Amman, Jordan, was calling a similar alert to the al Jazeera correspondent in his hotel room office.

It took the networks about an hour to prepare the story in their home offices, Atlanta for CNN and Doha for al Jazeera. Both slammed *Special Report* logos on their screens and broadcast the reports to millions of viewers. The twenty-four-hour cable news shows, already awash with Red Alert terrorism stories, would soon launch squadrons of talking-head commentators to argue with each other about just how soon war would break out between the United States and Syria.

The tent outside of Sa'ahn was an oven, and steamy mirages wiggled in the distance. Al-Shoum was sweaty, tired, and irritable from having been up all night. A folding cot was set up in one corner, and he lay down to catch a nap, with strict orders to be awakened if anything happened. He was not the one out there doing the searching, and his staff was running the map and radios, so there was nothing else he could do but wait. He could do that while sleeping. He checked for Logan and saw all three of the mercenaries lounging in the open bay of the helicopter, listening to music. Logan was smoking a cigarette. They were men bred for battle, dogs of war relaxing without a care while waiting to be unleashed. He looked at his wristwatch. Two o'clock. He would sleep no more than two hours.

General Hank Turner and Colonel Ralph Sims were asleep in the comfortable cabin of the little Gulfstream II-SP as it swept above the snowy peaks of the Rocky Mountains on its long flight from Alaska. Turner was dreaming of the moment when his big Boeing disappeared in a blast of flame. General Pete Brady turned the Gulfstream's controls over to his copilot and made his way down the aisle.

"Wake up, boys," he said, standing straight and stretching. "Shit's hitting the fan." He plopped down across from them as the two Marines blinked themselves awake and straightened in their seats.

Turner was instantly awake, but gave a shake of the head to clear it. *I should have been on that plane!* "What's going on, Pete?" Turner wanted to know. "Another attack?"

"Nope. Pentagon just relayed a call to you. Gunny Swanson contacted your *Blue Ridge* boat over a sat link. Apparently Middleton is with him. Swanson gave coordinates not too far from the Jordanian-Syrian border, so the wheels are turning to find some way to get them out of there."

"What do we have out there that can be deployed in a hurry, Ralph?" Turner stared hard at the MEU colonel. Sims had seen that battle stare from Hank Turner before. The man was getting ready for a fight.

"The Force Recon TRAP team is off the board because of the accident in the desert, but we wouldn't want to be stealthy this time anyway. I recommend sending in two full platoons, aboard several helicopters, with Cobra attack helicopters on guard and appropriate cover by fast-movers up top. Lay a secure box all around Middleton and the gunny, with nothing going in or out except us."

"How long would it take?"

Sims recalled the pre-mission briefing and did some silent calculations. "Depending on where the ships are, sir, they should be able to launch within an hour of getting the green light, since they know the coordinates. Less than an hour flying time in, no more than fifteen minutes on the ground, and then get back home."

Turner took out his fountain pen again and scribbled a note. He turned to Pete Brady. "Is Air Force One back in Washington yet?"

"No, sir. I just checked. They are over Arkansas."

"Okay. I need to talk to the President directly and divert Air Force One back toward us. Find me a secure air force base where they can put down with tight security and we can meet them as soon as possible."

"Got it," said Brady. "What else?"

Turner handed him the note he had written. "Transmit this to the Fleet and the MEU, with a confidential copy to the President, encrypted and for his eyes only. Launch the rescue immediately!"

Brady whistled. "Wow. Hank, you're taking a big chance here. You need some big-league paperwork to do this."

"Fuck it. We don't have the time. I'm sending the team in VOCO, on the Verbal Orders of the Commander. This comes straight from me, damn it. After you send it, have my staff alert the other chiefs."

Colonel Sims waited for Brady to step into the Gulf-stream's communications suite. "Good on ya, sir."

"Tired of all this fucking around, Ralph. I'm not going to lose those two brave men. When you wear four stars, sometimes you have to remember that you're a war-fighter, not a politician. Despite their bluster, the Syrians don't want a piece of us. So we kick ass first and beg forgiveness later."

The Vice President was unhappy. All of the important players on the National Security Council were present for the emergency meeting except for three. "The President is flying back from California and should be landing momentarily, and I will brief him when he arrives at the White House," he told the others. "General Turner is also flying back. That leaves us with an unexplained empty chair. Mr. Shafer, where is Mr. Buchanan?"

Sam Shafer rose and tugged at the hem of his jacket. "I don't know, sir. He is not in his office."

The Vice President's eyes seemed to smolder behind his rimless glasses. "Have you seen him at all today? Is he not aware that we're dealing with terrorist attacks on American soil, a major international crisis, and a hostile media that is going berserk with war talk?"

"Yes, sir. I spoke briefly with Mr. Buchanan at his desk at five o'clock this morning. As usual, he was going through the briefing papers. When I checked at six, he was gone, and I assumed he was having some breakfast in the mess or at a meeting. I haven't seen him since."

The Vice President growled, "Then go find him! I want him in that chair in five minutes. Do I make myself clear?"

"Yes, sir." Sam Shafer gulped, then hurried from the room.

"We will continue without Buchanan," said the Vice President. "State, you said you have something?"

The Secretary of State pulled her briefing folder close. "The Syrians are panicking. With the media carrying the story around the world, they apparently realize the error of their ways. Our Red Alert, the assassination of the Jordanian ambassador, the attack in Alaska, and the kidnapping of General Middleton probably was not the way they hoped things were going to come down. It's a major embarrassment, even for a state that sponsors terrorism. With our military ramping up for a hard response, Damascus wants to cut a deal and get out of trouble."

"What do they have in mind?"

"They will direct their military to help find and protect Middleton and the Marine who rescued him, and allow us to come pick them up without incident. They blame the whole episode on what they call foreign rogue extremists."

"What do they get in return?"

"No war, and a public statement of appreciation for their assistance."

The Vice President jotted the terms on his legal pad. "Sounds good to me. Any objections?" No one opposed the idea. "I will pass our recommendation along to the President. State, you tell the Syrians that if our men are harmed in any way, if this is a trap, the price for such treachery will be very steep indeed."

Murmurs of agreement around the table. "That's it, then. Get back to work." As he walked back to his office, he put his hand on the elbow of the chief of his Secret Service protective detail and drew him close. "Jim. I want you boys to find Gerald Buchanan and fetch him to me as soon as possible."

"Sorry, sir, that's not our job description."

"Oh, hell, Jim, I know that," said the Vice President. "You're a bright boy. You'll think of something. Just get his fat butt in here."

If Buchanan thinks I'm going to stick around and take this rap by myself, he's crazy. Sam Shafer went to the front hall, the thick soles of his polished shoes beating a tattoo on the marble, and signed out at the Secret Service desk. Then he walked down the long driveway and out the front gate of the White House, trying not to run, and cut across the open plaza into downtown Washington. Within two blocks, he hailed a taxi. "Reagan National," he told the driver.

As the cab crossed the Potomac, Shafer dialed his cell phone and Gordon Gates answered on the first ring. "He's gone," Shafer said.

"I expected it. Buchanan has the balls of a hamster," Gates replied. "You get on up to New York like we talked about and someone will meet your plane. Welcome to the Sharks, Sam."

CHAPTER 54

AN ARMED PERIMETER OF guards surrounded Air Force One as it stood alone on the tarmac of Minot Air Force Base in North Dakota at five o'clock in the morning. The President of the United States was as safe there as if he had been in a reinforced bunker two hundred feet underground. The base was isolated ten miles from the town of Minot, not far from the Canadian border, and even under normal conditions, security was always tight there. A hundred and fifty Minuteman ICBM missiles were buried in silos around the home base of the 5th Bomb Wing and the 91st Space Wing. Many of Minot's B-52H bombers carrying Air Launched Cruise Missiles were in the air. They were just drops in the bucket of what the President could throw at Syria if he decided to do so.

He was a quiet, thoughtful man, but during his three years in office, his dark hair had gone gray because of situations just like this. He read the note that General Henry Turner, the chairman of the Joint Chiefs of Staff, had given him. The words THE WHITE HOUSE were printed in blue across the top. Turner and a marine colonel who looked like he had been up all night sat in big chairs across from the desk in the plane's spacious office. "I did not order this," the President said. "This is the first time I have seen this extraordinary piece of paper."

"Never thought you did order it, Mr. President," answered Turner. "That's why I interrupted your itinerary to personally bring it to you. That is, however, Gerald Buchanan's name scrawled on the bottom."

The President passed the note to several other key people in the cabin. His chief of staff asked, "Why would he do this, General?"

Turner rubbed his hands together in thought. "Colonel Sims and I have been pondering the same thing. The kidnapping of General Middleton had to have some motive, and the most obvious one was probably to trigger a confrontation between us and Syria, which happened. This note indicates a deeper motive, so the confrontation might just have been cover. He says plain as day that if Middleton cannot be rescued, he should be killed. Why? We had no reason to think that the Force Recon team would not be successful. They ran into bad luck, that's all, or otherwise Middleton would be out of Syria by now. So why send one of the best snipers in the Marine Corps to make sure the general was dead? My conclusion is that Mr. Buchanan knew the rescue was doomed to failure anyway. Why . . . and how?"

The President tilted far back in his chair and crossed his arms. "Colonel Sims, do you think our rescue attempt was compromised?"

"Yes, sir. We had a good plan, we had good men, and the odds were overwhelmingly in our favor to be successful. We practice it all the time and use the same package to pick up downed pilots. I agree with General Turner. It looks like Mr. Buchanan had advance information that the mission was going to run into trouble."

"It's difficult to swallow. I've known Gerry Buchanan for years. He has always been rock-solid in giving me accurate advice. This just makes no sense."

The chief of staff spoke again: "Gerry is the only person who can answer these questions, Mr. President. Personal friendships aside, I suggest that we have him detained and questioned."

"The Vice President told me a little while ago that he has

given a similar order. Buchanan did not show up for the National Security Council meeting." The President, who had been a university president before going into the Senate and then into the White House, was known for his logical and scholarly mind, and always seemed a half-step ahead of everybody else. "Let's put it into context. Buchanan told me to ratchet up the alert status, and now I can no longer believe his counsel, nor his actions. Although we have had attacks on our soil, they have not been traced to any terrorists. I think the red alert was a diversion, part of some larger plan. The first thing we need do is loosen the tension beyond our borders. And we take the Syrian deal to help get Middleton released unharmed."

Turner looked surprised. He had not heard of any deal.

"That offer came in a little while ago, Hank. I got the call about the time you were landing. Good news on that, at least. State is working out the details. Now your rescue team can go in without guns blazing. I think the Syrian crisis has passed, thank the Lord. Now we are going to find out what, and who, is behind all of this."

"Awwright!" drawled Turner. Colonel Sims relaxed for the first time since the original mission briefing. It was almost over.

There was only one woman in the cabin, and the President locked his eyes on Senator Ruth Hazel Reed. "Well, Senator, it looks like General Middleton will be back in time for your committee hearing on the military privatization bill next week after all."

She had flown by corporate jet to her hometown of San Diego to bask in the President's popularity there and gather campaign donations, then joined him on Air Force One for the return trip to Washington. "Yes, Mr. President," she said. "I did not want to be without his expertise. This is wonderful news. He will need time to recover from his terrible ordeal, so I will postpone that hearing for a while." She glanced at General Turner, who smirked.

The President stood up and extended his hand to Ralph Sims. "Colonel, you did a courageous thing to get this out in the open. You are not under arrest or suspicion of any wrongdoing whatsoever. Go over to the visiting officers' quarters and get some sleep, and a plane will be waiting to take you back to the MEU tomorrow. Good job."

Then he shook the hand of General Turner. "Hank, see if you can still make that meeting in Beijing. We can handle the rest of this thing from here." He looked around the room. "Thank you all very much for your help during this crisis. Now if you will excuse us, I would like a private moment with Senator Reed."

Ten minutes later, Ruth Hazel Reed hurried down the stairs of Air Force One. The master sergeant guarding the bottom of the stairway saw that her cheeks were bright red. As she ducked into a waiting staff car, she was dabbing her eyes with a tissue.

CHAPTER 55

IT WAS A LITTLE BEFORE FOUR o'clock in the afternoon when an aide awakened Yousif al-Shoum with a tap on his shoulder. "General, you have a call from Damascus," he said. Al-Shoum blinked himself awake, feeling that the late-afternoon heat had grown intense. "I'm coming," he responded, pouring some bottled water into a cupped palm and rubbing it across his face. The aide handed him a headset with a microphone.

"This is al-Shoum," he said, and a distant voice replied, quiet, pleasant, diplomatic. The aide watched al-Shoum's jaw tighten and the dark eyes burn. "This is official?" he asked with sharpness. "Where does the order come from?" The aide did not dare move closer. "This is insane! At least let me continue the search until nightfall. We're sure to capture them!" Another pause, and deep breathing, al-Shoum's hands clasping both muffs of the headset hard, pressing them close to his head. "Yes. Of course. Very well. I acknowledge the order."

Al-Shoum slipped off the headset and tossed it to the radio operator, then looked at the map on the table. Still more red pins that signified . . . *Nothing!* Damascus had decided without his advice to cooperate with the Americans! The general and the sniper were not to be harmed! American military troops were to be allowed into Syria to pick them up! The map showed him nothing with which he could call back and demand that the orders be changed. He stalked from the tent without a word.

Putting on his sunglasses, he marched to the helicopter and noticed that two more mercenaries had arrived, a German and an Asian who had been one of the famous Nepalese Gurkha soldiers. Of the four men who were surrounding Logan, al-Shoum judged the small Asian fighter with the scarred face and the grim mouth and the huge curved *khukuri* knife hanging from his belt to be the most dangerous. Logan turned to meet him, holding a boxy object in one hand.

"A significant change of plan, I fear, Mr. Logan," said al-Shoum. "Radical, really. My government has been in direct diplomatic contact with the United States, and once again the diplomats have reached an agreement without consulting the soldiers in the field. My new orders are still to find the missing American Marines, but they are to be treated as guests and provided with protection until they can be evacuated." He spread his hands, palms up. "Nothing I could do."

An odd, twisting smile creased Logan's weathered face. The two men walked away from the others. "That's the government line. Do *you* still want these guys?"

"Yes, Mr. Logan, I want to kill them both. That sniper has made me look like a fool, and I cannot forgive that. This failure may cost me my career." He thrust his chin out toward the endless flat countryside. "We have spent a fruitless day on the hunt, with hundreds of men and dozens of helicopters and vehicles. They are obviously out there somewhere, but time has run out for me. My personal desires must now take second place to direct orders from my government. Even if I find them, I cannot kill them."

Logan understood the undercurrent of the conversation. "Right. You can't kill them. But did your orders say anything about *us* doing it? I want them, too. Real bad." He pointed a thumb over to where the other mercenaries were loading into the helicopter and getting it ready for liftoff.

"Let me show you something," said al-Shoum, and brought Logan under the tent. After clearing everyone else out, he had the mercenary look at the map littered with red stick pins. "Each of those is a white Toyota truck. We have no idea where the men are."

"Okay. From that, I see only that you have a bunch of Toyota trucks in Syria." Logan handed him a piece of paper. "Now look up these coordinates: north 32 degrees, 45 minutes, and east 36 degrees, 25 minutes." Al-Shoum traced the map grid with his finger and drew a circle with a black marker at a point midway between Dar'a and As Suwayda.

"Why this particular location?"

"That's them, General! That's exactly where they are! These boys who came over from Israel brought a GPS locator, and our home office in the States gave them the frequency for a signal being used by the sniper. So right now, they are sitting quiet in that little circle, waiting for night to fall. Or waiting for someone to show up and blow them away. So can we go get 'em?"

"I will not disobey my orders," said al-Shoum, hands on hips, staring at the American, loud enough for most of his staff to overhear. Then, much more quietly, he said, "I will shift my searchers away from those coordinates. If my people actually see the Marines, I will have no choice but to protect them."

"So you have no problem if I fire up the helo and haul ass down there and do what needs to be done, then go away so your boys can come in and make the big discovery of the dead bodies?"

"The two Americans are indeed in hostile territory, and perhaps might die at the hands of villagers who are outraged by the sudden appearance of Crusader forces in their midst. Just be aware that the Americans will soon be sending in another rescue team, this time with my government's permission and, of course, my utmost personal cooperation."

Al-Shoum had another idea flash into his head. "Wait just another moment. Perhaps all is not lost," he told Logan, and scribbled a note in Arabic. He gave it to the mercenary.

"Plant this on the bodies. It will be evidence that the deaths were the work of the Holy Scimitar of Allah, the militia group of the Rebel Sheikh. I need to settle a score with that scoundrel in Basra, so let us kill several birds with a single rock. He will have to answer for the slayings of the two Marines, and I will appear as a hero who did everything possible to save them. Damascus will be pleased."

Logan tucked the note into a pocket. "How long before the rescue team arrives?"

"I don't know exactly, but I'm giving you a one-hour head start, Mr. Logan. You must do it within that time, before anyone notices that I am keeping search parties out of the area. Then you and your men must vanish. I never want to see or hear from you again, and if I do, you will pay in full for killing that child in Sha'ra."

He raised his voice for the benefit of his staff, pointed toward the helicopter, and barked at Logan, "I am through with you worthless dogs. Get out of my country!"

"Color me gone," Logan said, turning and trotting toward the helicopter. He circled an index finger to the pilot to get the rotor turning.

CHAPTER 56

GENERAL BRADLEY MIDDLETON was testy. He and Swanson were free! The Gunny had been in intermittent communication via the satellite phone with the MEU, and had learned that the manhunt was over. Syria had agreed to settle things peacefully rather than have the United States bear down on them over something that Damascus had not been too keen about in the first place. The pickup was going to be unopposed, and Swanson had worked out a landing zone about ten kilometers to the south. Then the sniper went back to sleep, leaving the general on watch and ignoring Middleton's demand to move out.

"We go when I say go, General," Swanson had told him. "There's no guarantee that every Syrian soldier in this region has gotten the word not to open fire on us. I want to arrive at the LZ just before our choppers get there so we're not standing out in the open with our thumbs up our asses, just asking to be shot."

At least it wasn't very hot in the small tunnel in which they were parked, since it was shielded by the sun and cooler because of the foot of barely moving water. Middleton shifted the AK-47, sloshed from one end of the culvert to the other, and crouched behind some of the bushes Swanson had stacked on the left side as a makeshift hide. Traffic had been sporadic along the road, and they had grown familiar with the sounds of an occasional car, truck, or tractor passing overhead. Several helicopters had buzzed in the distance, but there had been no other military presence. A farmer driving a mule cart had taken forever to clatter by.

Middleton took a drink of fresh water and sloshed back toward the other end of the culvert.

"Stop!" Kyle Swanson reached out from the back of the truck and put a hand on Middleton's shoulder. He was sitting up, wide awake. "Hear that?" The sniper leaped from the truck bed with Excalibur in his right hand. "Incoming Huey."

Middleton had not heard anything at all, but now picked up the signature *whomp-whomp* of a Huey helicopter's blades. "Probably just following the road to see if he can spot any signs."

Kyle was already at the far end of the culvert, kneeling behind the bushes. "No, sir. He's too low and has been flying straight for the last few minutes, not running a grid search or following the turns in the road or checking any intersections. That's bad news."

"So what? Maybe he's just supposed to give us a ride to the pickup LZ." Middleton regretted saying that the moment the words left his mouth, and Swanson ignored him. "Yeah. That was stupid."

Victor Logan was leaning forward between the two men flying the Huey, calling out the GPS coordinates as the helicopter ran through the sky about a hundred feet above the deck. A strong wind whipped through the open side doors. He saw nothing moving down on the ground.

"Okay," he said into his microphone when the coordinates were exact. "Cut your speed and start making wide circles to the left. Look sharp." The clattering helicopter bent into a left turn as Logan made a final check of the controls he would use to fire the minigun pods mounted on each side of the chopper.

Relying on the GPS coordinates was helpful only to a point. Ten-digit coordinates were precise to within about a meter, but from an unsteady and moving airborne platform like the Huey, identifying that specific meter was virtually impossible. The most they could hope to pinpoint was a distance that would be about two football fields square. If they saw something, the chopper would have to stop, turn around, and go back to find the point where the crew might have spotted something suspicious. Lining up a shot was easy; finding the target was hard.

The terrain was flat and cut into rectangles of irrigated green fields, which told Logan there were a lot of ditches down there in which a Special Forces operator could hide. But Middleton was not an operator, was out of shape, and was injured. That should provide an edge that would allow Logan to find them.

"Hey, Logan," called out the Russsky co-pilot. "We're here. Where are they? You sure you plugged in the right numbers?"

"Yeah, asshole, I'm sure I plugged in the right numbers. Just fly this crate and keep looking." *Where the fuck are you, Sniper?*

After completing two wide circles, Logan decided to look into some of the bigger ditch lines. "There's a culvert at about two o'clock. Let's check it out."

As soon as he heard the pitch change in the blades, Swanson called over his shoulder, "Get in the truck and start it up, General. We're going to have to move fast."

Middleton argued, "I can help you. I'll spot for you. The two of us would put out more firepower."

"No! Damn it! Get in the goddam truck! You're just one more thing I have to think about!"

Swanson ducked deeper behind the brush hide. Stealth was his best weapon, being able to spot the enemy before being seen. The pitch of the rotor blades changed again, to a *THUD-THUD-THUD* sound that indicated that the helo was coming to a hover. If it was going to just hang up there, edging lower and lower, whoever was inside eventually would see the truck.

Kyle was feeling the hard downdraft as the blades pushed churning air against the ground and the ditch funneled the wind into the tunnel. He kept one hand on some of the bushes, but the others blew away, and he was partially exposed.

The helicopter was about thirty yards away from the mouth of the culvert, and about seventy yards in the air, in a hover and beginning a slow 360-degree spin to scan the entire area. The right side was toward him, and he saw the miniguns. *If they open up with those, we're cooked.*

Swanson let go of the other bush and brought Excalibur to his shoulder as he leaned his left side against the concrete curve of the underpass to steady himself. The scope was at his eye by the time the canopy of the helicopter swung around to face him, the chopper spinning to its left. He saw the pilot in the left seat and the co-pilot on the right and someone else between them, probably to fire the machine guns.

"Look!" the Russian yelled over the radio and pointed his finger. "There they are!"

Victor Logan leaned forward a bit more and could see one man in a tunnel beneath the road. It was the sniper, and he already had his long rifle up and pointed at the helicopter. "Shit!" he said, reaching out to fire the miniguns, knowing it was too late.

Kyle waited to squeeze the trigger until the last possible moment in a contest of nerves, speed, and physics. The co-pilot was clear and large in Excalibur's scope, which already had glowed with the blue firing stripe, but he wanted the armor-piercing .50-caliber bullet to do more than just take out one guy. When the angle was just right, he finished the shot.

The big bullet smashed through the Plexiglas canopy, caught the Russian under the chin, and tore off the back of his head. Then it continued upward through the roof of the helicopter and into the complex housing of gears and rods that controlled the rotors.

Kyle held the scope on the helo, jacked in another round,

and fired again, punching out another chunk of the canopy. The bullet ricocheted through the control panel. He managed to fire a third round before the pilot was able to snatch the nose back around to the right and break away, trying to get out of the line of fire and gain some altitude. Kyle emptied the rest of the clip at the retreating, wobbling bird.

"I'm losing rotor control!" shouted the South African pilot as the helo coughed and the controls stiffened. A loud ripping noise came from overhead, where the rotor gears were grinding themselves apart, and fire broke out in the cockpit.

He wrestled with the aircraft, trying to push it from hover to full power and then bleed off speed for landing. The Huey wasn't responding, and began tilting on its own.

"We're going in!" he screamed, and covered his face with his arms.

Victor Logan, strapped into a harness that had allowed him free movement, was sprawled on his back. He grabbed the metal struts of seats along the back of the cabin, pushing his feet hard against the bulkhead separating the front compartment just as the helicopter smashed nose-first into a green and soggy field. He blacked out.

Swanson was running to the truck before the helicopter crashed 400 yards away. Middleton had cranked it, left it in neutral, opened the driver's door, and slid across to the passenger side, where he buckled his seatbelt and pointed his Kalishnikov out the window.

The sniper piled in behind the wheel, pushed Excalibur over to the general, and tossed him a packet of ammo from his web gear. "Reload!"

Kyle jammed the truck into low gear and mashed the accelerator to the floor. The Toyota's powerful engine roared, the truck skidded a bit in the muck of the culvert and then the big tires took hold, and they crashed out into the daylight, throwing up a wave of water on each side. A curtain of spray coated the windshield. Swanson saw the downed chopper, but that was no longer a threat, so he twisted the steering wheel

violently to the right and the truck growled up the embank-
ment and skidded onto the paved road.

"Where are we going?" yelled the general as he pushed
five .50-caliber bullets into a magazine and loaded one more
into the raceway.

"Away from here! Toward the LZ." He brought the truck
under control and looked back in the mirror. Two figures had
crawled from the wreckage of the helicopter. "They had us
dead to rights back there, General. Bastards knew exactly
where we were."

Middleton propped Excalibur between them. "An old
chopper like that with no markings. Must have been mercs."

Kyle left the truck in four-wheel drive as they sped along
the pavement because he might have to go off-road again at
any time. He agreed with Middleton. "Yeah, I'd bet on the
Frankensteins, too. And I'll also bet there are more of them
converging toward us."

"Want me to call the Fleet and get some fast-movers in
here?" Middleton reached for the sat phone.

"No, don't do that. We would have to give a precise location, and it could be picked up by the bad guys. Not much
time before the scheduled pickup anyway, so we have to play
hide and seek until then."

"Where?"

"Beats me, pardner," Swanson said with a cowboy twang.
"I'm a stranger in these parts."

Middleton threw back his head and laughed.

CHAPTER 57

THE PLAN IS NOT YET FINISHED, Ruth Hazel. There are still things we can do." Gordon Gates IV had lost none of his silkiness, none of his controlled modulation. He might well have been discussing a high school football game.

Senator Reed did not see it that way. "It is for me, Gordon. It is not every day that I, me, myself, personally am threatened by the President of the United States of America. It was not pleasant."

They were in the privacy of the manicured flower garden behind Gates's holiday home in Aspen, Colorado. He talked while scraping the honed blade of a fighting knife back and forth across a sharpening stone. "He's bluffing. If he had anything, you would be in custody by now and not making this visit."

"Why do you think the game isn't over?"

"You don't need to know that." Stroke, stroke the blade, a comforting feel in the routine for a man very familiar with how to use a knife. "Just remember that Middleton and the sniper have not yet been rescued. A fatal accident may befall them before they are."

"What do I do, then? Gerald Buchanan will name both of us as accomplices when he is subpoenaed, just to save his own skin. He is a stupid man and we were mistaken to bring him in on this."

"Leave Gerald up to me. He poses neither of us any threat, although he may think otherwise. He really was stupid, wasn't he? An arrogant and stupid man. We should have found someone else."

Reed's voice had a quaver in it as she recalled the chewing-out on Air Force One. "The President was absolutely thunderous. He *yelled* at me! I never saw him show anger like that."

"What did he say?"

"The short version is that there will be a full investigation by the attorney general, and the President does not care who gets taken down. Also, the privatization bill is dead because they figure the Middleton kidnapping was part of a plan to keep him from testifying. The President swore that he would hold a national press conference to veto it should the bill come before him."

That stopped Gates in his tracks. "Interesting." He sharpened his knife and decided to abort Operation Premier. The kiddies could go safely to the latest animated blockbuster this weekend. No use pissing off the Prez even more by blowing up a couple of multiplexes. The guy had brains, but he would also leave office someday, and Gates Global would still be around, bigger than ever. "Well, that just means we put it off for a couple of years and try again. Try to get someone in the Oval Office who will be friendlier to the business community and private enterprise. Someone like you, Senator. It's the job you wanted, isn't it?"

Ruth Hazel closed her political career in that beautiful yard filled with blooming flowers. "No longer. I'll leave at the end of the year when my term is up, go home to California, and undertake a very low-profile life. The choice between my house in Del Mar and prison is a pretty easy one."

"Have you left any loose ends, anything with my name attached?"

"Not a one, Gordon. There is nothing in my files or notes or on my computer that mentions you in any questionable fashion whatsoever. I never had a whispered conversation with a lover, nor a private chat with an aide about our plans." She looked him directly in the eyes. "Even if I have to go on trial for something, I would never mention you. I've always understood that you would have me killed by a Shark Team if I put you in jeopardy."

"Now that's where you are wrong, my dear." Gates grinned at her, then whirled and threw the knife with force; it spun, end over end, and the point stuck deep into the trunk of a tree ten feet away. "It would not be a Shark Team. I would do it myself." He walked to the tree, pulled the blade free, and resumed sharpening it. "We do understand each other, then?"

"Oh, yes. Quite," she said. She reached into her shoulder bag for a tissue, and let her hand brush against the 9 mm pistol she had begun to carry. *I'll be waiting.*

CHAPTER 58

THEY SPED SOUTH DOWN THE highway, to the point where it intersected with a major east–west road. An unfenced area of tired old cars, wrecks, and abandoned mechanical devices and farming equipment was off to one side, a mechanical graveyard that had probably begun many years ago with someone's car breaking down on the road and being pushed to the side and abandoned. It had become a tangle of junk that spread over about ten acres, and Swanson steered into it, driving around until he found a crumbled old Mercedes cargo van that had rolled over in an accident and been hauled to the junk pile to rust in the punishing sun and wind.

Swanson stopped the Toyota next to the wrecked vehicle. "End of the line, General," he said. "We hump the rest of the way to the LZ, a few more kilometers."

"Why not just drive?" Middleton was out of the truck.

Swanson emptied his pack and picked out only a few things for them to carry. Water, more ammo, a few grenades, smoke grenades, and the sat phone. Each of them had a rifle, and he kept Excalibur over his shoulder and gave Middleton the pistol. It was time to lighten the load for the final dash, and if something would not fit on his web gear, he would leave it behind. When the pack was empty, he reloaded the computers in it, along with the sat phone, and gave it to the general to carry. "They will be looking for the truck now in a pretty narrow area, so we have to dump it and stay off the road."

Kyle had a drink of water and moved out, heading into the fields, and General Middleton followed. Swanson figured they were only about three kilometers from the landing zone, but could not go directly to it. He was considering how to circle wide around and come in from the side or the rear while keeping the sun behind him, when he found a small footpath that had been pounded out by generations of goats, sheep, and other animals and their keepers. *Probably leads to water.* "We're pretty near a population center now, so keep a sharp eye out for people moving about. We don't want to be seen."

One step at a time, he led them into the field and moved parallel to the path so as to leave no bootprints. The monotony of taking the slow steps helped him consider how the helicopter knew where to find them. There had been a Syrian army search going on, but that chopper flew in straight and was carrying mercs, and the more he thought about it, the more Kyle believed the Frankensteins knew where he was. He had to assume that someone had sold them out, just as the Force Recon rescue mission had been compromised.

He stopped, and Middleton stepped closer. They had walked about two miles from the junkyard, first through the fields and then tracking near the dirt path, which had narrowed as it went upward into irregular terrain when the cultivated area gave way to wrinkles of land that folded into distant hills. "We'll set up over there," he said, pointing to the first low rise.

A few minutes later, they reached the crest of the initial slope and Kyle got busy digging a hole for them while Middleton gathered bushes and stuck them into the ground in front of the hide. Swanson left Middleton lying there with the binos while he explored higher up the hill. Right behind their position, the little path ducked into a flat pocket of land that skirted a slightly higher hill. Kyle climbed it in five long steps, liked what he saw, and did some more digging, arranging a little wall of rocks and some brushwork, then came back down. He was careful this time to leave plenty of bootprints leading to the hide.

Then he went back off the trail and explored both sides of a small canyon that opened before him, and found a field of large rocks and boulders. He established a third hide there.

He trotted back to the original position. Both he and Middleton drank some more water, then lay side by side while they scanned the country they had crossed, Middleton with the binocs and Swanson with the scope of Excalibur, while Kyle explained the next step of the escape and evasion plan.

They saw it about the same time: a triangular dust trail rising from the road, kicked up by a fast-moving vehicle they recognized as the familiar shape of a Humvee. "Here they come," said Middleton. "With any luck, they'll stop and search the junkyard, or go highballing right on by us."

"Not a chance," Swanson replied. "Get on the horn and tell the MEU to come get us right now."

Victor Logan was in the passenger seat of the Humvee, with a map on his lap and the GPS locator box between his knees. He was sore all over from the crash, and his spine flared with so much pain that he believed he must have cracked something. At least he was better off than that Russky, who was shot in the face, and the pilot, who had two broken arms. The mercenary ignored his body and studied the readout. The numbers had been flashing steadily when the sniper was on the move, but had remained still now for more than a minute. Logan put a checkpoint on the map.

The big German was expertly handling the Humvee and the Gurkha was in the back seat, relaxed. Neither said anything. Logan saw that the road was flat and empty and straight, with some sort of clutter that looked like a stack of junk coming up on the right side in about a mile at an intersection. He located the crossroads on the map, then drew a line from his position on the road to the coordinates on the GPS. "Turn here," he told the German, and pointed off to the left at about a forty-five-degree angle.

The driver did not remove his foot from the gas pedal and

the Humvee went slashing into the field, the big wheels crushing a path through the cultivated plants.

"Damn!" Middleton exclaimed as the Humvee peeled away from the road. It had not even gotten to the junkyard, much less searched it. Instead, the vehicle was speeding straight for them.

"Yup," Kyle said. "Be ready to move out." He banished everything from his mind except the oncoming Humvee, and let time slow down on his internal clock as he took slow, deep breaths, never taking his eye from the scope. He let Excalibur do the math for a higher-to-lower elevation at two hundred yards.

The Humvee closed to three hundred yards, then two-fifty, and stopped.

Swanson released the scope to automatic range-finding. "That's fuckin' far enough," he said.

The German got out of the driver's side, and reached back inside to get a weapon. He had pale skin and a shaved head, wore narrow sunglasses, and apparently was chewing gum. The blue stripe flashed and Kyle took him out, the bullet crashing into his exposed left side beneath the arm and rupturing the heart and lungs. The big man was thrown sideways by the impact, dead before he hit the ground.

Middleton opened up with his AK-47 and Victor Logan dove from the other side and rolled into a drainage ditch, while the Gurkha went out the back and jumped to the opposite side of the vehicle. Both disappeared into the thick tangle of cotton plants.

Swanson put two more rounds into the engine block of the Humvee, and his shots were answered by searching, controlled, three-round bursts that pecked around their position. For several minutes, the firefight banged sporadically. Logan and the Gurkha were firing and crawling closer, trying to flank the hide.

A dark speck rose from the field and bounced toward them. "Grenade!" Kyle yelled and pushed Middleton down hard. The explosion shook the ground, sprayed a cloud of shrapnel, and blew up a cloud of dust and debris. Both attackers were up and running when the detonation occurred, then went back into cover and resumed firing.

"Go now," Kyle said. "You first."

Middleton pushed himself up enough to crawl backward out of the hole, turned, and sprinted up the trail. When he reached the curve, he knelt and called to Swanson. "Come on!" He fired short volleys into the fields.

Logan watched the readout when he saw the figure retreat, and the numbers had stayed steady. That was the general running. The sniper would be next. He took careful aim at a spot halfway between where the grenade had gone off and the spot where he saw the general disappear.

Swanson, with Excalibur in one hand and his M-16 in the other, took off, running low under the general's covering fire. Logan's bullets cracked around him, but he slid safely headfirst into the bushes beside Middleton. Both paused long enough to put more lead into the likely approaches to their old position.

"Drop the pack, take the sat phone, get back to the rocks, and pop a smoke," Swanson said. Middleton did as he was told while Kyle fired a few shots to keep the bad guys' heads down. He did not wait for Middleton to reach the new position. He ran forward, taking a couple of long strides up the little hill to where he had built the other hide, and lobbed the pack into it, then gripped Excalibur around the barrel and flung it into the hole, too. He sprinted back ten meters, dove prone behind some scrub brush, and began to crawl to his ambush point.

The Gurkha and Logan arrived at the original hide about the same time, and were moving fast. The American read the GPS numbers again and saw they were slightly different, but once again still, which indicated the sniper was in a new hide. While the Asian guy covered him, Logan crawled to the curve in the path and snuggled into some rocks and brush. He spotted the position: a hurriedly built hide bordered with rocks and bushes, with bootprints clear in the dirt.

He heard a pop and saw a stream of smoke rising from further up the trail. They had sent up a red smoke grenade, which meant that a rescue team was inbound and was to consider the LZ to be hot. Logan could not worry about that right now. Al-Shoum would be sending helicopters to the smoke, too, and the Marines and the Syrians could figure out what to do when they all arrived about the same time. Should be interesting, Logan thought, but he had to be gone by then.

He used hand signals to communicate with the Gurkha, who was on the ground about twenty feet away, and for the first time saw the man smile. Born in the Himalayas and growing up in the icy shadow of Mount Everest, the small commando felt more comfortable as the fight left the flat land and moved into some hills. His people had lived for centuries among the highest mountains in the world, and the spirit of these little hills spoke to him. He thought he could probably walk to the highest peak without breaking a sweat. Instead of moving directly up the path, the Gurkha crawled around to the left while Logan pumped shots up there to keep the Americans busy. He slung his rifle across his back and unsheathed his long knife with the thick curved blade. By custom, he could not put the *khukuri* away again until it tasted human blood, and he wanted it to taste Marine blood today.

It took him no more than a minute to come around a boulder and be within reach of the sniper's position. The Gurkha flipped a grenade into the secluded hole, ducked away to avoid the explosion, and was immediately up and charging, giving a chilling attack scream and slashing with his *khukuri*. There were no bodies, just the ruins of a long rifle and a backpack that had been shredded by shrapnel. The Gurkha realized his mistake just as Kyle Swanson came over the top, through the smoke, firing his M-16 at point-blank range.

Swanson was exposed during the attack for only a moment, but in that second, Victor Logan fired a quick burst at the shadow he saw moving through the dust of the explosion. Kyle felt bullets punch him in the stomach, and he was spun around, knocked over atop the dead Ghurka.

"Hoo-ah!" shouted Logan. "I got you, you bastard! I'm better than you!"

The mercenary felt cold steel at the back of his head. Before he could react, Brad Middleton pulled the trigger of the big pistol, and three shots pulverized the skull and the brains of Victor Logan. "No. You're not," said the general. "You're not even close to being as good as Shake."

Behind him, the sky seemed alive with approaching helicopters.

CHAPTER 59

CRISP FLIGHT ATTENDANTS welcomed Gerald Buchanan aboard the American Airlines passenger jet at Miami International and escorted him to a first-class seat aboard Flight 107 to Puerto Rico. After the dankness of Washington, he had been pleasantly blinded by the brilliant sun and the blue Florida skies. *Get used to it.* There were a lot of islands in the Caribbean and he planned to settle on one. He already had a new identity and a list of officials to bribe to avoid arrest and extradition. Marge and the kids would come down in a few months, and they would reestablish a home on a beach somewhere.

He was leaving behind his dream of being the behind-the-scenes king of New America, but felt excitement at moving toward a new dream, one of a long and comfortable life with plenty of money and a big sailboat on the Italian Riviera. He thanked the attendant, gave her a drink request, settled into the soft blue aisle seat, and buckled in. Another attendant was there immediately with an Absolut on ice with a twist of lime.

He looked over at the passenger in the next seat. His luck was already changing for the better, for next to him was an attractive woman in jeans and a loose T-shirt that showed a band of skin around her waist. Dark brown hair was pulled back in a ponytail, and she had kicked off her tennis sneakers to curl up in the spacious seat, working on a laptop computer balanced on the tray table. Graphs and charts and multipage reports danced on the screen as she clicked through whatever her project was. She was drinking a glass of white wine.

"Hi there," he said, taking a sip of his drink. Delicious. "May I ask what you're working on? It seems complicated."

"Oh, just some stuff about fish," she responded with a shy look. Not much makeup, and big wire-rimmed glasses. Intelligent blue eyes looked at him curiously. "Do I know you from somewhere? I mean, aren't you somebody famous on TV?"

Buchanan wanted to tell her everything, to impress her with his name and his title and his extraordinary reach and power. But that was all gone. According to his new passport, he was somebody else, moving toward a tomorrow to find new challenges to test his intellect. "No. Sorry." He extended his hand. "My name is Bob Walsh. I do oil exploration. And who are you?"

"Trish Campbell. Nice to meet you." She sipped her wine and pointed to the computer screen. "I'm a marine biologist up at Woods Hole in Massachusetts, and I've got to get out to the islands to tag some fish we believe are about ready to come off the endangered species list."

He noticed the huge wristwatch, a diver's chronograph with all sorts of dials. "Do you actually go swimming to find them?"

"All the time," she said and brought out a little tube of lotion, rubbing a dab on her cheeks. "That salt water and hot sun does a job on a girl's skin."

The doors closed, the pilot made his announcements, and she put away her laptop and removed the earplugs to the iPod that hung around her neck and dangled between her full breasts. The diving would explain the tightness of her body. He had no trouble imagining her in a clinging wetsuit with a scuba tank. Flight AA 107 was in the clouds a few minutes later. The seatmates chatted through the first drink, and Buchanan ordered another round.

"Are you going to hunt for oil down here?" asked Trish Campbell.

"No. Just burning off some accumulated holiday time, then I'm off to some other dismal place in the oil patch, possibly up in the North Sea to freeze my ass off," he said. "My family can't be with me for a while. Could I persuade you to have dinner with me tonight?"

She let the question hang as she studied his face, then she gave a warm smile and said, "Maybe."

Buchanan was regaining his confidence, which had been sorely tried by the setbacks of recent days. *That damned Sniper! I hope Gordon takes care of him in a most horrible way.* Of course Trish Campbell would dine with him. By the end of the evening, she would do anything he wanted. They always did.

The announcement came over the loudspeaker that it was permissible to use electronic equipment again, and Trish dug out her laptop and plugged in the iPod. A few clicks of the keyboard and she had MTV rocking, but only she could hear it. On the screen, a sexy girl was humping a boy wearing an oversize basketball jersey and a baseball cap turned to the side.

"What kind of fish are you going to tag?" he asked.

She glanced over and turned down the volume. "What?"

"Sorry. I asked about your job. What kind of fish will you be tagging?"

"Wrong question to ask a marine biologist," Trish laughed. She clicked off MTV and called up a program of big fish swimming slowly to and fro. "Sharks," she replied. "I'm into sharks. I don't want to bore you, but would you like to see something really hot?"

"Sure. I'm really interested." It was always a good play to pretend to be fascinated by a woman's work.

Trish slid the laptop onto his tray table and leaned across to insert the iPod buttons in his ears. He felt the weight of her breast against his forearm, and the clean smell of her perfume. He would gladly put up with MTV and fish for a roll in the hay with her.

"This is really good. You ready? Can you hear it okay?" When he nodded, she said, "Okay, watch and listen very closely," punched in a five-digit sequence, and clicked ENTER.

The fish dissolved slowly into a slide show. Buchanan was stunned as the pictures flipped past. The first was a full view of himself in the front yard of his home. Then came that picture of Marge that they always kept on the baby grand, and a photo of her playing with their dog, Rio. An action photo of fourteen-year-old Lester playing soccer. One of Missy studying in the library at Princeton, followed by a semi-nude picture of Missy on a bed, smiling sleepily at the camera. Photos of his cousin Florence and her kids, his brother and his family, and his bedridden mother in the assisted living facility.

The last picture was a live camera shot. Gordon Gates sitting at his desk, looking directly at Buchanan.

"Hello, Gerald," he said. "Going somewhere? Don't say anything out loud, just type your replies and look into the little camera button on the side of the computer screen. We will make this quick."

"Gordon? What is this!" he said aloud, but was pinched painfully under the arm by Trish, who pointed at the keyboard. "Type!" she said, and he did. WHAT IS THIS?

"That was a little photo album that we gathered of your entire family." Gates's voice in his ear was cold. "Did you like the one of Missy on the bed? Looks like your little princess just got laid, but never mind that for now. The young woman seated next to you and the big guy across the aisle, who happens to be the air marshal for this flight, are a Shark Team, ole buddy. They are there to make sure you do what you are told."

WHY ARE YOU DOING THIS?

"You bugged out on me, Gerald. Abandoned me to my fate, so to speak. That kind of made me angry, so you have to make things right between us."

I AM NOT GOING TO TELL ANYONE.

"That's for damned sure. By now, Trish should have a typed letter resting on her briefcase. It is a full confession that you were responsible for the entire Middleton kidnapping affair because you wanted to start a war as cover for a political coup in Washington. You realize now that you were wrong, that lives were wasted, that you misused your position and the power of the White House and besmirched the reputation of the United States. Noble shit like that. It's a good letter: says a lot in two pages. Your new Constitution will also be in the envelope. Sign it."

WE WERE IN THIS TOGETHER.

"After you sign, Trish will give you two little white pills. You will go into the bathroom at the front of the plane and swallow them. Within twenty seconds you will simply go to sleep, feeling no pain, and be dead."

HELL NO FUCK YOU GORDON.

"One second, Gerald, while I rearrange the screen." There was a scramble of the signal and a smaller picture popped into the lower right-hand corner. "There's dear old Mommy, Gerald, sleeping in that fancy old folks' home in Palm Beach. You just visited her about four hours ago, remember? Anyway, I have a nurse standing there taking this picture. You don't sign the paper, Mumsy is going to be put down like a dog with a needle filled with a medicine that will make her last moments hell. She will feel like she is on fire on the inside, and it will take her five long minutes to die. Next on the list will be your little soccer star, Lester, who will fall from a window in a tall building. How could you name a kid Lester, anyway? One by one, until they are all gone. Then the Sharks will kill you anyway."

DON'T PLEASE DON'T DO THIS.

"Sign the fucking letter. Take the fucking pills. Trish will let me know when it's over. You have three minutes before the nurse gives your mother the injection. Terrible way for the old woman to go. Goodbye, Gerald. Do the right thing."

NONONONONONONONONO.

The screen returned to the fish show and Trish pulled away the laptop and jerked the iPod buds from his ears. She slapped a letter on the plastic tray and put a pen on top of it. She made a show of clicking a button on her big diver's watch. "Two minutes and fifty-nine seconds . . . two minutes and fifty-eight seconds."

Gerald Buchanan felt a tear come to his eye as he scanned the letter. He would go down in history not as the savior of his country, but as its biggest traitor since Benedict Arnold. No! It was too much of a sacrifice! His reputation through the ages!

"Two minutes and thirty seconds," Trish said, now with a mocking smile on her face. She held up a small plastic bag containing two white pills.

He closed his eyes and put his head against the backrest for a moment, folding his fingers together tightly to keep from taking up the pen. *Everybody has to die sometime, including every member of my family. They are only mortal, after all. Death comes to us all eventually.* He could run to the flight attendant, but the passenger they believed to be the air marshal was actually one of the Sharks! He leafed through the alternatives. They couldn't kill him in the open cabin if he stood up and made a scene! Sure they could. They were professional killers. He was already a dead man. It was only a matter of choosing how he would go.

"Two minutes, darling," Trish whispered in his ear, and her breath was hot. "I'm afraid you won't be around for dinner tonight."

Buchanan looked at her. "Bitch," he said.

"Big Lenny over there and I will do Missy this weekend," she replied with a cold smile. "But your little whore will give us a good time first. An all-nighter. You only have one minute, fifty seconds. Your mutt gets poisoned tomorrow morning. Marge will be raped and then die when the house burns down around her. Cousin Flo and her family are going to have a tragic automobile accident . . . one forty-five."

Buchanan scrawled his name just to stop her awful recitation. Trish snatched the letter away and placed the two pills on the tray. He picked them up without a further word and made his way to the clean bathroom, filled a cup of water, and quickly swallowed the pills before the man in the mirror lost his nerve. Gates had lied. It was not painless. Buchanan went into spasms and convulsions and screamed in agony as fire coursed through his veins and he thrashed about the small toilet enclosure. When the alarmed attendants forced the door open, they found the bulky body of Gerald Buchanan curled into the fetal position. A soapy foam oozed from his mouth.

Trish looked across the aisle at her partner. "Fifteen seconds to spare," she said. She sent the confirmation signal to Gates.

CHAPTER 60

SIR GEOFFREY CORNWELL, Major General Bradley Middleton, and Master Gunnery Sergeant O. O. Dawkins were around a small table, watching the sun settle into the Pacific Ocean. The La Fonda restaurant, perched on a cliff, was almost empty at this time of day in the middle of the week. It was about two kilometers outside the Mexican town of Puerto Nuevo, and subsisted primarily on the weekend exodus of Americans who came down from California like clockwork to play along the coastline of the Baja Peninsula. Steep stairs chipped into the cliff face covered a vertical drop of some eighty feet to a white sandy beach, and beyond that, out on the water, a few surfers were still on their boards, waiting to catch a final wave before the sun set. They knew it was not safe to be on a surfboard after dark, for sharks like to feed at night.

The *Vagabond* was lodged securely in a nearby marina, and Cornwell took Lady Pat and his guests out for an early dinner of lobster tacos and cold Pacifico cerveza. Mariachi bands were playing in some other restaurants, and the songs drifted on the salty air. Lady Pat went shopping with Middleton's wife, Janice, and the three men stayed to drink beer. They raised their bottles in a salute. "To Gunnery Sergeant Kyle Swanson, USMC," said Sir Jeff, and the others said in unison, "Semper fi." Middleton added, "May he rest in peace."

They had all been at the funeral six months ago, and since Swanson had no family, the flag draped over the coffin was folded and given to Lady Pat, whose teary eyes were hidden by dark sunglasses. An honor guard fired a farewell salute, and the chairman of the Joint Chiefs of Staff, General Henry Turner, gave a brief speech before yielding the microphone to the President of the United States, who read the proclamation for a posthumously awarded Congressional Medal of Honor. The service was solemn and proper and very vague on details.

Now, with so much time having passed, Middleton took a long drink and gave a little laugh. "Shake treated me like a new recruit," he recalled of the Syrian fiasco. "I thought a couple of times we might shoot each other before anybody else got the chance."

"It was indeed a merry chase," said Sir Jeff, who had been briefed privately on the details of the mission weeks earlier to help solve the final mystery.

"Not so fucking merry at times," said Double-Oh. "When we came into the LZ it looked like a helicopter air show. The Syrians were facing us, and we were facing them, soldiers spreading out on both sides. Two lines and everybody was locked and loaded. Then those two Harriers came screaming in right overhead, no more than a hundred feet off the deck, and gave the Syrians an attitude adjustment. After that, we all got along just skippy."

The Englishman called for another round of beer. "I cannot tell you chaps how sorry I am about Excalibur. We have mended the problem, of course."

"I almost crapped my pants when I saw Shake throw the rifle and the pack with the computers into that hole. The grenade tore apart the most likely source of hard evidence against Gates. That's how the bastard skated free of charges."

"General," said Dawkins, "Kyle wasn't there to collect evidence like a cop."

"Of course. He knew that we were bugged, and the only

three things that could be giving off a signal were his long gun or the laptops. He didn't have a chance to figure out which, so all of them had to go. It worked. The Frankensteins bit, and went after the GPS position instead of us."

Jeff rolled a chunk of lobster into a warm flour tortilla and covered it with hot sauce. He took a bite, and it was a slice of heaven. After a drink of cold beer, he shrugged. "When we designed the GPS system for Excalibur, none of us even considered that it could be used against whoever was carrying the rifle. It was strictly to help with the computations and to help the shooter know his position, but we did not guess that it might be pirated. Only three of us knew about that capability anyway. Two of them are now dead. My number-one man, a delightfully solid former Para named Timothy Gladden, sold us out to Gates."

It was getting dim outside and only three surfers were left, and the waves continued to slope in irregular and small. "My own security team, making a scrub of our telecommunications systems, picked up that someone in our shop had called Gates. I was thinking it was just some industrial espionage going on, not unheard of in our business, until you told me about the GPS tracking device you found on the body of that mercenary. Excalibur's one flaw almost brought about an armed conflict."

"But it didn't," said Middleton. "And it won't again in the future."

"Right-o!" said Sir Jeff. "Unfortunately, Tim Gladden had a terrible accident on our trip across the Atlantic a few weeks ago. He fell overboard during some heavy weather and was never seen again. Tragic."

Only one surfer was left in the fading light, a bearded fellow with shaggy blond hair who seemed in no hurry to come back in. "Look at that lad," said Cornwell. "Sitting out there like he doesn't have a care in the world."

The surfer sat easily on his board, facing sideways between the setting sun and the cliff, waiting for a set of waves. Being dead wasn't all that bad. He could live with it. Anyway, without Shari, what was the point? He unconsciously rubbed the gnarly scars on the left side of his abdomen where the doctors had dug out the two bullets, and then had to go back in later to stop a raging infection caused by tiny threads of dirty cloth taken inside by one of the rounds. He had lost a chunk of his large intestine and his spleen, and a bullet fragment had ripped down far enough to crack a bone in his hip. That was only physical. Losing Shari was what really hurt.

His friends were waiting for him up in the little restaurant overlooking the K-54 beach, but his attention was on the patterns of the incoming waves. His recovery had been very slow, but he had recovered from wounds before. What would not heal was the part of his heart that was missing. Nothing would make that ache go away, but he knew of some medicine that would make it easier to bear.

A shadow curled below the horizon, a set coming in steep and flowing toward the beach with intense purpose. He saw them building and getting higher, and turned the board toward the beach and started to paddle. Then the first wave caught up and pulled the long board into its powerful center. He was riding with the break when he pushed up against his fifteen-year-old board, planted his feet, and stood, relaxed and perfectly balanced, and rode all the way in, wrapped in the pure essence and freedom of surfing.

The man who was no longer Kyle Swanson waded from the water and hauled the board up the worn stairs, bumping it a couple of times on the stones, as always happened at the K-54. It wore its scars with honor, just like its owner.

The following day, the *Vagabond* had snugged into a berth in San Diego after passing more naval ships at rest than most nations had in their entire fleets. Coming in from the sea instead of across by land at the San Ysidro crossing meant no border inspection. Two aircraft carriers were in port, Marine recruits were going through boot camp, and SEALs were training on a Coronado beach. Two-star general Brad Middleton examined the gathered vessels for a while with Sir Jeff, then went belowdecks and knocked on a stateroom door. Master Gunnery Sergeant Dawkins opened it, and Middleton stepped inside.

"You about ready?" Middleton asked. He and Double-Oh were on a unique shopping tour of elite units within the Navy and Marine Corps, looking to steal some hard-bodied warrior types for the general's new command. After the congressional hearings and subsequent investigations, Middleton "went black" and took Double-Oh with him as operations chief.

It had been decided that if Kyle Swanson remained dead and buried, a special unit would be built around the sniper, just as a professional football team could build a championship around a franchise quarterback. They could surround him with support players who were similar masters of their own specialties, and they would have a unit that could go anywhere and do anything, because the people on it did not exist.

Kyle had agreed, on one condition, and his wish had been granted. Now he was at a mirror on the far side of the stateroom with a splattered towel around his shoulders, the result of dyeing his long hair black. "I look like fucking Charlie Manson," he said.

"Naw, you don't have that little swastika thingie on your forehead," said Double-Oh. "You look like some heavy-metal freak."

"You ready for this?" asked Middleton, taking a seat on the bed. "Once it starts, you're on your own."

"More than ready, General. Jeff wants me to field-test Excalibur II. I'll be back in a few days and then we can get to work."

"Okay, Shake. I'll see you back here on the boat in five days." Middleton walked out.

Double-Oh popped Swanson on the shoulder with a balled fist and waved as he shut the door. "Later."

Kyle looked at the photograph on the California driver's license of James K. Polk. A Social Security card and two credit cards in the same name were on a night table, along with a thousand dollars. The dark hair of the man in the picture was pulled back in a ponytail, and the facial hair was neatly trimmed. He picked up the scissors and began to shape the beard.

Taped to the mirror were stories he had clipped from the society pages of *The Denver Post* and the *Rocky Mountain News*. After dinner with Jeff and Pat, he put Excalibur II into the trunk of a silver SUV and drove east. A stack of new CDs kept the music flowing, and he actually felt comfortable for the first time in six months.

EPILOGUE

ASPEN, COLORADO (UNP)—The body of missing billionaire industrialist Gordon Gates IV was found late yesterday in the rugged Rocky Mountains, police announced.

Law enforcement sources said that Gates had been killed by a single bullet to the head in an apparent hunting accident.

Gates, a decorated military veteran and avid hunter, was last seen Saturday night when he hosted his annual Christmas season fund-raising gala at his elegant home in this elite mountain resort. Some of the guests said he left about midnight in hopes of reaching a secluded canyon in which a rogue mountain lion recently killed two campers and mauled another.

"Gordon really wanted that big cat," said his attorney, Wilford Stanton, at Gates Global headquarters in Washington, D.C. "He spent a small fortune on guides and employed military-style detection equipment to track it to this particular location. He felt the lion was a danger to everyone in the area, and wanted to be the one to bring it down."

Sheriff Matt Randall said other hunters frequently had also been seen in the area stalking the mountain lion. "Mr. Gates was wearing a brush camouflage outfit, but not a brightly colored warning vest. Somebody apparently saw him move and took a hasty shot. The victim took a large-caliber round in the left temple and was dead by the time he hit the dirt."

A police search for other hunters was unsuccessful. "We are asking anyone with information about this unfortunate accident to come forward."

Gates Global, the multinational holding company, posted a reward of a million dollars leading to the arrest and conviction of the shooter.

Gates had recently been under intense government scrutiny for alleged corruption involving government contracts, and his firm sustained substantial public relations damage last year over alleged involvement in the kidnapping of Marine Brigadier General Bradley Middleton and the Syrian situation. The company insisted it had no knowledge of any involvement, and Gates invited the FBI to search its files and databases. Nothing was discovered that would link the giant corporation to the abduction.

Read on for an excerpt from the next book
by Jack Coughlin with Donald A. Davis

DEAD SHOT

Coming soon in hardcover from St. Martin's Press

CHAPTER 1

THE GREEN ZONE
BAGHDAD, IRAQ

IT WAS JUST A MATTER OF WAITING. Juba was good at
waiting. Patience was an important tool for him, as it was for
all snipers. The Iraqi desert sun baked and parched him, but
his soul remained calm, soothed by the instructions of his
two fathers and the sure knowledge that the hunt was on.
Once again, he was the sword of the Prophet. *God is great!*
he whispered, feeling guilty for breaking his oath and speaking the words of praise.

He had been in the hole for three days, shaded only by a
few bushes during the hottest part of the blistering after-
noons. He let his face and neck become sunburned and measured his rations carefully, eating and drinking only enough
to survive. The last chocolates from his field rations had
been eaten, and he had intentionally drained the last water
from his canteens the previous day. He was hungry, and
thirst clawed at his throat. Good.

Throughout the time in the hide, he had heard sporadic
traffic passing unseen only fifty meters away and the occasional boom of an explosion somewhere down the track.
Each morning an American patrol rolled past, clouds of dust

following the big vehicles. He could have gotten help anytime he wanted it. Didn't want it.

On the fourth morning, the sun was up and the temperature was climbing when he saw the faraway dust clouds kicked up by the oncoming patrol. No wonder they were so easy to ambush. He crawled from the hide, brushed away the signs of his stay by brooming the area with a bush, and staggered to the road. The vehicles now could be seen with the naked eye, which meant they could see him, too, a wobbling soldier alone in the desert.

He held up his hands as if in surrender to the first Bradley Fighting Vehicle that approached, with its .50 caliber machine gun trained on him. Then he collapsed. A lieutenant of the U.S. 1st Cavalry Division instantly recognized the disruptive pattern camouflage uniform and weathered beret worn by the British soldier and jumped down to help. They pulled him into the shade of the big vehicle.

Sweat caked the dusty face and dirt clung to the filthy uniform, and when they started pouring some water into his mouth, he greedily grabbed for the canteen. The American pulled it back. "Easy, pal. Just a little bit at a time. You're gonna be okay." He offered another sip. A medic smoothed a wet salve on the sunburned face, neck, and hands.

Juba slowly responded in a British accent, haltingly explaining that his sniper team had been discovered a week ago and his spotter killed in the ensuing fight. The Englishman had evaded the searching insurgents, found this road before dawn today, and walked next to it since then, hoping that a friendly force would spot him before the insurgents did. The Americans were unaware that his uniform and the rifle hanging from his shoulder had been stripped from a British soldier he had killed outside of Basra.

Juba was able to stand unaided by the time a helicopter arrived, and he thanked the American soldiers and climbed into the bird. Within thirty minutes, it delivered him to the landing pad of a military hospital inside the Green Zone of Baghdad. A stretcher team met him, but he waved them off, and they led him into a cool corridor, then into a big room where other soldiers lay on cots. A nurse helped him remove his tunic and stuck a needle into his arm to start a slow drip of hydrating fluids. He had been in the outside heat for so long that the fresh liquid going directly into his veins, plus the air-conditioning, caused a deep and instant chill, and he began to shake as if he were freezing. The nurse recognized the reaction as normal and wrapped a blanket around his shoulders as a doctor came over to check him. Exhaustion, sunburn, and dehydration, but no wounds. Juba lay back on the cot, enjoying the brief rest and the air-conditioning.

As the IV drip was finishing, a courteous U.S. intelligence captain came to his cot, having already notified British commanders that their man had been rescued. "They thought you were dead," said the captain, settling into a chair. He thought the guy looked like hell. "So what happened out there, Sergeant?"

The officer took a few notes as Juba repeated his tale of a mission gone wrong. "Sorry about your buddy," the American said and put away the notebook. "Bad shit."

"Part of the job, mate." Juba sighed and leaned back on the green sheet of the metal-framed cot.

"Your instructions are to rest up and then return to your unit as soon as medically fit," said the captain.

The busy doctor in uniform came by just long enough to look him over for a final time and remove the needle. "I've signed your discharge slip, Sergeant. You're going to be fine except for a few aches and pains and that sunburn. Drink a lot of water and have some chow. Here's some ointment for the burn, and if you need more, just come by the pharmacy. You want something to help you sleep tonight?"

"No, sir. I've dealt with worse than this."

"Okay, then. You're free to leave. Good luck."

The intel officer was still there. "Come on with me, soldier, and I'll take you over to the mess hall, then give you a chit for a bed tonight in the guest quarters. Your orders from British HQ are to rest up and then report back to your unit. Meanwhile, you're a guest of Uncle Sam."

Juba pushed himself from the cot, acting wobbly, then

drew himself erect and stretched, turning side to side. The body was lean and muscular. He put on his tunic. "Thank you, sir, but I plan something a little more upscale. I'm going to get a hotel room, raid the minibar, take a long shower, get some decent food, and then sleep for two days."

"I hear ya," said the officer. "I've got everything I need. Stay safe." He waved Juba through the door. The sniper ducked into a bathroom, locked himself into a stall, dropped his trousers to retrieve some documents from a plastic bag that had been tucked just above his right boot, and put them in his shirt pocket. He came out, signed for his rifle at the makeshift armory, and left the hospital. Back on the hunt. Closer than before.

He took his time crossing the military areas of the Green Zone as he made his way over to the new Nineveh Hotel, a five-star, four-hundred-room edifice that offered safety, opulence, an indoor Olympic-sized swimming pool, a gourmet restaurant, and other luxury conveniences to foreign visitors, diplomats, and business executives. The gleaming signature spire and a communication array on the roof made it the tallest building in Baghdad.

Despite the outward appearances of commerce, Baghdad remained a military town, and it was not thought strange at all when Juba unfolded the papers that he had carried in the plastic bag and handed them to the concierge of the Nineveh. The documents allowed him to commandeer the corner suite on the twelfth floor for an unspecified "military necessity," the code that unlocked any door in the city. The civilian led him to the suite and joked during the elevator ride about how things were improving. Soft music played in the background.

Juba thanked him, locked the door, and dumped his gear and clothes. He showered, shaved, cleaned his uniform, and put it back on. He snatched three pillows from the bed, piled them on the small dining table in the center of the suite, and stacked his pack atop them to provide a solid support for the long rifle. Crawling on his knees, then his stomach, he moved to the sliding glass door that led onto the balcony and pushed it open by a narrow six inches. Then he wiggled back about seven feet and stood in the shadows of the room, overlooking the neat front garden with lawns of grass that was irrigated to a deep lush green.

Juba lifted his L115A1 long-range rifle, made by Accuracy International UK, the standard weapon of a British sniper. It fired a .338 Lapua Magnum round that was accurate up to 1,100 meters, and it had a Killflash silencer on the muzzle and a bipod. He had zeroed the weapon two days ago and was confident it would hold enough for the task today. From his position, he could see the outside world, but no one on the ground could see him.

Juba had exchanged the standard Schmidt & Bender PM II telescopic sight for the better Zeiss version used by the Germans, and he peered through it to examine the foot traffic along the pathways. A wolf eyeing a flock of sheep. The people below seemed startlingly close through the clear optics. The first potential target to stroll through his kill zone was a civilian wearing a loud Hawaiian shirt and tan trousers. Too easy: a foreign contractor who meant nothing, and killing Americans was not his mission today. It had to be the man with the secret. Sooner or later, he would come along, if the intelligence was correct. Juba would wait. He knew how to wait.

He put down the rifle, sat in a soft chair, and flipped through the English-language newspaper that had been delivered free to the hotel room and checked the football scores to see if Manchester United had won.

He sipped chilled water from a plastic bottle. Scorching outside air oozed through the slightly opened door and did battle with the room's buzzing air conditioner. The flat-screen color television set mounted in the wall was on, and he adjusted the volume slightly to the loud side. News readers rattled on about next week's royal wedding in London, elevating the event steadily so that by Tuesday, the marriage of the prince and his girlfriend would be considered the most important thing in the world. Millions of people would watch. As a British subject, he vividly remembered the legends of the glory days of the monarchy, lessons that had been pounded into him as a student and later as a soldier defending the Crown. He planned to be there for the wedding.

Juba was slightly under six feet in height and slender at 170 pounds, with the fair hair of his British mother and the dark eyes of his Arab father. His skin was several shades darker than the normal Briton, more of a nice California tan that had been darkened even more by his work in the desert. It helped him move with ease in the twilight gulf between Christians and Muslims. Juba could be anybody he wanted to be, and for the past few days, he had again chosen the familiar role of a British Army sniper. It was his best disguise, because he once had been awarded the coveted sniper's patch of two crossed rifles with an S between the barrels.

After reading the sports in the newspaper, he put his eye back to the scope and considered the next possible target, an approaching soldier who, despite the midday heat, wore a helmet and a flak jacket. This had once been the safest place in Iraq, the International Zone, home of the giant U.S. Embassy. It once had been known as the Green Zone, and although bureaucrats changed the name to better claim that the war was the effort of many nations, the Green Zone name stuck. Juba was tempted by the soldier, for he always enjoyed the challenge of placing a bullet in the small gaps of the armored vests or between the ceramic plates. Not the mission: Let him pass.

An hour before sundown, four soldiers in full armor appeared, moving in a box formation as they escorted a smaller man toward the Coalition Headquarters building where the first formal interrogation was to take place. The soldier on the left front corner was talking and making sharp, descriptive motions with one hand, probably an officer directing the prisoner transfer. Except that the man was not a prisoner, more a valuable guest of the Coalition. He had arrived yesterday in Baghdad, with the secret locked in his head. The Iraqi physicist planned to hand the information to the Americans and the British officials, but he had made too many mistakes in escaping from the laboratory in Iran. The biggest error was in trusting his coworkers, who were able to provide almost a minute-by-minute schedule for the defector. Then Juba had been summoned.

The traitor could not be allowed to reach the interrogation room alive. Juba pressed his cheek into the cool stock, his fingers roving with familiarity over the rifle to make sure it was ready. They were three hundred yards away, and he checked the flags on the government building. He estimated the wind at seven to ten miles per hour full value, right to left, which would move the fired round two inches to the left at two hundred yards. He adjusted the scope to compensate. Humidity was zero.

He settled the scope on the officer and looked for a weakness. The waving arm! The officer was describing something, and his right arm windmilled to make his point. Juba exhaled and let his heartbeat slow almost to nothing. Under the arm, that's the place.

At two hundred yards, almost point-blank range, he squeezed the trigger back, slow and steady and straight, just as the American raised his arm above shoulder level. The big rifle fired, and the Killflash ate up the noise as the bullet entered beneath the right armpit of the officer, smashed down through the rib cage and exited out of his lower left side, crushing bones and shredding every organ in its path. The officer died before anyone could reach out to help him.

Juba accepted the light recoil and cycled another round into the chamber as the startled group stopped in its tracks. He brought his scope to the small man in the middle. They had heard nothing, but the colonel had just been shot! The soldiers spun around, looking for the threat but leaving the target uncovered. The Iraqi automatically bent down, turning to aid the fallen American. That exposed the left rear side of his neck, and Juba centered the crosshairs right there and pulled the trigger again. He was able to see the vapor trail of the bullet, which impacted right below the base of the skull and ripped out the throat when it came out the other side. Two catastrophic kills.

Juba put aside the rifle, ducked down to the floor, crawled forward, and reached up to slowly close the door to the outside patio. He went back, retrieved his kit and the rifle, tossed the pillows back onto the bed, and left the room.

He increased his pace through the lobby and hurried outside with other armed soldiers and civilian private security company guards who were moving into the attack area. A Quick Reaction Force would arrive within minutes, and uniformed men would be all over the place, with all sorts of weapons pointing everywhere, and Juba would be just another soldier with a gun. He made his way through the crowd and walked out of the Green Zone unmolested.

That evening, a small Royal Jordanian Airlines Fokker plane took off on schedule from the Baghdad International Airport. On its manifest was a quiet Canadian civilian engineer with fair hair and dark eyes. Juba was going to London.

The secret that Saddam Hussein had taken to his grave remained safe. The Palace of Death was secure.

CHAPTER 2

CAPTAIN SYBELLE SUMMERS of the U.S. Marine Corps walked purposefully into a secure briefing room at Incirlik Air Force Base in southeastern Turkey. Many of the combat-ready Marines who were to conduct the mission recognized her immediately, and the others knew her reputation as operations officer of a special operations unit known as Task Force Trident.

"Oh, oh. It's the Queen of the Night," muttered a lance corporal. "We've stepped in it. They don't use the Bride of Dracula on small jobs."

"Count Dracula divorced her for spousal abuse," whispered the man next to him.

"Shhh. Summers will kick your ass if she hears you."

The experienced warriors of the Marine Special Operations Command (MARSOC) normally shied away from taking orders from women, but Summers was different. She wore a black jumpsuit with the silver railroad tracks insignia of her rank glinting on the collar of a turtleneck sweater and projected a maximum "don't give me any shit" attitude as she walked to the podium and flipped open a file folder. Her short black hair, dark blue eyes, and lithe figure disguised the fact that she was the only woman ever to make it through Force Recon training.

"Settle down," she snapped, and the MARSOC team quieted. "We are going after a High Value Target tonight in Iraq, and I don't want any of you jarheads to screw this up. Mustapha Ahmed al-Masri has surfaced again, stirring up the Kurds in northern Iraq, and the intelligence pukes have pinpointed his location. They list him as the number two for al Qaeda in the region, which is why he has been designated an HVT and we have been assigned to stop him."

She walked around the podium to the front and nodded to her left. A door opened and a man stepped in, also wearing a black jumpsuit and with his face covered by a pull-down mask. A long rifle of a sort they did not recognize was slung over his shoulder. Sniper.

"Batman?" whispered the lance corporal.

"Maybe a holdup," joked his partner.

"CIA spook. Definitely."

Summers spoke. "You guys will assault the house at 0500, and I'll leave it to the other briefers to give you the details. By the time you arrive, this gentleman and I will already be on the ground, closing the back door. He is masked simply because you do not need to know who he is. The two of us have been attached as special operators for this mission. Far as you are concerned, we aren't here, and we will go in and extract on our own."

As she finished, other briefing officers came forward with their maps and timetables. The lights started to dim. "If you see al-Masri, kill him. The best bet is that he will haul ass once the attack starts, and we will be waiting. You absolutely must remember that this is friendly territory and be sure not to have civilian casualties. If you screw up and shoot at us, even by mistake, he will shoot back, and I guarantee that you don't want that to happen. Be very careful when you pull the trigger. Know your targets. That's it. Good luck and good hunting. Captain Barnes will continue your brief." She spun on her heel and disappeared out the door with the masked man.

Once they were in the Humvee and driving to the helicopter pad beside the ten-thousand-foot runway, Kyle Swanson rolled up the mask, changing it into a watch cap. His face itched. "Damn, Sybelle, you are a woman of few words." He changed his voice to imitate her grim briefing cadence. " 'Shoot at us and he will shoot back!' Way to inspire confidence in the troops."

They both laughed. "I had to get their attention. We don't want any mistakes out there."

"I knew about half the guys in that room," Swanson said. "Worked with some of them. It's always strange not letting friends know who you really are." In special ops, he had a million aliases but no real name at all because he was officially dead.

The Turkish night was crisp and starlit, with a slice of a coasting moon. A giant Air Force cargo plane roared overhead on its landing approach, hauling more material from the States into Incirlik, a major supply dump that fed the war in Iraq. Adana, a modern city of a million people, was less than ten miles away, and the Mediterranean washed onto beaches within casy access. For special operations types, it was a good location. You could get a decent hamburger and a cold beer, jump on a bird and fly off on a quick combat mission, and be back in time for a hot shower and a movie.

Swanson brought the Humvee to a halt beside a hangar, and they both got out and suited up with their web gear. Summers removed her shiny captain's bars because they were entering the world of hiding, blending, and deceiving, a dark place where nothing must reflect light. She had assigned herself to this mission for several reasons, one being that she still spoke the language of her childhood, although her Kurdish last name had disappeared when her father had died and her mother remarried an American. It was a welcome asset.

A U.S. Air Force lieutenant approached, saluted, and introduced himself as their command pilot. He would not be going with them, however, and behind him sat a tiny HTX-I helicopter, the rotors already turning lazily on battery power. Commonly called a TAXI, it would be controlled by pilots far away from the action, with this lieutenant in charge of getting them launched and then handing the flight over to another controller cruising far overhead in an electronics warfare plane.

The TAXI had been perfected by the U.S. Special Operations Command as a revolutionary tactical delivery system for particular missions and could deliver up to four operators to an exact point, then speed away to some nearby isolated site and shut down, roosting there patiently for days if need be, while solar panels recharged the batteries. When summoned, it would zip back in to pick them up. Except for the reconfigured overhead rotor, it hardly even looked like a helicopter. With no pilot, copilot, or loadmaster and with the giant internal combustion engines gone, weaponless and without armor, the unique helicopter was a blend of ultralight, stealth, and modern fuel cell and electronic technologies. It possessed extraordinary range and was virtually invisible to searching radar while its passengers sat in pairs, side by side, encased in a sleek aerodynamic bubble. The HTX-I wore the X designation to indicate it was still in the experimental stage, nothing more than an idea on the drawing boards. The media had never even picked up a scent that it was already operational.

Swanson and Summers climbed in, checked their gear, buckled up, and put on their headsets as the flight engineer closed the hatches and backed away, speaking into a radio to the controller. The reaction was immediate, and they heard no roar of engines as the TAXI rose from the landing strip like a quiet elevator, with only a slight whipping sound from the rotors, then flitted away on its run to the border. Swanson watched the lights of Adana disappear behind them. It was like sailing on a quiet lake.

At an exact GPS location, the TAXI slowed to a crawl and went close to the ground and then into a motionless hover. They jumped out, boots crunching desert sand, and ran to some nearby clusters of trees. The contact who had alerted the Americans about the presence of Mustapha Ahmed al-Masri was waiting, and Sybelle spoke to him in Kurdish, apologetically explaining to him that she was just a mere translator for the man with her.

Satisfied that as a woman, she was still an underling, the man guided them into the village and pointed them to a flat place in a ditch. The road beside them ran straight for a while, then bent right, and at the curve was the house that was to be attacked.

Sybelle and Kyle slid into the dry gully, and Swanson unlimbered some of his gear, setting up shop. Sybelle thanked the guide profusely and told him he was now free to go and wait for the main force that would be coming in on the other end of town. The guide disappeared into the night.

"Let's move," she said.

Kyle was already packing. They had no intention in staying in a place known to a local. Trust went only so far. "That house on the left. We go over the wall and get some protection, and I can brace the rifle on top of it."

They moved out quietly, and Sybelle spider-dropped over the wall and landed without a sound on the far side. Swanson turned the knob on the gate, opened it, and walked through. Sybelle raised her middle finger in response.

During the next hour, they created a hide by using material found around the yard, and Kyle placed his personal space-age sniper rifle, the Excalibur, on a solid rest. Sybelle set up a spotter's scope. Both had a clear view of the target building. They created a range card by measuring distances to points in the target area as they waited in the early morning chill.

At five o'clock, dawn was only an hour away, and parts of the village stirred as men and women prepared for the coming day. Kyle and Sybelle received a radio alert that the assault team was on its final approach, and almost immediately, the attack began with the buzzing approach of two big troop-carrying helicopters. Lights began snapping on throughout town by the time the birds landed on a soccer field a block east of the target. As the other Marines charged for the house, one of their snipers found a high position and took out the al Qaeda guard in front. Swanson and Summers, in the rear of the house, never took their eyes off of the target area.

"I have movement at the door," whispered Sybelle. "Tall man. Must be al-Masri's huge bodyguard."

"I see him," responded Kyle. In the scope of Excalibur, strings of numbers scrolled in constant movement as the computer measured the distance and figured the trajectory. So close, wind would not be a factor. Swanson held his fire.

"Second target. I identify him as al-Masri."

Kyle studied the figure. "I confirm. Target in sight."

As gunfire snapped in the house, the two men ducked into a small automobile, with the bodyguard driving, and the vehicle charged into the street with its lights off. Once again, the foot soldiers of al Qaeda were left behind to become martyrs while the leader escaped.

"Not this time," whispered Kyle. He pulled the trigger. The .50 caliber weapon fired with a jarring *BOOM*, and the recoil kicked his shoulder as the big bullet slammed into the engine block hard enough to make the vehicle jump. A second round then went through the windshield and shattered the head of the bodyguard as the out-of-control car swerved sharply and slammed into a parked truck with the crunch of metal and glass.

"Target down. Other one getting out." Sybelle's voice was perfectly calm, a monotone devoid of emotion.

"Confirm the other one is getting out." Kyle took his time racking in a third round, giving the man a moment to open the door. Al-Masri was alone in the empty street. His men were all dead or captured, and he knew that an American sniper had him in plain view. It was time to quit. He dropped to his knees and held his hands high over his head.

Kyle shot him through the chest, and the al Qaeda officer flopped over on his side. A final shot went into his head.

"Both targets down," said Sybelle.

Kyle grabbed his rifle and pack, and Sybelle picked up her scope and gear and called out the signal for the controller to send in the TAXI for pickup. They hustled out through the gate and back to the landing zone, where the little bird arrived two minutes later. They jumped in and were gone.

The fighting was over in the house. The nest of terrorists had been wiped out to the last man, and the Marines would secure the area.

"Was he trying to surrender?" Sybelle asked, wiping some camouflage greasepaint from her face. "Might have given up some intelligence."

"I saw a weapon," Kyle said.

"Yeah," she said. "Me, too."